THE
MONEYLENDER'S
DAUGHTER

WINDJAMMER

THE MONEYLENDER'S DAUGHTER

Book 2

V.A. Richardson

BLOOMSBURY

First published in Great Britain in 2006 by Bloomsbury Publishing Plc
36 Soho Square, London, W1D 3QY

A CIP catalogue record of this book is available from the British Library

Hardback
ISBN 0 7475 7017 5
9780747570172
Export paperback
ISBN 0 7475 7819 2
9780747578192

All papers used by Bloomsbury Publishing are natural, recyclable products made
from wood grown in well-managed forests. The manufacturing processes
conform to the environmental regulations of the country of origin.

Typeset by Dorchester Typesetting Group Ltd
Printed in Great Britain by Clays Ltd, St Ives Plc

1 3 5 7 9 10 8 6 4 2

www.bloomsbury.com
www.HouseOfWindjammer.com

For my mother K
and for Janie

With special thanks to
Michael Cripps Esq. Royal Navy (retired)

My soul, like a ship in a black storm, is driven,
I know not wither.
John Webster (*c.* 1580–1625), *The White Devil*

Contents

Draco, Amsterdam 1697

Preface

On the 20th June 1637 the ships of the Spanish fleet set sail from Havana for Spain, loaded with treasures from the new world of the Americas.

The Silver Fleet, as it was known, sailed north along the Florida coast following the currents of the Gulf Stream towards Cape Fear before turning east across the Atlantic. Waiting for them was an assortment of pirates and privateers – men from many nations in ships of all sizes – desperate to steal their fortune. And it is here, off a point of land known to them as Hell's Rock, on the deck of the French frigate *Requin*, that this part of the Windjammers' story begins with the blast of war …

1. The Silver Fleet

The cannonball passed close to the bow and smacked into the water, exploding up into the downpour.

'To windward, Captain!' The lookouts in the rigging began calling down warnings. 'The galleon's breaking formation! Coming around fast on us!'

The boy paused briefly to look out over the ship's rail. Through the rain he saw the sudden flashes and bursts of smoke from the Spanish guns. His breath caught in his throat at the strange fizzing noise of cannonballs in flight. Cold dread gripped him as the shots fell all around, lifting sudden fountains out of the rolling grey-green ocean.

On the quarterdeck above him stood Jacques Talon, captain of the *Requin*, privateer turned to private business, opportunist, *boucanier* and self-appointed governor of more islands of the Americas than he could remember. He cursed under his breath when he realised he had sailed too close.

'The *Gran Carlo*.' He breathed the galleon's name in an I-might-have-guessed sort of way.

Jacques Talon's respect was grudging but genuine. A

galleon of the Imperial Spanish Fleet made a fine sight, and they didn't come much finer than the *Gran Carlo*. One thousand two hundred tons of floating fortress, four masts crowded with sails and long battle standards trailing from her mastheads. Even dulled by the rain, the ornate carvings that gilded her from forecastle to raised stern made her seem gold plated. With bronze guns on three decks the *Gran Carlo* had the *Requin*'s twenty-eight cannons out gunned almost three to one.

'Don Hernando de San Juan – must I cut your beard again?' he called to the Spanish captain and spat over the side before turning to the men around him. 'Well, what are you waiting for? Run out the guns!'

Suddenly there was movement and noise everywhere. The boy remained on deck just long enough to see the galleon moving to protect the rest of the fleet from the *Requin*'s attack, then he went bounding down the companionway into the run of water sloshing along the gun deck below.

'Blasting powder, boy!' '*Here*, damn you!' 'Be quick about it!' The gunners cursed him as they worked on the line of twelve-pounders in the cramped heat. The gun ports were thrown open. The cannons rolled forward on their wooden wheels, emerging like so many dark lidless eyes.

The boy had learned enough French in the long months he had been with them to understand most of what they said. He knew better than to anger these hard men. Some of them were bringing up dry powder in kegs from the magazine in the hold below. Others were dealing out canvas packs, each cartridge charged with the right amount of powder to be tamped down

14

the barrel before the cannonball and wadding. The boy helped carry the charges to the guns, stacking them by the flat wooden trays containing the iron round shot.

'Fill it!' a man shouted, hurling a wooden pail at him.

The boy was sent staggering to the water barrel. He filled the bucket and others too, dragging them back to the gunners so they could sponge the barrels of the guns when they became red hot. The rope handles cut his hands raw and the heat and the work left him gasping for breath, but he dared not stop.

'Prepare matches!' the word was passed along the line. The gunners calibrated their guns, kneeling to squint down the barrels, adjusting the height and trajectory with the wedge-shaped *quoins*, before standing back ready.

The slow-burning fuse matches left firefly trails in the half-darkness as they were lit and passed from hand to hand. The gunners blew gently on the glowing tips and pressed the cords into the forks of their iron fire-sticks.

'Here, boy!' A wild face – a dirt-smeared, sweating, bearded face – half man, half creature of that terrible underworld, came close with a hiss of stale breath. 'You be ready to bring blasting powder when I call for it,' said the man he knew only as Saindoux. 'And it'd best be dry or it won't be the Spaniards that'll cut out that Dutch tongue of yours.'

Saindoux fetched him a clout that sent him staggering against the shaft of the mainmast and set tiny coloured lights popping behind his eyes.

'And you stay where I can see you, Hollander,' Saindoux warned.

Along the length of the cramped gun deck the men stood, sweating in the gloom as they bent over their cannons. Tension spliced the moments together while they waited. The *Requin* rolled to starboard, tilting the muzzles of the guns towards the waves until the downward motion reached its lowest point. A pause – a seemingly endless stretch of time – then the ship began to roll back, bringing the line of twelve-pounders up towards the galleon.

'Give *fire*!' the order came down from above.

And suddenly their wooden world shuddered as the air was split by the thunderous roar of the guns.

The boy didn't know how long it lasted. It might have been a trickle of sand or a full turn of the hourglass. He only knew that it felt as if he had been sucked down into some dark hellish place; a place filled with images he saw only in the flashes of the guns. Staccato images. Grim, grimacing faces. Twisted shadows in the smoke. The gunpowder crackled and spat, bursting into life at the touch of the glowing matches.

Again and again the guns erupted, belching fire and smoke. They slammed back, recoiling against the ropes that secured them, spitting twelve-pound balls of cast iron from their muzzles. The blast seared his eyes and blackened his skin. The smoke and the smell of men's sweat choked him. And the noise – the noise was like nothing he had ever heard before: like the roar of some giant invisible wave breaking eternally on a reef.

There was nothing noble in it. The fight was neither fine nor heroic. It was just fire and stench and noise and fear and death; until at last he could bear it no longer. Saindoux's warnings were forgotten. His only thought was to get out alive, to escape the inferno. His nerve broke. He turned and made a sudden dash for the companionway that led up to the deck above.

'You get back here, you little rat!' Saindoux loomed out of the smoke in front of him.

The man made a terrifying sight, his face was streaked with dirt and sweat and blood. The boy backed away in terror, tripped over some cordage and fell. He lay, helplessly opening and closing his mouth, pleading silently, the words choked-off in his throat.

'Get up! Bring blasting powder, damn you!' Saindoux kicked him. '*Now* or I'll –'

An explosion rocked the ship, blowing huge splinters off the hull, sending them bursting across the gun deck. Saindoux's head snapped back and his back arched. He stood for a moment, staring wildly up as if he had just caught a glimpse of something truly wondrous far above him, then his knees buckled and he dropped with the force of a man who'd been pulled down.

Blood appeared on the deck, seeping; a red bloom. The boy recoiled from it, scrabbling away until his back came up against the shaft of the mast once more. Saindoux groaned.

'Help me, Hollander,' he gasped, reaching out.

The hand hooked at the air then dropped, the fingers curling in spider-like. The boy's terror gripped him again and he came to his feet, stumbling blindly away through the smoke. Ahead of him the guns roared and recoiled. Behind him, another explosion ripped through the hull. Men cried out. The blast washed over him and he fell forward, only vaguely aware that something heavy had hit his leg.

He felt no pain, but his own blood was in the water

now. He left a trail of it on the companionway as he crawled up to the open hatch above. Step by step, he dragged himself up until at last he emerged into the maelstrom of rain and lead sweeping the open deck.

'Follow me if you dare, Don Hernando!' a voice rose defiantly against the noise. 'Follow me all the way to Hell's Rock if you must!'

The boy looked up to see Jacques Talon standing at the forward rail of the quarterdeck above, oblivious to the musket balls that were plugging into the wood all around him. He was unarmed, gripping the forward rail, shouting his defiance. The storm seemed to gather over him, setting his eyes alight with reflected fire. To the boy it was as if the Devil himself had risen out of the carnage of the battle to guide the *Requin* away from the great warship.

The Spanish guns flashed and flickered, but they soon became strangely distant to the boy as he stumbled among the shattered spars and tangled ropes. He fell heavily, his strength draining away in bright crimson drops. He called out in a voice that grew steadily weaker until at last the darkness came to gather him up. And in that moment his fear left him.

2. Cape Fear

Adam Windjammer came out of the darkness suddenly, arching up from the table with a gasp. He struggled, still caught in the net of his dreams until the phantoms that haunted his sleep fled from him once more.

He sat dragging for breath, sweating in the stifling heat of the Long Cabin. The map was still spread out on the table in front of him, weighted at each corner. The light from the lantern slid across the ragged coast-line. He was still wondering how long he had been lying with his head on the table when he realised he wasn't alone.

'Who's there?'

The Frenchman sat forward out of the shadows.

'Monsieur Valoir. What are you doing there?' Adam said.

'As God loves me – I could not sleep,' Victor Valoir replied. He glanced towards the line of leaded windows in the stern. 'You heard the guns. They mean trouble. Big trouble.' He spoke a low, guttural French that was hard to understand even for Adam who had grown used to it. 'Your friend Monsieur Honthorst – he doesn't like it either. He's out there right now stirring up trouble again.'

'Slowly, Monsieur Valoir, speak *slowly*,' Adam said. 'I can't understand when you speak too quickly.'

The Frenchman wiped at the sweat on his top lip with the back of his hand and spoke deliberately. 'What do you dream about, Adam Windjammer? Fame? Fortune? Or maybe it's a girl, hey?'

'I don't know what you're talking about.'

'You speak French well enough.'

Adam pushed back the bench and stood up, stretching the stiffness out of the muscles in his back as he gauged the movement of the ship. He crossed to the line of windows in the stern and brushed aside the trailing leaves of the botanical specimens growing in pots on the transom. Through the swirls and bubbles in the thickly leaded glass he could just make out the widening expanse of the ocean spreading away behind them, cut by a line of moonlight.

When he had fallen into an exhausted sleep, the *Draco* had been making its way cautiously along the coast of the Americas, sailing on the very edge of their world, following the currents north towards a place known as Cape Fear. Now the crew had reduced sail and the *Draco* was moving sluggishly, riding on an uneasy swell. With each dip and sliding roll, the ship's timbers creaked, the ticking sounds stringing themselves together to necklace the shadows like black pearls.

Somewhere on the deck above he heard the night watchman call the third hourglass of the middle watch.

'Three o'clock.' His breath misted the glass as he spoke.

'It'll be dawn soon,' the Frenchman said. 'Then we'll see.'

Adam turned to find Victor Valoir watching him intently under hooded eyes. Long straggling hair, sweating jowls – the Frenchman had a hunted look about him as if he carried the memories of the various pursuits of his life in bulging bags under his eyes.

'It's *gold*, isn't it?' he breathed. 'That's what you dream about. *That's* why we've come here.' His lips pulled back in a lop-sided grin. 'All this talk of finding your uncle and his crew,' he laughed, 'it's just a cover, isn't it – a ruse to throw others off the scent.' He leaned closer as if frightened of being overheard. 'You can trust me with your secret.'

Adam doubted it. 'There's no gold, Monsieur Valoir.'

'Silver, then. Stolen from the Spanish maybe?'

Adam shook his head.

The Frenchman's smile faded and he hunched away. 'Then you're just plain crazy to come here. And so am I!'

Adam rolled up the map, put it with the others in the mapmaker's wooden chart box.

The Frenchman lit his clay pipe and breathed out smoke. He seemed to come to a conclusion and wheezed into a laugh. 'You're a clever one, Adam Windjammer. Oh yes! You almost even had me believing you there. But you don't fool me so easily.' He tapped the side of his nose. 'No! You don't fool old Victor.'

Adam headed for the door.

'As God loves me – and he does – I want to help you,' the Frenchman called after him. 'I am your friend, Adam Windjammer. Not like the others out there! You go and listen – you'll see.'

Adam closed the door behind him and leaned back. He took a deep breath. The Frenchman had a bad smell about him that seemed to linger, especially down there in the fetid heat below decks. He looked along the passage. Curtains screened the cramped cabins on either side where the paying passengers slept – the widow and her maid, the tobacco planter and his family, the wanderer, the puritan and his God – crammed into their narrow hutch-like cabins, sweating in the heat.

'I tell you this is madness. *Madness.*'

Adam could hear voices coming from the cabin he shared with the company men. Hendrik Honthorst was doing most of the talking and what he was saying drew Adam along to listen.

'This whole area is crawling with Spanish,' he heard Honthorst say. 'I tell you, we're sailing into a war. I say we go on deck this very moment and tell the captain to end this foolish quest before it's too late.'

'He'll never agree,' another voice spoke up – it sounded like the quartermaster. 'He has his orders, you know that. We're to look for them ships if we can. And then there's the lad aboard. It's his uncle lost out there – who can blame him for wanting to search?'

Adam had reached the place where the shaft of the mizzen mast rose through the decks when a third voice spoke up:

'Aye, and the Frenchman swears it's the *Sirius* –'

'Well, I for one don't trust that Frenchman,' Hendrik Honthorst snapped back. 'How does he know this God-forsaken place so well? He says he trades meat this way – but who with, I ask you? Master Adam is too trusting – always asking for news of his uncle's lost ships at every port. Even in the taverns in St Christophe! And suddenly our Monsieur Valoir turns up. Drunk. Shouting his mouth off about a wrecked Dutch ship.'

'The boy won't give up now,' the quartermaster said.

'Master Adam's been filled with false hopes, that's all,' Honthorst said. 'But he isn't captain of this ship. He might have a powerful benefactor back in Amsterdam, but he's aboard to learn to be a merchant. So I say it's time we showed him that there's more to this voyage than searching for a lost uncle and his dead crew.'

The curtain was drawn back suddenly and Honthorst emerged from the cabin. Adam ducked into the shadows behind the mizzen mast, crouching by the water barrel.

Hendrik Honthorst steadied himself against the roll of the ship. 'Who'll come to the captain with me now?' he asked. 'None of you? Very well, then, I'll just have to go myself.' He let the curtain fall and made his way unsteadily along the deck. He reached the water barrel and paused, muttering before lifting the lid and taking down the ladle.

Something brushed against Adam's leg and he looked down to see Admiral Heyn. The ship's cat had a huge black rat by the neck. Adam recoiled from it in horror, pressing his back against the mast, relieved the rat was dead.

'No beer and only scum to drink,' Honthorst muttered. He saw the cat and kicked out at it in frustration. Admiral Heyn hissed and spat back furiously, causing Honthorst to drop the ladle and retreat in alarm.

'The very Devil's aboard this ship!' he cursed before hurrying off towards the light of the helmsman's lantern.

Adam smiled his thanks at the cat and eased out of the shadows to follow Hendrik Honthorst along the covered part of the main deck past the cannons. He stepped back when he saw Honthorst stop to talk to the helmsman.

'I'm sorry, sir,' the helmsman said as he kept a firm grip on the whipstaff pole of the tiller. 'But I've had no orders to change course.'

Honthorst glanced up at the grill hatch. The lantern swung from side to side, sliding its yellow light across his face. He drew in a deep breath of the cooler air coming down from the quarterdeck above. 'I can smell something. Dear God! It's land, man! *Land.*'

He broke through the circle of light, ducked under the steps leading up to the quarterdeck and vanished into the open area of the main deck known as the waist. Adam followed him. He ignored the helmsman's bewildered look, ducked under the steps and stepped out under the sails. He sucked in a deep breath and caught the hint of something unmistakably green after so much blue. It set his heart pumping.

The masts jumped skywards as he looked up. Only the topsails were set; the sheets high up on the fore and main masts were pale in the moonlight. The criss-cross of the rigging was blotted here and there by the silhouettes of men hanging in the ratlines. Others had gathered at the bulwarks on the port side. Only the animals stirred in their pens at the foot of the main mast: the chickens and ducks fluttering their wings in their wooden cages, the pigs shifting and grunting as if they sensed the danger somewhere out there in the darkness.

Adam took the steps up on to the quarterdeck three at a time. The stern lanterns hadn't been lit and the moonlight made statues of the men of the nightwatch. Among the shadows he picked out the short, bow-backed shape of the captain standing at the ship's rail. The mapmaker – taller and wearing a hat and cloak – was at his side. Hendrik Honthorst had joined them and was talking urgently.

'I must speak with you, Captain. It's a matter of utmost urgency –'

A stream of cloud covered the moon and plunged them into sudden darkness. It silenced Honthorst and left the men shifting uneasily. It was as if a heavy curtain had descended to rob them of their senses. For what seemed an eternity they were blind, that stretch of time filled with unseen terrors. Then finally, to the relief of all, the moon broke free and spread its pale light in glints across the liquid blackness once more. Only now the darkness lingered across a narrowing stretch of water.

The breath jammed in Adam's throat as he pushed past Hendrik Honthorst to the ship's rail and looked out. The land seemed to loom out of the sea ahead of them like the ridged back of some great slumbering leviathan.

'Cape Fear.' The mapmaker spoke the name without taking his eyes off the brooding mass.

'And may God have mercy on our souls,' Captain Lucas said quietly. He had just turned to give his orders, when he stopped and called for the men to be still again.

As they strained to listen now, they heard the sound of a bell striking faintly at the air. It came calling out to them across the water, like a death bell.

'Looks like that Frenchman of yours was right, Master Windjammer,' the captain murmured.

For there, at the foot of a great cliff known as Hell's Rock, at a place Victor Valoir had marked on the map with a simple cross, they found the wreck of a galleon.

3. At the House on the Street of Knives

The double doors opened and Hugo van Helsen's servant slipped quietly into the dining room. Goltz approached the table with the air of a man bringing important news.

Jade van Helsen sat in her place at the other end of the long table and pretended not to be interested as their servant leaned close to speak in her father's ear.

'The *Sirius*?' she head her father say. 'Are you sure?'

'I have the news straight from the waterfront, sir,' Goltz said. 'A ship just returned from the American Islands brought the letter.'

The letter was produced, read and then folded again carefully.

'Then they've gone in search of ghosts,' Jade heard her father murmur. He sat in silence for a while, considering the implications of the news before he spoke again. 'Send for Cornelius Yort,' he said at last. 'Tell him to come at once. *Tonight*. We will have need of him now if we are to move quickly and take advantage of this news.'

Goltz bowed, took several steps back, turned and

left as quickly and as quietly as he had come. Jade heard the doors close and resisted the urge to look up as her father laid his napkin over his left shoulder to protect the lace collar of his shirt and the fustian weave of his coat. He lifted the metal cover off the dish in front of him in the way of a man with renewed appetite, only to pause.

'*Fish*,' he said, his expression changing to a scowl. 'Why must it always be fish?'

Jade looked up from her plate and forced a smile. 'Fish is good for you, Father. Agnes says a fish a day will keep the plague away –'

Her father slammed down the lid, making the pewter jump. 'I don't care what *Agnes* says! If I eat another fish I swear I'll grow fins.'

Jade lowered her gaze to the herring on her plate. It stared blindly back at her with an opaque white eye. Cooked with onions and shallots, it would never know the vital part it was playing in her escape from the house on the Street of Knives.

Her father tore the napkin from his shoulder and hurled it on to the table. 'I have business to attend to,' he said, sliding back his chair. He stood up. 'When you have finished your dinner you will go straight to your room.'

'As you wish, Father.'

He gave her the suspicious look of someone who had expected a protest. Jade stood in a show of politeness and respect she didn't feel.

'And you can tell Agnes,' he went on, 'there is to be no more fish. Tomorrow we will eat meat. *Meat* – do you understand? Tomorrow, the next day and the day after that until I say it should stop!'

'Of course, Father – meat, tomorrow.'

Another suspicious look followed, then her father crossed the dining room, pausing only when he reached the doors. 'If I didn't know any better, Jade …'

He left the accusation hanging and walked out. The door closed and Jade threw herself back into her chair only to sit forward again almost at once. She snatched up the knife and stabbed it into the fish's eye.

By tomorrow she would be gone.

Jade stopped dead as the sound of raised voices burst on her ear.

'I'm *begging* you, sir. *Please*, reconsider. I need time to find that amount!'

'You've had time enough, merchant. I want my money.'

Jade stepped back at the sound of her father's voice. She stood in the shadows by the door, gripping the cloth bundle under her arm as she listened.

'But, Mr van Helsen!' the merchant was saying, almost pleading. 'You know very well I lost a fortune when the market in tulips crashed.'

'Then blame your own greed, not mine.' Her father's voice was cold, dead flat.

Jade had seen and heard it all many times before. Another unfortunate merchant had fallen on hard times and had been called to the house on the Street of Knives to plead for his old life and living back. And it had been worse since her father had brought her back from England. For this was the summer of 1637. The tulip fever that had gripped Holland and beyond was over. Fortunes had been made and lost, and it had been left to men like her father to pick up the pieces.

And the pickings were rich indeed.

'But, Mr van Helsen,' the merchant's voice rose in alarm, 'if you insist, it will ruin me and bring down the House of Yort!'

Once, not so long ago, Jade would have felt sorry for him. No longer. After all, one person's loss was another's gain – if nothing else, she had learned that from her father over the years. If the cruel twist of fate that had brought the merchant to the house on the Street of Knives late that evening helped her to escape, then so much the better for her.

Had she had time Jade might have wondered when she had begun to grow so hard. Had she had time she might have wondered when she had started justifying her actions with a philosophy that was all her father's. But time was running out for Jade van Helsen.

She stirred uneasily and glanced back along the passage. As she had passed the kitchens she had seen the maid her father had paid to keep watch on her. Agnes had been sitting on the knee of the fish seller, her white cotton cap pushed back, her broad face flushed pink with the heat of the fire and his kisses. Two fish lay among the onions on the wooden chopping block on the table, side by side like spent arrows, their silver scales turning dull with time spent lying together. Jade knew the fish seller wouldn't keep Agnes from her duties much longer now. She pushed open the door and moved on.

This was Goltz's place, a waiting room – a limbo of space – next to her father's accounting chamber at the front of the house. Goltz's desk faced the door leading to the Street of Knives. Jade's heart was drumming, her stomach filled with froth and bubble. To her right, another door was cut into the wooden panelling. It led into her father's accounting chamber and place of business. The men's voices were coming from inside.

'We had an agreement, merchant,' her father was saying. 'If you cannot pay, I will be forced to take action. This loan is secured on your properties and businesses.' He snapped his fingers. 'Remind him, Goltz!'

Goltz started reading from a list, running through it quickly, half under his breath: '*A fine house on the Prinsengracht. A coach and two horses. Silverware to the value of 4,500 guilders. Chinaware and furniture ...*'

Jade pinched out the candles on either side of Goltz's desk. Instantly shadows filled the room around her and a stripe of light from her father's accounting chamber fell slanting across the flagstones.

'*... Interests in a cheese business in the town of Gouda ...*'

She crept to the edge of the light and looked in cautiously. Her father was sitting at his desk. The merchant – a thick-set man with a grey beard and a large gut – was standing in front of them with his back half turned to her. Goltz was reading from a parchment:

'*... A pewter factory in the Jordaan. A cloth bleaching company ...*' Goltz's voice grew louder as he completed the list. 'Not forgetting, *A sizeable investment in the Quadrant Shipping and Trading Company.*'

'As you can see, Mr van Helsen,' the merchant spoke up, sounding more confident now. 'I still have some worth –'

'*I* will be the judge of that!' her father snapped. He rose to his feet abruptly and went to stand before a large map pinned to the wall. He kept his back turned towards the merchant and he studied the map with minute interest.

In the drowning pool of silence that followed, Jade could do little but stand very still. Her heart punched painfully at her ribs. She held her breath until her lungs began to burn. Then at last the merchant spoke and when he did there was a world of weariness in his voice.

'What do you want of me, van Helsen?' he asked. 'Why did you call me here at this late hour? Why *tonight*?'

Jade moved on.

The door leading to the Street of Knives was heavy and studded with huge iron nails. It wasn't the easy way out, but Goltz had already made his rounds. She knew all other doors would be locked, the keys on Goltz's belt. Only this one offered her any hope of escape, secured as it was with a key that out of habit remained in the lock when her father was at work. She turned it quickly. Now only the heavy iron bolt and the invisible force of her father's will secured the door to the street outside.

The merchant's voice rose out of the murmur behind her. 'But *why*? You are a banker, not a merchant.'

'I am a man of vision!' she heard her father correct him. 'A man of ...' he chose the word carefully, '*destiny*.'

'And to fulfil this *destiny* of yours, you need a ship?'

'Not just *a* ship. I wish to build a shipping empire.'

Jade reached up and tried to ease the bolt back. It wouldn't budge. She put down her cloth bundle and took hold of the haft of the bolt with both hands. It grated stiffly as it began to move.

'But surely there are other companies – *other* ships,' the merchant said. 'Why choose the Quadrant Shipping and Trading Company?' He paused then added. 'I beg you to reconsider – haven't you benefited enough from the Windjammers' misfortunes?'

Jade froze at the name, hanging on the haft of that bolt as she listened to the merchant.

'It has been barely a year since they lost their fleet to a storm and all their money and property here in Amsterdam to you. Adam Windjammer's father fell dead before his eyes! And now, just when he has a chance to restore his family's fortune, you –'

'*Enough.*' Her father brought his fist down heavily on the desk. 'This is business – just business. The boy has made a mistake by going off in search of ship-wrecks and I intend to profit by it. I care nothing for Adam Windjammer or his lost ships.'

'You care enough to put a spy aboard, it seems!' the merchant said.

Her father's answer was well practised. 'In knowledge there is power. In power, *money*.'

'No, there is more to it than that, van Helsen. For some reason you fear this boy – why else would you keep such a close eye on him? What is it that frightens you so?' The merchant paused for a moment, before coming to a sudden conclusion. 'Unless … yes, perhaps it's true what I've heard said – about Adam and your daughter …'

There was a dangerous pause. Jade remained very still, dreading what might come next.

'And what *exactly* have you heard?' her father asked, tight-lipped.

'Only that she tried to help him against you.'

'Lies! All lies!' her father cut him dead. 'Jade is my daughter. She is a van Helsen – a good and faithful daughter. She cared *nothing* for Adam Windjammer when he was in Amsterdam and she cares *nothing* for him now.'

'And yet I think I am closer to the truth than you would like to admit. But it matters little now.' The merchant let his bitterness show. 'I cannot stop you seizing my share of Quadrant, van Helsen. So why don't you just take it and be done with the talk?'

'My reasons are none of your concern, merchant!' her father roared. The outburst was followed by silence. When he spoke again it was with more control. 'For now, let us just say, I would rather my interest in Quadrant was to go ...' He took a pause before finishing the sentence. 'Unnoticed.'

'*Unnoticed?*' the merchant repeated, glancing at the map. 'I do not know what game you are playing, van Helsen. I do not understand this talk of your *destiny* – but I'm telling you now, I want no part of it.'

'This is no *game*,' her father snapped. 'I intend to make money – a great deal of money. But to do so, I have need of some secrecy.'

'You are asking me to do your dirty work.'

'I would look kindly on the debts of a friend.'

'A *friend*?' the merchant repeated the word bleakly. 'The Windjammers are my friends. Bartholomew de Leiden is my friend. I gave him my word that I would protect Adam, his mother and sisters. I will not break my oath. I'll go to the old man now. I'll tell him everything.' He forced a laugh. 'Do you think he will stand idly by and let you take Quadrant after all you've done?'

It was Goltz who spoke up now. 'Then it seems you have not heard, sir.'

'Heard? Heard what?' the merchant rounded on him. 'Speak up from the shadows if you must!'

'Bartholomew de Leiden is dying,' Goltz said. 'I have it from the old man's physician himself. It will not be long before they turn the pictures to the wall at his house on the Keizersgracht.'

The merchant staggered back as if he had been slapped in the face – *hard*.

'You're lying!' he hissed. 'You're just saying this to make me do what you want. Well, I've heard enough.' With that he drew the remnants of his self-respect about him like a threadbare cloak, heeled around and started towards the door.

Jade saw his silhouette loom suddenly large against the light and she panicked. There was nowhere to hide. She could only attack the bolt in a last, desperate attempt to get out. Then relief came suddenly as the merchant stopped at the sound of her father's voice.

'Only a fool nails his feet to the deck of a sinking ship, merchant,' her father said.

Cornelius Yort stood very still, framed in the doorway. He didn't turn. He didn't look back.

'When the old man is dead – what then for *you*, merchant?' her father went on. 'Think of your family. Think what it will be like for your dear wife and daughters in the House of Correction on the Heiligeweg.'

The merchant's shoulders sagged slightly. His resistance seemed to leak out of him in a sigh. He stood for a moment longer then slowly turned back to face the light, a beaten man. But he was not finished yet:

'One day, van Helsen,' he warned quietly, 'you will push someone like me too far. God help you when that day comes! Because all your money will not protect you then –'

Crack! The bolt moved suddenly under Jade's weight. Metal snapped against metal, as sharp as a pistol shot. She stumbled and almost fell.

'Who's there?' Goltz called out. He pushed past the merchant and peered into the shadows. He cursed the candles on his desk and went to fetch a lantern.

Jade heaved open the door, slipped out through the narrowest of gaps and pulled it closed again before Goltz had a chance to return with the light. Then she was running, her cloak streaming out behind in the moonlight, her footsteps smacking echoes from the walls as she fled through the shadows that filled the Street of Knives.

Hugo van Helsen burst into his daughter's bedroom. He was breathing hard. He lifted the lantern high, setting the shadows leaping around the walls as he crossed the room. He began a search that ended as he tore aside the folds of damask cloth that looped around the four posts of the bed. Jade had left no obvious clues to follow. He turned his fury on the maid.

'I pay you to watch her, woman, not entertain the fish seller!' he snarled at Agnes. He laughed – it was a sound completely without humour. 'I see now why my daughter wanted me to eat more *fish*. Only Jade could think of matchmaking using a herring!'

He ordered Agnes out of the house, ignoring her pathetic pleadings as he stormed from the room. His shadow followed him, faithful and lumpen on the wall in the lantern light. He had just reached his desk again when Goltz returned, having seen the merchant out.

'I found this by the door,' his servant said, placing a cloth bundle on the table.

Hugo van Helsen fumbled in his hurry to untie the straps. He rummaged through Jade's things, pulling back his hand when he came across the comb that had once belonged to his wife. He couldn't bring himself to touch it. Instead, with obvious relief, he reached for the purse he found there, weighing it in his hand, estimating the amount inside without the need to count it.

'She won't get far without money, Goltz,' he said quietly. 'Go to the waterfront. Have our people watch for her. The little fool will probably try and stow away aboard one of the ships.'

'I will spread the word at the taverns, sir.'

'No.' Hugo van Helsen stopped him. 'I will *not* be made to look a fool in front of all Amsterdam by my own daughter. We must keep this quiet, Goltz. Use only the best – send for Mother Race and her brood.'

'That witch of a seer, sir? But surely –'

'Do not argue with me, Goltz!' Hugo van Helsen interrupted. 'Do I need to remind you that we are just back from England? The ink is barely dry on the agreement I signed with Henry the goldsmith! Jade will marry the Englishman and I *will* have his business.' He spoke through gritted teeth, his fury growing with every word. 'I want this to be a wedding to remember! Yes! Something that'll make all the fine merchants and burghers of Amsterdam take notice of me. I want them to see what I've made of my life – despite everything.' His fist thumped down on the table. 'How will it look

37

for me if word gets out that I have lost the *bride*!'

Goltz retreated quickly, ducking into a bow before withdrawing from the room. The banker leaned back in his chair. He sat staring at the bundle in front of him for a long time after his servant had gone. At last, he reached out and picked up the comb. His hand was trembling slightly as he held it up so the tortoiseshell caught the lantern light.

'It isn't easy being the father of a daughter.' He spoke as if to a ghost. 'I would we'd had a son to follow me.' He thought for a moment before adding, 'A *boy* – like Adam Windjammer.'

His fury came upon him again suddenly. He swept the table clear and slammed his fists into the wood, cursing. 'What use is this girl to me?'

4. Stowaway

Jade van Helsen stood with the torchlight flickering in the green of her eyes. Her back was against the wall and the darkness around her felt stifling. The night was still but for the insects drawn to the flames burning in the iron brackets along the canal. A moth singed its wings and fell spiralling out of sight into the water below.

Her head was spinning with what she had overheard in the house on the Street of Knives. She understood little of it. Now her father's voice came echoing back to her. He kept repeating Adam Windjammer's name accusingly. It grew louder and louder, until she was sure her thoughts would explode: 'She cared *nothing* for Adam Windjammer when he was in Amsterdam,' that voice was incessant, 'and she cares *nothing* for him now.' *Nothing … nothing …*

'Nothing.' The word burst from her lips. She knew it was a lie.

She pressed back against the wall and closed her eyes, trying to calm the race of her heart. The cold reality came upon her then. She was as much to blame for the Windjammers' ruin as her father. For almost a year she had carried that secret deep in her heart like the broken point of a knife. And if Adam Windjammer had ever felt anything for her then, it could only be hatred now.

The mournful blare of the timekeeper's horn broke into her thoughts. The sound signalled the turning of the hourglasses to mark the end of the first hour of her freedom. She came out of the shadows, determined that it would not be her last.

It was a strange feeling to have nothing, to own nothing, to be ... What was she? She didn't know yet. She wondered if she could ever be anything more than just a moneylender's daughter.

Even the few things in the bundle she had left behind seemed wealth beyond belief now they were lost. Her plan had been to buy her passage on the first ship she could find, but there was little hope of that now. With no money and only the clothes she was wearing she knew she wouldn't get far. However, it never occurred to her to go back. To give up, to return to the stifling oppression of her father's house, to condemn herself to a future chosen for her, was more than she could bear. What choice did she have but to go on? Where could she go but the waterfront?

The pipe dens on the Kalverstraat were still open for business. The sounds of laughter and voices mingled as she made her way down the long thoroughfare, her shoes crunching on the sanded cobbles. There was danger there and yet safety too among the red-faced pot-bellied people milling among the ale houses. The tobacco smoke silvered the air, darkened here and there by the belch of the peat fires and spiced with the rich bloody scent of spit-roast meat gone cold. She felt the men watching her. She turned her face down to the points of her shoes and the hem of her black dress and hurried by.

'Hey you! Girl! Where are you going at this time of night?' the sound of the voice startled her.

She did her best to ignore the question, but a man lurched into the street. He stood, swaying slightly, thick lips pulled back in a lopsided grin. She could smell the beer on his breath and tried to pass him, but the man caught her by the wrist and held her back.

'Not so fast, my dark-haired lovely,' he said. 'Where's the harm in talk?'

Her chin lifted slightly as she answered him with a defiant look. The man seemed to recognise something in it – something desperate, perhaps – and let her go, forced to laugh it off with a glance over his shoulder at his friends. Jade stepped around him only to find herself mixed up with some street players, actors with powdered faces playing for the crowd. They drew her into their small drama briefly, turned her in a circle under the public gaze, before releasing her.

'My Aphrodite!' one called after her as she fled his outstretched hand. 'My muse lost to the night!'

Men laughed. She didn't look back until she reached the corner. By then the Kalverstraat had forgotten her.

The houses along the Rokin were mostly closed up behind wooden shutters. Only here and there on the other side of the river could she see squares of fugged yellow light, diamond panes spilling brightness across the cobbles in patches. She crossed the bridge near the university. The water under the bridge was full of reflections, streaks of torchlight mirrored darkly, wavering: cold fire, out of reach.

The old part of the city opened to her, then closed quickly behind. These were streets she had explored secretly by day, but night filled them now. Darkness lurked around corners and down alleyways. She heard footsteps and voices: familiar sounds made hollow and sinister by the shadows. She made her way down past the barges and river boats on the Rokin, avoided Dam Square and followed the Damrak, staying close to the old city walls. Torches lit her way, set at intervals in iron brackets, burning on the walls of the Bourse and over the door of the Old Church, leading her down to the waterfront and the tall ships waiting beyond.

The *Batavia* was tied to the quayside in the area known as Lastage. Jade was drawn to her. Blazing iron braziers stood guard on either side of the gangplank. The flames drew her. She knew the danger. She knew her father's people would be looking for her, but the light was dazzling, irresistible – a flame of freedom which seemed to beckon her.

She approached cautiously and hid in the shadows behind a stack of empty barrels. The waterfront was strangely quiet now. Gone were the crowds and the daytime hustle; gone were the merchants, sailors, traders and hawkers. The warehouses were closed and the wooden walkways that crossed between the islands of the docks and the shipyards were deserted. Even the taverns had finished business for the night, leaving a few drunks wandering home. Only the *Batavia* seemed alive, the crew still taking on stores as the bellman on the Schreierstoren tower marked the midnight hour.

She watched the men working, their shadows distorted and made grotesque by the firelight, and soon gleaned from their talk that they were preparing to sail on the morning tide. She studied the ship carefully. The decks were awash with light, the three masts up-lit, rising to be lost in the darkness above. The *Batavia* was a merchant ship, smaller than a galleon but designed to go just as far, and that suited Jade.

The ship's quartermaster was checking the barrels and sacks piled on the quayside. His lantern cast a ring of yellow light as he paused here and there to study his manifest.

'A word with you if you please, Mr Johannes,' his voice carried on the quiet.

One of the men loading the barrels stepped into the circle of light. The others continued up the gangplank, carrying an assortment of goods on to the ship and disappeared from view. The way aboard was open.

Before she could change her mind, Jade slipped out of the shadows and ran lightly and silently across the open quayside to rest behind some barrels. The quartermaster and the man called Johannes had their backs turned to her and were arguing over some detail on the manifest. She took a deep breath and crept towards the gangplank. A pause, a final look around, then she started up the plank, flitting between the fiery pillars.

The sound of men's talk above her on the main deck brought Jade to a sudden halt halfway up. For an uncertain moment she just stood caught between the old world and the new, yearning to go on, knowing this might be her only chance, but in the end – inevitably – forced back the way she had come. She turned in a whirl of skirts and, in several leggy bounds, was back on the quayside among the sacks and barrels and the safety of the shadows.

'Get on with it, you idle wharf-rats!' the quarter-master grumbled as the men started down the gangplank.

Jade heard him mutter something about it taking them all night at this rate and drew back as the light from his lantern touched the darkness around her. She looked again.There had to be another way.

Beyond the low forecastle, the bowsprit angled up into the darkness as if pointing the way to a promised land. She studied the curving beak of the prow; her gaze travelled to the anchor that hooked over the side, and made the jump to the rope hawser. Twisted hemp thicker than her arm tied the *Batavia* to the quayside, stretching down to thread her to new hope.

From the barrels to a pile of sacks, from the sacks to more barrels, she ran in short bursts, keeping her head down. A pause at each brief stop, then on again. She ran until she reached the squat leather-capped post where the rope was tied and curved up to the prow above.

Jade could hear the water slapping at the keel as she slithered out on to the thick rope. She pulled herself up hand over hand, locking her feet on to the twisted hemp to stop herself slipping back. Exposed to the flickering light, she was unable to do anything but keep climbing until she came level with the shank of the anchor. Her arms and legs were aching as she eased across and slipped on to the hook. It was easier after that: a simple matter of pulling herself up to reach some trailing rigging. And suddenly, incredibly, she was aboard.

She lay very still, straining to hear past the sound of her own breathing. Finally she eased up from the deck and sat with her back to the mighty shaft of the ship's bowsprit, hiding in the shadow of the forecastle. The relief was so intense it was painful. She had made it. She was free. And at that moment Jade believed – yes, she truly believed – there was nothing she couldn't do.

Jade came awake suddenly. She struggled to pull her senses together with the sound of a bell tolling over her as if somehow it had escaped her fleeting dream. She shook off her tiredness with difficulty, remembered where she was and how she had got there, and sat up, listening intently, furious with herself for having drifted into sleep.

The heat had gone out of the night and the ship was quiet in the cool hours before the dawn. She chewed at her fingernail for a while, hardly daring to move, gripped by the dread of being caught and sent back, until at last she climbed up and risked a look over the forecastle. The decks were deserted as far as she could see. The men had finished loading and had pulled in the gangplank while she had slept.

She eased up and over the bulwark. Her feet made no sound as she landed, crouching, alert, listening before she risked crossing the fore deck to peer down into the waist around the main mast of the ship. The stern lanterns were still lit and there was enough light to see. The light reflected on the barrels of the cannons set at intervals on either side between the masts where rigging – like spun webs of silver – seemed set to snare and entrap her.

At first she didn't see the nightwatchman. He was on

the main deck, leaning comfortably against a coil of rope close to the place where the gangplank had been. Only the sound of his snoring alerted her to his presence as she crept down the steps from the forecastle. There were animals in pens and they shifted uneasily at her approach. She stood very still, hoping they would settle again, but the nightwatchman stirred. His breath caught in the back of his throat, a sudden snort loud enough to impress the pigs, and he came awake with a start.

Jade dropped on to her haunches, crouching where she had stood, watching through the gaps between the animal pens as the man stood up and scratched vigorously at his chest lice. He stamped the feeling back into his legs and went to the side. Jade heard a trickle as he urinated into the water and she moved on quickly while he was too busy to notice.

There was a grating over the main hatch, but it had been raised on its hinge and she could see steps leading down into the dimness of the decks below. Even as the nightwatchman finished and turned back, she was ducking into that hole, vanishing down the steps into the hold below.

The smell that wafted up out of the bowels of the ship was so bad it made her breath catch in her throat. She gagged at it and buried her face and nose in her hand. The stink of the bilge water which had gathered at the bottom of the ship was overwhelming. It mixed with the stench of ancient sweat, wet wood and vermin, in a cloying, fatty, evil concoction that smelled like filthy wet wool. It seemed to attach itself to her face like a suffocating invisible mask. She had to fight back her rising feeling of panic as she forced herself to go on down.

A lantern was hanging on a hook lighting a distant end of the deck below. The tallow candle was lit and Jade was still wondering why when she heard someone moving about among the labyrinth of stores. She stopped halfway down the steps and peered under the beams. A shadow was dragging itself about, sometimes upright against the stores, sometimes leaping back against the curved ribs and boards of the hull. The quartermaster came into view. If he had slept at all it couldn't have been for long and now he was making his final checks of the stores they had loaded aboard, making very little noise for a large man in such a confined space.

Jade risked a step, then another. The tread creaked under her weight and she froze as the big man paused. He didn't look around, but she could tell he was listening. He stood with the lantern light cutting down one side of his face, picking over the sounds of the ship as if he could make sense of every noise he heard except this one.

'Mr Johannes? Is that you?' No answer came back so he returned to his work.

Jade slipped quietly into the maze of barrels and sacks. Her passing was little more than a whisper, a stirring of the stale air, but the quartermaster was alert now and he must have sensed something because he turned, took down the lantern from its hook and started back along the narrow passageways between the piled-up stores. Jade fled ahead of him, going deeper into the hold until she found a hollow behind some sacks just big enough for her to hide in.

The quartermaster's huge knuckles floated above the light as he held the lantern ahead of him on a crooked arm. The shadows pooled in the sockets of his eyes and drew down his nose and chin into a fleshy grimace. Jade pressed her cheek against the coarse hessian of a sack and listened as he passed so close she could have reached out and touched his sleeve. Then with a slow, deliberate tread he moved on and she breathed again.

The light faded and the shadows returned. But Jade resisted the urge to look. Only when the lantern had stopped moving did she ease her cramped legs and start searching for a better place to hide. By now the lantern was back on its hook and she crept out from her hiding place, determined to stay as far away from the light as possible. As she made her way through the labyrinth, however, she hadn't reckoned on the quartermaster's cunning.

The blade rasped slightly as it came out of the big man's belt. Jade heard it, too late. She stopped dead at the touch of the steel against the soft skin just below her right ear.

'Well, well,' the quartermaster said quietly. 'And what have we here?'

The door opened and the quartermaster ducked in. Jade saw a way out into the passage and hurled herself at the gap. She kicked and scratched in her desperation to escape, but he was too strong for her. He caught her by the wrists, dragged her out of the hold and up the narrow companionway on to the main deck.

'What did I tell you?' the quartermaster panted to Johannes. 'Caught myself a real wild cat here.'

Jade glared at him. They had kept her locked in the hold for over two hours in the hope that she would calm down. Still she struggled. Still she tried to break free. But the quartermaster and the man called Johannes carried her between them, kicking at the air, to the captain's door.

'Here's your stowaway, Captain,' the quartermaster said through gritted teeth as they dragged her in. 'But a word of warning – we'd best tie her up.'

'Thank you, quartermaster. That will not be necessary.'

The quartermaster wasn't so sure. 'Just as you say, Captain. But I want it known I found her – that way if there's a reward I'll get my share.'

Captain van der Leck was breakfasting on boiled mutton and onions. He went on eating, speaking as he chewed without looking up.

'What is your name, girl?'

Jade's chin came up slightly.

He leaned back in his chair and looked at her. Jade would never forget those dark eyes as she stood in front of him.

'No name, no home and no money, I suppose?' he said, without much surprise.

The fight went out of her then. Her despair swamped her and robbed her of the will to go on. She just stood weakly waiting to hear her fate from a man she had never met, while he casually began paring the nails of one hand with the point of his knife. He studied the results briefly then looked up. 'Did my men hurt you?'

'Hurt *her*?' the quartermaster shook his head. 'She's a wild cat, Captain, I swear it! And I have the bruises to prove it,' he added, starting to pull up the legs of his breeches.

'Thank you, quartermaster, but that will be all,' the captain said, waving him away.

'But, Captain …' the quartermaster protested.

'I said that will be all! Go back to your work. And you, Mr Johannes, make sure the men are aboard. We sail with the dawn.'

The quartermaster turned to Johannes with a shake of his head. Together they left, closing the door behind them.

After they had gone the captain fixed Jade with a heavy look. 'You know I could have you arrested? I could call an officer of the guard and turn you over to the authorities as a stowaway. I daresay time spent in the dungeon of the arsenal would loosen your tongue.'

He helped himself to an apple from a bowl on the table in front of him. Jade watched him polish it on the sleeve of his coat. He bit out a large chunk, chewed and swallowed. 'Are you hungry?'

Jade lied with a shake of her head.

The captain pushed the bowl of apples towards her and she couldn't resist the urge to take one.

'Take two or three! Take the whole bowl, why not?' the captain said. 'You obviously expected such charity from us.'

Jade realised she had fallen into his trap and put the apple back. 'I would have worked for my passage.'

'And what work can a girl with no name do?' the captain enquired.

Jade hesitated. The captain removed a piece of apple pip delicately from the tip of his tongue using his thumb and forefinger. He flicked it away.

'You have spirit, no-name,' he said. 'But spirit is not enough.'

'Don't send me back!' she burst out, gripping the table, unable to contain her desperation.

The captain leaned forward and caught hold of her hand. He pulled her towards him and studied her face intently. For a moment she thought she could see real compassion in his dark eyes. Then he spoke.

'I would not take you with us even if I could,' he said. 'This is no game – no romantic adventure for a girl. You know nothing of the voyage we are about to undertake. You know nothing of the burning heat of the southern seas or the terror of the Cape of Storms.'

'I'll take my chances,' Jade said. 'Please, you *have* to help me.'

'And when your teeth start to rot and fall out with the scurvy, what then, no-name? When you are puking your guts on to the deck or stricken by the Bloody Flux, what will you say to me?' He let her hand go. 'No, I would not take you with us, because if I did you would be dead within six months. You would not reach the Cinnamon Isles and I will not sign the death warrant of one so young and full of life.'

Captain van der Leck came to his feet abruptly. He took his hat down from a peg and paused. 'Whatever it is you are running from, it must be bad if you are willing to risk so much,' he said. 'But you cannot run for ever, no-name. One day you will have to face the thing you fear most. So take the advice of one who has seen something of the ways of this cruel world and find a way to face it – in your own time and on your own terms.'

A sudden impulse made him pick up the apple. He pressed it into her hand then strode past her to open the door. He stood back politely to let her pass through first then ducked out on to the quarterdeck and settled his hat. They were met by the quartermaster and, further off, the man called Johannes.

'See she gets ashore,' the captain said.

'You're not just going to let her go, are you, Captain?' the quartermaster complained.

'What do you expect me to do, quartermaster?'

'But *look* at her, Captain!' the quartermaster insisted. 'She's got money written all over her. You can see from her clothes she's not just one of the girls from the waterfront. If you ask me, she's a runaway. Probably from a fine house. That means someone will be looking for her. There's sure to be a *reward*.'

'Is it not reward enough that you have saved her life, quartermaster?' the captain said. He looked to the rigging. 'Make ready! Raise the yards!'

The quartermaster clamped a blunt-fingered hand around Jade's arm and led her away. The captain didn't turn to look as she descended the steps to the main deck. Only when she passed under his gaze and glanced up did he speak again.

'Good luck, no-name,' he said quietly. 'I have a feeling you are going to need it almost as much as we will.'

The gangplank had been run out to allow the men who had spent their last night ashore to come aboard. A crowd of people were now gathering on the quayside where the quartermaster and his stores had been. Some had faces so lined and wizened they might have been carved and weathered by the wind and the salt and sea itself. The old, the women and the very young had come to watch their men go. They stood quietly, stiff and silent as if they had come to observe some final funeral rite.

'The captain's a good man,' the quartermaster

grumbled as he pushed her ahead of him down the narrow plank. 'He's a man of principle, no doubt, but principles don't make you rich, now, do they? It's cold, hard coin that matters.'

He held on to her, reluctant to let his prize go. Finally Jade pulled free and backed away. She turned and pushed through the people gathered there. They hardly seemed to notice her, standing like so many statues, their faces drawn and pale in the morning light.

Jade reached the corner of a warehouse and looked back. She could see the quartermaster talking to someone and pointing after her. Already men were leaping up into the *Batavia*'s rigging, climbing towards the white birds that wheeled over the masts.

She felt her failure like a dead weight. It settled on her and deepened her despair as she forced herself to move on again. She couldn't bring herself to look back so she didn't notice the ragged boy sitting cross-legged on a wall. He watched her thoughtfully for a while, then stood up, dusted off the seat of his breeches and began to follow.

5. One Door Closes ...

'Fresh fish!' 'Get your drinking water here!' 'Clean rooms to let!' 'Hello, sailor, want to meet some nice girls?' Laughter and the cry of seagulls burst on the salt air.

The sounds of the waterfront swirled around Jade, wrapping about her like a living thing, scooping her up, drawing her into the crowd as she walked along the quayside avoiding the nets of goods and stores as they were loaded and unloaded from the ships.

The dawn had brought new life to the waterfront. In a few short hours it had been transformed. She felt the buzz, the excitement. A small fleet of narrow-decked Fluyts had sailed in on the colours of the new day. Others came singly: a merchant carrack wearing her years at sea, several barks and a galleon marked with a golden lion – the lion of Holland – on her stern. Jade had watched them sliding in from the stretch of open water to the north they called the Zuider Zee. They had sailed up the narrowing channel to find berths among the hundreds of ships that were already jostling along the waterfront of the port of Amsterdam.

Now the warehouses had opened their doors for business and the quayside was littered with goods: grain from the Baltic, timber from Sweden and Moscovy, beer from Hamburg, spices from the East, chests of sugar from the West, iron ingots, bricks, wool, rope and more – much, much more. She picked her way between the barrels, the horse-drawn sledges of the delivery men and the handcarts of the peddlers, trying hard to be just another face on the waterfront, remaining as inconspicuous as possible, as she worked out what to do next.

Her chances weren't good. Her father had eyes everywhere and she knew it wouldn't be long before they searched her out. Everywhere she looked people seemed to be watching her: the old woman selling chickens and ducks from a stack of wooden cages, the man with the handcart who had stopped to light his pipe, the sharp-faced trader standing with the small group of merchants who had gathered around a warehouse door. At any moment she expected to be stopped and challenged. It only surprised her that it hadn't already happened. It was a risk just being there, but she had little choice now. If she couldn't buy her freedom and she couldn't steal it, what else could she do but *earn* it?

It seemed impossible. How could *she* hope to earn a life? She had nothing – least of all time – but she wouldn't give up. She wouldn't beg, borrow or steal, she wouldn't sell herself for the amusement of others. She would find another way. And if at that moment it seemed hard, she did have one advantage: she had visited the waterfront before and with time and a quick eye had learned its ways. She knew it to be a cruel hard place, a dangerous place, but with that danger came *opportunity*.

Jade didn't notice the merchant at first. He was in a hurry, pushing his way through the tight groups of traders on his way somewhere else. He kept his face turned down, his gaze fixed firmly on the cobbles in front of him. A tall man, greying, unremarkable but for the way his shoulders sagged and leaned into his walk as if he were dragging an invisible weight behind him.

Jade still might not have seen him as she stopped briefly to eat the apple the captain had given her. She chose one of the alleyways that led off the waterfront as the safest place. From there she could watch without being seen, and it was pure chance, a twist of fate, a coincidence of time and place that brought them together.

It must have been some hint of a likeness, some expression or feature on her face that made him stop and look again. Her immediate reaction was to hide her face, to step back, to move away into the shadows. But as he continued to stare at her, she suddenly recognised him. He ran a hand over his mouth and down to the grey point of his beard as if trying to wipe away his troubles. He didn't know Jade because he had never met her, but she knew him from her father's house. And she even remembered his name. Cornelius Yort had come to the waterfront.

He hurried away, glancing back more than once until the crowd swallowed him up. Jade dropped the remains of the apple and, without really knowing why, began to follow him. She kept her distance, turning away whenever he looked back. What she hoped to gain, she didn't yet know. She had only a vague idea, an instinct, that there would be some advantage in it. It left her tingling slightly with excitement, because she knew his secret and she had heard her father say himself that in knowledge there was power and in power – *money*.

The courtyard of West India House was even busier than usual. Serious-looking merchants had gathered under the lines of rectangular windows and were standing around in small groups, talking in hushed voices.

Jade stopped at the edge of the Herenmarket and watched the merchant hurry on into the courtyard. She couldn't follow him into a place where only men of business were allowed. So she watched as the other merchants turned to greet him. Cornelius Yort hardly seemed to notice them, such was his preoccupation and haste, and soon he had disappeared through the arched doorway into the hall beyond.

Jade glanced about. It suddenly occurred to her that she had been careless. She had been so intent on following that she had forgotten she might have been followed herself. The Herenmarket was busy with traders selling from brightly painted stalls. A fresh catch of herrings had just come in and business was brisk at the fish sellers. A fishwife was gutting and salting fish, laying them out in lines on wooden tables. A small boy caught her eye. He had stopped to drink from a drinking trough and was looking at her as he wiped his mouth on the back of his hand. He vanished into the crowd and she relaxed a little.

When Cornelius Yort emerged from the offices of the West India Company again he was carrying an armful of papers. He clutched them to his chest; his face was set, his expression grim as he made his way across the Herenmarket and hailed a boat at the canal's edge.

Jade followed the boat, staying as close as she dared to the canal. She went from doorway to doorway, stopping to see which way the boatman would take him before moving on again. She was on the bridge as the boat passed right under her feet, turning up the Keizersgracht canal. Soon after that the warehouses gave way to houses that grew taller the further away from the waterfront they went.

Elm trees lined the canal making it easier for Jade to follow without being seen. She picked her way down the line of fine flat-fronted houses where household servants were still going about their morning duties, scrubbing and sanding the steps and cobbles. The canal was crowded with boats and for a while she was forced to stop when a boat jam formed.

'Can I help you, miss?'

The sound of the voice startled Jade. She spun around, her heart hammering at her ribs. Two men were busy hauling goods up to an attic storeroom in one of the houses. The one on the end of the rope had paused to look at her, a barrel swinging dangerously overhead.

'You look lost, that's all,' he explained. 'Only if you are, don't ask them boatmen to help you. They're all mad.' He nodded towards the snarl of boats. 'Look at them – everyone one of them thinks he owns the canal. Why only last week my boat was nearly driven into the bank by a madman who called himself van Mann.'

'Boat rage,' his companion confirmed it. 'We never had that when I was a lad …'

Jade fled to the next corner and pressed her back to the brickwork of a house, fighting a rising feeling of panic as she checked both ways along the canal to see if anyone had noticed. The men had begun hauling on their rope again and the boatmen were still busy arguing. Only a small girl sitting on the canal side had given her a second glance and she was soon forgotten as Cornelius Yort's boat finally worked itself free of the others and began pulling up the canal again. Jade moved on.

Soon after they had passed within sight of the bell tower of the West Church, the boatman steered into the side. Cornelius Yort clutched his papers and stepped out of the rocking boat. Jade watched from a safe distance as he crossed the street to a large house with tall, mullioned windows and a fine gabled roof. The shutters were closed over many of the windows and there was a cold, sunless feel about the place. It was only after the merchant had climbed the steps, knocked at the front door and had been ushered in that she began to wonder what she had hoped to achieve by following him.

She approached the house, at first unaware that the boatman was still sitting in his boat. He lit his pipe and leaned back as if he had nothing better to do until Cornelius Yort returned.

'Who lives in that house?' she asked, causing him to look up.

He removed his pipe from between his teeth. 'It's the house of Bartholomew de Leiden, miss,' he said. He regarded her thoughtfully before adding, 'But if it's the place you're wanting, then you've come on a bad day. This is my fourth fare here this morning and there'll be more before the day's done. From what I hear the old man isn't long for this world.'

'You mean he's ill?'

'*Dying*, miss.' He nodded and patted his purse. It seemed a boatman's business was always brisk to death's door.

Jade watched the house from the canal side. She sat with her back to an elm. She had been waiting for over an hour with one thought above all others keeping her there. Perhaps it was bred out of the same impulse that had caused her to follow the merchant from the waterfront in the first place. Perhaps it came out of some deeper instinct for survival. Whatever had spawned it, she was certain of one fact: that this was the house of her father's *enemy*.

She had met Bartholomew de Leiden only once. It had been on the Herengracht almost a year before when the Windjammers had finally lost everything to her father. He was an old man, but he had proved himself to be a friend of the Windjammers then and in so doing made himself a powerful enemy of her father.

'But why would he help *you*?' a small voice in her head kept asking the same question over and over again. 'You're a van Helsen, remember.'

Jade convinced herself the answer to that question lay in what she had overheard in the house on the Street of Knives.

A bell was striking ten, a slow deliberate tolling, as the front door opened and Cornelius Yort stepped out. He stopped to breathe as if the air inside was rank, settled his hat and came down the steps.

Jade watched him drag his invisible burden back to

the waiting boat. She had already made up her mind that she had no more use for him. Without him knowing it, the merchant had served his purpose. So now she waited until the boatman had pulled out among the other boats before slipping out from behind the tree and approaching the house. She knew the risks she was taking by seeking help from this old man. Nevertheless, she climbed the steps, took hold of the door knocker and sent brittle echoes to shatter the quiet within.

A manservant with a sharp face, long slicked-back hair and a pronounced widow's peak opened the door. He stared at her from under hooded eyes. 'Yes?'

'I have ...' she started uncertainly, '... a message – for Mr de Leiden.'

'I will see it gets to him,' the manservant said holding out his hand as if expecting a note or letter.

'No. You don't understand. I must *talk* to Mr de Leiden himself.'

'Quite impossible! No one can see Mr de Leiden. He is not well. Doctor's orders. He must not be disturbed on any account.'

Jade glanced over her shoulder. She was conscious of standing too long at the top of those steps for all in the street to see. 'This is important – it's business.'

'*Business?*' The manservant frowned and looked at her as if he doubted it. 'Then, if it is a business matter I suggest you see Mr Cornelius Yort about it. He is my master's partner in business.'

'His *partner?*' Jade glanced after the merchant's boat.

'Yes, miss. That's him there. A fine, upstanding gentleman if there ever was one, and you'll still be able to hail his boat if you're quick about it ...'

'No,' she said. 'I mean ... thank you, it can wait.'

The manservant gave her his best then-stop-wasting-my-time sort of look and closed the door. Jade retreated down the steps. She became aware that the manservant was watching her now through a window and she moved around the corner into Wolf Street, heading in the direction of the Herengracht. There she stopped and leaned back against the wall, trying to make sense of what she was doing.

But what *was* she doing? The small voice began whispering questions in her head again. This was madness, it said. What did she know that could possibly be of interest to a man like Bartholomew de Leiden? She tried to think it through. Cornelius Yort had fallen into her father's pocket, of that much she was sure. She had heard a name – a company name she couldn't quite remember – and knew that Adam Windjammer was somehow involved. It didn't seem to amount to much and yet it was all she had. It had to be *worth* something, she decided, even to a dying old man.

'And if it is I'll make him pay to hear it,' she hissed under her breath, finally silencing that voice of doubt. With that money she would buy her passage on a ship and *never* come back.

Nevertheless, even with her mind made up and filled with a new determination, she knew she would never get past the manservant. It left her wringing her hands in frustration, pacing to and fro. But with no money and no other prospects she had nowhere to go. So it was, inevitably perhaps, that she was held by that sunless house – until it occurred to her that there was another way in.

The alleyway led off Wolf Street, twisting away, running down the backs of the tall houses overlooking that part of the Keizersgracht. To the right, there were gardens and small allotments that served the big houses with fresh fruit and flowers. To the left, the high walls closed off a line of courtyards. All the doors looked alike, making it hard to tell which would lead into the back of Bartholomew de Leiden's house, and Jade would have had great difficulty finding the right one had a servant not emerged from one of the courtyards further along.

Jade saw the maid coming and walked on. The girl was in a hurry to fulfil some errand. As they passed each other Jade saw the girl's eyes were red and her face was puffy with weeping. The girl held the corner of her apron to her nose and hurried by without a second glance. Jade waited until she was out of sight before slipping quietly back to the courtyard door.

The house that rose above the high wall had that same dead feel about it and many of the windows at the back were closed behind wooden shutters. Jade pressed her ear to the door and listened before trying the latch. The door came open easily and she pushed it gently with the tips of her fingers. A cobbled courtyard opened to her, with a gutter running away to a stone water trough outside a door.

One final look around and Jade stepped in from the alley outside. She went to one of the windows and cupped her hands around her face to look in through the small leaded panes. The kitchen of the house swam in the swirls of the thick glass. She could see pans hanging from iron hooks along one wall. A brace of ducks hung from a low wooden beam along with several haunches of smoked meat and sausages. On the table a huge loaf of rye bread lay in a pannier, the crust broken and picked at. A cloak lay discarded over one corner of the table: the red cloth flowing on to a bench seat then down in suspended ripples to the blue Delft tiles, pooling on the floor like spilt wine. The narrow closet bed to one side of the fireplace was empty, the sheets crumpled and thrown back. The kitchen maid was nowhere to be seen and the fire had been allowed to burn low. The heart of the house was going cold.

Jade tried the door. It came open easily and she stood on the threshold, listening. A strange expectant hush hung over the house as if it was filled with a sense of the inevitability of the event that was coming. A surge of panic left her wondering if the old man had already died.

She picked off a piece of bread in passing, realising just how hungry she was as she chewed it. She tore off a larger chunk and bit into it, washing the mouthful down with a swallow of water from a pitcher. A flag-stoned passage led to another door, which in turn opened under the stairs. Beyond lay the main hall of the house with the front door directly opposite. Several rooms opened off the hall on either side and she stepped back briefly as someone moved between rooms with a soft tread. There were hats and summer capes on pegs and walking canes in a stand by the door and men's voices were coming from a room at the foot of the stairs. Jade eased out a little and caught a glimpse of some men sitting around a table playing dice. The manservant who had opened the door was serving them beer in pewter mugs and from their talk Jade gleaned that the large red-faced man among them was a doctor.

'I would bleed him more if I thought it was any use,'

she heard him say, 'but I fear it will do the old man little good now. More ale here, Voorhuis!'

The servant obliged.

The doctor drank and wiped his mouth. 'Does not the Bible allot us three score years and ten? The old man has done well to exceed that span by almost nine.'

Jade looked up the stairs. Many pairs of eyes followed her: the eyes of long-dead ancestors staring down from portraits on the walls. She started up, leaving the sound of the men's voices behind as she reached the floor above. A passage led away to a window at the end. The shutters were closed and the only light came from the candles in the brass chandelier. A door was half open and she had already taken several steps towards it when she noticed the dog.

The wolfhound lifted his head and regarded her briefly with rheumy eyes. The tail flapped lazily. *Thump, thump, thump*, like the beat of a heart. She remembered the bread and carefully put it down. The dog was tempted away from the door, moving stiffly, claws clicking on the floorboards. She stroked its head and edged around to take a quick look in through the open door.

The old man was lying propped up on a pile of pillows. The shutters were closed over the windows, but enough daylight was coming in between the cracks for Jade to see his eyes were closed. He was very pale and she could smell his age: it was a dry dusty smell – like old books – that couldn't be masked by the scent of the rose water sprinkled on the pillows. He seemed so small and withered, and yet this dying old man seemed to fill the entire room with his presence.

The dog flopped down in its place across the doorway. There was no other sound, but the drone of distant voices below. Jade crept closer and peered at the old man, certain she had come too late until he startled her by speaking without opening his eyes.

'Do not be frightened, girl.'

Jade took several steps backwards to the door.

'Wait!' The old man raised a hand to stop her. 'Please. Before you go.' His trembling hand pointed towards the windows. 'I would like to see the light again.'

Jade glanced at the shutters.

'It's that fool of a doctor,' the old man explained. 'He would have me in the dark before I'm ready.'

She hesitated, saw no harm in it and crossed the room. The windows opened inwards, but she had to lean out to push aside the boards. The shutters folded back, to left and right, along the bottom half of the oblongs of glass. The sunlight was sudden and dazzling. It caught in sharp glints in the diamond panes, filling the room with a dappled light. She closed the windows and turned to face the old man.

'Can you see the boats?' he asked.

'Boats?' Jade glanced over her shoulder. 'Yes. There are boats.'

'Tell me what you see.'

She stood uncertainly for a moment. 'I see … nothing much. Just boats and trees and people, I suppose.' She gave up with a shrug. 'That's all.'

'Look again, please,' the old man insisted. 'Describe it to me so I might see it one more time through your eyes.'

Jade hesitated. She wasn't good at this. She tried to find words to describe what she saw, but it sounded so flat and inadequate. A boatman had lost his oar and was trying to get it back. 'He can't quite reach it ...' she ended feebly and would have given up there if he had let her.

He made a winding motion with one hand, indicating for her to go on. So she tried again.

The sun was fast cutting back the shadows on the eastern side of the canal where the house stood. The light was catching on the water, filling it with reflections. She was struck by the impression it gave of the boats sailing on the trees and houses. What had looked ordinary suddenly seemed less so and she found herself telling the old man just how it looked to her. When finally she turned to him again she found him lying with his eyes closed, a slight smile drawing at the corners of his mouth.

'Mr de Leiden?' she whispered.

No answer.

She crossed the room to the bed and touched his hand. His skin felt cool and waxy.

'I was wrong to come here.' She spoke the thought aloud.

'I will be eternally grateful that you did,' the old man said, startling her once more. 'You have done more for an old man in these few short minutes than any of those fools downstairs, Jade van Helsen.'

Jade stepped back from the bed in surprise. 'You know me?'

'I'm old, I am dying, but I am not stupid. It was not so long ago that your father brought you to the Herengracht; to the house that once belonged to the Windjammers.'

'I was there,' Jade nodded. 'But I'm not like my

father!' she added quickly.

The old man tried to laugh, but wheezed painfully instead. For a while he drifted off then came back. 'I like to see the boats on the canal,' he said.

Jade stood there, not knowing what to do or say next. In the end she decided he was too old, too vague to help her. She made up her mind to leave and started towards the door.

'Why did you come here, Jade van Helsen?' the old man stopped her.

She paused. It was hard to tell him the real reason: that she was on the run, desperate and needed money. Instead she just said, 'I came because … because I had to.'

'You have not answered my question.'

'Because … I need help – *money*,' she admitted. It was easier after that. 'I'm leaving Amsterdam,' she explained. 'I'm going far away and I'm not coming back. But I've lost my money and I thought …' Her voice trailed away.

'You thought that I might help you?'

Jade's chin came up slightly. 'I'm not asking for charity. If you help me, I'll help you.' She was defiant. 'It's business, that's all – just *business*.'

She realised her father often justified himself in exactly the same way. She had said it without thinking and sensed that the old man had noticed too, so she went on quickly, 'I overheard something at my father's house – something that could be important to you. But you'll have to pay to hear it.'

'*Pay?*' The old man's eyes opened again. She noticed they were piercingly blue. 'And why would I do that?'

This surprised her. 'Because it's important.'

'I am dying,' he pointed out. 'Why should I care

what goes on in the Street of Knives?'

'Then I'll go,' Jade said. 'I'll go and you'll never know.'

'Of course, that is your right, Jade van Helsen.' He clasped his fingers over his chest and closed his eyes.

'I mean it – I'm leaving.' She didn't move.

The old man remained very still. She wondered how he could be so calm about dying.

'It may surprise you to know that I respect your father,' he broke the silence between them suddenly. 'I do not agree with his business methods or his thirst for wealth and power, but he has made much of his life and, by so doing, *yours* also.'

'My father doesn't care about me. He thinks only of his money,' Jade snapped back.

'Ah yes, *money*,' the old man sighed. 'It means so little to the dying ...' He paused then added. 'There are many who would envy you your gilded cage, my dear.'

'They can have it!' Jade said. 'My father would have me married off and gone to England. He would rather have an alliance with a rich family in London than a daughter living in his house.'

'And I take it you have decided against this marriage?'

'Henry the Goldsmith is more than three times my age! He's an old man! He makes my skin creep.' She hugged her elbows. 'Excuse me, but it's true.' She began to pace. 'How can I love him? I've hardly even met him. How can I live a life like that?'

'Have you considered that your father may simply be doing what he thinks is the best for you?'

Jade looked away. It wasn't supposed to go like this. Why did he make her feel like she was some sort of

Judas? Why did he make her feel she was betraying her father? Her confusion turned to resentment.

'You are old, Mr de Leiden, but you don't know everything.'

'How true,' he conceded.

'I heard my father talking,' she went on, determined to make her point. She wanted to hurt him back a little. 'Your business partner, Mr Cornelius Yort, owes my father money – *a lot* of money.'

'Cornelius Yort is an old friend. He would have told me if he was in trouble.'

'You don't know my father. He *buys* people.'

'Cornelius was here less than an hour ago. He would have said something.'

'He can't, don't you see? My father has the power to destroy him. I overheard them arguing. That's why I followed him here.'

The old man struggled up on his pillows and studied her face. 'You *followed* Cornelius Yort here?'

Jade nodded. She refused to admit it had been upon impulse alone. Instead she countered his accusing look with a question. 'You say he is your friend, but he was at my father's house last night. Did he tell you that?'

The old man eased back on to his pillows. 'Go on.'

'Don't you see – I know my father. He finds a way to make people do things – things they don't want to do ... *Promise* me you'll pay.'

'I promise nothing,' the old man said sternly. 'And you are not in a position to insist. If you were, you would have left by now.'

Jade chewed at her fingernail. She knew it was true. This awkward old man was her only hope.

'They were talking about money,' she started reluctantly and went on to tell him what she had seen and heard at the house on the Street of Knives. 'Cornelius Yort lost a lot of money on tulips.'

The old man nodded. 'I have heard some such rumour.'

'He borrowed from my father and now my father has called in the debt. I heard my father saying something about needing a ship. There's a company – I can't remember the name, but I know it has something to do with Adam Windjammer.'

'Adam Windjammer?' At this the old man sat up again. His eyes showed some spark. 'Are you sure?'

'All I know is that my father wants the company, but he doesn't want anyone to know about it.'

'And that's where Cornelius comes into it, I suppose?' the old man murmured. 'Why didn't he tell me? Why didn't he come to me?' He deflated back on to the pillows with a sigh. His eyes closed and his face collapsed into wrinkles, creasing as if in sudden pain. It was some time before he spoke again. 'This company, this name – was it the Quadrant Shipping and Trading Company?'

Jade remembered it then: *Quadrant*, that was it. But she held back. 'First you must pay me!' she insisted.

The old man sighed and sank deeper into his pillows as if she had already told him all he needed to know. He drifted away, murmuring about the boats for a stretch of time, before coming back with a start.

'So it goes on,' he murmured wearily. 'And my work is not yet done.'

'*What* goes on?' Jade asked. 'What work? I don't understand.'

'Your father is a rich and powerful man, my dear,'

71

the old man said. 'But for all his money he has one great weakness: he believes that everything and everyone has a price.' He looked at her. 'That's not true of you, is it, my dear? And yet, yes, perhaps even you ...'

Jade shifted uncomfortably. 'Why are you looking at me that way?'

'What would you give for your freedom, Jade van Helsen?'

'Anything – *everything*.'

'Even the love of a father?'

Jade felt a jolt. 'I've told you already – my father doesn't love me,' she said flatly.

'Perhaps, perhaps not,' the old man said. 'But how will you ever gain his respect if you run away?'

A hundred questions ran through her head all at once, but only one found its way through the turmoil of her thoughts to her lips. 'What do you mean – his *respect*?' she asked in a whisper.

The old man beckoned her to come closer. 'Stay a while and I will explain, Jade van Helsen. But to understand what I am about to say, you must first know a little more about Adam Windjammer and the Quadrant Shipping and Trading Company ...'

6. Adam Windjammer and Co.

The longboat heaved up, then dipped sharply. From stern to bow, it rocked as the first of the big waves moved under the keel and rolled on towards the shore.

'This is it, lads!' Mr Glass, the *Draco*'s first mate, raised his voice above the noise of the surf. 'We're going in.'

Adam Windjammer sat in the bow of the longboat and watched the wave roll on ahead of them, rising steadily to meet the land. For a while he lost sight of the rocks; the water stood tall in a sparkling array of reflections as if the dawn itself had rolled out of the sky to break on the shore. Then, at last, the wave tripped on the shallows, curled and fell with a booming *crump* that sent fingers of pinkish-white spray to claw the air.

The sea drew back again, foaming around the rocks. The reef was nearer now. The sight of it left Adam feeling squeezed inside.

'Pull, you sheep-heads, *pull*,' Mr Glass encouraged the eight men sweating at the oars. The first mate stood gripping the long arm of the tiller-oar, steering the longboat towards the froth and boil of the surf.

The wreck lay ahead of them, half-hidden in the mist. Once, she had been a fine ship, a merchant galleon built in the old Spanish style: tall forecastle and sloping poop deck, three masts, square top and main sails. Now she lay trapped between the reefs, driven up on Hell's Rock by the relentless pounding of the waves, her decks awash and her keel lost for ever to the fish. Blasted and bleached, the galleon's main mast had been smashed away and what was left of her sails fluttered in rags on her foremast and broken mizzen. And as the waves surged with spent force around her keel, she rolled gently so that with each shift of the rotting hulk the bell on her mizzen mast tolled out as if it had been struck by a phantom hand.

'It's like the Devil's calling us, brothers,' one of the men at the oars spoke up.

'Like he *wants* us to follow,' another agreed.

And sitting in the longboat with the dawn bleeding into the mist it was easy to believe the men's talk. The galleon seemed to be moving ahead of them as if somehow it had been condemned to sail on to eternal destruction.

'That's enough of your talk,' the first mate broke the spell the wreck had cast over them all. 'This here's just a ship broke on the rocks, that's all. A sad sight, it's true – but a ship, nothing more. Isn't that so, Mr Merrik?'

Merrik the mapmaker looked up from the notes and small sketches of the bay he had been making with some difficulty ever since they had left the ship. He lifted his lenses in their wire rims and peered at them with two enormously magnified eyes.

'As a man of science,' he said, 'I find it hard to believe in ghosts.' He attempted to engage the

Frenchman huddled beside him on the bench in the conversation. 'The phantoms, Monsieur! Pfff! No?' he said in bad French.

Victor Valoir cast him a suspicious look, crouching under the wide brim of his hat. He glanced towards the trees that fringed the shore and hunched his shoulders. 'As God loves me, I want more money for this,' was all he said.

An uneasy silence descended on the longboat after that as they rowed, cutting the water with their wooden blades. Mr Glass struck a rock-like pose at the tiller as if nothing could trouble him, but Adam noticed the way his knuckles stood out white as he steered. The first mate was sweating under his helmet and iron breast plate, and it wasn't just because he was dressed and armed for a fight.

Ahead of them the land rose sharply from a curving beach, through the scrub and salt oaks to a cliff that formed the point of land to their right. Beyond, bluish with distance, lay the vast brooding land they called America. Mysterious and unexplored, it stretched away on either side as far as they could see.

Adam glanced back over his shoulder. Some way behind them now the *Draco* lay at anchor in the mouth of the bay. He could still make out the figures standing at the ship's rail watching them go. And even though he believed the moment had come at last – the moment he had been waiting for – he still couldn't quite shake off the feeling that somehow, by doing what was right, by trusting a Frenchman he hardly even knew, he was making the biggest mistake of his life.

It hadn't been easy. The debate had raged across the

map spread out on the captain's table, with Hendrik Honthorst doing most of the talking as usual:

'This is madness, Captain!'

The small man had paced the width of the captain's cabin, turning on his heel as he reached the mapmaker. Adam remembered the way he had glanced at the widow, Madam de Witte, before striding back towards the first mate, returning to face the captain across the map once more. His fist thumped down.

'Do I need to remind you, Captain Lucas, that *I* am the representative of the shareholders of the Quadrant Shipping and Trading Company?'

'How could I forget when you remind me so well and so often, Mr Honthorst?' the captain had replied drily. He sat back. His cheeks were pocked by the scars of smallpox and there was still an unhealthy pallor to his skin. He looked tired, very tired.

'I have my responsibilities, Captain.' Honthorst had puffed up with self-importance. 'As you know, men like Bartholomew de Leiden and Cornelius Yort have invested a great deal of money in this venture and they rely on *me* to look after their interests.' He took a deep breath and regained his composure with effort. 'So I am asking you once again, Captain – bring an end to this fool's errand and make for New Amsterdam. We must reach the safety of the Hudson River while we can. We must stop chasing ...' he searched for the right word and found it, '*phantoms.*'

Even now, as Adam sat in the longboat, he remembered the burning feeling deep in the pit of his stomach at the thought that they might have sailed on without stopping.

'We don't know they're dead,' Adam had spoken up.

The widow's gaze flicked to him.

'That'll do, Master Windjammer,' the captain said.

Hendrik Honthorst turned to him, 'I understand this must be very painful for you, Master Adam,' he had said. 'But there's more than just the Windjammers' family honour to consider now. I know you feel it is your duty to find your uncle's lost ships, but surely you can see it is time to think of the *Draco* and her crew. We could lose everything by going ashore – is that not so, Captain?'

Captain Lucas made no attempt to deny it.

'Do not misunderstand me,' Honthorst appealed to them. 'I am as concerned as anyone here for these poor lost souls. But even if the wreck we have found is the *Sirius* – and we only have the word of that Frenchman out there that it is – how long do you think the crew will have survived here? A week? A month? It's been almost a year since we last heard from the Windjammers' lost fleet. A *year*. This is Cape Fear. If they haven't starved, then animals or natives or the pirates that infest these bays will have got them – I'm sure of it.'

'You seem sure of a good many things, Mr Honthorst,' the mapmaker had spoken up, 'but my maps show good water here –'

'Your maps!' Honthorst made a *humph* sound in the back of his nose. It was a habit he had grown into of late.

'And what's that supposed to mean?' the mapmaker asked, peering at him through his lenses.

'I simply wish to point out that mapmaking is neither an exact science nor, judging from these,' he pointed at the pictures of the sea monsters around the edge of the map, 'a passable form of art.'

'How dare you insult the noble craft of Ptolemy and Mercator!'

'Gentlemen, please! There is no time for your arguments now.' The captain stopped them before they had come to blows. 'Remember there is a lady present.'

'*Ladies*,' the widow corrected him. She was sitting to one side of the captain's table with her African maid, Clara, standing behind like an exotic shadow.

The captain had glanced briefly at Clara, hesitated, then nodded his apology to the widow only. The widow's irritation at this slight to her maid showed.

Hendrik Honthorst leaned close to the captain's ear. 'You would do well to be a little less abrupt, Captain.'

'I am well aware of the importance of Madam de Witte's business to you, Mr Honthorst,' the captain hissed back. 'But this is a company matter ...'

The widow shot a despairing glance at her maid and cleared her throat.

Hendrik Honthorst gave a guilty little start. 'I was just reminding our captain here,' he declared in a voice that always rose an octave in alarm whenever he spoke to her, 'how we at the Quadrant Shipping and Trading Company always put the customer first.'

'And will you, Captain?' the widow had asked. '*Will* you put my interests first?'

'It is time to make our decision,' Captain Lucas nodded. 'I take it, Mr Honthorst, you are against sending the longboat ashore?'

Hendrik Honthorst had pulled himself up to his full, not very impressive height. 'If this is a matter of duty, we owe it to the living now, not the *dead*, Captain. For

the good of the company we must honour our contracts with Madam de Witte and deliver our goods on
time to the people of New Amsterdam. To delay in
these waters would be madness – pure madness!'

The captain had made a note in the ship's log and
looked to the first mate.

'The men don't like it much, Captain. Their heads
are full of ghosts,' Mr Glass said. 'But they'll do as
they're told, I'll see to that.'

The captain nodded as if he expected nothing less
and turned to the mapmaker.

'That wreck out there proves the Frenchman was
telling the truth, Captain,' Merrik the mapmaker said.
'We all know that the Windjammer fleet was heading
for New Amsterdam. If Lucien Windjammer's ships
were caught by a storm they could easily have been
blown off course.' He stepped up to the map and
traced a line until it touched a jutting point of land.
'They do not call it Cape Fear for nothing.' His finger
tapped down. 'So I say *this* is where we'll find survivors, Captain – *if* we dare to look.'

Hendrik Honthorst turned away in frustration even
before the mapmaker had finished speaking. He caught
hold of Adam by the arm, his grip so tight it hurt.

'One day, Master Adam,' he whispered urgently,
'God willing, you will take control of the Quadrant
Shipping and Trading Company and then your family's
fortune will be restored. But to do so, this first voyage
must be a success. We need Madam de Witte. She can
open many doors for us in the Americas trade. So I
am begging *you*, Master Adam, for the sake of the
business and your fortune, think carefully before you
speak now.'

Honthorst moved aside and suddenly Adam found everyone was looking at him. The widow's silence was ominous, her stillness – but for the flick of those dark eyes – unnerving. In those moments he decided she was the scariest woman he had ever met.

'Well, Master Windjammer,' the captain had asked after a pause, 'and what do *you* say?'

The great disc of the sun broke up over the far horizon and climbed ponderously over the eastern edge of the world. The brightness obliterated the *Draco* and forced Adam out of his thoughts. He looked away with dark sun spots jumping before his eyes.

'Be ready with your grappling iron, Master Windjammer,' Mr Glass raised his voice against the boom of the surf. 'It's up to you to get a line aboard.'

Adam unhooked the fingers of one hand from the boat just long enough to make sure the three-pronged hook was within easy reach. The grappling iron was attached to a length of rope tied to the bow. He couldn't help wondering how he was going to stand up and throw it aboard the galleon if he could hardly let go of the gunwale for more than a moment.

Water exploded over the bow. The spray stung his eyes, soaking through his coat and into his sun-bleached shirt. The salt prickled his skin. The water chased down the small of his back, dripping through the waistband of his breeches, and raced down the backs of his legs, soaking his long socks and filling his boots.

All the while the wooden blades flicked away the sunlight, dipping and rising and dipping again.

'We'll ride the next wave in – nice and easy,' Mr Glass said as he stood at the tiller. He seemed oblivious to the bucking longboat beneath him. 'Ship oars when I give the word!'

Behind them the sea moved and began to rise. A wave reared up, stretching away on either side as far as the eye could see. It was beautiful and terrible all at once: misted here and there with bursts of sand and trails of dredged-up seaweed, sparkling, shimmering, rolling in with all the majesty and power of the distant storm that had given it life. And in its roar it was easy to believe they could hear the voice of some vengeful native god.

'Break your backs now!' The first mate called for more speed as he timed their run. 'Pull for your lives. *Pull. Pull. Pull.*'

The wooden blades picked up speed. The ocean seemed to suck in an enormous watery breath. The stern dipped, the bow came up then dropped again almost immediately as the long boat was dragged backwards up the face of the wave.

'Now, lads, *now,*' Mr Glass roared and eight oars came out of the water, thumping on to the gunwales as the men laid the blades flat to the sides and braced themselves.

The wave rolled on, scooping them up and thrusting them forward as if some beast had suddenly reached up out of the deep and picked up the longboat with one foaming claw. It hurled them towards the reef, pushing them on. The lip curled over them. It rolled in on itself from right to left, turning over, faster and faster, until suddenly it was thundering down at terrible speed. And the wave was at its most awesomely beautiful in the moments before its self-destruction.

Adam clung to the gunwale. He had lost sight of the line of dark water that marked the channel between the reefs. He searched for it desperately, his head full of the roar of the wave that threatened to crash down and swamp the longboat and hurl them on to the pocked and razor-edged reef.

The longboat bucked, caught suddenly by the surge. It shot forward in a sudden gut-wrenching rush, bursting out of the seething white spume, past the rocks at the mouth of the channel and into the gap between the reefs. The current had them then. The race of the water set them rocking wildly from side to side. The gunwale struck a rock and glanced off, tearing splinters away as long as a man's arm. On they raced, on and on towards the galleon.

'Make ready, Master Windjammer!' Mr Glass's voice came out of the tumult.

Adam's head was pounding. His hand was shaking as he took up the heavy grappling iron. The points of the curling hooks were wickedly sharp. Half crouching, he rode the storm, braced against the gunwale like a harpooner ready to strike at a whale.

They came in fast, approaching the wreck of the galleon from astern on the starboard quarter. Everywhere he looked he could see evidence of the ship's violent end. The rail and bulwarks had been smashed away in places and he could see silver fish moving in and out of the seaweed growing out through the gaping hole in the galleon's side. They passed into the shadow of the cliff and instantly the mist and shifting patterns of reflected light conspired to play tricks on his eyes. He blinked hard, trying to judge the distance. And all the while he could hear the bell tolling mournfully, calling them.

'Now! Master Windjammer! Now!' Mr Glass roared.

With one swift movement Adam came to his feet, stretching as he hurled the grappling iron with all his strength. The hook disappeared over the wooden wall of the bulwark and landed with a thump on the deck. The longboat surged on past the galleon at a level just below the quarterdeck. Adam gripped the rope tightly. He felt the iron catch briefly then slip to catch again.

The rope came taut so suddenly it jerked out of Adam's hands and almost pitched him overboard. He found himself clinging to the side and just had time to pull his head back before he was crushed between the gunwale and the galleon. His senses came together to the sound of the rope burning out over the side of the longboat. A moment later it reached the end and came taught against the bow. It stretched, humming with the tension, sending droplets of water showering away, and just when he thought it was sure to snap, the longboat juddered and began to turn.

Slowly at first, the bow swung around until it was pointing back the way they had come. The longboat bucked from side to side. The current threatened to swamp them by the bow, until suddenly they were out of the current and into the dead water where the galleon lay. At last they came alongside, wood scraping on wood. The exhausted men slumped forward over their oars.

'*Nice 'n' easy*, that's what he said, brothers.' A man called Allart was the first to complain.

The surf boomed on the outer reef. Another surge of water raced down the channel, streaming past the galleon, shifting the wreck and the longboat together.

'For the love of God,' Mr Glass said, 'will someone not silence that bell?'

7. Leviathans

The bell fell to a single cut from Govert's blade. It dropped with a clatter and a clang and, before he could stop it, a sudden shift of the wreck sent it rolling down the slope of the deck, trailing a jangle of cracked notes behind. It reached the port side where the ship's rail and bulwarks had been smashed away and dropped, still clanging, into the water to sink without a trace.

A sudden, eerie quiet enveloped the wreck, deepening the sense of gloom the cliff cast over them.

'I said silence it, not throw it overboard!' Mr Glass snarled at Govert. The first mate's threats to come aboard and shake some sense into him were interrupted by the sound of the bell as it came echoing back from the cliff.

'That's done it, brothers,' Allart spoke up gloomily. 'The bell's gone, but it *still* keeps calling us.'

'Don't start that again!' Mr Glass rounded on him.

The men exchanged uneasy glances over their oars. It seemed everyone regretted disturbing that rotting tomb.

'Forget the dead!' Mr Glass said, glancing towards the shore. 'We'd better hope that fool Govert hasn't woken the *living*.' He looked back up at the young crewman he had sent aboard. 'Can you see a name anywhere? Anything to tell us what ship this was?'

'Yes, Mr Glass,' Govert called back, brightening. 'There was a name on the bell. I saw it – as clear as anything.'

'On the *bell*? Good lad!' Mr Glass sounded pleased. 'What did it say?'

There was a long pause. 'I don't rightly know, Mr Glass,' Govert's pitiful answer came back at last. 'No one never did teach me lettering.'

Mr Glass pinched the bridge of his nose in a tired sort of way. 'If you want something done properly ...' he muttered through a sigh before making the jump on to the galleon's side.

Adam didn't hesitate. He followed close behind, leaping across the gap and scaling the ship's side on to the quarterdeck.

'A hand here!' the mapmaker said, rocking the boat by deciding to go too. Before Mr Glass could stop him, he had clambered out over the oars and was climbing after them. Once on the quarterdeck he settled his wide-brimmed hat and fumbled for his lenses that hung on the chain around his neck.

The wreck shifted under Adam's feet. He steadied himself and looked around. The splintered end of the broken rail and bulwark caught his eye and left him wondering what terrible struggle of life and death had happened there.

'More lettering, Mr Glass!' Govert said, pointing at the name carved into the split and weathered lintel over the door that led into what had been the captain's cabin.

The first mate called Adam over. But Adam already knew the truth. He had known it from the moment he had set foot aboard.

'So the Frenchie was telling the truth,' Mr Glass said. 'It's the *Sirius* all right. And it looks like we're not the first to set foot aboard her since she ran aground. She's been stripped clean and only the bell left as a warning, I'll wager.' He strode to the side and looked down into the longboat. 'Here, Manfred! Bring that Frenchie aboard! I want a word with him.'

Manfred, a big Rhinelander, lifted a startled-looking Victor Valoir over the side and Mr Glass took hold of him by the collar, hauling him aboard.

'So who's been here, *Mon-sewer*?' the first mate asked. 'Who's salvaged this ship to her boards?'

'Mr Glass! That is quite enough,' the mapmaker interceded. 'You will treat Monsieur Valoir with respect.' He peered apologetically at the Frenchman. 'I pardon you, Monsieur,' he said.

The Frenchman looked even more surprised. He wiped at the sweat on his top lip and muttered. 'There'd better be gold ...'

'What he say?' Mr Glass growled.

The mapmaker attempted to ask him with only a scowl for a reply.

The first mate scratched at his beard. 'He don't understand much French for a Frenchie, do he, Mr Merrik?' he said, never considering it might be the mapmaker's language skills that were at fault.

'Perhaps it was the *Sirius*'s crew,' the mapmaker said. 'Perhaps they escaped in the ship's boat and came back later to salvage what they could.'

'If it was them, they didn't use the boat,' Mr Glass said, nodding towards the tangled wreckage piled up against the forecastle. 'It looks like the main mast crushed it when it fell.'

'But there must be some chance!' The mapmaker attempted to keep the hope alive for Adam's sake.

Mr Glass looked doubtfully towards the shore. 'I've yet to meet a sailor who can swim more than a dozen strokes,' the first mate said grimly. 'And, as God is my witness, the currents around here could take down any man.'

'I'm sure Lucien Windjammer, like Adam here, was well versed in the watery arts.'

'The question is, Mr Merrik, would the boy's uncle have been the sort of man to leave his men to save himself?'

And no matter how much Adam wished the map-maker was right – no matter how much he tried to hold on to the hope – he knew, deep inside, that Lucien Windjammer would never have willingly abandoned his men.

'Now,' the first mate said, 'if this Frenchie knows so much about this wreck, I'll wager he also knows what happened to the crew.' He turned to the Frenchman. 'The crew, *Mon-sewer*? The *crew*?'

The Frenchman shook his head and shrugged.

'Surely, Monsieur, to the beach some of them arrives?' the mapmaker questioned him.

In the silence that followed a breath of wind lifted off the water and stirred across the decks. They shifted uneasily.

'I don't like this place, Mr Glass,' Govert said.

'Maybe it *is* cursed.'

'Did I ask *you*?' the first mate growled. 'Now get up into the stern and keep watch or you'll be visited by the curse of my boot!'

Adam felt the mapmaker's hand on his shoulder. He shook it off and crossed the quarterdeck to push at the broken door into the captain's cabin. It juddered back. The reality of the wreck was undeniable. The utter deadness of it overwhelming.

He retreated from the empty cabin and moved back across the quarterdeck. The wreck shifted under his feet and he steadied himself by holding on to the forward rail.

He wondered now what he had hoped to find. In his wildest imaginings he hadn't expected to come aboard and find Lucien Windjammer and his crew sitting around, waiting to be rescued. But neither had he been prepared for this – this *nothing*. Above all else he feared that nothingness now. In nothing there could be no end and no beginning. No release.

His grip tightened on the rail in front of him and he fought the tears that burned suddenly at the backs of his eyes. Furiously he told himself he was almost sixteen – no longer a child. But the truth was, deep inside, he felt he was still just that same frightened boy who had watched his father die. He closed his eyes and instantly his thoughts were sucked far away ...

... The old house on the Herengracht. The Windjammers emerging with the dawn to go down to the waterfront. Adam could see his father, sombre in black, walking with his mother. Their faithful servant, Gerrit, was there. His sisters too – the twins laughing and skipping. Even Uncle Augustus walked with them.

'Yes, yes, indeed,' Augustus was saying. 'It is a fine day for the beginning of such a great enterprise.'

He saw the waterfront now: crowded and busy, full of life. For most there it was a day like any other. Unknown to the Windjammers, for them it was the beginning of the end. A day in early spring almost two years ago. The day Lucien Windjammer led the Windjammers' Star Fleet away from Amsterdam for the last time.

Only now it was him – not Lucien Windjammer – who was standing on the quarterdeck. The *Sirius* seemed to come alive under Adam's feet as his mind ran free like a white bird on the wind. He heard voices, voices of men he knew were dead, chanting voices singing shantys as they hauled on the ropes. And just for a moment, he began to believe that somehow he had fulfilled his duty and had brought the *Sirius* back from the dead. Then he heard Mr Glass speaking as if from a great distance ...

'We've seen enough here,' the first mate said.

The voices faded. Adam was drawn back with a rush. He opened his eyes. He was still standing in the wreck of his old life. Inexorably his gaze was drawn up to the face of the cliff that loomed over them. He saw it then for what it was: a giant gravestone, a blank monument to Lucien Windjammer and his crew and a blunt end of life he had once known.

He tried to deny it, of course. He was not ready to let go. 'There has to be more,' he breathed, turning to the Frenchman. 'There just *has* to be.'

'What about the natives?' Allart asked as he helped unload the powder and shot from the longboat. 'What about *them* – that's what I want to know.'

'Natives?' Govert yelped, clutching his musket. 'I don't see no natives.'

'Course you don't,' Allart said as if he carried all the wisdom of the world in his head. 'You don't *see* them. You don't even *hear* them – not until it's too late.' He drew a finger across his neck and made his eyes bulge out of his narrow face in a peculiar way of his own. 'But you mark my words, brothers, they'll be here,' he looked towards the line of trees, 'watching, *waiting*.'

Adam glanced up. From the moment he had helped the men pull the longboat up out of the shallows on to the sand, he'd had the uncomfortable feeling they weren't alone. By now the sun was beginning to climb on to the shoulder of the cliff, forcing the shadows to retreat into a darker line under the trees. The canopy steamed a gentle mist, the myriad shades of green cut here and there with the blur of colourful wings. This strange, unexplored land was alive with movement and unfamiliar bird calls.

'I've heard stories, that's all,' Allart went on. 'Tales about the Indians that'll make your toes curl up and drop off.'

And no one seemed to doubt him on that point – no one but Merrik, that is.

'I couldn't help overhearing what you said,' the map-maker spoke up as he settled the strap of his wooden map box over one shoulder. 'And I believe there is much misunderstanding here. For a start it is incorrect to call the natives of these parts "Indians". We are not in the Indies, so how can they be Indians? They are natives of the Americas and I have heard much to make me believe them to be noble and civilised tribes.

Perhaps a good deal *more* civilised than we Europeans who come to their shore with powder and shot.'

The men glanced at one another, not sure what to believe. The mapmaker, after all, collected plants and insects wherever he went and was clearly a man with strange ideas about the natural order of things. Nevertheless, there was some half-hearted thanking of him for shutting Allart up at least. The mapmaker beamed his pleasure at being able to shed a little light in the darkness of their ignorance, shifted his wooden map box on to his hip and started towards the trees, leaving Allart looking foolish behind him.

'Well, maybe he's right about the Indians, brothers,' he said, before adding, 'But what about the tribes of cannibal giants with no heads that live here? What about them? That's what *I* want to know.'

'*Cannibals*,' Govert gasped. 'No one said nothing about *cannibals*.'

'Not to mention the giants,' another agreed.

And so the debate would have gone on around the longboat had Mr Glass not appeared from the trees at that moment and set off towards them across the sand.

Adam could see from the first mate's expression that something was wrong. Mr Glass paused briefly to talk to the mapmaker, who in turn spoke to Victor Valoir, before continuing. Two men with muskets followed him until he pointed first one way and then the other, sending them to keep watch from nearby rocks. Mr Glass's heavy advance brought him down to the longboat, his boots lifting sprays of sand off the toes at every step until at last he filled Adam's entire vision and stopped.

'You best come and take a look at this, Master Windjammer,' he said.

The whale had been cast up on the shore, hurled up long ago by some time-forgotten storm as if the sea itself had felt the need to make an offering to atone for the damage it had caused to the land. The carcass and blubber had rotted away, leaving the ribs exposed to the encroaching creepers and strangler vines. Over the years, curved whale bone had been drawn in and sown impenetrably together, until it had become part of the jungle itself, forming a vaulted chamber that stood twice as high as a man. And it was there – in a tomb befitting a sailor king – that they found the skeleton.

'By all the saints – it's *Jonah* himself,' Allart muttered.

They crowded in under the trees, craning their necks for a better look, until Mr Glass pushed them back to allow Adam to step forward alone.

'Take a look at the mark on his belt, Master Windjammer,' the first mate said.

Adam moved without feeling, one step then another taking him towards the whale's great skull. He hesitated, steeling himself before he reached out and pulled back the trailing creepers.

No flesh. The skin rotted and fallen away. Only empty sockets where eyes had once been. A skull face greeted him with the jaw fallen open as if uttering one last command. He had been a tall man, big-boned and strong, and his coat still clung to his ribs in patches, his bone fingers emerging from brass-buttoned cuffs at the end of sleeves that had yet to decay. One boot on, the other lost. The heat and humidity and the ants had done for the rest, stripping away all that was fine and graceful from him, leaving little but stark bones and the leather of his broad belt where a brass-plate buckle bore a mark.

Adam's hand went to the ring he wore on the chain around his neck. He felt the same mark engraved there: the W bearing the weight of the globe. It was the mark of what had once been a great merchant house – the House of Windjammer. And in that instant he knew the search for his uncle, Lucien Windjammer, was over.

Adam stepped into the belly of the whale and stood very still. Invisible creepers seemed to twist around his ankles, drawing him down into the earth. And all the while the blank, eyeless skull just stared back at him, grinning in the certain knowledge of all that was eternal and secret.

Outwardly, calm. Inwardly, Adam was running – running through a blizzard of thoughts – shouting in the wilderness of some great empty landscape. He had built pillars of hope to support castles of dreams, only to have the flat reality of death reduce them to a heap of bones.

It left him feeling strangely empty. He found himself wondering how this pile of bones could be the man he remembered, the man who had carried him high on his shoulders, the laughing uncle who had taught him to sail and swim and throw a knife.

His anger came as a relief. It was easier to feel something rather than nothing and he let it rage silently in a torment of frustration.

'I'm too late – too *late*!' he hissed. He wanted to kick away the bones, to scatter them and trample them to dust. Then as quickly as it had come, his fury left him and once again he felt the weight of his emptiness. He eased down on to his knees and bowed his head.

'I needed you, Uncle,' he whispered. 'We *all* needed you. Everything's gone. The house, the business – *everything*. The banker Hugo van Helsen took it all after we lost the fleet. And now Father's dead and Gerrit too ... just like you.' A pause. His voice came back strongly. 'And don't think Uncle Augustus will help us. He ran away when we needed him most. Now there's only me and my mother and sisters left. You remember Rose and Viola, Uncle? They're just children. How can *we* rebuild the House of Windjammer alone? How can we become strong again without you?'

Death just continued to grin back, mocking him, and Adam felt the full weight of his self-pity and loneliness. And there perhaps his search might have ended with part of him tied for ever to a place called Hell's Rock, had it not been for the men of the *Draco*.

'How do we know he didn't just crawl in there and die?' one asked.

'Take a look for yourself,' another answered. 'It's like a tomb in there.'

'Natives?'

'Can't be. He's been laid out east to west – a Christian's done this.'

And suddenly it was as if Adam's eyes had been opened. Now as he looked around he saw beyond the bones. What had appeared to be a litter of flotsam became much more. With a start he realised they had been placed there with utmost care: a pewter mug, a black bottle, pulley-blocks from a ship's rigging and more, much more. He looked up and saw shells hanging over the bones. Dozens of them. They had been tied into lengths of creeper and threaded on twists of dry grass, and he reached up and brushed them, setting them knocking together so they tinkled like tiny bells. There was something about this simple gesture, something naive and adoring – almost child-like – and then the full meaning of what it all meant rocked him back suddenly.

The answer came like a hand out of the darkness, a lifeline thrown to him in the moment of his drowning. Adam came to his feet. He stood for a moment longer before turning away. He pushed through the men pressing in around the entrance to the tomb. They parted on either side as he stepped out and moved through them, searching for Victor Valoir.

'Has anyone seen the Frenchie?' the first mate asked, looking around.

'He's gone,' Govert said.

'Vanished, brothers,' Allart agreed.

'Why weren't you keeping an eye on him?' Mr Glass snarled.

Adam headed for the beach.

'Where are you going, Adam?' the mapmaker called after him.

'Someone survived the wreck, Mr Merrik – they must have done. Whoever it is, I'm going to find him.'

'But, Master Windjammer –' the first mate objected.

'He's right, Mr Glass,' the mapmaker stopped him. 'Someone must have lived to lay out his uncle in this tomb.'

'But surely we're to fetch canvas and bury your uncle first, Master Windjammer?' the first mate called out.

Adam looked back at the whale. He knew no marble tomb could have been carved better. He shook his head. 'Leave the dead in peace, Mr Glass,' he said. 'It's the living we have to find now.'

He walked on without looking back again. Trees loomed and passed as he moved through the shadows and out into the light. He stopped when his boots sank into the sand. The surf flicked and fell on the reef close to the wreck and he breathed in the rhythm of the ocean. He felt strangely calm now and in that moment he knew Lucien Windjammer was finally at peace.

8. An Unwelcome Visit

The pig burst out of cover ahead of them. It squealed loudly as if in pain and ran, unseen except for the swathe of destruction it caused in the undergrowth.

At the head of the line, the big Rhinelander called Manfred came to a halt, his blade still raised as if expecting an attack. Further back, Adam stopped as the men in the line ahead of him bunched up. They stood and listened to the wild pig crashing through the undergrowth with a mixture of relief and regret. Relief that it wasn't the ambush they feared. Regret because they were all hungry for fresh meat.

'You mark my words, brothers. It'll be us roasting on spits soon, not porkers.' Allart was his usual gloomy self.

'I pity the poor cannibal who has to eat you, Allart,' Mr Glass growled as he went striding past. 'You're enough to give anyone a belly ache.'

The men around him laughed and the tension eased a little. Mr Glass ordered the men to move on and Manfred let his blade fall, hacking into the creepers. The line started forward again. They fell silent as they worked their way through the dappled world under the spread of the trees.

Two hours had passed since they had begun their search. They had said a few words over Lucien Windjammer before closing up his tomb and leaving him where he lay. Govert had been left to guard the longboat and to keep watch for signals from the *Draco*, while Mr Glass had led the search along the shore for any sign that the survivors might have left for them to follow. They had found no sign of the Frenchman, nor any sign of shelters or a camp that might have been built by the survivors of the *Sirius*. Now they walked in silence, alert to the sounds around them, cutting their way through the undergrowth and the clouds of blood-sucking insects that had come out to torment them.

'Do you remember the story of Prometheus, Adam?' the mapmaker asked, breaking a silence that had lasted between them for some time. 'The story of the young Titan who stole the fire of the gods?'

The mapmaker paused, leaning heavily on the stick Mr Glass had cut for him. He shifted his mapping box on to the other hip, wiped his forehead with the sleeve of his coat and fanned at the mosquitoes with his wide-brimmed hat.

'If I remember rightly,' he said thoughtfully, 'Zeus, the king of the gods, punished Prometheus by chaining him to a great rock. And each day an eagle would come and tear out Prometheus's liver and each night his liver grew back so his torment could begin all over again the next day.'

It was a myth, nothing more – one of many Adam's ancient tutor, Meister Bloem, had tried to teach him.

'I imagine Prometheus's rock to be a little like this one,' the mapmaker said, lifting his lenses to peer at the cliff that loomed over the trees above them. He sighed. 'But then the past can be like a rock – is that not so, Adam?'

Adam regarded him warily, knowing that there was some message for him in this. The mapmaker patted him on the shoulder with a wry smile.

'I have grown to like you on this voyage, Adam,' he said. 'So take some good advice. However this turns out – whether we find anyone alive here or not – let that be an end to your searching. For your sake as well as your family's, do not chain yourself to the past for ever. I fear it will cost you dearly.' There was something in his look that seemed to say there was more to it than what had been said, but already the men ahead of them were fast disappearing into the undergrowth and the mapmaker sighed, adding, 'And now it seems we must *both* move on.'

Soon afterwards they reached a stream and a halt was called to allow the men to rest and refill their water skins. Impatient not to waste time, Adam walked on a little way and climbed on to some rocks. Allart watched him go and spat.

'You mark my words, brothers,' he said. 'A Windjammer brought us here and a Windjammer'll bury us here too if we aren't careful. I seen it in that boy's eyes. It's like a worm that's got into his head.'

'That's enough from you, Allart,' Mr Glass said. 'And you'd do well to show Master Windjammer some respect.'

'Respect now is it, Mr Glass?' Allart replied. 'And there was me thinking that was something to be earned like everything else in life.'

'That tongue of yours'll get you hung for a mutineer one day,' the first mate warned. 'Now you leave the boy alone.'

'And what's he to you, Mr Glass?' Allart asked. 'It's plain you've been keeping a close eye on him ever since he came aboard.'

'Don't be a fool!' the first mate growled.

But Allart wasn't the sort to give up. He turned to the men around him. 'I'll wager a Spanish gold ounce that there's more to this than Mr Glass wants us to know.'

'And where would you get a Spanish gold ounce from?' Mr Glass tried to laugh it off. But others were left wondering.

Adam stood on the rock, unaware of the resentment simmering behind him. He studied the line of the ridge above them. From there he knew he would be able to see a long way. He tried to pick a way up to it through the trees. But he couldn't shake off his growing sense of foreboding. He heard a shriek, and high above there was an explosion of feathers as a huge bird burst up from the ridge.

'A sea eagle!' he heard the mapmaker shout. 'Look at it! What a bird!'

The eagle rose over Hell's Rock, spiralling up, black and white against the metallic blue of the sky until it turned away to vanish like the piebald incarnation of a great spirit. Adam's gaze fell back to the trees. The shadows seemed deeper after the brightness of the sky, the undergrowth more impenetrable and tangled. He shivered despite the heat and jumped down from the rock, slipping back to the stream where the men were gathered.

'You've sensed it too, Master Windjammer,' the first mate said, glancing up at the ridge. 'There's more than just us here, that's for certain.'

Almost as he spoke a shot cracked at the air. The sudden report of the gun startled them all, scaring brightly coloured birds out of the trees. The men snatched up their muskets and cutlasses and drew into a defensive circle, facing out in all directions. Tense moments passed before a second shot sent echoes ricocheting around the cliffs.

'It's the signal,' Mr Glass said. 'We're being called back to the longboat. Right, lads, get back into line and keep your eyes skinned!' He started pushing the men into some semblance of order. 'Light the fuse on that musket, Manfred. I'll wager a pound of salt there'll be trouble before this day's out.'

'We can't go back yet!' Adam said. 'We have to get up to the ridge. It isn't far and we'll be able to see everything from there.'

'I'm sorry, Master Windjammer,' the first mate shook his head, 'but I have my orders.'

'But we're so close!' Adam insisted. 'This could be our only chance.'

'There's not a man here who'll say we haven't tried, Master Windjammer,' Mr Glass said. 'But them bones down there speak for themselves.'

'Mr Glass is right, Adam,' the mapmaker agreed. 'We've done everything we can. If someone was here they'd have seen us. There's no shame in looking to the *Draco* and her crew now.'

'Then I'll go alone,' Adam said. 'It won't take me long and I can meet you back at the longboat.'

Mr Glass laid a hand on his shoulder. 'I'm sorry, but

the captain put me in charge and I've said my final word on it. Now we're all going back together even if I have to carry you every step of the way.'

Adam's eyes flashed his fury and frustration. He stood his ground defiantly for a moment longer. The mapmaker took him by the arm and attempted to steer him back the way they had come. Adam shook him off furiously, shot a final despairing glance at the ridge and pushed past them, heading back down the trail they had cut in the undergrowth.

'In time he'll come to understand we have no choice, Mr Glass,' the mapmaker said. 'Adam's young – impetuous.'

'I know that, Mr Merrik,' the first mate said. 'I was told to watch for it even before I signed aboard for this voyage.'

Mr Glass strode away, but the mapmaker paused.

'*Before* you came aboard, Mr Glass?' he called out, trying to catch up.

'It's the *Draco*, Mr Glass!' Govert greeted them with the bad news as they reached the beach.

'What about her?' Mr Glass hissed.

'She's cut her anchor, sir. She's leaving!'

'*Leaving?* Don't be a damn fool!' Mr Glass pushed past him and strode down the beach. He stopped and shaded his eyes, looking out to sea.

'He's right,' one of the men said to the others as they crowded on to the sand.

Already they could see the sails unfurling on the *Draco*'s masts. Nothing happened for a moment, then a cry went up. They broke into a run, swarming down to the water's edge to take hold of the gunwales and heave the longboat off the sand into the shallows.

Mr Glass strode in among them, urging them into the boat. He managed to instil some order into the launch and soon the men were back at their oars. Adam slid into his place in the bow and the first mate had already taken up the tiller, when they realised the mapmaker was missing.

'He'll have to take his chances, Mr Glass!' Allart spoke against going back for him. 'You can see for yourself the captain's cut and run.' He looked to the men for support. 'What's to stop him keeping right on running to New Holland – I ask you that, brothers?'

Others nodded and growled their agreement.

Mr Glass silenced them. 'The Frenchie can look after himself, but I'm not leaving Mr Merrick behind, by God!' He let his gaze travel over them, daring any among them to argue. They shifted under the weight of his stare, but said nothing. Mr Glass grunted. 'Master Windjammer, you'll be quickest. Run back and find him, if you would!' He glared at the men, daring them to disagree. 'The boat'll be waiting for you when you get back, I give my oath on it.'

Adam jumped down into the shallows and splashed ashore again. He raced up the beach and plunged into the trees, following the trail they had cut through the under-growth. He hadn't gone far when he found the mapmaker kneeling, bent over the spilled contents of his map box.

'My precious inks, Adam,' he gasped. 'I dropped them. I can't leave them. You have no idea how valuable they are.'

'There's no time, Mr Merrik,' Adam said, pulling him to his feet. 'The *Draco*'s set full sail.'

'*Full sail*. Surely not!'

'If we don't go now, Mr Merrik, we'll be marooned here.'

The mapmaker managed to stuff several more ink bottles into his map box and came to his feet. Adam hurried him down towards the beach. They burst out on to the sand and were greeted by the shouts of the men, urging them to be quick.

'Leave me, Adam,' the mapmaker panted as he struggled to keep up. 'Go on – save yourself.'

Adam caught hold of his arm and dragged him on faster down to the boat. At last they were splashing into the shallows. Mr Glass reached out and hauled the mapmaker aboard with little ceremony.

'Oh my goodness!' the mapmaker gasped. 'Really, Mr Glass, is that necessary?'

Adam pulled himself up out of the water and rolled into the bow, falling between the thwarts into the bottom of the boat, gulping for breath. He sat up and took one last look for the Frenchman.

'Row!' the first mate roared. 'Put your backs into it, lads! Row like the very Devil!'

But it was already too late. Even as they drew level with the wreck of the *Sirius* and plunged into the seething white waters around the reefs, the *Draco* was beginning to turn towards the open sea.

Allart saw what was happening and came to his feet shouting. Others did the same, and the longboat rocked violently as the men shouted and whistled until their voices echoed around the face of the cliff as if there were an army of lost souls begging not to be marooned on Hell's Rock.

'Steady, lads!' The first mate had difficulty regaining order.

The men, desperate, set to the oars again and sent the longboat plunging into the surf. The bow came up sharply against a wave and almost tipped them all out. The boat was forced back with a lurch and they tried again only to be hurled back once more by the next wave. Time after time it was the same. Finally, exhausted, they were forced to admit defeat. But their troubles had only just begun.

'*Spaniards*,' Mr Glass shouted as a galleon burst around the headland, all sheets to the wind.

The warning struck terror into the hearts of the men. They twisted their necks to see for themselves as the great golden galleon turned into the bay in pursuit of the *Draco*.

'Oh, that's all we need,' Allart groaned. 'A visit from the most Holy Order of the Spanish Inquisition.'

'Back to the shore!' Mr Glass shouted, slamming the tiller hard over.

The longboat began to cut a turn though the water and Adam found himself staring back over the heads of the men as they rowed. He had seen great ships before, but never a galleon of King Philip IV's Imperial Navy. The ship was as fine as it was awesome, a machine of war, armed and ready for the fight. Her four masts were crowded with sails, her mastheads trailed long battle standards and on her mainmast flew the flag of the radiant Madonna and Christ child, as if to prove that this Spanish captain even had God on his side.

'They've seen us,' Mr Glass raised his voice. 'Make it lively, lads! It'll go ill for us if their gunners catch us out in the open.'

'But we've done nothing to the Spanish, Mr Glass!'

the mapmaker yelped, his hand clamped down hard on his hat.

'You're forgetting the *Draco* flies the Dutch flag, Mr Merrik,' Mr Glass said grimly. 'We were at war when last I heard and I'll wager King Philip's men think so too.'

As if to prove him right, the galleon was already making a pass into the bay to bring her guns to bear on the longboat. Adam could see men in the rigging and others on deck. A moment later there was a puff of smoke from one of the cannons in the forecastle. The cannonball raised a spout close enough to cause some of the men at the oars to miss their stroke. A wave caught them; Adam tried to hold on, but such was the force of the water he was hurled over the side head first.

He came up to see Mr Glass reaching towards him. 'Catch hold, Master Windjammer!'

A rope snaked out, splashing down in a line across the water. Adam made a lunge for it, but couldn't reach. Mr Glass drew it in, looping it quickly in one hand and let it fly out once more. It fell short again. Another cannonball landed close by, the explosion throwing up a rush of water that knocked Mr Glass over backwards into the bottom of the boat. In the confusion that followed the longboat was caught by the current and sucked away at frightening speed.

Adam was left treading water helplessly. He looked around and saw the wreck of the *Sirius*. He struck out for it, swimming strongly with the current now, arm over arm, until it loomed over him. He caught hold and pulled himself up on to the side. It took all his strength to drag himself out of the water. Gasping for breath, he heaved himself up and clung there until a crackle of musketry reminded him of the plight of the others.

By the time Adam reached the quarterdeck and had leapt up the rotting steps to the poop deck, the Spanish galleon had begun its run as close as it could to the line of the reef. The sunlight struck sparks from the helmets and weapons of the soldiers lining the decks. Spanish marines were lined up in the forecastle, their muskets levelled on wooden stands. On the commands of their officers they were laying down a withering fire that set the water seething around Mr Glass and the others as they cowered helplessly in the longboat not far from the wreck.

Almost without thinking Adam leapt up on to the stern and took hold of the broken lantern. Frantically he waved, shouting insults in an effort to attract attention and draw the fire away from the longboat. At last someone aboard the galleon noticed him and pointed. After that everything changed.

Adam saw the gaping mouths of the cannons as they were run out on the galleon's upper gun deck. A line of them, twenty at least were aiming right at the *Sirius*.

'That *can't* be good!' he yelped. He abandoned the lantern and leapt down, hit the slope of the poop deck and took the steps three at a time. The rotten timbers of the quarterdeck splintered as he landed and took off at a run. He had no time to think, he just launched himself out over the water as the very fabric of the world was ripped apart by the roar of the guns.

The shock of the blast rolled over Adam. It sucked the breath from his lungs and sent him far beyond himself. He shot away into some strange grey middle-distance and, for what seemed an eternity, he thought he would just keep on going. Then he caught a glimpse of something he had left far behind. It was only a speck at first, but as he looked it suddenly became much closer. He recognised the wreck and there, flying through the air from the quarterdeck, arms and legs flailing, he was amazed to see himself. An instant later he hit the water and the shock brought him back inside himself with a rush.

Down he went. Down into the race of the water, down into the swirl and swish with his head ringing as if it were filled with a million bells. His senses began to come together and he became aware of a burning sensation in his lungs. He kicked hard and began to rise until at last he burst up to drag in a breath. Immediately the noise engulfed him.

Adam couldn't see the Spanish galleon. The *Sirius* was in the way, shuddering continuously as gaping holes appeared in the rotten hull. A deadly rain of iron and splintered wood showered down into the water. Something heavy speared in close by and Adam grabbed it as it came up. It was a piece of broken spar and he hugged it to his chest. The current had him again and he went with it.

The end came quickly then. Deep in the heart of the wreck something cracked. What was left of the *Sirius*'s hull bulged, held together for a moment longer, then burst open like a rotten carcass. The rush of the water forced the wood apart. It broke up into jagged pieces that rolled and tumbled into a deadly churning mass, engulfing everything.

Adam let go of the spar and struck out for the shore with all his strength. The great weight of water and wreckage hit him. He was sure his arms and legs would be torn from their sockets. He went under and came up and was dragged down again even while he was trying to snatch a breath. Something caught him a glancing blow and everything was swallowed up in the shock of the violence. Dark shapes loomed and passed. He kicked out at them, struggling in the broiling, riotous, spinning world that engulfed him and went on and on and on, until his soul seemed to blend with the water as if it were the only thing he had ever known – and would ever know again.

9. At the Stroke of the Noon Bell

The water shimmered in the sunlight. Jade stood at the window and looked down through the trees at the canal beyond. She watched the boats passing. Outside, life went on.

'I pray to God that Adam Windjammer survives the dangers of this voyage.' Bartholomew de Leiden's voice scratched at the quiet of the room. 'But it is by no means certain. There are so many dangers ...' He was speaking more to himself than Jade as he leaned back on the pillows of his death bed.

'I have lived a long time and I have some regrets, it's true,' he murmured. 'I was never blessed with a family of my own. Perhaps that is why Adam has become so important to me.'

Jade turned to find him watching her. 'I have to go,' she said.

She didn't move.

'His father was my friend, you know,' the old man said, 'but I did not do enough to save the House of Windjammer from ruin. I blame myself for much of what has happened since and I am sworn to make

111

amends for it by helping the boy restore his fortune. But I fear, when I am gone ...' His voice leaked away in a breath.

Jade wondered if it had been his last and was about to step forward when his eyes suddenly opened, piercingly blue.

'I should have known your father would have a spy aboard the *Draco*,' the old man said. His look softened, 'But then I have my spies too ...'

'I'm not your *spy*,' Jade protested, stepping back. A sudden pang of guilt stabbed into her. 'I didn't come here to betray my father.'

'I did not mean you.'

'And I don't care about Adam Windjammer! Why should I? I'm a van Helsen and he *hates* me for what my father did.'

'Perhaps, perhaps not,' the old man mused. 'Adam Windjammer has his faults. He is young and impetuous, but he is loyal and honest too and I believe in time he will learn that life has many twists.'

Jade was getting fidgety. She had already stayed too long.

'We are all searching for something in life,' the old man continued. 'For some, like Adam Windjammer, it is the past. Others,' he looked directly at her, 'it is a future. Me?' A faint smile played across his lips. 'I have found out too late in life that the only place we can really truly live and be happy is the present.'

Jade glanced up at the sound of voices. They came echoing up the stairs from the hall below.

'I have to go,' she said. 'I've told you everything I know – now will you help me?'

The old man's gaze remained fixed on her face. She

was sure he would refuse. Then an ancient hand lifted off the sheet and, with a finger so gnarled and arthritic it reminded her of a twisted stick, he pointed towards an oak chest beneath a tapestry hanging on the far wall. He nodded and muttered something about a purse.

Jade wasted no time in heaving up the lid. She searched through the clothes until she found a leather pouch, clutched it to her briefly then hurriedly pulled it open and let the coins spill into her palm.

'Take it,' the old man said. 'Take all of it. There is enough there to buy you passage on any ship. But be warned, Jade, running away will not help you. That is why you must find another way.'

'What do you mean?'

The hand lifted off the sheet again, but this time the old man raised it to touch his forehead. 'You are an intelligent girl. You've already proved that by coming here today. It's time you started using your head.'

'That's what I'm doing,' Jade said. 'That's why I'm leaving Amsterdam and *never* coming back.'

'And tell me, my dear, what do you hope to find out there that is not here?'

Jade hesitated then her chin came up slightly. 'A life of my own,' she answered him squarely.

The old man sighed and closed his eyes. 'Your father is a powerful man. You will never truly be free of his shadow. He will come after you and, sooner or later, he will find you and bring you back.' He nodded. 'Then it will be worse. That is why you must stay and face him.'

'*Stay?*' She hid the purse behind her back as if the word itself could rob her of it and all it promised.

'How else will you gain his respect – which is what I

believe you want more than anything else. Am I right?'

'I hate my father,' Jade snapped back. 'I'm just another investment to him, something to be married off and bargained away. I *never* want to see him again.'

'And yet despite that, you still feel guilty for coming here and talking to me.'

Even as she denied it, Jade was wondering if somehow the dying had the power to see into the souls of the living.

'Forgive an old man for speaking frankly, my dear, but you could make much of your life if you gave yourself a chance.'

But Jade had her chance – the money was in her hand. Her heart was racing. The stale, dead air in that room was making her feel light-headed and confused.

'I see you do not believe me,' the old man said.

'I don't know *what* to believe any more.'

'Then start by believing in *yourself*,' the old man said. 'Why do you think your father is a successful man?' She made no attempt at answering so he did it for her. 'Because he believes in himself, despite what others think. I admit I do not agree with his methods but, even now, a part of me admires his sense of timing and ruthlessness. He has made something of himself and he has done it the hard way. How can you gain the respect of a man like that by running away from him? You must face him, but it must be in your own way.'

Bartholomew de Leiden sank back into his pillows exhausted by the effort. He suddenly seemed so very frail.

'I have to go,' Jade said. She thanked him for his kindness and headed for the door.

'Of course, I cannot stop you,' the old man called

weakly after her. 'I cannot make you listen. But perhaps I can help you prove you are more than just your father's daughter.'

Jade stopped, but she didn't turn.

'At least say you'll stay long enough to hear me out,' the old man said. 'Promise me you'll do that for a dying man.'

'I promise *nothing*.'

The old man smiled. 'I am beginning to like you, Jade van Helsen. You're strong and you learn fast. So listen now to what I have to say and then I will let you go.'

Jade hesitated; in the end she turned.

'You were right about Cornelius Yort,' the old man said. 'He came here trying to buy my share of the Quadrant Shipping and Trading Company and he used our friendship to make a powerful argument that it would be in the best interests of the Windjammer family if he took control of the company until Adam was older.' He shook his head. 'I did not sell to him. But there are others who will – especially when the rumour gets around that the *Draco* is overdue or even lost. It seems only your father and Cornelius Yort will know the real truth.'

'I have to go,' Jade insisted.

'Then run away, if you must!' The old man came up off his pillows in one last brief burst of life, a cold fire burning in his eyes as he reached out to her. 'But as you go listen well to the tolling of the noon bell, Jade van Helsen, because it will toll for you as well as the Windjammers.'

'The noon bell? For me? I don't understand.'

'At the stroke of that bell, the gates of the Bourse

open on the Rokin,' the old man explained. 'Do you know the place? It is not far from the Old Church where the Windjammers now live.'

Jade knew the place. She had often walked by the large building and the great clock tower where the businessmen of the city congregated to trade in commodities and stocks and shares.

'Cornelius Yort will go there next in search of a man named Ahmed the Turk,' the old man went on. 'I have done business with him in the past. He was once a tulip trader and a rich man. Recently he has fallen on hard times. However, I believe he still owns a sizeable holding in the Quadrant Shipping and Trading Company.'

Jade grew impatient again. 'What has this got to do with me?'

'Everything,' the old man said, 'because this is your chance to make a difference. That is why I am asking you to go to the Windjammers with this message.'

'Why would the Windjammers listen to me? I am a van Helsen, remember.'

'It is time to bring an end to the rivalry between your families. It is time to let the past go and begin again. Adam's mother, Mary Windjammer, is an intelligent woman. She will understand and she will listen if you make her.'

'You just want me to betray my father.'

'No, I want you to make things right. Call me selfish – but I want to die in peace.'

A pause. 'What message?' Jade asked at last.

The old man seemed relieved. 'You must tell Adam's mother to go to the Bourse on the stroke of the noon bell. If there is trouble, tell her to say to the officials at the gate that I sent her. Once she is inside she must search out the Turk. He is well known. He should not be too difficult to find. She must warn him not to listen to Cornelius Yort. She must persuade him that his good fortune, as well as hers, depends on it.'

'And what's in it for me?' Jade asked.

'Ah yes, *you* ...' Here the old man paused and collected his thoughts before he spoke. 'If nothing else, my dear, you will prove I am right about you – that you can be so much more than a runaway child. Trust your instincts, Jade. I believe they are honest and good. Show your father that he has underestimated you as a person as well as a daughter. In that at least, you will gain his respect. And who knows what might come of it – for without respect there can be no love or affection between you.'

Love and *affection*. How could she know the meaning of those words when she hadn't experienced the feelings they described. She wanted to know, but the effort of speaking had exhausted the old man. The fire suddenly burned out in his eyes and he collapsed back on to his pillows. Only then did Jade become aware of the sound of voices again and realise that someone was now coming up the stairs.

'I'm sorry,' she shook her head. 'You're asking too much. You'll have to find someone else to take your message.'

If the old man heard he didn't show it. He was murmuring about the boats again.

The sound of the voices grew louder. Jade recognised one as the doctor's, the other as the servant who had opened the front door to her. They were talking in hushed tones as they approached along the passage. The dog was cursed for being in the way and Jade had just enough time to slip behind the door as it opened inwards.

'Voices, Voorhuis. I'm certain I heard *voices*,' the doctor was saying as he walked in. 'Someone has been disturbing my patient. And who opened those shutters? Did I not expressly say they should be closed until we need to bleed him again?'

Bartholomew de Leiden's servant followed close behind apologising. 'I shut them, doctor, I swear it,' he insisted. 'It must have been that stupid girl, Martha. Just wait until she comes back ...'

The doctor went to attend to Bartholomew de Leiden while Voorhuis hurried to close the shutters.

'The boats are sailing on the houses and trees,' Jade heard the old man muttering. 'In all my years, I've *never* seen it that way ...'

'Now, now, Mr de Leiden, calm yourself,' the doctor said, patting his hand. Then, in a lower voice, he added behind the back of his hand, 'He's rambling like an old fool – going fast, I fear.'

Voorhuis crossed to stand at the bed. The men had their backs turned and Jade saw her opportunity. She came out from behind the door and slipped into the passage. As she went she caught a glimpse of the slight smile that had frozen on the old man's lips. He was already dead.

Jade fled silently down the passage to the stairs. Behind her the wolfhound sat up and began to whine, staring into an empty space as if something had just followed Jade through the door and stood, invisible, close by.

'You didn't promise anything,' the same small voice

whispered incessantly in Jade's head as she made her way back through the streets towards the waterfront. 'All you needed was the money. You don't have to take his message to anyone.'

She was moving fast, desperate to be away from the Keizersgracht, determined to seek out the anonymity of the crowds. She kept clear of the western docks in case she should see Cornelius Yort again and cut across the canals, first the Herengracht – close to the place where the Windjammers had once lived – then the Singel. She was forced to stop whenever she reached a bridge, looking around each time to be sure she wasn't being followed. She only saw a few small boys playing pebbles against part of what had once been the city walls.

Jade cursed herself for being a fool. She had stayed too long listening to the ramblings of the old man. Now she found it hard to shake the feeling that the net was closing about her. It was time to think of herself – to take the money and run. She found some comfort at least in the weight of the purse. It felt pleasingly heavy in her hand as she gripped it tightly under the folds of her cloak and hurried on.

She avoided the crowds in Dam Square and cut down the back alleys behind the New Church, passing the small graveyard on her left. She felt the weight of the church and longed to break free of its shadow. It reminded her of the marriage she dreaded – and yet even as she fled from it she found herself wondering if there could be any hope of salvation now for a faithless daughter.

It only occurred to Jade as she reached the wide avenue by the canal that the way she had chosen was, quite by accident, taking her right by the Bourse. She kept up her pace as the fine two-storey building came into view, trying not to dwell on the old man's dying words again.

The Bourse stood just to the north of Dam Square between the busy Rokin and the stretch of the river leading to the waterfront known as the Damrak. Narrow streets snaked all around crowded with shops and taverns. Among the confectioners and sellers of expensive sweetmeats, there were shops selling blue and white china, fashionable clothes, lace, furs and more. Well-dressed citizens paraded the streets in an area grown rich and prosperous on the money generated within the great building that dominated its surroundings.

Jade kept her face turned down as she made her way quickly along the street until she reached the cupola bridge at the end where the great bell tower rose over the entrance. The gates were closed.

'The old man's dead, dead, *dead*,' the voice repeated, thumping out its fatal message with every step she took now. She crossed the bridge and turned away quickly. Good sense told her to forget Bartholomew de Leiden; to take his money and run. But things had been said – powerful words that lingered:

'Show your father that he has underestimated you as a person as well as a daughter ...' the old man's voice echoed in her memory. 'For without respect there can be no love or affection between you.'

Finally it brought her to a halt with her back once more pressed to the wall.

'Why did he have to say *that*?' she hissed. She turned to rest her forehead against the cool brick. The voice of freedom spoke to her now. *Why should you help the*

Windjammers? They wouldn't help you. She squeezed her eyes closed and banged her head against the wall to make it stop. 'All I want is a sign,' she gasped through gritted teeth. 'A sign that he cares – is that so much to ask of a father?'

'Are you all right, my dear?' someone asked gently.

Startled, Jade spun around to find a small group of women had gathered around her and were watching with mild surprise. She nodded and thanked them for their concern, made an attempt to smooth her dress and act normally as she escaped from their enquiring gazes into the surrounding streets.

'*Damn* you, old man!' she breathed as she stumbled on. '*Damn* you, Adam Windjammer!'

Gone was the wealth. Gone the fine house. Jade looked around the square and was confronted by the reality of what it meant to fall.

A rented house, built on two storeys, its narrowness giving it a slightly squeezed, top-heavy feel. Jade didn't know it, but these houses had been built with Bartholomew de Leiden's money, forming a small square, or *hofje*, close to the Old Church. They were modest and neat, built among the slops and stews of the city for the betterment of the poor and those who had fallen on hard times.

It was the loss of their fleet that had brought the Windjammers down. Jade had often heard her father say it was so and – perhaps to make it easier on herself for the part she had played in their downfall – she had allowed herself to believe him. Now she was faced with the consequences of what had happened, forced to look in the certain knowledge that she had once had the power to prevent what had happened to them. For when the moment had come, the moment she'd had the rare and valuable Black Pearl in her hand, she had stolen it from Adam in the vain hope that she could somehow use it to buy herself back into her father's favour. How wrong she had been.

Now the Windjammers had every reason to hate her and it would have been easier to hate them right back. And yet ...

The tinkling sound of young children's laughter echoed eerily around the square. Jade could see two small girls – identical twins aged six or so – playing with a wooden toy on the doorstep. They had long yellow hair, plaited and tied back under cotton caps and were dressed identically in red, cheap-dyed dresses under off-white aprons. They might have looked like any of the other poor children that lived there, but their leather shoes spoke of a richer past life.

Jade recognised them at once and stopped. At first they didn't see her. The front door of the house was open and a woman was sitting on a milking stool, preparing vegetables into a pot at her feet. She didn't notice the twins looking up. Jade beckoned to them. The twins exchanged glances then, still unnoticed by the woman, came to see what Jade wanted. They walked side by side, with small, quick steps, hands hanging loosely in the folds of their skirts.

'Rose. Viola.' Jade greeted them as they approached. She crouched so she could look at them. 'Do you remember me?'

'There's dirt,' Rose said.

'On your face, she means,' Viola explained.

Jade touched her cheek self-consciously. 'You've

grown,' she said. It had been almost six months since she had seen them.

The twins beamed at the compliment.

'He's not here,' Rose said.

'Adam, she means.' Viola felt bound to explain everything her sister said.

'He's gone ...'

'... to the Americas.'

'I know,' Jade said. She couldn't resist asking. 'Have you had news from him? A letter, perhaps?'

They shrugged.

'He'll come back one day,' Rose said simply.

'He promised,' Viola agreed.

'He won't leave us.'

'Not like father.'

And in their strange connected way, Rose and Viola told it how it was with a genuine honesty that's often only ever found in the very young or the very old.

It left Jade feeling deeply uncomfortable knowing their troubles were far from over. And yet she could also see now that Bartholomew de Leiden had been right. She *could* make a difference.

'Is your mother at home?' Jade asked. 'It's important I see her.'

'She's not in.' The sound of a woman's voice cut over their heads. Jade came to her feet as the woman called the girls back, scolding them for leaving the front doorstep.

'I wouldn't hurt them,' Jade assured her. 'They know me. My name's –'

'I know who you are, Miss van Helsen. I was looking after this family when the old master was alive and I'm not about to stop now,' the woman said with

123

barely disguised dislike. 'So what do you want? Why have you come here?'

Jade's chin came up slightly. 'I have a message for Mary Windjammer.'

'She's not in,' the woman repeated bluntly. She gathered up Rose and Viola and ushered them towards the house. The twins cast wondering looks back over their shoulders.

'Wait!' Jade went after them. 'How long will she –' The door banged shut in her face. '– be?'

Jade's fury drove her back along the street. She had gone quite some way before sense prevailed and she stopped. As she struggled to regain control of her thoughts she caught a glimpse of her reflection in a window. The face that looked back at her was hard to recognise. Her hair hung down lankly in rats' tails and dirt was smudged on her cheek and forehead. But it was her eyes that startled her most: they seemed to bulge right out of her head in a wild, hunted look.

Further along the street a stone lion was spurting water from its mouth into a trough. She went to it now and washed her face, trying to scrub away that look. The water cooled her fury. She wiped her face on her dress, looking up, startled by the sound of the bell. She counted each of the strokes until the last rang out and faded.

'The noon bell,' she murmured. It was *already* too late. She thought of the girls and wondered what would happen to them when her father won – as he inevitably would. 'No!' The word burst out of her.

Jade made up her mind as she always did – quickly – and then gave herself no chance to change it. Strangely, she felt nothing of the enormity of the moment in which she stopped running and turned to face her life. There was just a sense of calm, of something cool and powerful within her. It seemed to grow, spreading through her veins until it touched and hardened her heart.

'I'll show him,' she murmured. 'I'll show them *all*.'

10. Trading in the Wind

Jade stood at the end of the alleyway and looked out into the wider street with the canal beyond.

'Repent! Before it's too late! For you cannot serve God and mammon!' A Calvinist was raining down warnings on the people in the crowd.

Jade let her gaze travel over the group that had gathered to listen to him, then her eye was drawn to the flow of people heading for the Bourse. The gates were open. She took a deep breath and stepped out into the stream of life, hoping that there would be some safety at least in the crowd. She was only vaguely aware of the small boy sitting cross-legged, leaning against the iron rail of the bridge, as she walked by.

Beyond the bridge, at the foot of the tall bell tower she had passed earlier, the gates into Amsterdam's Bourse stood open. Through the arch, Jade could see a large quadrangle. It was rapidly filling up with men and there was movement and noise everywhere. There were a few women, but they stopped at the gate, forming little groups as they waited for the men to return. Jade worked her way through them and kept her head down, making herself as inconspicuous as possible to the dark-suited officials at the gate. She waited for the fattest merchant she could find and fell in step just behind him, screened by his jollity and bulk as she followed him in.

Jade sensed the excitement the moment she stepped inside. The quadrangle was filled with the buzz of expectation. Voices echoed, rising up the inner walls of the building like a swirling vortex that pulled the ear in all directions. The building seemed to come alive with it, feeding on the noise as if the stones themselves were mortared together by secrets.

Jade could see people standing at the windows that lined each side of the quadrangle. On the floors above, richer merchants – city burghers and aldermen – gathered and remained aloof from the deals that were being struck on their behalf by the brokers on the trading floor. Everywhere men were gathering in small groups, talking urgently over ledgers or papers or parchments with wax seals, the groups breaking up and reforming elsewhere in different combinations of faces, only to break up just as quickly and move once more.

A bell marked the opening of trade and after that they were all too busy to notice her. But Jade took in everything with a quick eye. It was the men who stood out in brightly-coloured coats that seemed to be doing most of the business. They were the brokers – members of the Bourse – and they were 'trading in the wind': buying and selling shares on behalf of their rich clients in cargoes and commodities carried by ships sailing all over the world. They owned these cargoes briefly on paper, in part or whole, without ever seeing or touching or tasting the sugar and spices that would be traded on to the highest bidder.

Strangely, even though Jade had never set foot in that place before, even among all those businessmen, she instantly felt at ease. It was as if somehow she belonged to this place, as if she had been born to it all and she was one of them. She shared their thrill, marvelling at the speed with which deals were struck and money was made or lost. She noticed the signs: the pull of an ear or nose, the touch of a shoulder, the nod or shake of a head. She saw the deals being chalked up on slates and rubbed out on the slap of a back or shake of a hand. It left her feeling slightly light-headed and breathless.

'Can I help you, miss?' a sharp-faced, dark-suited official asked as he approached.

Jade shook her head and tried to pass him. The man barred her way. His gaze ran over her from head to foot then back to her face, leaving her feeling very uncomfortable.

'And what business do *you* have here, miss?'

Her chin came up slightly. 'My own.'

He caught her by the arm. 'Well, perhaps you'd better come with me and explain it to my master.'

She twisted and broke free. 'Leave me alone! I'm looking for someone – it's important.' She remembered something the old man had said and added, 'Bartholomew de Leiden sent me.'

'Mr de Leiden!' The official stepped back. '*You* know him?'

Jade nodded. 'If you stop me, Mr de Leiden will want to know the reason for my delay. I'm sure your master would explain …'

'My master?' The man suddenly sounded more than a little unnerved. 'No, on second thoughts, there's no need to trouble him.'

Jade resisted the urge to smile. 'I'm looking for Ahmed the Turk,' she said. 'Do you know him?'

The official nodded. 'You'll find him over there, miss. Close to the arches at the end,' he said, pointing. 'And I hope you'll forgive my –'

'You can be sure Mr de Leiden will be eternally grateful,' she said.

Ahmed the Turk was a tall man with a big dream and, like many who came to Amsterdam's Bourse, a cash-flow problem.

'Coffee,' he was saying with great certainty to the men gathered around him, 'is the drink of the future.'

The men listening weren't quite so sure.

'You say you *drink* beans?' a man – a furrier by trade – said, eyeing the coffee beans in the sack Ahmed had at his feet with great suspicion. 'That's hard to swallow.'

'*After* they have been crushed and boiled in water,' Ahmed said. He stood on a stool to address them. He was wearing long, flowing robes and a turban that was beginning to unravel. 'Hot and strong,' he said. 'Coffee is delicious.'

'But Beelzebub and all the fiends of darkness savour the juice of this bean,' a cloth merchant spoke up, apparently with great authority on the subject. 'Everyone knows that.'

'Beelzebub? Who is this Beelzebub?' Ahmed looked puzzled. 'If he drinks coffee I would like to invite him to my coffee house when I open on Kalverstraat.'

The men laughed. 'Not unless you want your beans roasted in the pit of eternal fire!' the furrier said.

'And be condemned by your coffee to the abyss where no one ever sleeps,' the cloth merchant agreed.

'Enough of your Christian ramblings!' Ahmed said. 'Coffee is a drink, made from beans and water, not witchcraft and magic!'

'Yes, but will it cure the plague?' a new voice joined in as the laughter subsided.

'The plague?' Ahmed picked out the apothecary who had stopped to listen. 'How could it cure *plague*?'

'Fevers? Gout? Bilious colic?' The apothecary was clearly unimpressed.

'It's a drink, not a medicine,' Ahmed said.

'And you expect people to pay good money to drink the juice of the damned when they can buy ale for a tenth of the price?' the furrier came back with.

There was a general shaking of heads in disbelief and wonder.

'Take it from me, Ahmed,' the cloth merchant said. 'This coffee stuff will never catch on. Now, if you were to rub it on to your chest ...'

The circle began to break up around him, the men discussing among themselves the best possible uses for coffee.

'I have a horse with a boil,' the furrier was saying.

'Maybe Ahmed's brew would be good for that,' the merchant suggested.

'I swear by dead cats,' the apothecary disagreed.

'Then don't use coffee.' The cloth merchant laughed. 'Put the cat on the boil instead.'

They found that very amusing. Ahmed raised his hands as if appealing to God for help in their enlightenment. He begged them to stay and listen, but they went off in search of other, less outlandish ideas than coffee. Ahmed stepped down from his stool with a scowl and went about tying the neck of the sack of beans. Only then did he notice Jade.

'Do you want to buy, miss?' he asked. He looked at her dishevelled appearance. 'No, perhaps not.' He went back to tying the neck of his sack.

'Are you Ahmed the Turk?' Jade asked.

Ahmed paused. 'Who wants to know?'

'The tulip seller?'

He came up straight and looked at her suspiciously. 'Do not talk to me of tulips! They are the Devil's flowers! Their flaming petals have burned my fingers just like everyone else. So if you bought from me and have lost all your money, I cannot help you.' He shrugged and took on an air of wounded righteousness. 'How was I to know the market would crash? How was I to know I would lose a fortune and a good little business too?'

'It's not about tulips,' Jade said.

Ahmed's eyes narrowed. 'Then what? Who are you?'

'My name's not important. I have to talk to you.'

'Names may not be important to *you*, maybe,' he said, returning to his sack. 'Me – I like to know who I'm dealing with.'

'I have a message. A message from Bartholomew de Leiden.'

'Bartholomew de Leiden?' Ahmed sounded surprised. He frowned. 'It is true that I know him. But I have not done business with him for some time – he is not a well man.'

131

'This is important,' Jade said. 'It's about the Quadrant Shipping and Trading Company.'

'The Quadrant Shipping and …' Ahmed the Turk cast another despairing look skywards. 'Have you come here just to taunt and torment me? I never want to hear that name again. Everyone is talking of it and the news is all bad. The *Draco* is lost – lost with all hands they say. The company is finished. It seems, once again, all I have left is tied up in worthless agreements and pieces of paper. So don't talk to me about *Quadrant*.'

'You shouldn't believe all you hear,' Jade said. 'The rumours aren't true.'

Ahmed forced a laugh. 'Forgive me, child, but why should I believe *you* when important men say otherwise?' He flapped a hand at her. 'Why don't you run along now? Why don't you go back to wherever it is you came from and stop meddling in grown men's business?'

Jade's eyes sparked. 'If you don't believe me now, then perhaps you will when a merchant called Cornelius Yort comes to see you. He will try to buy your share in Quadrant. Do not sell to him. Your good fortune depends on it.'

'My good fortune? And why should you care of that?'

'Just promise me you'll remember what I said. If I'm right, this merchant will come to you soon – today.' Jade glanced around. 'He may even be here now.'

'You expect me to believe this … this …?'

'If Cornelius Yort comes, you will know I'm telling the truth,' Jade pointed out. 'Then you will also know the rumours about the *Draco* are untrue. Once you believe me, go to the Windjammers. They live close to the Old Church. Do you know the place? Tell Mary Windjammer what has happened. Together you can save Quadrant *and* make your fortune back.'

'And what, may I ask,' the Turk was cautious, 'is in this for you?'

A pause. Jade shrugged and told the truth. 'I don't know yet.'

Ahmed regarded her thoughtfully before shaking his head. He gave her a look as if to say her business was all about plaguing poor, hardworking ex-tulip sellers. Then he picked up his stool and set off with his sack.

'But you *have* to believe me!' Jade went after him.

He stopped and turned on her. 'Why?' He balanced the sack on one shoulder and waved the stool about at the crowd. 'This place is full of people who say they know something when they don't. Are you any different? I doubt it. Now, be gone with you before I have you thrown out!'

He moved on through the crowd and she would have gone after him had she not seen Cornelius Yort. She hid her face quickly as the merchant passed close by. She retreated to the pillars. From there she could see him working his way through the crowd. It was clear he was looking for someone. He spotted Ahmed the Turk and finally the two men met. Jade watched as they spoke briefly. Even from a distance she saw the surprise on Ahmed the Turk's face. He even half-turned as if to look for her. Then the two men moved away together towards a door.

The door opened to Cornelius Yort's knock and immediately one of the dark-suited officials relieved

Ahmed of his sack and stool before he was ushered inside. The door closed and Jade caught fleeting glimpses of them through the small, mullioned windows as they climbed a spiralling stair to the first floor and were gone.

Gone, yes, and all that could be done had been done. The old man was dead. The Windjammers were on their own now. Jade decided she had done enough. Nevertheless, the uncertainty of the outcome left her with a feeling of disappointment. There was more to it than just the nagging doubt that Ahmed the Turk still hadn't believed her. She had felt a thrill she had not known before – the thrill of being able to change the destiny of others – and strangely she felt closer to her father for it. As she looked around now she realised this was his place, a part of his life he had never let her into before and she wanted to know more – much more. For by knowing the secrets of his business, she felt as if she could know him.

She glanced up at the windows that surrounded her and imagined herself up there with her father. She decided then that it would happen, that one day she would take her place as a van Helsen among the great merchants and burghers of the city. But for now, she knew she had a lot to learn.

So it was that Jade van Helsen began to look around and take in as much as she could of the business of that place. And, inevitably perhaps, she soon found herself drawn away from the trading floor to the edges of that great building. It was there, under the arches around the quadrangle, that she stumbled on a different world. The world of the sharp-players who congregated in side rooms and on the shadowy side of the pillars, like ragged and unkempt strays come to feed on the scraps and titbits that fell from rich men's tables. They were the gamblers, the risk-takers: they were the people on the make.

Jade only noticed the youths when the noise of their cheers or groans became so raucous it stood out even against the noise of the trading going on in the main quadrangle. They were crowded around an open window, pushing and shoving one another in their efforts to gain a clear view of something taking place in a back street outside.

She couldn't see what was happening, but whatever it was it had the full attention of the young men hanging out of the open window or fighting for position on the pile of wooden crates and barrels stacked up against the wall. Here money was changing hands – fast.

A larger, older, fatter man was sitting at a table behind a delicate arrangement of weighing scales. He sat back with his hands on his hips, his coat open and his gut bulging out, accepting bets on a word or a nod. As the coins were slapped down, he weighed them with exquisite delicacy for a man with blunt fingers before pocketing the proceeds. It wasn't long before his sharp eye picked Jade out in the crowd.

'Make way for the little lady!' he bellowed.

When no one paid any attention, he reached up to one of the young men who was balanced precariously, struggling to see over the backs of the others, caught him by the belt and, with surprising strength, heaved him down. The youth fell with a startled cry and the big man heaved several more down on top of him.

'What's the matter, Books?' a youth spluttered. 'I paid good money to watch and I've a right –'

'It's *Mr* Books to you, Luckless!' the big man rumbled, still sitting. He pointed Jade out with a delicate gesture of his hand. 'A little more respect for the lady, if you please.'

The one called Luckless slapped the backs of several of his companions. They turned and when they saw Jade there was a sudden hush.

Books told them to make way and several jumped down, until Jade could see the open window. She could hear noise in the narrow street beyond.

'Take a look, miss,' Books encouraged her. 'No charge.'

Books nodded to the youths and before Jade knew what was happening they had closed ranks behind so she couldn't escape. Some helped her up on to the boxes while others immediately crowded around the table making bets.

'I have 5–1 to say the little lady takes the bird!' Books said, starting a rush of coins on to the table.

In the street outside, men, women and children were gathered in a tight semi-circle against the wall. Directly below the window Jade could see two bloodied cockerels strutting on the cobbles. The birds were wearing strange little leather caps – one red, one black – that went some way down the long feathers of their necks. As the birds came together suddenly, claws up and pecking in a flurry of feathers, she noticed the pointed iron spurs tied to their legs. The small crowd cheered each bloody strike. The birds came together again and again, eyes wide and shining like purple-black beads. Then suddenly it was all over and the bird with the red cap lay fatally wounded, fluttering pathetically on the cobbles.

The half-dead cockerel was snatched up and held aloft for all to see. Some cheered, others who had lost their money shook their heads, wondering where it had all gone wrong. The bloodied bird was passed around the circle and thrust up at Jade as she stood at the window. Before she knew it, the bundle of feathers was fluttering weakly in her hand. She stared numbly at the blood oozing out between her fingers, then someone reached over her shoulder caught hold of her wrist and forced her to turn to face the gathered youths.

'I win again, I think!' Books bellowed and beamed.

The bird was snatched away and paraded around until finally it was hurled dead on to the table.

'Sable Coxcomb wins!' Books declared, whereupon Jade was forgotten in the rush of those who had gambled on black and wanted to be paid.

'Out of my way!' Jade hissed and fought her way down off the boxes, pushing through the crowd, feeling the weight of their indifference and their shoulders pressing against her.

She retreated to the pillars. There was blood on her hands. She had nothing but her dress to wipe them on. Her hands shook as she rubbed at them furiously. The blood was sticky and already congealing.

'You shouldn't mind Mr Books. He'll take a bet on anything.'

Jade turned to find one of the young men had followed her. He had long fair hair and was wearing a knee-length, wine-coloured coat. She tried to ignore him and walked on.

'Cockfights, dog races, the age of a horse, marriages, births, deaths – you name it, Books will take your money,' he said, falling into step beside her. 'I bet on you taking the bird – I could tell you would.'

'How can you bet on things like that?' she rounded on him.

He shrugged and glanced around. 'It's not so different from what the fine merchants are doing over there. It's all a game of chance around here. All you need is a quick eye and a sharp ear – oh, and a bit of luck. And that's what you brought me.' He smiled. 'Valentino's the name. And that's Tobias and this is Aert.'

Two others appeared in front of her. Suddenly Jade found herself surrounded by overfriendly, enthusiastic and completely unwanted attention.

'Not forgetting Raphael ...' Valentino pointed out a third. 'He's the quiet one. Moody. A writer, always late – you know the type.'

'What about me?' another said.

'All right, Luckless, I haven't forgotten you.' Valentino introduced him with a toss of his head. 'Luckless Rony, we call him.'

Luckless Rony waved a contradictory finger. '*Luckless* no longer, I says.' He produced a handful of coppers and held them out. 'I bet on the girl too, see. Seven *duits* – that's nearly a whole *stuvier*.'

There was something deeply unpleasant about him as if his ugliness wasn't just skin deep. He had slicked back his hair with goose grease and his coat was worn and dirty. He wasn't tall, he wasn't short, neither narrow nor broad, just average in so many ways – except, perhaps, for the bad luck that followed him around like a rancid-smelling dog.

'Luckless won!' Tobias whistled softly. 'Then our luck *must* have changed.'

'And it needed changing, I can tell you,' Aert agreed.

'I don't care about *you* or your luck.' Jade pushed Luckless Rony's hand away as he attempted to show her his winnings.

'But you can't go – you're our lucky charm,' Tobias said.

'Charm*ing* too,' Aert said, batting his eyelashes.

'I'm not anyone's anything,' Jade hissed. Luckless Rony was closest and he bore the brunt of her anger. 'Your pathetic gambling makes me sick, do you understand – *sick*.'

Valentino glanced at Tobias, Tobias at Aert, Aert at Raphael. Then they all looked at Luckless Rony. Tears began to well up in his eyes.

'Now, now, Rony.' Tobias put an arm around his shoulder.

Jade softened slightly.

'Oh, don't you worry,' Tobias said. 'He's just a sensitive soul. You see no girl has ever said anything as nice to him before.'

'I wasn't being *nice*.'

'Come to think of it, no girl's never said *anything* to our Rony before,' Aert agreed. He slapped Luckless Rony on the shoulder. 'It must be love.'

'Well, they say love is blind,' Tobias laughed. 'We'll get Raphael to write you a sonnet, hey?'

Jade realised they were mocking her. She stamped her fury into the flagstones as she stormed away. They followed like a pack of hounds on the scent.

'You can't go. Not without telling us your name,' Valentino said.

'Where do you come from?' Tobias said. 'Never seen you around here before.'

The questions kept coming. People were beginning to notice. She stopped and faced them.

'Surely there's some poor bird you want to kill? Why don't you go back to your *sport* – if you can call it that.'

'I'm not sure she likes us,' Tobias said.

'No? Do you think?' Aert said.

'Why can't you just leave me alone!' Jade said, glancing about nervously.

'Anyone would think she's got something to hide,' Valentino mused. 'She a mystery all right.' He looked her up and down thoughtfully. 'Let me guess – you've run away.' He reached out and tested the quality of her cloak between his thumb and forefinger. 'From a good life by the look of it.'

'You don't know anything about my life,' Jade said, snatching away her cloak.

'Don't be so sure,' Tobias said. 'Valentino here can read people like a scroll.'

'He's never wrong,' Aert nodded. 'Take that merchant over there – the one with the fine clothes. You would think he has all the money in the world, but you'd be wrong.'

'As soon as he started wearing his best clothes to the Bourse I knew he was in trouble,' Valentino said, inspecting his fingernails casually. 'Turns out he lost a fortune in the Americas.'

Jade had heard enough. 'And this is supposed to impress me?'

'You may not think much of us,' Valentino said, 'but we know more about what makes this place work than most of these fine merchants you see. There are more shady deals and schemes going on here than you can throw a cat at. And many a fine businessman who'd have done better to lower himself a little and come to talk to us first before throwing his money down the drain.'

'If you're so clever why aren't you rich?' Jade asked.

There was a long pause. Valentino shrugged. 'Sometimes you need luck too.'

A shout went up from around Mr Books's table. Valentino glanced over his shoulder. With a slight nod of his head he dispatched Luckless Rony to find out what was going on. Luckless soon brought the news back.

'It's just Books taking bets on the old man,' he said. 'He's offering 20–1 that he'll live until noon tomorrow.'

Jade, meanwhile, had seen her chance to get away from them. But this new level of callousness stopped her. 'You mean – they're betting on the time someone is going to *die*?'

'Now look what you've done, Luckless!' Tobias said. 'You're gone and offended the girl.'

'How could you?' Jade asked.

'Oh, don't look so shocked,' Valentino said. 'The doctors are in on it too. They like a cut of the winnings. They tell us who's dying and Books bets on when it happens.'

'Of course, it gets more interesting if it's someone rich or famous who's doing the dying,' Aert said. 'Take that old man up on the Keizersgracht – he's rich *and* well known around here, but –'

'The *Keizersgracht*?' Jade interrupted. 'An old man?' She had to swallow hard as bile started to come up into her throat. 'Do you mean Bartholomew de Leiden?'

'That's the one!' Luckless Rony said.

There was a pause. Suddenly they were all looking at her with great interest.

'Do you know him?' Valentino asked.

'There's something wrong with you,' Jade said quietly, '*All* of you – really there is. Why can't you just leave an old man to rest in peace?'

'Then you *do* know him,' Valentino said.

Jade glared at him. 'Stay away from me!' She spun on her heel, turning back just as quickly to jab a finger at them as if it were a blade. 'If any of you follow me I'll ... I'll ...' She balled her fists in frustration, gritted her teeth and left the threat of the punch swinging in the air behind her.

'Was it something we said?' Tobias asked as they watched her go.

'Rest in peace, hey?' Valentino repeated. He reached into a hidden pocket of his jacket and produced a coin. He gave it a thoughtful look then flicked the silver piece off his thumb. It went spinning up in the air for Luckless Rony to catch.

'Tell Mr Books I wager everything I have that the old man called Bartholomew de Leiden is already dead,' he said.

Luckless Rony tested the coin between his teeth. 'Where are you going?'

Valentino ignored the question and posed one of his own instead. 'Now why do you think a girl like that would come here – to the Bourse of all places?'

They shuffled their feet, trying to think of an answer, but couldn't.

'My thoughts exactly,' Valentino said. He sniffed and glanced about as if trying to catch a scent. 'Can you smell it, my friends?'

They all sniffed loudly.

'What is it?' Tobias asked. 'What can you smell, Valentino?'

'*Opportunity*,' was all Valentino said.

11. More Ways than One to Cook a Fish

'What went wrong?' Hugo van Helsen asked, his voice dangerously quiet.

'I don't know,' Cornelius Yort spoke up as he stood by the door with Goltz lurking behind. He was still wearing his cloak and had his hat in his hand. He fingered the brim nervously. 'I did everything you asked of me. I spread the rumours, just as you told me to. For a while everyone believed the *Draco* was lost. Then, well ...'

Hugo van Helsen was sitting in a high-backed chair staring into the fire. He was dressed for bed in a long burgundy-coloured robe and a cap and silk slippers of a similar colour. To one side of the fireplace stood a portrait on an easel, the canvas covered with a velvet cloth.

'I hope you are going to tell me you managed to buy the Turk's share of Quadrant,' the banker said in that same dangerous way.

A pause. Cornelius Yort seemed to be having difficulty getting the words off his tongue. 'I tried,' he said with an effort. 'But he wouldn't sell.'

'*Wouldn't* sell?'

Cornelius Yort explained in a rush. 'He said someone had told him I would come. There was a mysterious girl. He didn't know her name. He said she had come to him like a vision. She had warned him not to be hasty and sell to me.'

'A girl?' Hugo van Helsen cut in. 'Are you sure?'

'That's what he said,' Cornelius Yort nodded. 'But you know what these Turks are like. They are wily businessmen – they'll say anything if it'll get a better price. I almost had him persuaded when –'

'I know the rest.'

'But you've never seen anything like it!' Cornelius Yort was desperate to explain. 'Somehow word must have got out. You know what the Bourse is like. There are ears everywhere.'

'I was wrong to trust you with this, merchant,' Hugo van Helsen said.

'No! It wasn't my fault – I swear. Someone knew something. It started among the traders near Books's table. There were questions about Bartholomew de Leiden. It wasn't long before they found out he was a shareholder in the Quadrant Shipping and Trading Company. I don't know how, but someone must have worked it out. Word spread that something was going on. Others started to question whether the rumours about the *Draco* I put about were true ...'

The merchant twisted the brim of his hat miserably. 'What could I do? I had to admit I didn't know for certain. It all happened so fast. Before I knew it, speculators started trading in the wind while the price was cheap. People were *buying* not selling Quadrant stock as they were supposed to. The price just went up and up. What could I do? What could I do?'

'You've been fooled, Cornelius Yort – *fooled*.'

'But, Mr van Helsen! I am not to blame!'

Hugo van Helsen eased out of his chair and crossed to the portrait. He pulled back the velvet cover with a flick of his hand. 'Tell me, merchant – do you recognise this girl?'

The merchant stared at the painting. 'Why, yes ... I have seen her. I don't know where, but I do know that face.'

'Was she at the waterfront, perhaps?'

Cornelius Yort considered it for a moment before remembering. 'Yes – yes, that's it. She *was* there.' He frowned. 'But I don't understand – who is she? What has she got to do with any of this?'

'This girl followed you from the waterfront to Bartholomew de Leiden's house.'

'Followed me? Why would she do that?'

A thin smile pulled at Hugo van Helsen's lips. 'Because she has been one step behind you and one step ahead of me all day.'

The girl's green eyes stared back at the banker, fixed on some point in the middle distance as if they could see right through him. The face seemed to shine out of the darkness of the brushstrokes that surrounded it, effulgent with some inner light.

'So you overheard us talking, did you, Jade? Well, you're clever at that,' van Helsen stooped to whisper to the portrait. 'Even so you could not have understood the importance of what you heard until you talked to the old man. That meddlesome old fool! So he told you about Quadrant, did he? And you decided to get back at me by helping Adam Windjammer. Mother Race said you'd been seen near the Bourse. Yes, you're clever, my dear, very *clever*.' He forced a laugh. 'It seems I have underestimated the daughter and overestimated the merchant.'

'But I don't understand,' Cornelius Yort spoke up, unnerved by this monologue. 'What has this girl got to do with anything?'

Hugo van Helsen glanced over his shoulder. 'Cornelius Yort is leaving, Goltz. See him out!'

The merchant was stunned.

Hugo van Helsen turned on him. 'You were supposed to secure the old man's agreement to sell, but you failed. Then you *failed* to buy the Turk's share of Quadrant for me. Now the advantage I had in this matter has been wasted and if I make a move on Quadrant everyone will know of my interest in the matter. I told you before I cannot afford any questions!'

'If you'll just tell me what secret business you have undertaken and why you need the *Draco*, perhaps I can help.'

'You had your chance, merchant.' The banker dismissed him with a flick of his hand. 'But rest assured, this is not the end of it. If necessary I will just have to see this Turk myself and invest in his coffee.' He glanced at the painting. 'There are more ways than one to cook a fish – if nothing else I have learnt that much from my daughter.'

'Your *daughter*?' Cornelius Yort was astonished.

Hugo van Helsen pulled the cover back over the canvas. 'Our business is concluded,' he said. 'Get out.'

'You can't throw me to the dogs like this, van Helsen!'

The merchant strode towards him. The banker stood with his back to the fire. His face was cast partly in shadow, the yellow light licking at his cheek.

'Must I call the Civil Guard?'

Cornelius Yort came up against the banker's unflinching stare. He stood for a moment before sense seemed to prevail and he staggered back.

'I don't suppose I will ever fully understand what has gone on today, van Helsen. But I warn you now – I refuse to be treated like an animal.'

Hugo van Helsen's fingers snapped. Goltz stepped forward.

'Stay away from me!' the merchant rounded on Goltz with a snarl. 'I'll see myself out.' Even so he hesitated slightly as he reached the door, as if expecting some final reprieve. None came. His look hardened. 'You'll pay for this, van Helsen!'

Cornelius Yort hurled back the door on its hinges with a crash and stepped out into the Street of Knives. Goltz hovered behind him in the shadows. The merchant turned away and the door thumped closed. Suddenly the emptiness of the street engulfed him and the full reality of his ruin dawned. He tore at his collar, raising his voice to a starless sky in a cry of impotent rage. Then the fight just seemed to go out of him and he let his arms drop, staggering away like a man who had been poisoned.

A voice rose into the night. It was a terrible sound – like an ox bellowing its last breath – filled with agony and despair. Jade stopped dead, listened then stepped back quickly into a doorway. Her heart was pumping, her blood thumping in her ears. A man was staggering along the middle of the street. At first she thought he was drunk. He was moving slowly, unsteadily as if he had to drag himself along with every new step. At first he was only a silhouette and she didn't recognise him. It was only as he stumbled past that she saw it was the merchant. He looked like a man who'd been badly beaten.

The shadows of the doorway were enough to hide her and yet Jade felt utterly exposed. Not to the eyes of others, but to herself. For she knew the part she had played in the merchant's fall and regretted it. Even as she had fled from the Bourse, she had heard the whispers. The name of the Quadrant Shipping and Trading Company seemed to be on everyone's lips. It spread behind her like a wave. Only later, as she had sat in a quiet place by a canal, did Jade have time to think about what she had set in motion. Surprisingly, she had no sense of success, no feeling of victory over her father, just a certainty that she had betrayed him.

She had taken out the pouch of money the old man had given her and as she had weighed it in her hand the dead man's words had come back to her.

'Your father is a powerful man,' his voice had echoed from beyond the grave. 'You will never be truly free of his shadow. Sooner or later, he will find you and bring you back. Then it will be worse.'

How could it be worse? she had wondered.

It had started to rain.

And there, sitting by the canal, huddled against the steadily falling rain, she had come to a stone-hard conclusion. With trembling fingers she had pulled open the strings of the purse and had let the coins spill into her hand. She knew then that freedom came at a much higher price. One by one she had let the coins drop into the water to sink.

Now Jade stood in the doorway and looked along the length of the Street of Knives. Her father's house stood at the far end. The lights were on in the windows. She thought of him sitting in his accounting chamber. Even though she had made up her mind she still had her doubts. Could she really go back and face him? Would he respect her any more now for proving she could think for herself?

Perhaps not, she reasoned, but at least going back to him of her own free will would prove something. He would *have* to see that. And in this at least she knew she would be able to face him on her own terms.

Jade stepped out of the doorway and started across the road. She didn't take much notice of the small boy who was hanging around the corner on the other side. She had gone on some way before she stopped and stood very still. Slowly she turned to look at the boy. Had she seen him somewhere before? He was only small – no more than eight or nine years old – but there was something unnerving in the way he was watching her so intently.

'Holaaaaaaaaa!' A coachman's call startled her and sent her staggering back. A carriage drawn by two horses rattled along the street.

Jade spun in a whirl of skirts and broke into a run, but already the net was closing. The children came out of the shadows ahead of her. She saw them and immediately turned away down the nearest alleyway. She ran on, stumbling through the darkness, her only thought to escape them. She didn't know who they were, only that they had been sent to take her back.

She stumbled and fell, skinning her hands and knees painfully on the cobbles. Gasping in pain she pushed herself to her feet. A woman had appeared at the end of the alleyway in front of her. She stood with the light behind her so Jade found it hard to see her face. She just stood there, one hand resting on the shoulder of a small boy, the other clutching a hooked staff.

'No!' Jade gasped. 'I have to go back on my own.'

She turned to retreat the way she had come, only to find more than a dozen children blocking the alley behind her. They stood in silence, watching. Jade backed up against the wall and she heard a sound she would never forget – the sound of the children whispering her name. Softly at first. It became a hiss – like the wind in dry grass – growing louder until their voices rushed around the walls as if the bricks themselves were speaking the name Jade van Helsen.

Jade pushed her fingers in her ears, retreating before them until they stopped suddenly. As their voices died, she heard the long drawn-out steps of the woman shuffling towards her, clogs scuffing, hooked staff tapping on the cobbles.

'Jade van Helsen,' the woman said, 'your father's been looking for you.'

Jade stared at the woman. The hag was completely blind.

'You don't understand,' she pleaded. 'I was going back to my father. It's the truth! *Please!* You *have* to believe me! You have to let me go on my own.'

Some time later at the house on the Street of Knives, Goltz made his way through the shadows. His nerve had been severely tested that evening and his hand was trembling slightly as he held up the lantern. He reached the double doors leading into a large room in the heart of the house. The shadows were leaping up the curving stairs at the far end, licking at the gallery above that ran around the four sides of the room. His master was seated again in brooding silence.

'I have locked Jade in her room, sir,' Goltz spoke up, fearful of his master's unpredictable mood.

Hugo van Helsen nodded and for a while the only sound came from the crackling of the fire.

'How could she betray me, Goltz?' the banker spoke at last. 'I am her father. Have I not always had her best interests at heart?'

'She says she was on her way here when Mother Race and her brood found her,' Goltz said.

'And you believe her?' The banker came to his feet slowly. 'She has lied to me. She has disobeyed me. She has deliberately meddled in matters that are none of her business and has cost me a fortune. Why, Goltz, *why*?'

'Perhaps you should ask her yourself, sir.'

'The time for talking is over! See that Mother Race is well paid for her work. Then bring me the belt.'

'The belt, sir?' Goltz flinched slightly. 'If I may say, sir, perhaps more might be gained if you are a little less hard –'

'How I deal with my own daughter is my affair,' Hugo van Helsen snapped. 'Jade is a van Helsen. It is time she started acting like one. I will make her see that her duty lies with me, her *father* – not the Windjammers! If nothing else tonight I will teach her *never* to take sides against me again.'

Jade sat on the edge of her bed, head bowed, her hands resting loosely in her lap. She stared at the dirt on her fingers, only looking up when she heard the sound of footsteps in the passage outside. The key turned in the lock and she came to her feet as the door swung inwards. Her father stepped in and closed the door again behind him. He put down the lantern. His expression was set, his eyes pale and cold.

Jade's chin came up defiantly when she saw the belt in his hand.

12. Lost and Found

The dream was made vivid by pain: Adam Windjammer saw himself running along the side of a sunlit canal, darting between lines of lime trees, crossing bridges, running by churches. He knew he had to be somewhere but he didn't know where. He just kept running until at last Dam Square opened to him. And there – waiting for him as always – he found Hugo van Helsen and his beautiful, green-eyed, treacherous daughter, Jade.

Adam felt the rain on his face and stirred. Big warm drops splashing down. He opened his eyes and blinked until the sky formed itself out of the blur into a heavy grey mass.

He tried to move his legs, but couldn't. Cramp gripped him suddenly and he twisted in agony to spew a gush of sea water before collapsing back on to the sand exhausted by the effort. A wave ran up around him and washed the sand clean, sinking back with a hiss of tiny bubbles.

He just lay there for a while, his back pressed into the hard wet sand, catching the drops of rain on his tongue. The water cooled his throat. His first clear thought sent his hand to the ring on the chain around his neck. He felt the weight of it and wrapped it in his fist. It was some time before he found the strength to move again.

When he did, he came up on to the points of his elbows. He was lying among the wreckage of the *Sirius*. Debris from the wreck was piled up all around him and along the water's edge as far as he could see. A piece of decking pinned his legs into the sand. He made a concerted effort to free himself with a combination of shuffling and twisting movements and managed to ease one leg out then kick away the rest. He fell back, fighting for breath, until at last he was able to sit up.

The pain hit him again. The backs of his hands and forearms had been burned in the blast that had ripped through the wreck. His skin was blistered, his coat torn and seared away into great holes. But the fine weave of the wool had saved him from worse. He sloughed off the coat like a reptile skin and tore out strips of the silk lining to bind his hands. He ached in more places than he could count and was covered in small cuts and tender places that were rapidly developing into bruises. When he probed with the tips of his fingers he found a patch of hair above his right ear had been singed completely away to the scalp. He tore out another strip, trying it around his head in a bandana to protect the livid sore.

He looked around. 'Mr Glass? Mr Merrik! Monsieur Valoir! *Anyone?*'

No answer.

By now the rain was falling heavily, drawing grey

veils down around him. The beach was deserted as far as he could see. The bay was empty too: the wreck, the longboat, the Spanish, the *Draco* – they had all vanished. A claw of panic hooked into him. He had no way of knowing how long he had been lying there. For all he knew the *Draco* might have returned and taken the others aboard. For all he knew he might have already been given up for dead.

'I'm alive!' It burst out of him, then again, '*Alive.*'

The rain dragged the words down and drove them mercilessly into the oblivion of the sand. He reached for the handle of the knife in his belt, found some comfort in being armed in some small way, but when he looked towards the line of trees he shivered. He was scared now.

He judged from the face of Hell's Rock that he must have been washed further along the beach into one of the many smaller inlets there. He stood up, swaying unsteadily until he had his balance, then he started back along the beach, stumbling as he turned in slow circles every now and again: one moment fearful of the brooding, steaming darkness under the trees to his left, the next filled with forlorn hope that he might suddenly see the *Draco* sailing into the bay to his right. He felt very alone.

Misty shapes ahead of him in the rain soon formed themselves into rocks. They jagged up out of the sea and disappeared into the trees only to burst up again further back, rising into the sheer face of the cliff. Adam climbed up on to their sharp-edged slipperiness and stood among the rock pools where all reflections were destroyed by the rain. As far as he could tell, the rocks marked the place on the reef where the wreck of the *Sirius* had been. He shielded his eyes with his hands and looked both ways along the beach. Thunder rumbled in the bellies of the clouds and lightening struck down, forking at the ocean in half a dozen places at once in a sudden cage of light.

He noticed something protruding from among the rocks further along and climbed down to investigate. As he slithered over the rocks and on to the sand he saw it was the gunwale of the longboat. A hole the size of his head had been punched through the side and the boat had been washed up and left by the ebbing tide. Here and there he could see oars, some snapped. He looked for footprints. If there had been any, the rain had obliterated them long ago.

The lightning flickered and a glint caught his eye. Something was lying half-trodden into the sand. He eased gingerly down on to a knee. One lens was cracked, the glass shattered into a star, but there was no mistaking the mapmaker's lenses. With clumsy, bandaged hands, he brushed away the sand and picked them up, then came to his feet calling Merrik's name.

'It's me – Adam Windjammer!' he shouted.

'*Windjammer Windjammer Windjammer*.' The echoes snapped back from the face of the cliff. The thunder rumbled. A feeling of hopelessness swamped him. He eased down, crouching among the rocks, staring at the lenses. The mapmaker would never willingly have left them behind – if he was certain of nothing else he was certain of that – and in that lonely moment, he convinced himself the mapmaker and the others were dead.

'I should've listened to Hendrik Honthorst,' he murmured. 'We should *never* have come ashore.'

He hugged his knees, rocking gently as his tears mingled with the rain. It took an effort of will to shake off his self-pity. When he did, he stood up and faced the trees. His gaze climbed to the ridge above. He made up his mind to try and reach it to see what he could from there. He slipped the lenses into the pocket of his shirt then reached for his knife. This small gesture of defiance gave him strength. He started up the beach, but he hadn't gone far from the rocks when a movement in the undergrowth made him forget everything else.

Adam scuttled the rest of the way up to the trees and ducked into cover. He looked around a trunk, watching as a man appeared from one of the pig-runs that criss-crossed the undergrowth. From that distance, with the rain falling in sheets, it was hard to see the man's face under the flopping brim of his hat. Several others followed him on to the sand. Adam didn't recognise any of them. They were all heavily armed with muskets and cutlasses and they started moving along the line of the trees towards him.

His heart was thundering as he eased out of sight and pressed his back to the trunk of the tree. Now as he listened he could hear movement in the undergrowth to his left. He risked another look around the trunk and ducked back again. The men were moving fast, crouching over their weapons as if expecting an ambush. They spotted the longboat and spread out quickly across the sand. Adam could do little but wait. He shrank back as a big man wearing an oiled coat passed close by – so close he could hear the man's breathing, see the rain streaming off the brim of his hat and dripping from his beard.

Adam tried to make himself as small as possible. He wished the tree would open up so he could hide inside.

The surf boomed on the reef. Closer, the rain drummed on the foliage, forming into small pools in the green funnels and curves of the leaves until they dipped to release tiny waterfalls of crystal.

At last, the man moved on. Adam breathed again. He waited a little while to be sure, then eased out from his hiding place, crawling some of the way before coming to his feet. He plunged into the undergrowth and pushed his way through into the strange half-lit world under the trees.

Stumbling, he broke into a run. The rain drowned all other sounds but his own tortured breathing. He blundered on, dodging first one way then the other as he tried to get as far away from the beach as possible. He tripped and fell, wincing as the pain shot up his arms. He came to his feet again and stumbled on until he was gasping for breath. The lightening flickered and the thunder rumbled. The rain was streaming down his face and running into his eyes. Still he pushed on through the undergrowth without knowing where he was going; his only thought now was to get away. Then suddenly a man stepped out in front of him.

It happened so fast Adam didn't have time to react. Before he knew it, the knife had been knocked from his hand and he had been pulled down. His startled cry was cut off as his back slammed into the soft earth and a hand was clamped over his mouth. He felt the touch of steel at his throat and stopped struggling. Then just as suddenly, the weight lifted off his chest.

'As God loves me ...' a voice breathed.

'I thought you were food for the fish, Windjammer,' said the Frenchman after he'd helped Adam to sit up.

Adam leaned back against the trunk of a tree. It had taken same minutes for him to recover his breath 'Monsieur Valoir – where have you been?'

'That was a brave thing you did back there – I saw it all,' the Frenchman said.

'Who were those men?' Adam gasped. 'What are they doing here?'

No answer.

'If you saw it all then you must have seen what happened to Mr Glass and the others,' Adam said. 'Did they get ashore? Were they taken?'

The Frenchman spat. 'Who cares about them? Call me sensitive, but I have a feeling that Mr Glass of yours didn't like me.'

Adam stood up stiffly.

'Where are you going now?' the Frenchman asked.

'To look for them, of course. Dead or alive, I have to find them.'

Victor Valoir shook his head. 'I didn't save you from *them* just to let you go and get yourself killed. Besides, you'll not find your friends now.'

Adam paused. 'Why? What happened to them? Tell me!'

The Frenchman didn't reply but glanced up at the ridge.

Adam followed the direction of his glance. 'Those men – who were they? They weren't Spanish, that's for certain.'

Valoir shrugged. '*Boucaniers.*'

'Buccaneers?' The name was enough to kick Adam's heart against his ribs. The reputation of those French sharp-shooters was well known to him. They were wild, dangerous men, living on the edge of the world, hunting everything that moved for their skins and meat.

'While you were chasing ghosts back there, I went up to take a look,' the Frenchman explained.

'You went up there! Then you must have known those men were here.'

Victor Valoir nodded.

'Why didn't you tell us?'

'As God loves me, I had hoped to keep Jacques Talon and his men out of this for the sake of the gold,' the Frenchman said sadly. 'But those Spanish guns have put paid to that now.'

'I don't understand – who's this Jacques Talon?'

The Frenchman forced a laugh. 'Captain Talon, late of the King Louis's navy. A privateer turned to private business. I've traded with him in the past and he's a hard man to do business with. As God loves me, he'll already have your men if any of them survived.'

Adam looked away up the slope towards the ridge.

'Don't be a fool! You can't go after them now,' the Frenchman said. 'If we're lucky, they won't find out about us or the gold.'

'How many times do I have to tell you –'

'I know – there isn't any gold.' The Frenchman tapped the side of his nose.

'You can stay if you want to, but I'm going,' Adam said, pulling himself up.

Victor Valoir watched him set off. Then he sighed and stirred himself. 'This had better be worth my while, Adam Windjammer,' he muttered and began to follow.

Adam eased aside the tangle of undergrowth to reveal the open space ahead of them, a long scar in the vegetation caused by a rock slide. The rain had stopped and the clearing was now bright with watery sunlight – exposed – a jumble of recently broken stumps steaming in the heat and shimmering with the buzz of insects. Not far above them, the ridge he had seen only in fleeting glimpses through the canopy, angled up out of the trees, jutting grey against the backs of the retreating clouds.

Victor Valoir eased down on to one knee beside him and shook his head.

'What's up there, Monsieur Valoir?' Adam asked.

'As God loves me, I am your friend. I don't want to see you killed.'

'Then if you won't tell me, I'll just have to find out for myself.'

Before Victor Valoir could stop him, Adam had stepped out into clearing. Nothing happened. He took several steps and paused. He was just beginning to think that this Jacques Talon was some elaborate fabrication made up to scare him, when somewhere among the rocks on the ridge above there was a puff of bluish smoke and a flash. The crack of the musket smacked at the air, scaring colourful birds up from the trees around them.

The musket ball struck sparks from a rock close by Adam's foot and sent him diving for cover behind a boulder. Brightness destroys detail in the shade and even from that short distance, he could hardly make out the Frenchman hidden among the leaves.

'Maybe you'll listen to me next time,' the Frenchman called to him. He pulled a filthy rag from his pocket, found a suitable stick and tied it to the end.

'What's that supposed to be?' Adam asked.

'A flag of truce,' the Frenchman said. He pushed the rag out through the bushes and gave it a shake. 'Don't shoot!' he called. 'We're coming out!'

Victor Valoir eased out of the bushes, waving his flag with great swinging movements of his arm to be sure they understood his peaceful intentions. Step by tentative step, he moved to Adam's side and helped him up. Together they came out from under the trees into the full glare of the sun, picking their way through the rocks, expecting at any moment to see the puffs of smoke of the shots that would cut them down.

Adam shaded his eyes, looking through his fingers into the glare. After the rain the sun seemed to have been polished to special brilliance as it began its descent, dipping into the afternoon beyond the ridge. It was shining into their eyes and making it hard to see anything much around the rocks above. Faceless, the enemy was terrifying.

'We are unarmed!' the Frenchman called. He had some difficulty proving it while still holding the flag, but with a clever use of his chin to grip the stick he managed to hold up both hands at once and then told Adam to do the same.

Nothing happened.

The Frenchman wiped the perspiration from his top lip and tried calling again with the same result. They stood, exposed, sweating in the sun. Adam's mouth was parched. His tongue felt as if it had swollen to fill his mouth. He couldn't tell how long it lasted, but the end came suddenly as someone stepped out from behind one of the rocks.

The man came to stand at the edge of a large flat rock, his legs apart, one hand on the hilt of his sword.

His hair was cropped short against his head, but his beard was long and bushy and he was carrying a long-barrelled musket, the butt resting on one hip, the muzzle pointing at the sky.

'Who are you?' he called down to them in guttural French.

'It's me – Victor Valoir!' the Frenchman called back.

'Victor?' the man sounded surprised. 'Victor Valoir – the meat trader? Are my ears playing tricks on me!'

The Frenchman forced a laugh. '*Lamont?* My old friend –'

'You're no friend of mine!'

The Frenchman swept his arm across his mouth again. 'Still sailing with the *Requin*, Lamont?' he asked weakly.

'The very same, Victor.'

The Frenchman groaned. 'And I suppose … *Jacques* is with you?'

'Why don't you come up and see for yourself, Victor?' The one called Lamont waved them up.

'Just let me do the talking, Windjammer,' Valoir hissed out of the corner of his mouth.

Together they started up, the Frenchman stopping to wave his flag of truce at intervals just in case. Adam climbed after him through the rocks. Valoir was breathing hard by the time he reached the top and pulled himself up on to the flat rock with some difficulty. Adam scrambled after him and stood up to find himself caught in the sights of half a dozen muskets.

'Don't shoot!' the Frenchman pleaded. He forced the end of the stick into a fissure in the rocks and left his flag drooping on the crest as he shuffled forward, making nervous little scooping motions with his hand to be sure Adam followed him.

At once the view beyond opened to them and fell away down a wooded slope. Lamont and the musketeers stepped aside to reveal a man standing with his back to them, one eye pressed to an enormous brass telescope set on a stand.

'Well, well, Victor,' Jacques Talon said without looking around. 'This *is* an unpleasant surprise.'

13. Jacques Talon

'Do you like my contraption, Victor?' Jacques Talon asked, perhaps a little too casually for comfort. 'Have you seen one before? I doubt it. They call it a telescope. You see, it works by an ingenious positioning of polished lenses. Here and here.' He pointed them out, one each end of the brass tube. 'Perhaps you would care to try it, Victor? Before Lamont takes you away and hangs you for a liar and a thief.'

'No wait!' Victor Valoir gasped as Lamont stepped forward and took hold of him by the arm. He struggled, trying to break free. 'Don't you want to know why we've come, Jacques?'

'Not particularly.'

'You'll be sorry, Jacques. As God loves me, you'll be sorry ...'

Jacques Talon raised a hand in a sign to Lamont. Victor Valoir was released and immediately began thanking everyone effusively. 'You won't regret this, Jacques – I swear it.'

'I already am,' Jacques Talon said drily. 'You owe me, Victor. You owe me for one hundred barrels of salt beef, if I remember rightly.'

'Was it my fault that Goulan turned out to be a pirate? He didn't pay me, Jacques – you ask anyone on St Christophe –'

'I'm not interested in excuses, Victor. I want my money.'

'And I have it now, Jacques, every last *sou*,' Victor Valoir assured him. 'Yes, I have all of it – in gold.'

'*Gold?* I see no gold, Victor.'

'It's safe, Jacques. Buried. I just have to get it, that's all.'

'Hang him!'

'No wait! I'm serious, Jacques. You know me – I am your *friend*.'

Jacques Talon laughed. Once again he waved Lamont back. 'I am not interested in friends now, Victor. I need a ship.'

'A ship? But what about the *Requin?*'

'Take a good look! She's sinking into the mud.'

Adam followed the direction of his outstretched hand. Below, he could see a hook-shaped bay. A bulge of the land jutted to make a good anchorage behind. It was almost invisible from the sea and easy to miss. The trees clustered on the slopes, growing right to the water's edge: ancient forests of cedars and pines camouflaging the settlement. The houses were built from logs and roofed with bark, crowded together behind a wooden palisade. The largest building stood in the middle overlooking the natural harbour where a badly damaged frigate listed, lying low in the water.

Victor Valoir stared at the vessel, cast a thoughtful glance in Adam's direction and then looked out to sea. '*We* have a ship, Jacques,' he said. 'A fine ship too. As

God loves me, the *Draco* would suit you well.'

'What do you mean?' Adam hissed. 'You've no right to talk about the *Draco* like that!'

Jacques Talon looked at him. 'And who is your friend, Victor?'

Adam answered for himself.

'Jacques Talon at your service,' he introduced himself in return with a bow. 'Captain of the *Requin*. Late of His Majesty King Louis's navy. And you speak good French.' Talon seemed impressed. 'Much better than the other one.'

Adam gave him a hard look. 'What other one? Do you mean Mr Merrik?'

Jacques Talon stared back but didn't answer. If he was a pirate he didn't look like one. He was squat and balding with more of an air of a town clerk about him than of a buccaneer. His nose was a little too large and his jaw a little too short, but there was an air of intelligence about him that made him stand out from the hard men around him. He was dressed in a long-tailed blue coat that had seen better days in the French navy, a shirt that was high at the neck – tied and pinned with a gold clasp – a pair of breeches that had once been white, and knee-length boots. But it was his eyes that struck Adam most. They were dark and quick under the brim of his hat, so that it seemed he missed very little of importance. Surprisingly, he was smiling now.

'For once in your life, Victor,' he said without taking his eyes off Adam's face, 'I think you've done something right.'

'I have? I mean … yes, of course … Jacques.'

'What are you talking about? You leave my ship out of this!' Adam interrupted.

'*Your* ship?' Jacques Talon picked up on it at once. His eyes narrowed and he looked Adam up and down, noticing the bandages. 'There is clearly more to this boy than meets the eye.'

Valoir was quick to assure him there was.

Jacques Talon bowed his head politely to Adam. 'Welcome to Fort Louis, Adam Windjammer,' he said, and pointed towards the settlement below. 'It is not much, but it is all I have.' He turned to Valoir. 'Now about that ship ...'

Adam's whole body was trembling. He balled his fists until the damaged skin underneath throbbed and split. He didn't want anyone to see how badly his hands were shaking. But it wasn't fear that made him quiver – it was utter fury. If he'd had the chance he would have launched himself at Victor Valoir and torn out his treacherous tongue, then and there. But the Frenchman kept at a safe distance as if he expected just such an assault. It took a great effort of will to remain calm and think, especially when Jacques Talon clamped an arm around Victor Valoir's shoulder as if they were the oldest of friends, reunited after a long time spent apart.

'We have much to talk about, Victor,' he heard Jacques Talon say.

'We do?' the Frenchman sounded less certain. 'I mean – yes, we do, I suppose. Like I said, I'll get your money –'

'Oh, don't you worry about a little thing like *money*, Victor,' Jacques Talon said. 'We've other things to discuss now.' He turned to Adam. 'Lamont, here, will show you the way down. If you do not cause trouble, I give you my word that you will not be harmed.'

Adam could only stand and watch as Jacques Talon took the well-worn path down the other side of the ridge. Victor Valoir went with him, reluctantly it was true, casting meaningful glances over his shoulder, but right then Adam was too angry to wonder about that.

The butt of a musket pushed into the small of his back. He stumbled and almost fell. They started down the path, walking in single file, led from the front by Lamont and guarded at the back by his men. Two were left guarding the ridge and two more trailed some way behind, struggling under the weight of Jacques Talon's telescope as the group went winding down the path, until the trees and the heat opened to swallow them once more.

They approached a gate in the palisade. There, a watchtower rose above the wooden wall of sharpened stakes. The gates below were open and Adam could see huts built among the trees inside. They made their way down a rutted track towards the large house overlooking the harbour. This, it turned out, was the main street; the house, Jacques Talon's.

Piles of equipment salvaged from the sinking frigate had been stacked up around the jetty close to a number of long open-sided huts. Large charcoal fires had been recently put out and the wooden smoking racks were still laden with strips of half-cured meat. It was pork mostly – *boucan*, the French called it. Adam knew it as bacon.

Now men with faces smoked black from the fires, were hurriedly lifting the meat down, chopping and sawing at the bones. Under a dark cloud of flies, the *boucaniers* were working hard to store as much of the meat as they could, hammering closed the barrels and branding them with the symbol of a dragon's claw and Jacques Talon's name. There was a sense of suppressed urgency about their work, an air of resigned desperation, as if this had all happened before and would, no doubt, happen again.

The sight and smell of so much food made Adam stop and stare until he was forced to move on again, prodded from behind by the butt of a musket. He walked on, trying to take in as much of his surrounding as he could. He studied the frigate. She had been blasted full of holes and her foremast shot away. If these Frenchmen were leaving it was clear they wouldn't get far aboard their own ship. He passed under the stoic gaze of some natives squatting in the shade, then close to the crooked arm of a gallows. Finally, he reached a hut. The door was kicked open and he was pushed in.

Adam stood for a moment as his eyes adjusted to the dim light inside. Then familiar faces swam out of the shadows around him.

'Well, if it isn't Master Windjammer, brothers,' Allart said. 'Come back from the dead.'

'Stand back, everyone! Give the boy some air!' The mapmaker pushed through the knot of men and took Adam by the shoulders. 'Adam, my boy, you're *alive*.' He looked him up and down. 'Alive – but hurt.'

Mr Glass appeared in front of him. 'I would never have believed it if I hadn't seen it with my own eyes. You must have the luck of a cat, Master Windjammer.'

The others crowded around to see for themselves. The crew of the longboat were all there and, apart from a few minor wounds, had all escaped the Spanish attack with their lives.

The mapmaker made Adam sit down and explain

what had happened and how he had got there, while he untied the bandages around his forearms and inspected the wounds.

'Just wait until I get my hands on that Frenchie,' Mr Glass muttered ominously when Adam had finished.

Adam remembered the eye pieces and dug them out of his pocket with some difficulty. The mapmaker's relief was obvious. He bent the wire frames back into some semblance of shape and perched them on his nose, blinking one eye heavily behind the starred glass as he inspected the burns.

'We'll need to ask for fresh water to bathe them, Mr Glass,' he gave his opinion, glancing up. 'But you've been lucky, Adam. Those burns would have been a whole lot worse if the sea water hadn't drawn out the heat. They'll be painful until they heal, I'm afraid, but at least the salt will stop the infection.'

'It was a brave thing you did back there, Master Windjammer,' Mr Glass said. He turned to the others. 'Now, not so long ago, Allart said respect was something to be earned. Well, I'm telling you there's not a man among us who don't owe his life to Master Windjammer's quick thinking back there. If he hadn't drawn the Spaniards' fire on to the wreck, I'll wager none of us would be alive to tell of it.'

Allart scowled and spat. 'Alive, yes – but for how long now, brothers? If it's not cannibals, it's Spaniards, and if it's not Spaniards it's cut-throats –'

'That's enough of your talk, Allart,' Mr Glass interrupted. 'We'll get out of this all right.'

'But what if that Spanish galleon catches up with the *Draco*, Mr Glass,' Govert asked.

'She'll be back, don't you worry, lad,' Mr Glass

reassured him.

'Aye and they'll find the longboat shot to pieces, brothers,' Allart pointed out. 'These Frenchmen have us all prisoners. So who'll raise a signal to the *Draco* now? That's what I want to know.'

'We could fight our way out,' one suggested.

'I'm not paid to fight pirates!' replied Allart.

Others agreed.

'Call yourselves *Dutchmen*!' Mr Glass hissed. 'Where's your courage, men?'

They shifted uneasily under the weight of his stare. Govert started to say something, thought better of it and stopped.

'Well, lad, what is it? Speak up!' Mr Glass said.

'It's just that, er ...' Govert spluttered, '... Manfred's not Dutch. He's from the Rhineland. And Copenhagen, there ... well, he's from Denmark.'

'For the love of God will you shut up!' Mr Glass growled. 'Where we've come from don't change the fact that we're here.'

'And why *are* we here?' Allart asked. 'Maybe you can tell us, Mr Glass! Because the way I see it, at the moment we're risking our lives for nothing.'

The mapmaker intervened. 'We have enough troubles without fighting among ourselves.'

Mr Glass nodded and assured them they would think of a way out of it. But before a plan could take shape they heard guards approaching and the door to the hut swung open.

'*You*,' Lamont said to Adam, 'and you,' pointing to the mapmaker. 'Come with me! The rest – stay here.'

Mr Glass was reluctant to let them go.

'What about the others?' Adam asked.

'They will eat,' Lamont said. He addressed the men and spoke slowly. 'You ... eat.' He made movements towards his mouth. '*Eat. Drink.*'

'The last meal of condemned men, brothers,' Allart gloomed.

Just at that moment Adam couldn't help wondering if he was right.

The air under the trees pulsed with the noise of insects. It was oppressively humid and sultry after the rain. Adam's shirt stuck to him, his hair ran with sweat. He walked beside the mapmaker, following Lamont through the settlement. Barricades had been thrown up at strategic points between the huts, and cannons from the frigate had been placed in line between gabions – defences made of earth and stones formed by filling huge wickerwork cylinders. Other guns had been mounted on the corner towers of the palisade wall overlooking the harbour. It was clear they were expecting an attack to come from the sea.

They turned the corner and moved into the trees and it was there, hanging by his ankles from the crooked arm of a gallows, that they found Victor Valoir.

'You sons of dogs! You cut me down! I'm an honest man.' Victor Valoir was wriggling, cursing anyone who came near. It seemed Jacques Talon wasn't quite so forgiving after all. The Frenchman saw Lamont and changed his tone. 'Lamont! My old friend. Won't you help old Victor?'

Lamont walked on by without a second glance.

'Adam Windjammer! Help me!' Victor Valoir pleaded. 'Make them cut me down! As God loves me ...'

'From what you've told us, Adam, I'd say it serves

174

him right,' the mapmaker said.

At first Adam thought they were being taken to the biggest house in the settlement, but when they approached he saw that it was filled with wounded men. They lay in bloody lines near a table where someone he assumed was a doctor was working under the jutting roof of the veranda. The man was filthy with blood and even as Adam watched, he stood back from the table with a shake of his head. Two assistants in leather aprons stepped forward, heaved a groaning man off the table and took him away. Further on Adam came across the newly dug graves.

It was a relief to get away. Adam took a deep breath, but the smell of death remained. It made him wonder how the bay could look so beautiful. He recognised the promontory and realised he was standing on the bulge of land that protected the bay from the sea.

Jacques Talon was seated at a table under a spread of canvas sail that had been roped at the corners between the trunks to form a tented roof. The table was covered with quills and inks and a number of grim-faced men were gathered around a map. He had taken off his coat and rolled up his shirt sleeves, now looking even less like the pirate that Adam was still convinced he must be.

'Thank you, gentlemen,' Jacques Talon said as the meeting broke up. 'Prepare the signal and the longboat. You know what to do.'

The men nodded and talked in low voices as they took their leave in different directions. The last to go – a man with long grey hair – paused for one final word. 'I still say we should take the ship and run for Martinique, Jacques.'

'And how long will it be, Henri, before Don Hernando follows us there? Today it is Fort Louis. Tomorrow, St Pierre and Fort Royal? You heard what the Spanish did to Tobago not four months since. They will not stop until they've driven us all out of the Americas for good.'

'Then I pray to God you know what you're doing, Jacques.' With that the man fixed Adam with a stern look and strode on by.

Jacques Talon stood up from the table and beckoned to them.

'You leave this to me, Adam!' the mapmaker said. And with that, he pulled himself up to his full height, stepped up to the table and fixed Jacques Talon with a weighty stare. 'You, Monsieur,' he said in his very worst French, 'are nothing but a *parrot*.'

There was a long pause. Then a smile caught the sides of Jacques Talon's mouth. He guffawed and suddenly he was laughing.

'I think,' he said, 'the word you are looking for is *pirate*. But then one man's pirate is another man's privateer, wouldn't you say, Lamont?'

Lamont grinned and nodded. The mapmaker stood stiffly, looking blank. He hadn't understood a word.

Jacques Talon sighed. 'Alas, I have no Dutch to make myself understood.' He switched easily, trying several other languages: 'Spanish? Latin? English, perhaps?'

'My mother is English,' Adam said. 'My father was Dutch.'

'Ah yes, *English*.' The mapmaker sounded relieved. 'I am off course. In speaking English is like a fine fellow.'

Jacques Talon sat down and rubbed his forehead

with the tips of his fingers. 'I can see this is going to be harder than I thought,' he muttered. He dismissed the mapmaker as an irrelevance with a flick of his eyes and studied Adam.

'I regret that you have come at such a difficult time, Adam Windjammer.' He spoke in almost perfect English now. 'If things were better I believe we would find we have much in common, you and I.'

'Why are we being treated like prisoners?' Adam asked.

'Prisoners? No. Guests.'

'We are locked up.'

'A precaution – for your own safety, that's all.' Jacques Talon waved the accusation aside easily. 'My men are jumpy with the Spanish about. I would not want a misunderstanding to arise.'

Adam stood stiffly. Every instinct warned him that this man was not all he seemed to be.

Jacques Talon sighed as if he could read Adam's thoughts. 'Why is everyone so obsessed by pirates these days?' He asked the question more of himself than Adam, and leaned over the table, his knuckles pressing into the map.

'See these colours? They represent the different countries fighting for control of the New World of the Americas. The English are in New England to the North.' His finger came down. 'You Dutch here around Hudson's River. The Spanish are here in South America and in the Caribbean – in strength in Havana, Hispaniola and Puerto Rico. We French are here in the lands to the North,' he pointed to the St Laurence River, 'and here in the Gulf and on the islands of Guadeloupe and Martinique. Even as we speak, the

Dutch, English, French, Danes, Swedes, Portuguese and a few others besides are settling on the islands of the Americas.'

He shook his head sadly and looked back up at Adam. 'Are we all pirates? No. When the history of this new world is written, I hope it will be recognised that it is brave men – men of vision – that are carving out empires, not just kings and queens. *Businessmen* – with companies and shareholders and financial backers. Men like us. Risk-takers – like you and me. It is people like us who are bringing civilisation to these lands.'

'Mr Merrik wouldn't agree,' Adam said, trying to sound calmer than he felt. 'He says we are taking these lands from the natives.'

Jacques Talon glanced at the mapmaker. 'Your Mr Merrik has the luxury of an education, it seems. And yet still somehow he is a fool – a clever fool, perhaps, but a fool all the same. They are the worst sort.'

Jacques Talon took out a bulbous black bottle, poured the liquor and offered it. The mapmaker softened immediately and took a glass for medicinal purposes. Adam refused.

'Despite what you may think,' Jacques Talon said. '*I* am *not* your enemy.' He drained his glass. 'And I shall prove it. Our friend Victor has been squawking like a parrot. He has told me all about you, Adam Windjammer, and your quest. Of course, Victor being Victor believes you have come in search of sunken gold – but I know that part is not true.'

He paused to allow Adam to translate for the mapmaker's benefit before continuing:

'A worthy and noble cause brings you here, but

unfortunately you have stumbled into a war. You saw my wounded men. Like you, we have been attacked by the Spanish.' He poured another glass, replenished the mapmaker's as it was quickly offered, then raised a toast to the frigate in the harbour. 'To the *Requin*! May she rot in peace.'

He drained the fiery liquid in a single gulp and breathed hard.

'We were minding our honest trade in meat when the Spanish surprised us – just as they surprised you. They attacked us just west of Cape Fear, blew holes in my ship and killed or wounded over half my crew. What chance did we have against Don Hernando? What chance did we have against a ship like the *Gran Carlo*?'

Adam frowned. 'You know this Spanish captain?'

'Ah yes, Don Hernando and I go back a number of years. He is a ruthless man, a slaver who has grown rich in the service of King Philip, and now he captains one of the finest ships ever to sail out of Havana: the *Gran Carlo* – a thousand tons of warship, carrying sixty guns or more. They say she cost one hundred and fifty thousand gold pieces to build. When she catches the sun she looks as if she is fashioned out of pure gold. Ah! I could rule the New World with a ship like that ...'

His voice trailed away as if he had said a little more than he had intended. He stood up and went to look out at the widening bay towards the open sea.

'At this moment, Don Hernando is somewhere out there preparing to attack Fort Louis. It was only your arrival and our good fortune that stopped him finding Fort Louis earlier. Had your ship not caught his eye we would all be dead men by now, or chained and destined for the salt mines or slave galleys.'

He turned abruptly. 'But Don Hernando will grow tired of chasing shadows and he will be back. Do you know how long Fort Louis will last when he returns? *One* hour, maybe two if we are lucky. First he will bombard the settlement. Then he will send his marines ashore. Believe me, they will not take kindly to anyone they find here. You see, like your friend, it seems Don Hernando also thinks we are little more than French pirates.'

'I came to find my uncle's ship,' Adam said. 'We have no quarrel with this Don Hernando – it's not our war.'

'Not *your* war?' For the first time Jacques Talon showed a flash of anger. He controlled it. 'This is the year of our Lord 1637, Adam Windjammer – war is the *fashion*. The Spanish are at war with us because France has declared against the Austrian House of Habsburg. The Catholic Habsburgs are at war with the protestant Germans of the north. The Germans have allied themselves with the Swedes and Danes and so the Swedes and Danes have declared war against Spain and the Papal States for supporting the Habsburgs. The Pope, in his wisdom, supports the Habsburgs and the Spanish in their war with you – the Northern Dutch states – and the Northern Dutch are, in turn, supported by the French. The French have made peace with the English now that there is a French queen on the English throne. But the English are as divided as the rest of us over religion and soon, so I hear, will be at war with themselves.'

Jacques Talon paused for breath, filled his glass again and drained it. '*War*,' he spoke the word as if it tasted bitter to him. 'Such a ridiculously small word for something so gargantuan and terrible, do you not think?'

Adam noticed the musket leaning against the trunk of a tree. Jacques Talon saw the flick of his eyes and followed the thought.

'It seems the urge to fight is within us all.' He picked up the musket and weighed it in his hands. Then put it to his shoulder and sighted down the barrel, before surprising Adam by offering it to him. He wouldn't take it. Jacques Talon shrugged.

'When we came here I hoped I would not need to use this again except for hunting. I thought – at last I have found somewhere I can live and grow rich. But I fear Don Hernando has other ideas.' He fixed Adam with an enquiring look. 'Is it so wrong to fight for what you believe is yours?'

'No,' Adam said after a pause.

'Somehow I knew you would say that.' Jacques Talon slanted the musket over his shoulder easily and led them to the water's edge. He pointed the barrel out towards the open sea. Adam squinted until he spotted the sails of a ship coming in on the dying rays of the day. He pointed her out to the mapmaker.

'It seems your captain has not forgotten you,' Jacques Talon said. 'Although who can say what he will think when he sees your longboat among the wreckage on the beach back there ...'

Adam glanced around at the cannons commanding the bay.

'I think now perhaps,' Jacques Talon spoke without looking at him, 'you see the business at hand, Adam Windjammer. It is clear, is it not, that you need us as much as we need you?'

'Need *us*? What for?'

Jacques Talon shrugged casually. 'It's true. I could order my men to light a beacon and draw your ship in close. I could send my men to fight their way aboard. But there would be loss on both sides and just at this moment I cannot afford to lose a single man unnecessarily. Besides, have I not already explained – we are *honest* businessmen.'

Adam's throat was dry. He swallowed hard. 'Then what *do* you want?' he asked at last.

Jacques Talon smiled. 'I knew we could do business. So here is the deal – you help us to escape Don Hernando and I guarantee to let you and your men go freely on your way with your ship and cargo. I will also give you signed letters saying you should be granted safe passage through all French waters and that your company should be allowed to trade freely in all French ports. Such letters will help make you rich.'

'How do I know you will keep your word?'

'We will shake on it.' Jacques Talon held out his hand.

'Why do you ask me? I'm not the captain.'

'You are educated. Intelligent. Victor told me how you risked your life to save your men. True – you are young. Still learning the ways of the sea perhaps. But like I said, there is more to you than meets the eye.'

'Even if I agreed, there's still the captain and Hendrik Honthorst. They would never let your men aboard.'

'They will if you persuaded them,' Jacques Talon said. 'Of course, I cannot *make* you do it. But I think you will, all the same.'

Adam took some time to translate the proposal for the benefit of the mapmaker, who had been nodding along in an effort to show he knew what was being said.

'We cannot trust him!' the mapmaker said, when he finally understood what was being offered.

Jacques Talon nodded. 'I see you still need convincing,' he said and called over Lamont who had been standing nearby. His lieutenant stepped forward and the two men spoke quickly together. Lamont was then ordered to take the mapmaker and wait with him outside, and when they'd gone Jacques Talon fixed Adam with a look. 'And what would you say if I could help you in your quest for your missing crew?' he asked quietly. 'What then, Adam Windjammer?'

The boy was lying on a low bed in a tent that had been erected some way from the other wounded. It was clear that he had been moved away from the others only recently. He was no more than nine or ten years old, thin and small with fair hair matted to his forehead. As Adam approached, he could see from the sweat on the boy's face and the high colour in his cheeks that he was caught in the grip of a dangerous fever. He was mumbling, delirious.

'Why'd you bring me here?' Adam asked. 'I'm not a doctor.'

Jacques Talon's reply was grim. 'There isn't a doctor within a hundred leagues of here.'

'Then who's that?' Adam pointed to the man working at the table.

'The ship's carpenter. He has to saw bones as well as wood.'

Adam looked at the boy. He had seen enough illness and death in his short life to know the lad wouldn't last long. He found it hard to watch his suffering and turned away.

'Why, you ask, do I show you this pitiful sight?' Jacques Talon called him back. 'Let me tell you. A year ago, a Dutch merchant galleon ran aground out there on Hell's Rock. There had been a great storm then fog so thick you could barely see your hand in front of your face.'

The steady blood-thump of Adam's heart quickened and he turned to look at him.

'The first we knew of the wreck was when the boy stumbled out of the woods into Fort Louis. When we went to look, the currents had rammed the ship up on to the reef. We buried the dead we found, salvaged what we could and left her there to rot.'

Adam stared at the boy. 'What's his name?'

'He was half starved,' Jacques Talon said. 'We took him in, fed and looked after him.'

'He must have a name,' Adam insisted.

'At first we called him Hollander, because he was from a Dutch ship. Eventually he told us his name was Hobe.'

'Hobe,' Adam repeated it. 'This is *Hobe* – the ship's boy from the *Sirius*.'

'You know of him?'

'His father is a shipwright in Amsterdam. He helped me once when my family had lost everything. In return I swore I would do everything I could to find his son.'

'Then I have it in my power to help you fulfil that promise.'

Adam knelt beside the boy. 'Hobe.' He spoke the boy's name quietly. 'Hobe, can you hear me? My name is Adam Windjammer.'

The boy's eyes flickered and opened. He stared through his fever. 'Captain?' he whispered. 'You came back for me?'

A feeling of helplessness washed over Adam. He remembered the tomb in the belly of the whale. 'It was you, Hobe, wasn't it?' he breathed. '*You* buried my uncle there ...'

He looked down at the coarse blanket crumpled over the boy's legs. With a trembling hand he pulled away the cover and stood back. A gasp escaped his lips at the sight and smell. The boy's right leg was badly swollen and wrapped in bloody bandages to the knee.

'He was aboard the *Requin* when we were attacked,' Jacques Talon explained. 'So perhaps now you see that war makes few distinctions.'

Adam retreated from the boy in horror. He fought back tears of frustration. Had he come so far just for *this*? And yet, even at that moment, he knew this simple ship's boy meant everything now that all else was lost. His hopes, his dreams of restoring his family's fortune, became nothing to Adam then. For suddenly, no success seemed to compare with restoring this ship's boy to his father.

He dropped to his knees again and took the boy's hand. 'I'm taking you home, Hobe,' he whispered. 'I give you my word on it.'

'Home,' Hobe muttered and a smile caught at his lips before his eyes closed again.

'If the Spanish take Fort Louis this boy will die,' Jacques Talon said. 'After all, what use is he to Don Hernando's slavers without a leg?'

A pause. 'Prepare your beacon,' Adam said quietly without looking up. 'Please, do it now.'

14. Men of War

The flames from the torches leapt up, reflecting in Adam's eyes as he stared at the fire.

'Adam,' the mapmaker whispered urgently. 'You don't have to do this.'

Adam found it hard to drag his gaze from the flames.

'I understand how you feel,' the mapmaker went on. 'But he's only a ship's boy, when all's said and done.'

But Adam knew Hobe had become so much more than that to him now. The boy was rapidly becoming the difference between success and failure of the voyage. Lucien Windjammer and the rest of the crew were lost to him, but in this small way at least Adam *could* make a difference. Alive, this boy had the power to bury the ghosts of the past. Dead, he would become just one more phantom to haunt Adam's dreams.

'And you would you entrust the *Draco* and the lives of all aboard on the word of this ... this ...' The mapmaker glanced at Jacques Talon. 'Well, you tell me what he is.'

Adam wiped his mouth on the back of his hand. That hand was trembling. The moment had come and it left him feeling weak, and yet he knew he had no choice. He couldn't let the boy die. Whatever Jacques Talon was or wasn't – whether he would keep his word or not – he was the only man alive who could help now.

'I gave Hobe my word,' he said. 'I'm taking him home.'

'But, Adam,' the mapmaker reasoned, 'once these Frenchmen are aboard and the ship is taken they could murder us all.'

Adam closed his eyes. The responsibility was terrible, but his mind was made up. He gripped the torch and held it up to the iron brazier that had been set on the point. The fire licked at the tar-soaked wood in the iron basket, then caught and the flames leapt up. The signal had been lit – a beacon to bring the *Draco* into the bay.

Adam dropped the torch and turned on his heel. He strode back up from the water's edge to the tent where Hobe lay. The boy was mumbling, making no sense, his eyes half-closed as he slipped in and out of consciousness. Adam put a cup of water to his lips, but it choked him and dribbled away down his chin. With trembling fingers, Adam mopped up the drips and smoothed them across the boy's brow.

'Don't die, Hobe,' he said. '*Please* don't die.'

'Take him to the table,' a voice said in French.

Adam looked up as two men in leather aprons ducked in under the canvas. Outside, the carpenter of the *Requin* stood talking to Jacques Talon.

'I may not be a surgeon,' the man was saying, 'but I know when a leg is rotted. It'll have to come off – even then he will probably die.'

'No!' Adam came to his feet with a burst of furious energy that set him snarling a denial. 'He mustn't die.'

However, he could only watch and follow as the men carried Hobe to the table. They cut away the bandages and what was left of the boy's breeches to reveal the wound in all its putrid ugliness. To one side an array of carpenter's tools had been laid out on another table. The saws, knives and other tools seemed macabre and evil now – more like implements of torture than surgical instruments.

'Here, drink this, boy,' the carpenter said, forcing the neck of a bottle between Hobe's lips. Hobe choked on the fiery spirit. The carpenter forced down some more, then handed a piece of leather to Adam. It had been cut from a length of a belt. 'Put this between his teeth and make sure his tongue is underneath.'

Adam was horrified.

'Do you want the boy to choke on his own tongue?' the carpenter insisted.

Irons had been heated in the glowing charcoal of a fine and a pot of tar was bubbling to seal the wound. The oiliness of the melted tar was choking. The points of the cauterising irons glowed red hot. Adam's head began to spin. He found it difficult to open Hobe's mouth.

'I'm sorry,' he said, 'I have no choice …'

Words. What were words worth? Nothing, it seemed to Adam at that moment. They just scratched at the ear like dead leaves on glass. And yet as he spoke quietly in Dutch, the boy's eyes flickered and opened once more. It took a moment for them to focus.

'It'll be all right,' Adam promised, knowing it wouldn't.

Hobe caught sight of the irons and twisted away in

terror, writhing suddenly as the doctor's assistants took firm hold of him. He was too weak to resist for long. Adam gripped the boy's hand. And the carpenter took up his saw, spat on the blade, and went about his bloody business.

The *Draco* came in with the dusk, sailing slowly into the bay, drawn in by the signal fire. Now she stood out on the water, her masts dark against the fading light. Every now and again the sound of a voice drifted across as an order was called and there were the telltale trails of glowing match-fuses. The crew of the *Draco* was expecting trouble.

Jacques Talon's men assembled on the shore by the boat that would take them out to the ship. Sparks flared up from the torches that had been lit along the water's edge, the flames slanted their shadows over the rocks as the men obeyed Jacques Talon's orders and left their weapons and muskets behind before filing down the wooden jetty.

'Just look after Hobe until I get back,' Adam told the mapmaker. 'Don't let him die.'

'Alas, Adam,' the mapmaker said, 'that's up to Hobe now.'

A lantern was hung in the bow of the French long-boat. It cast an eerie light over the faces of Jacques Talon's men as they settled on to the thwarts and prepared their oars.

'It's time,' Jacques Talon said, striding out along the jetty. He stepped down into the boat and had just taken his position at the tiller when a shot was fired. Suddenly there were shouts from the huts and the sound of scuffles.

'It must be Mr Glass,' the mapmaker said. 'He's trying to break out with the men.'

Jacques Talon remained aboard, ordering Lamont and some of the men left ashore to see what was happening. The men went bounding away, but hadn't gone far when Mr Glass appeared, leading the others out of the trees. They had overwhelmed the guards and were armed and carrying blazing torches.

'Mr Merrik! Master Windjammer!' the first mate called to them. 'You best get over here. They may get us, but they'll not take the *Draco*.'

'No, Mr Glass! Wait!' Adam said. 'You don't understand.'

'It's plain enough to us, Master Windjammer. These Frenchies want to take our ship.'

'They're unarmed, Mr Glass!' Adam spoke up. 'We're going out to talk to the captain. Jacques Talon gave his word.'

'It's the Devil's word, Master Windjammer, and it's not to be trusted.'

'They aren't pirates, Mr Glass.'

'If it looks like dung and it smells like dung, then I'll wager it's –'

'That's enough, Mr Glass!' the mapmaker stopped him.

The sound of the water lapping on the shore filled the silence that followed. Once, not that long ago, Adam had watched his father face a hostile crowd. It had been in front of the old house on the Herengracht. Adam recalled the scene well. He remembered how his father had faced them alone; how his father had believed in himself even when the crowd had turned against him.

'I'm going with them,' Adam said.

'Willingly, Master Windjammer?' Mr Glass called.

Adam nodded. 'Yes, Mr Glass – *willingly*.'

'What did I tell you, brothers?' It was Allart who spoke into the pause. 'It's a Windjammer that brought us here and it's a Windjammer who'll bury us here too.'

Adam stood in the bow of the longboat and steadied himself against the gunwale. Ahead, the shadow of the *Draco* had grown; it seemed to fill the whole bay. The ship was ominously dark and silent. He took up the lantern and swung it from side to side in a clear signal. The light caught in glints on the water and stretched the shadows around the men crouching over the oars.

'Captain!' he called, his voice sounding small. 'It's me – *Adam*.'

No answer.

Adam raised the lantern as high as he could. The darkness thickened around the longboat. He called again. At last the answer came.

'Who's in the boat with you, Master Windjammer?' Captain Lucas's voice carried across the water.

'Frenchmen, Captain, under the command of Jacques Talon.'

'Are you a prisoner, lad?'

'No, Captain.'

'And where's Mr Merrik? Where's Mr Glass and the others?'

'Ashore, Captain. They're being treated well.'

'We heard shots, Adam. Musketry.'

'No one was hurt, Captain. I give you my word on it.'

A pause. Then the captain called again: 'How do I

know there's not a knife to your throat, Master Windjammer?'

Adam swung the lantern around so the light flickered over the men behind him. 'They're unarmed, Captain.'

Another pause. 'Very well, then. Come aboard.'

Adam sat down and Jacques Talon gave the order. The oars dipped, swirling the darkness into ripples about them. When they were close enough, the men shipped their oars and the longboat eased in until the gunwale nudged up against the ship's side. A ladder was sent down, unravelling until the thick knots of rope thumped against the *Draco*'s rounded belly.

'Bring this Jacques Talon aboard, Master Windjammer,' the captain called down. A light appeared at the ship's rail.

Adam caught hold of the ladder and stepped over the gap. His shoulder thumped into the wood as he swung in the ropes. The coarse hemp creaked under his weight. He began to climb, pausing when he came up alongside the open gun ports to be sure Jacques Talon was following him up. Below him the boat seemed to float on a sea of black. Further off he could see the beacon on the promontory and the torches of the men waiting on shore reflected in the water. He started up again and soon hands were reaching down from above and helping him over the bulwarks.

But when at last he dropped on to the deck Captain Lucas didn't greet him as he had expected. Instead, a grey-haired Frenchman and at least twenty armed men stood there. They had come aboard secretly on the other side and taken the *Draco*'s crew by surprise.

'No!' Adam gasped and spun on his heel just as

Jacques Talon climbed up on to the ship's rail behind him. 'You gave me your word!'

'So I did, Adam Windjammer,' was all Jacques Talon said. 'So I did.'

'Have you any idea,' Hendrik Honthorst said, doing his best to control himself, 'how *much* a ship like this is *worth*?'

Adam stood in front of them, alone, silent.

'What good will this talk be now, Mr Honthorst?' Captain Lucas said. 'There are fifty armed men aboard. The *Draco* is lost.'

Hendrik Honthorst ran a hand back through the sparse hairs on the dome of his head, making the calculations under his breath. '*Lost*. Yes! Ninety thousand guilders for the ship, then there's the fittings and fixtures, the value of the cargo, not to mention Madam de Witte and the other passengers ...' He looked at Adam. 'And you just gave us up to a French pirate because he gave you his word!'

'He isn't a pirate,' Adam said, defending himself weakly.

'Not a pir—' Honthorst spluttered. 'Master Adam! I expected more sense from you. He's played you for a fool! Do you think his men could have sneaked their way aboard so easily had it not been for you? You did just what they wanted of you – and you did it willingly.'

Adam focused on the one thing he could. 'Jacques Talon gave me his word – I believe him.'

'Oh, you do, do you?' Honthorst laced his words with sarcasm. 'Well, I'll take that comfort with me when I have to tell Bartholomew de Leiden, Cornelius Yort and the other shareholders that we've lost their money.'

'He'll keep his word,' Adam insisted, but it was hard to believe that now.

Hendrik Honthorst rounded on the captain. 'I warned you, Captain Lucas! I said this fool's errand was madness from the start. So I am holding you personally responsible. *Personally.* Yes! If we ever get back to Amsterdam I'll have you on a charge for letting these ... these ... *filibusters* aboard. I'll see you never captain a ship again as long as you live. We have lost the *Draco*, all for what? A ship's boy! A ten-to-a-copper-*duit* ship's boy with one leg!'

'His name is Hobe,' Adam said.

Hendrik Honthorst glared at him. 'Your father was a great man, Master Adam. I had hoped some of his intelligence and judgement might have rubbed off on you, but I can see I was wrong. You will never be like him – *never.*'

Adam looked away. He had a metallic taste in his mouth. He wondered if it was the taste of failure.

It had been some time since they had been herded down into the Long Cabin. Adam, the captain, Hendrik Honthorst, Madam de Witte and her maid along with the rest of the paying passengers had been sent down to sweat out the night below decks under guard. At first they heard very little, then the activity on the decks above increased until it became evident that the crew of the *Draco* was being sent ashore. But it was only later, as the first hint of the dawn broke in the east, that Lamont and two of his men came for them.

They were led out to an uncertain fate. Adam stood stiffly, unable to look them in the eye as they filed into the passage. Only the widow paused.

'All this for a ship's boy?' she repeated. She reached out and lifted his chin, forcing him to look at her.

'I gave him my word,' he said.

She held his gaze for a while longer, then nodded. 'It is good to know that the given word still means something in these troubled times.'

The widow moved on and Adam followed her out. Admiral Heyn watched them go from his place on top of the water barrel at the mizzen mast; the cat's bright eyes catching the dim light in green glints. The helmsman was not at the tiller and the whipstaff pole was tied. They made their way past the cannons on the main deck and Adam was last to duck out under the steps into the waist. The animals had been cleared from around the mainmast and more of Jacques Talon's men had come aboard. Now fifty or more sat around cleaning and preparing their weapons.

On the quarterdeck above, Jacques Talon was standing at the forward rail looking down. He was dressed in a fresh uniform and there was a sword hanging from the leather baldric that cut diagonally across his chest. Under the blue of his long coat he had a pistol-sized blunderbuss tucked into his belt. With the wide brim of his hat turned up and a feather catching the breeze he looked to Adam uncomfortably like a pirate now.

'Your men are waiting for you ashore, Captain,' he spoke to Captain Lucas in English. 'But be warned. I will be keeping two hostages aboard to ensure you do not attempt anything reckless while I am gone.'

'Then I'll stay.' Adam stepped forward.

Jacques Talon smiled. 'I expected that. But I have others in mind. You two!' He pointed out the widow and Hendrik Honthorst. 'You will stay. The rest of you will go ashore at once.'

'Me? *No*,' Honthorst gasped when the news was translated to him. 'I'll not stay with this madman! He can't make me!' It took two of Jacques Talon's men to prove him wrong. 'I am the representative of the shareholders of the Quadrant Shipping and Trading Company. I demand some respect. *Respect!*' Still shouting, they dragged Honthorst away.

All eyes then turned to the widow and her maid. Clara refused to leave her mistress and this time it was Lamont who dragged them apart.

'Come on, slave girl!' he mocked her.

'Leave her alone!' Adam snarled, stepping forward.

'Thank you, Master Windjammer, but I will deal with this,' the widow said. She switched into perfect French. 'Clara is not a slave – she is my friend and companion. And I'm warning you, Captain Talon, if anything should happen to her while she is ashore you will answer to me personally.'

Jacques Talon regarded her thoughtfully. 'She will be well treated as long as you do as we tell you.'

The widow nodded. 'Very well, then.' She spoke quietly to her maid and, weeping, Clara went with the men. They were pushed towards the ship's side and Adam had little choice but to follow. Clara's eyes were wide with fear as she was helped down into the waiting boat. One by one the others followed – the tobacco planter and his family, the wanderer and the Puritan – all descended the ladder.

Adam waited his turn, noticing the four large barrels that had been loaded aboard during the night. Each barrel had been stove in at one end and ropes had been attached. He was still wondering why when he reached the ship's rail. There he found Victor Valoir waiting for him. It seemed he too had joined Jacques Talon's crew. Adam glared at him and swung easily over the side. His heart sank with every step down the rope ladder, until at last hands reached up and helped him aboard.

'Cast away!' Jacques Talon called and spun on his heel.

The lugger eased off the *Draco*'s beam and Jacques Talon's men went about raising the small triangular sail. They picked up speed, tacking away across the harbour towards the beach where a crowd had gathered. Behind them the ladder was being drawn up the *Draco*'s side. Adam's gaze flicked to the anchor rope leading up the galleon's bow. He looked at the faces of the tobacco planter's children sitting around him miserably. Clara sat among them, still weeping silently.

'I'll look after your mistress,' Adam whispered.

He eased off his boots, made sure Jacques Talon's men weren't watching and slipped over the side into the water with hardly a ripple. He held on to the gunwale briefly before letting go and ducking under the water. The lugger sailed on. When he came up, Clara had moved to fill his place and was watching him out of the corner of her eye. He ducked under once more, swimming hard until he was under the *Draco*'s prow.

Above him the *Draco*'s dragon figurehead seemed to uncoil before his eyes and spread its gilded wings. Already he could see men climbing the masts and setting the top and sprit sails. The men chanted as they turned the capstan, hauling up the anchor. He watched the rope tremble and pull taut, the tension sending beads of water springing away, as the great iron hook shifted and stirred the water cloudy with sand. The ship came alive as the anchor came up out of the water, trailing seaweed and a stream of diamond drops. It was too easy. Adam caught hold and hitched a ride back aboard.

So it was that Adam Windjammer – not yet even sixteen years old – found himself going to war for the first time.

15. The Line of Fire

The sea beat up in billowing waves: blue-grey, flecked here and there with white. The dragon on the prow seemed to take flight below him as Adam rode the bowsprit.

The order of sail had been given and relayed in a series of shouts to the men in the rigging. Adam had been forced to hide as Jacques Talon's men leapt up on to the yards to release the sheets. With sails spreading to a prevailing south-westerly the *Draco* had come about and was headed for the open sea. Now Adam felt as if he was riding the great beast itself, as if he were some great mythical hero of the past, flying low over the water in one long dazzling breathless rush. Strangely, now faced with death he had never felt so utterly alive.

Slowly, however, the reality of his situation began to dawn on him as his thoughts turned to Hobe once more. The memory of the boy's terrible injuries began to colour his thoughts red. His excitement turned cold and he was forced to push his growing uneasiness to the back of his mind as he climbed up to look over the forecastle to see what was going on.

He found himself looking back down the length of the ship. The forecastle was deserted and he couldn't see into the dip of the waist where the heavily armed Frenchmen had been assembled. Beyond, however, he could see men on the slope of the quarterdeck and poop deck behind. He caught a glimpse of Jacques Talon at the forward rail and ducked back quickly, fearing he might have been seen.

When nothing happened he dropped on to the bowsprit once more and sat there wondering what to do next. His plan was only vague – to get the *Draco* back somehow – but he hadn't a clue how to do it. He didn't even know for certain where they were going or why, only that Jacques Talon and his men were planning some kind of attack. He was still wondering when he became aware that they were sailing around in circles.

Adam came to his feet with his back against the forecastle. As they came up on Hell's Rock again he was left in no doubt. He decided to risk another look to see what was happening on the decks behind him and climbed quickly up. When he reached the bulwark he listened, but heard nothing, so he stuck his head up over the side and came face to face with one of Jacques Talon's men.

The surprise was mutual. The man uttered an oath and tried to grab him. Adam dodged back down a little too quickly, missed his footing, slipped and fell heavily, slamming into the shaft of the bowsprit. As lights burst in front of his eyes a sudden lurch of the ship sent him slithering down into the crossbeams of the prow where he hung, as helpless as a fish gasping in a net, with the rush of white water coming off the bow of the *Draco* below. By the time he had pulled the rags of his breath together and sat up, the bulwark above him was crowded with faces looking down.

The men above parted and Jacques Talon appeared among them. 'Well, well,' he called down. 'Why am I not so surprised to see you?'

'I want my ship back,' Adam hissed as he was dragged up on to the deck.

'Oh, come now, Windjammer,' Jacques Talon said reasonably. 'Do you really think you can take it?'

'You gave me your word.' Adam was unable to bite back his bitterness any longer.

'Would you not have done the same? Fort Louis and everything I have is threatened. Do you honestly think I have time to make bargains with bean-counters and widows?'

'You still lied!' Adam flew at him, but was easily restrained by the men around him.

Jacques Talon seemed amused. 'Perhaps I was not quite truthful when I said that the Spanish attacked the *Requin* first. We were, I admit, sailing after their Silver Fleet.'

'You *attacked* the Silver Fleet? No wonder the Spanish are after you.'

'Men like Don Hernando grow rich and fat on the suffering of their slaves in the silver mines at Potosi. They steal the gold from the Incas and melt down their treasures. Does that make them any more *honourable* than us?'

'I don't know and I don't care,' Adam said. 'You told me you were a businessman. You told me you wanted to escape from the Spanish.'

'And I meant it – just not the way you took it.'

'You *tricked* me.'

'You believed what you wanted to believe, Windjammer. Besides, sometimes the only way left open to us is to fight for our freedom.'

'But the *Draco* is a merchant ship. She'll be blown out of the water – just like the *Requin*!'

'This time I'll win.' Jacques Talon regarded him thoughtfully. 'Let me give you a piece of advice,' he said after a pause. 'If you can fool your enemy, you can outmanoeuvre him.' He reached up and touched his temple. 'You have to out-think him. Predict his next move. And *I* know just what Don Hernando will do. He is a greedy man. His men are slavers. He will see the *Draco* as a fat prize. That is why I expect him to try and board us.'

'*Board* us?'

Jacques Talon looked pleased with himself. 'Once he brings the *Gran Carlo* in close we can bite back.' He glanced up at the sails and for a moment the rigging held his attention. When at last he spoke it was in a softer tone.

'Perhaps one day you too will be faced with a difficult choice such as I have been. When that time comes, I wonder if you will think of me and of what happens here. Perhaps then you will understand that sometimes the choices are hard, but in the end we all do what we have to do to survive – right or wrong.' He gave a slight shrug of his shoulders and forced a laugh. 'Yes, if you live long enough, Windjammer, life will probably make a pirate of you too.'

The lookouts on the maintop raised the cry within the hour. 'Spaniards, Captain!' The warnings came down thick and fast. 'The *Gran Carlo* on the starboard quarter!'

Suddenly there was movement and noise everywhere as the men ran to their stations of battle. Adam leapt to his feet and pressed his face against the window, trying without success to see the Spanish ship as she came up behind them. He had been sitting in the captain's cabin for the best part of that hour, faced with Madam de Witte and Hendrik Honthorst, and compared with them an attack by a galleon of the Imperial Spanish Fleet almost came as something of a relief.

It had been the longest of hours in the longest of days. Hendrik Honthorst had passed the time by heaping complaints upon accusations until even the widow said enough was enough.

'Will you stop that incessant whining?' she hissed. 'We're here now and we'll have to make the best of it.'

'My thoughts exactly, Madam de Witte,' Honthorst said, and with a bow he proved the depths of his obsequiousness.

Soon after that, Jacques Talon opened the door and stepped in. He was carrying an iron helmet under one arm. He tossed the helmet to Adam. 'Put it on and tell the others to follow.'

'They are going to hang us for sure!' Honthorst whimpered as they stepped out on to the quarterdeck.

Jacques Talon pointed at the steps leading up to the poop deck above and asked Adam to translate his orders: 'Tell them they are to stand in full view in the stern by the lanterns. I want Don Hernando to see there are passengers aboard.' He waited for Adam to relate the message and silenced Honthorst's protests by pulling the blunderbuss from his belt. 'I do not have time to argue.'

Honthorst understood that part without the need for translation and scuttled up the steps with the widow following more sedately behind.

'What about me?' Adam asked.

'It seems you have made this your fight too, Windjammer,' said the French captain. 'So you may as well make yourself useful with a cannon.'

'A *cannon*.'

Jacques Talon nodded. 'Lamont will keep an eye on you.'

High above the lookouts were pointing somewhere off to starboard and Adam crossed to the ship's side to see the *Gran Carlo* for himself. The Spanish galleon was bearing down on them fast, her battle standards flying and her sails billowing in the wind; the sun glinted on the ornate gilding that adorned her woodwork as she made her inexorable advance.

Adam settled the helmet on his head. It was too big and he had to push it back to see out from under the metal rim. He had never felt more like a small frightened boy.

He tore his gaze from the ship with some difficulty and looked along the length of the decks. The sight of Victor Valoir stopped him dead. The Frenchman was with the armed men crouching behind the bulwarks along the starboard side. Valoir caught his eye and looked guiltily away. Adam spotted more men hidden in the forecastle and under the cover of the main deck and down in the hold. On the poop deck above him, Madam de Witte and Hendrik Honthorst were standing by the lanterns in the stern in full view. Jacques Talon was at the forward rail, preoccupied now with something happening on the main deck below them.

Adam heard a repeated 'Heave!' and *splash* and realised that the barrels he had seen earlier were being thrown over the side. Two went over on the port side and two more on the starboard. There was the sound of ropes burning out over wood before a shudder ran through the whole ship. Adam felt the change at once.

The *Draco*'s forward motion checked as the barrels filled with water and acted like drogues, bleeding the ship's speed with their drag. The galleon's movements became sluggish and soon she was wallowing and rolling on the swell, so much so that had they thrown out the log to measure her speed, Adam was sure it would barely have shown any forward movement at all. He didn't yet fully realise that the *Draco* had just become bait.

His gaze was sucked back to the Spanish galleon. His mouth was dry. He felt light-headed. This was all wrong. This wasn't how it was supposed to be. He had often imagined fighting in a sea battle and he had always seen himself as brave – a true Windjammer, like his father – standing defiantly on the deck fighting like a hero. This was all so different. He felt like he was in the middle of a bad dream, only this was one night-mare from which his mother wouldn't wake him.

He stood, wondering if he would ever see his mother and sisters again, and his mind fled away down sunlit canals, across bridges and under elms to Dam Square where inevitably his thoughts met Jade van Helsen again.

The report of the gun brought Adam back with a rush. There was a sudden explosion. It was a ranging shot, a warning of the storm to come, and it fell well short. But that shot claimed its first casualty in Hendrik Honthorst. With a gasp he fainted clean away on the spot, landing supine with a thump, his arms and legs spread like a star.

'Leave him!' Jacques Talon ordered.

The cannons were loaded at the muzzle: first the gunpowder charge then twelve pounds of iron ball and finally pieces of cloth wadding. Skilled hands could load in about a minute, tamping the barrel before the pan was primed with gunpowder and the cannon rolled forward to fire. The *Draco* had four guns on either side of the waist, three more to port and starboard on the covered part of the main deck where the helmsman stood, four more on the forecastle and two on the quarterdeck where Adam now stood. There were four smaller falconet cannons mounted on the ship's rail and, surprisingly, these all had been placed on the port side – the side *away* from the enemy.

Every cannon was loaded now as the *Gran Carlo* came in range. The men were ready. They watched the great warship tacking across the wind on a course that initially had her almost at right angles to the *Draco*.

'Hold your fire until I give the command!' Jacques Talon passed his order to Lamont. In a quieter voice he said, 'It's time to see if Don Hernando means business.'

Almost as he spoke the Spanish warship began to turn broadside on. From bow to stern, puffs of smoke appeared one after the other along the line of her upper gun deck. Cannonballs started smacking into the water to Adam's left and right; one fell close in front and made him flinch. Everywhere he looked he could see plumes of water rising in a sudden parade.

'You can do better than that, Don Hernando!'

Jacques Talon shouted. He strode across the quarterdeck. 'I think it's time to give him some encouragement, don't you, Windjammer?'

Jacques Talon caught him by the arm and led him to a cannon. Lamont and his men moved aside as their captain knelt and squinted down the barrel, made some small adjustment of calibration to ensure the angle and range were correct before standing up. He took a slow-match from one of the gunners and inspected the glowing tip in its wooden holder. The glow grew fiercer as he blew on the end. He held it out to Adam.

Adam didn't move. He *couldn't* move. Jacques Talon reached out and took his hand, pressing the holder into his palm and closing the fingers tight around the blackened shaft.

'Touch the spark to the powder and stand well back or that gun will grind your bones.'

Adam stared at the glowing match. It might as well have been in someone else's hand for all the control he had over it. He felt a surge of panic.

'It'll be easier when it starts,' Jacques Talon assured him. 'Even brave men are scared at times like this – God knows I am.'

Adam turned to look at him in surprise, but already the French captain had moved away.

'Clear the decks!' Jacques Talon ordered.

The widow fought off Lamont's attempts to hurry her down the companionway. She descended from the stern with dignity. Lamont went back for Hendrik Honthorst, returning to shake him and slap his face.

'I would like you to have this for your protection, Madam.' Jacques Talon offered her the blunderbuss from his belt. 'You may have need of it.'

The widow took the weapon. It was a short-barrelled pistol loaded with shot, with a flared end not unlike a bugle. She weighed it in her hand and looked at Jacques Talon. 'I could shoot you down on the spot,' she said.

Jacques Talon nodded. 'You could, Madam.'

The widow regarded him thoughtfully then turned to Adam. 'If it makes any difference, I believe you might be right about this Frenchman. May God protect us all!'

She continued down the next companionway into the waist. Her step was unhurried and her manner calm. She paused to look around before ducking under the steps in the direction of the Long Cabin.

'I would I had a hundred men as brave,' Jacques Talon murmured.

Hendrik Honthorst came to with a gasp. He sat up, rubbed his head and looked around, remembered the *Gran Carlo* and jumped to his feet.

Jacques Talon ignored him and took position at the forward rail to make his address. 'To defeat Don Hernando we need to make him think he has us beaten before we start,' he called down to the men in the waist. 'We will give him one round from each gun – and one round only. Don Hernando will judge us on our speed and our ability to reload. If we do not fire again he will think little of us as fighting men. Let him! I want him to believe he has nothing to fear from this Dutch merchantman.'

It was a strange command and Adam was still wondering if he had understood correctly when Hendrik Honthorst appeared at his side. He had managed to escape Lamont and played a game of dodge until he leapt down the steps on to the quarterdeck.

'Surely he's not going to make a fight of it, Master Adam!' Honthorst caught hold of his sleeve and tugged hard. 'Have you *seen* the size of that warship? It must have a thousand guns! This is madness.'

'On my signal!' Jacques Talon gave the command.

Honthorst looked horrified. 'Captain Talon! I must protest. Have you any idea how much a cannonball costs these days? Not to mention the gunpowder we will be wasting. It must *all* be accounted for.'

Honthorst remembered Jacques Talon couldn't understand him. 'You speak his infernal tongue, Master Adam. Tell him that my shareholders will not tolerate waste of any kind.' He fought the motion of the ship, gripping the ship's rail as he looked with obvious alarm at the Spanish warship bearing down on them. 'We must strike our colours and a bargain. We must surrender!' He turned several circles on the spot in the hope of finding someone who might agree, before taking his protest back to Jacques Talon. 'This is a Dutch ship. You have no right –'

'Did I not order the decks to be cleared? Now get this infernal bean-counter off my quarterdeck!'

Lamont did his best, but nothing inspired Hendrik Honthorst to resist as much as wanton waste. Adam might have found it funny to watch had he not been so scared. The moments spliced themselves into knots in his stomach. He noticed the tiniest of details: the smell of the gunpowder, the metallic click of the cannonballs, the smouldering trails of the slow-fuses. And most of all, the sickly-scared thump of his own heart as he waited now for the order to fire.

On every deck, at every cannon, the men crouched ready. They waited as the *Draco* rolled to starboard, tilting the muzzles of the guns towards the waves until the downward motion reached its lowest point. The ship began to roll back, bringing the muzzles of the twelve-pounders on the *Draco*'s starboard side up towards the galleon.

'This has gone far enough –' Hendrik Honthorst decided.

'Give fire!' Jacques Talon's hand came cutting down.

The rest was lost in the roar of the guns.

The cannon slammed back against the ropes that secured it to the bulwark. It belched smoke and pieces of burning wadding as the gun recoiled. Adam was momentarily blinded. He tasted the burnt powder and his ears were ringing with the noise. But he was relieved that he had managed to fire the gun without making a fool of himself.

The men leapt forward to reload. One sponged out the barrel, another pushed in the charge and tamped it down. The cannonball followed and then the wadding. Jacques Talon's men were well practised and Adam was soon helping them roll the cannon forward into position once more. This time, as he stood back, he did so with new confidence. But the order to fire again didn't come.

The smoke cleared and Adam looked around. Hendrik Honthorst had fainted once more and was lying flat out on the deck. No one else seemed to notice him. All eyes were now on the Spanish warship. Adam wasn't sure what he had expected to see, but it wasn't this: their broadside seemed to have made no impression on the galleon at all. He didn't know it at the time, but this was exactly as Jacques Talon had intended. Right then, Adam could only stand and watch as the *Gran Carlo* began to make a turn. Her sails caught and billowed with the wind as she manoeuvred to run on a parallel course to the *Draco*.

'Steady as she goes, helmsman!' Jacques Talon called down though the grating in the deck. 'On my order we'll take her hard to starboard.' He stood back. 'I want every stitch of sail up! Everything she carries. Let Don Hernando think we've something aboard worth catching.'

Lamont knuckled his forehead by way of salute. 'You heard the captain!' he roared.

Instantly, men leapt up into the rigging, climbing the rope ladders and out on to the yard arms to release the last of the sheets. Jacques Talon pulled himself up on to the bulwark, clinging to the ratlines of the mizzen mast so he could see the Spanish warship behind them.

The break and slope of the poop deck now blocked Adam's view. He could only stand at the cannon with the men and wait as the French captain leaned out over the side, looking aft. Hendrik Honthorst groaned and came around for a second time and sat up, rubbing his head.

'She's shortening sail!' Jacques Talon called over his shoulder. 'Don Hernando's afraid he'll run past us!' He jumped down on to the quarterdeck. 'He's taken the bait.' He laughed. 'He thinks we're nothing but a fat little merchant ship ripe for the plucking. Well, it's time we taught Don Hernando what happens when you underestimate your enemy. Make ready!'

'What did he say?' Hendrik Honthorst asked, getting

to his feet. 'What's happening? Where are the Spanish?' He noticed several long tears in the mainsail. 'Oh my goodness! This is terrible. How will it look if we arrive in Amsterdam with a ship shot full of holes?' He ran his hand back through the greying hairs on his glistening head. 'I only hope she hasn't been holed at the waterline. We're probably sinking even as I speak!'

'Does he *ever* shut up?' Jacques Talon growled at Adam.

It took the sight of the *Gran Carlo*'s mighty bow to silence Hendrik Honthorst. He saw it spear into view and his jaw dropped. Suddenly masts were towering over them, the yard arms almost touching the *Draco*'s mizzen. He stood and stared at the warship: 'We're done for,' he murmured. 'We're all going to die.'

'Get that fool out of the line of fire!' Jacques Talon shouted.

Adam leapt over and pulled Honthorst down as shots began to pepper the deck. Together they scrambled back to join the men crouching by the cannon in the cover of the bulwark. Musket balls tore splinters from the ship's rail.

'Oh my goodness,' Honthorst groaned. 'They'll ruin the woodwork.'

Adam could see the glint of helmets in the *Gran Carlo*'s forecastle. Sharp shooters with long muskets called harquebuses were up in the galleon's rigging and on the fighting tops, laying down a withering fire across the deck.

Suddenly the air was filled with the skip and whine of lead. A man caught out in the open was cut down. Adam heard the strange hollow knock – like bones on wood – as the musket balls struck and plugged, sending splinters flying. Another man went staggering back and fell, blood oozing from his head. Another took a musket ball to the shoulder and cried out. Everywhere men were shouting, screaming. Only Jacques Talon seemed oblivious of the fire as he strode across the quarterdeck.

'Don Hernando de San Juan de Ulua!' he raised his voice to the *Gran Carlo*. There was a lull in the firing as he called to the men in the forecastle. 'Tell your master that Jacques Talon wishes to speak terms with him!'

This caused a stir among the group of men gathered at the warship's quarterdeck rail. They were dressed for the fight, wearing armour and leather tunics. Their burgonet helmets caught the sunlight, the panache plumes making a bright display. They parted ranks as Don Hernando himself stepped up to the ship's rail. He was a tall man dressed in richly embroidered clothes and a breastplate. A proud narrow face looked down at them from under a golden helmet. His beard was dark and pointed, his gaze sharp.

'Well, if it isn't Jacques Talon himself!' he called back in perfect French. 'Running away with the women on a Dutch ship like the cowardly rat you are?'

'Here are my terms, Don Hernando,' Jacques Talon called back.

'Terms? I hardly think you are in a position to bargain, Frenchman!'

'Turn about, Don Hernando! Take your slavers with you!' Jacques Talon went on regardless. 'Leave Fort Louis in peace and we'll spare your lives.'

There was a pause, a brief moment as this was translated into Spanish for the benefit of the men aboard the *Gran Carlo*. Then suddenly there was the sound of laughter. It started on the *Gran Carlo*'s quarterdeck among Don Hernando's lieutenants and rippled away through the men standing at the bulwarks until it seemed everyone aboard the galleon was laughing at them.

Jacques Talon remained unmoved. 'I must have your answer, Don Hernando!'

'I'll give it to you when you're jumping on the end of a rope, Frenchman!'

'I can see I need to teach you some manners, Don Hernando.'

More laughter.

'And just how are you going to do *that*?' Don Hernando asked.

'With them,' Jacques Talon said simply and gave the signal.

Along the length of the *Draco*'s bulwarks, Jacques Talon's men came to their feet on his command. Adam could only imagine what it must have looked like to Don Hernando and his men. One moment they were looking down at what seemed to be a defenceless merchant ship, the next fifty or more heavily armed men – some of the most feared marksmen in all the Americas – appeared as if out of nowhere. The volley of shots tore into the closely packed marines with deadly effect. Men died where they stood without even knowing what had hit them.

'Cut away the barrels!' Jacques Talon roared.

Adam heard axes fall. The ropes parted and, released from the drag of the barrels, the *Draco* leapt forward. With all sails up she raced ahead of the warship even as Don Hernando's men were still reducing sail in order to avoid running on past. The surprise was total.

The *Draco* cleared the *Gran Carlo*'s bow and Jacques Talon unleashed his own brand of hell.

'Hard to starboard!' he shouted. The helmsman pulled the whipstaff hard over and the *Draco* responded with a turn that took her directly across the *Gran Carlo*'s bows. 'Make ready!'

Hendrik Honthorst was dragged out of the way as the gun crew leapt up to man the cannons once more.

'Give fire!'

Adam remembered he had the slow-match in his hand and made a lunge at the cannon. A hand caught his and took the fire-stick. Jacques Talon himself put fire to the powder and the cannon roared, jumping on its trunnions and slamming back against its ropes. The gun crew melted away as the men raced to the guns on the port side. The *Draco* was already turning to catch the wind, bringing her loaded port-side guns to bear on the *Gran Carlo*.

The Spanish warship burst through the smoke, her forward momentum taking her past as the *Draco*'s sails began luffing in the wind. Having blasted her bow, now Jacques Talon's manoeuvre had brought them in behind. The gunners had a clear shot at the enemy's rudder and the vast windows in her stern. Don Hernando's men didn't even have the time to run out their massive array of guns on the starboard decks to face this new threat.

Another thunderous broadside belched from the *Draco*'s guns. Then another. It was Jacques Talon himself who put the match to the cannon that took the *Gran Carlo*'s rudder clear away and left her drifting helplessly. The *Draco* steered in for the kill, running in fast against the Spaniard's starboard quarter.

'Prepare to board!' The order was passed down the line.

Twenty iron hooks were hurled on to the *Gran Carlo*, then twenty more. The two ships closed until they were locked together. Jacques Talon's musketeers fired another deadly volley, then they drew their cutlasses and gave a cheer as they swarmed up on to the galleon and poured over the side. Suddenly everywhere men were fighting in a desperate hand-to-hand battle. Screaming. Falling. Dying. Adam caught a glimpse of Jacques Talon – he had lost his hat and blood was pouring from a wound on his face. He led the charge with his sword drawn, and right behind him – much to Adam's amazement – went Hendrik Honthorst. Wielding nothing more than a bucket, Honthorst had pushed the cowering Valoir aside and leapt after the French captain.

Instinctively, Adam started after them only to be met by a counter-charge from the Spanish galleon. Men came swinging across on ropes to drop on to the *Draco*'s deck. One came at him with a knife and it was only then that Adam realised he was completely unarmed. He dodged one way, then the other, reached the forward rail and vaulted over, dropping easily into the confusion of the waist below. Half a dozen of Don Hernando's most fearsome men had fought their way aboard the *Draco* led by a giant slaver. A furious hand-to-hand battle had broken out around the main mast. There was the clash of steel and the ringing sound of metal on metal. Adam looked up to see one of the men raise a musket and aim straight at him.

He had no time to move. It all happened so quickly and yet every detail of what happened next was instantly burned into his memory. Flame burst from the muzzle. He felt a searing pain as if a red-hot poker had stabbed into his head. The impact hurled him off his feet, slamming him into the steps leading back up to the quarterdeck. He slithered to the deck dazed, unaware that the helmet had saved his life.

The slaver came out of the smoke with a rush. He was wielding two cutlasses, slashing and chopping at anyone in his way. Adam just managed to roll aside in time as one of the blades cut down, slicing clean through the step where his head had just been. The blades flashed again and he scrambled under the companion way on his hands and knees. The slaver came in for the kill.

Adam flinched, unable to avoid the slash and stab. And there he would have died had it not been for Victor Valoir. He heard the shout and looked up just as the Frenchman hurled himself from the quarterdeck to land on the slaver. The two men went down, grappling until Valoir sent the giant staggering back with a thunderous blow. They clashed again, locked in a deadly fight, when suddenly something heavy fell between them fizzing at their feet. The slaver's eyes opened wide in surprise and he broke free, diving away to his left, leaving Valoir standing, staring at the round ball with the sparking fuse.

'As God loves me ...' Adam heard him say just before the grenade exploded.

The explosion hit the Frenchman hard. It lifted him high in the air and hurled him across the deck. He didn't utter a sound, he just flew backwards and landed with a dull thump.

'*No!*' Adam came out from under the steps. He ran

to Valoir and knelt at his side. He had never seen so much blood. He looked around, calling for help. No one came.

The Frenchman's eyes flickered and opened. He stared at Adam then his hand came up and caught him by the collar. 'Tell me, Adam Windjammer,' he gasped through gritted teeth. 'I have to know – it was gold that brought you here, wasn't it? *Gold*.'

Adam hesitated, staring into that man's desperate face. Finally he nodded. 'Gold – yes, Monsieur Valoir. Treasure like you've never seen. That's what we came for.'

The Frenchman's lips pulled back in a grin. 'I knew it,' he tried to laugh. 'I said you couldn't fool old Victor.'

'No – I couldn't fool you.'

'Then I'm a rich man,' the Frenchman said. He held on for a moment longer then relaxed back on to the deck with a long breath. 'Rich, at last,' he murmured and closed his eyes.

Adam heard a voice – a voice filled with a mixture of rage and despair – it sounded like an animal howling. He realised it was his own voice and he staggered back across the deck, turning just as the slaver rose out of the carnage in front of him.

Don Hernando's henchman came at him with a rush. The cutlasses cut arcs in the air and Adam only just managed to avoid them. Terror gripped him then as he was driven remorselessly back towards the steps where he had been hiding. He fled along the covered part of the main deck, past the whipstaff pole and the guns that now stood smoking and abandoned as Jacques Talon's men had gone to join the attack.

Adam ran for his life, just managing to dodge around the shaft of the mizzen mast as the slaver made a slashing cut. One blade sank deep into the mast, scaring the ship's cat from where it had been hiding behind the water barrel. The cutlass stuck fast and the giant abandoned it, hacking into the curtains on either side of the passage with the other blade in a wild flurry that shredded the brocade. Adam reached the door into the Long Cabin and hit it at a run. It wouldn't budge. He fumbled for the handle desperately, but couldn't open it in time. He spun around and pressed his back to the wood.

The slaver's lips pulled back into a leer. His eyes were gleaming with a mad, blood-lust glow. The cutlass traced deadly little circles in the air. Adam shrank back and was only saved when the man stood on Admiral Heyn's tail.

The cat snarled and reacted by digging its teeth and claws into the slaver's leg. The man uttered a curse and tried to kick it off. Luckily for Adam, Admiral Heyn was the sort of cat that held a grudge. It was enough to save Adam's life. At that moment the door behind him came open and he fell backwards into the Long Cabin.

The slaver shook off the cat with a snarl. Adam scrabbled back, crab-like on all fours until he thumped up against a bench.

'Stop or I fire!' Madam de Witte's voice cracked over his head.

The slaver hesitated as she calmly faced him across the table. An evil smile spread across his face when he realised she was alone. He breathed a stream of words and came on, blade glinting.

'It's all right, Madam de Witte,' Adam gasped, coming to his feet between them. 'I'll think of something.' He was still trying to do just that when she lifted the gun.

'Stand aside, Adam!' she said, her voice low, her intent deadly.

The widow raised the blunderbuss in one hand and took careful aim down the barrel. And if a thought passed through the giant's head in the moment that he charged in, it must have been that he had come face to face with the Black Reaper at last. For his life was lost in the spit and roar of that gun.

The slaver was thrown back, hurled out through the door and dead even before he hit the deck. Madam de Witte stood very still briefly before carefully placing the gun on the table.

Adam stared at her, fighting back the tears. His whole body was shaking.

'It's all right, Adam,' she said, folding him into her ample bosom.

In the passage outside, Admiral Heyn emerged from the shadows, glanced at the dead man and strutted away on silent paws.

The sounds of the battle above began to fade and the news of their victory reached them through the cheering of the Frenchmen. The widow stood back and looked at him.

'It's been interesting sailing with you, Master Windjammer,' she said, 'but I'm getting a little old for all this excitement. So perhaps we could go on our way before anything else happens ...'

The longboat ran up on to the sand and spilled men on all sides. Adam jumped down with the rest of them and splashed ashore through the shallows. On the beach, the crowd that was waiting for them surged forward. A triumphant cry rang out as they were mobbed like returning heroes.

Adam felt strangely unmoved by it all. He was relieved to be alive, but a small part of him – perhaps the last vestige of the boy he had been – had died that day, killed in the heat of the battle.

Faced by such a deadly attack, Don Hernando had struck his colours and surrendered. The *Gran Carlo* had been taken and towed to Fort Louis as a prize, and now the *Draco* lay safely at anchor in the harbour.

'Master Windjammer! Thank God!' Mr Glass greeted Adam as he strode across the sand.

'What did I tell you, brothers?' Allart spoke up. 'I said this Windjammer could do it.'

Mr Glass took Adam by the shoulders, looking him over for wounds. 'Like I said, Master Windjammer,' he grunted, 'you've the luck of a cat.'

'A cat? Yes, Mr Glass,' Adam nodded. 'A cat by the name of Admiral Heyn.'

The musket ball had left a dent the size of his fist in the helmet and a sizeable lump on his head. It had cut to the scalp in a streak that would grow back as a silver flash in his dark hair. It was almost as if he had been marked by the god of war himself.

'Valoir is dead,' he said quietly.

'Dead?' The first mate's face fell. 'Pity. That Frenchie and I was just beginning to understand each other.' He sighed and looked out to sea.

Hendrik Honthorst was coming ashore in the next boat. He stood in the bow with one foot up on the gunwale, posing like the conquering hero.

'We did it, Captain! We saved the *Draco*!' he called out as he jumped down and punched the air. 'Did I not always say we could?'

The change in him was startling. From the wheedling man of figures he had been transformed. There was a definite swagger in his step now, one hand gripping the hilt of a sword he had taken from one of Don Hernando's men. He swept off his helmet and tucked it under one arm before giving them all a flourishing bow. The men crowded around him, wanting to know what had happened.

'Has anyone got a bucket ...?' he started and wasted no time in telling them.

Jacques Talon stood on the jetty and watched the line of captured Spanish nobles being led from the boat. He stopped Don Hernando and the cheering around them died away.

'I am a practical man, Don Hernando,' Jacques Talon said. 'And enough of a businessman to know that Fort Louis will not prosper long if King Philip comes seeking revenge. So I have decided to spare your lives and ransom you and your men back to your king. We will take the *Gran Carlo* as payment for the loss of the *Requin* and change her name to the *Valiant*.'

Don Hernando's eyes flashed his fury, but he could only grit his teeth, saying nothing.

'And what of our friends the Dutch?' Jacques Talon raised his voice to the crowd. He pointed Adam out. 'I made a deal with that boy and we shook on it. He kept his side of the bargain and I'll keep mine. The *Draco* is free to go on her way with her cargo intact. What's more, I have promised Adam Windjammer letters to ensure that the name of Quadrant will be well received in all French ports ...'

'What's he saying, Mr Glass?' Govert asked.

'I don't know, lad,' the first mate answered him, 'but it sounds good – even in French.'

Adam was forced to wait until Jacques Talon had finished. His only thought was to find the mapmaker and to see Hobe. At last he broke free of the crowd and into a run that took him up to the makeshift tents under the trees. He was greeted by Merrik.

'His fever has abated a little, Adam,' the mapmaker said. 'I think he's going to make it.'

Adam fell to his knees at the boy's side. 'We're going home, Hobe,' he said. It was part-laugh, part-sob of relief. 'Just like I said we would. Home.'

16. The Will to Live

The doctor inhaled deeply, sucking the heat from the flaming taper into the chip of tobacco in the bowl of his pipe. He breathed out a stream of bluish smoke.

'And my daughter?' Hugo van Helsen leaned forward impatiently.

The doctor sucked on his pipe thoughtfully before giving his diagnosis without looking around. 'I am sorry to say, Mr van Helsen, your daughter is definitely not well.'

'I know that!' The banker's voice rose. He controlled his temper with some difficulty, 'What I want you to tell me is *what* ails her, man?'

Doctor Fabious Munck considered the question, blowing acrid-smelling smoke out of the corner of his mouth. He regarded Jade with a look of learned interest, tapped his lip with the long stem of the clay pipe, his expression brightening before his eyebrows finally dropped over the bridge of his long nose in a look of intense puzzlement.

'*That*, Mr van Helsen,' he concluded, 'is the million guilder question.'

Hugo van Helsen breathed through his frustration and returned to pacing the length of Jade's bedroom. He reached the window and looked down though the leaded panes into the Street of Knives. Below, the shops that gave the street its name were opening their shutters. He watched the butchers hanging up their knives, his attention caught briefly by their activities, before he returned to the problem of his daughter.

'I'm paying you a fortune, Doctor Munck,' he said. 'At the very least I expect your potions and inhalations to bring about some change. But it's been weeks – *weeks* – and still no improvement.'

Doctor Munck was not the sort of physician to be intimidated easily. 'That is just the problem, Mr van Helsen,' he answered. 'I administer to the *sick*.'

'Are you saying she isn't? Look at her, man! See how pale and thin she has become. Is that not sick enough for you?'

The doctor regarded Jade thoughtfully then nodded. 'You misunderstand me – Jade is indeed sick. But her sickness is not of the body.'

'Not of the ...?' Hugo van Helsen cast a look skywards. 'Is this some kind of doctor's double-tongued way of saying you have no more idea what ails her than I do?'

The doctor was unmoved. 'Hers is a sickness of the heart, Mr van Helsen. And hearts, as we all know, cannot easily be cured – no matter how much they bleed.'

Hugo van Helsen glared furiously at him.

The doctor tucked his thumbs into the lapels of his coat and gave his professional opinion. 'I suggest you look elsewhere if you wish to restore your daughter to health.'

Hugo van Helsen strode back across the room and pulled aside the damask curtain that looped around the four posts of Jade's bed. She was just as she always was when he came to visit her: lying pale on her pillows, her eyes fixed as if gazing into the distance.

'This has gone far enough, Jade,' he warned through gritted teeth. 'If you think you can defy me by ... by ...' He broke off in frustration and turned to the doctor. 'Well, don't just stand there, man! Do something! This girl will be sixteen in less than a month and her wedding dress is made.'

'Mr van Helsen, I don't think you quite understand,' Doctor Munck tried to reason. 'No matter what I do, I cannot cure someone who has lost the will to live.'

'Lost the will to *live*?'

Doctor Munck took him to one side and lowered his voice in the way of someone imparting a great professional secret. 'There are humours of the brain. Yes, it has been proven. Indeed, I have heard tell of the natives of some islands in the far Pacific that, for whatever reason, just lose the will to live and lie down and die.'

'Don't be a fool! My daughter cannot ...' he lowered his voice too, '... *die*?'

'We all die.'

'Some more quickly than others if they are in your charge, I shouldn't wonder, Doctor Munck!'

The doctor's expression took on a lofty look of disdain. 'If that's the way you feel, perhaps you had better instruct another physician.'

'No, wait. I'm sorry,' Hugo van Helsen apologised. 'I am a man of business, not a learned man of science like yourself. I am just disappointed there is no potion or elixir that we can give her.'

The doctor softened a little. 'I could suggest vervain and betony, spiced with a hint of nutmeg.'

'Herbs and spices? I pay you all this money and you can suggest nothing stronger than a tonic. Well, I'll pay you ten times more than what we agreed if you'll just stop my daughter wasting away!'

'Alas, Mr van Helsen,' Doctor Munck said with a sigh, 'there are some things in this world that money cannot buy.'

Hugo van Helsen's gaze slid from the doctor to his daughter then back again. His feelings of powerlessness were obvious. It wasn't something he was used to.

'There is, however, one course of action,' the doctor admitted after a pause for thought. 'I can't guarantee it will work, but I think it might help.'

'Yes, yes – anything. Tell me!'

The doctor came closer. 'May I suggest that you could show your daughter a little more ... how can I put it ... affection?'

'Affection! God damn it, man! Are you accusing me of not caring for my own daughter?' The banker cast around for proof and settled for the obvious. 'I'm paying you a fortune to heal her, aren't I? How much more proof of my affection do you need?'

'Forgive me for saying this, Mr van Helsen,' the doctor said quietly, 'but I do not believe that *I* am the one who needs convincing.'

Hugo van Helsen followed the doctor's eyes as they swivelled towards the bed. He stared furiously, turned away then turned back at once. He ran his hand over his mouth and glanced towards the bed again. 'Why?' the word burst out of him. 'I mean, what good would it do to be more ...'

The doctor shrugged his shoulder slightly. 'Who knows, perhaps if you let her into your life a little more?'

'Let her into my life? Don't be ridiculous! My life is *here* – in this house and she's already part of it.'

The doctor stepped back and began gathering up his instruments.

'Where are you going?' Hugo van Helsen said. 'I thought you came here to bleed her again?'

'It'll do no good …'

'Bleed her, damn you! Vent the bad blood in her veins and she will be well.' He turned to the maid who had been standing quietly in the corner throughout. 'What is your name, girl?'

'Gert, sir.' She bobbed into a slight curtsy.

'Well, Gert, I have employed you to keep watch on my daughter. I expect you to do so. You will sleep outside her door, do you understand? All night.'

The maid bobbed again.

Hugo van Helsen glanced at his daughter. 'I want to know what she does, what she eats, what she says – *everything*. And be especially vigilant, Gert! Keep this door locked at all times during the night.' He turned to the doctor. 'Carry on, Doctor!' he said and stormed out.

Doctor Munck reluctantly took up the small brass bleeding bowl. Jade didn't flinch as the knife sliced into her forearm, opening one of several cuts already there. Crimson drops welled on her skin and began to drip into the bowl.

When he had finished his work, Doctor Munck stemmed the flow by placing his thumb on the vein until the blood began to clot. He studied the contents of the bowl.

'There is bad blood here,' he spoke quietly to Jade, half under his breath, 'but I do not believe it is running from *your* veins, my dear.'

The bell on the church was striking midnight and Jade was at the window again. She was just standing there in her long nightdress, ghostly in the moonlight.

Every night it was the same. When the house finally slept, she rose from her bed and went to the window to look out. The street below was deserted now, filled with shadows that grew fat around the flat patches of light thrown down by a sickening moon.

Across the room a long mirror caught her in its reflection. Beyond the glass – in that mirrored world where all things had always seemed possible even for a girl of her age – her other-self gazed back at her intently: a fading spirit, a pale reflection against the stifling half-darkness of her room.

She moved silently on bare feet, crossing the room to the wall near the fireplace. Her weakness felt overwhelming. It seemed to have taken root deep inside her like a strangler weed that had sent invisible tendrils curling around her arms and legs. She ran the tips of her fingers over the smoothness of the oak panelling until she came upon the split in the dark wood that armoured the walls. She eased the broken piece out and looked into the hole behind. There, among the few precious things that had belonged to her mother, she found the knife.

'Pick it up!' her reflection urged. 'End it tonight.'

Jade's hand seemed to move of its own accord as she drew the blade out of its sheath. It was long and thin and deadly sharp. Across the room her mirrored spirit stared at the point of the blade as she turned it to her breast. The moonlight set it in blinding silver, it blurred before her eyes and she felt the bite of the point in her flesh. Then a cloud crossed the moon and plunged her briefly into darkness. By the time the moon returned and her reflected self reappeared the moment had passed.

A single tear broke from one eye, tracing a line down into the hollow of her cheek. She forced her fingers to release the knife, laying it carefully back in the hole in the wall and slid the panel closed. Then she returned to the window, to watch once more.

'So you see, Mr van Helsen, my client, the States General, is offering a return of seven and a half per cent on your initial investment. What do you say to that?'

No answer.

The notary tried again. 'Seven and a half per cent ...'

Still no answer.

The smile faded from the notary's lips. He glanced at his assistant, then at Goltz, who was standing behind his master's chair.

'Mr van Helsen?' The notary's voice took on an I've-other-banks-I-can-offer-this-to sort of tone. He repeated the offer, louder this time and finished with, 'It's a good return on your money. I'm sure you'll agree ...'

Hugo van Helsen didn't – he didn't do or say anything. He just sat twisted away in his chair, his chin resting on the heel of one hand as he chewed at a fingernail without appearing to notice anything that was going on around him.

Goltz cleared his throat in an effort to gain his attention. The banker stirred, his pale eyes flickered and his gaze settled on the notary sitting across the table. The notary's assistant produced a parchment.

'It has been approved by the State Assemblies and ratified by the House of Orange itself,' the notary said proudly. 'Unlike tulips, this investment will provide blooming returns!' He tittered a laugh at his own joke.

Hugo van Helsen took the parchment, glanced briefly at the eminent signatories, then casually tossed it aside. He settled back into his chair and his eyes took on that distant look again.

'Am I to take it that the Banking House of van Helsen is not interested?' The notary's astonishment was obvious.

Another lengthy pause. Goltz broke the uncomfortable silence by stepping forward and picking up the parchment.

'Thank you, gentlemen,' he said. 'Mr van Helsen is clearly *very* interested but would like to give your proposals some more thought. We will let you know our decision just as soon as we can.'

'Clearly very interested ...' the notary spluttered. 'I'm not sure Mr van Helsen understands the honour involved in doing business with the House of Orange.'

They looked at the banker, who was muttering to himself now.

'Mr van Helsen is not himself today,' Goltz apologised, gathering up the papers. 'He has had much on his mind of late. His daughter has not been well, you see –'

Hugo van Helsen's mutterings grew louder then stopped suddenly. He banged his hand down on the desk so the quills jumped and the inkwells spilt. He glared across the table at the notary. 'This has gone on long enough!' he said.

The notary looked positively alarmed. 'I beg your pardon, sir?'

The banker rose from his chair. 'Where's that girl?'

'Girl, what girl?' the notary stammered. 'Mr van Helsen – have you lost all reason?' He came to his feet too and cowered behind his assistant.

'Gert! Geeeeeeeeeeeeeeeeeeeert!' Hugo van Helsen roared. He nodded to the notary as if he had just remembered him. 'Good day to you, sir.' And without a word of explanation he stormed out.

Jade didn't know why she had been summoned from her room. She resigned herself to it like everything else, allowing her maid to dress her and comb her long dark hair.

'We have to have you looking presentable for your father,' Gert said, fussing nervously about with the hairbrush.

Jade sat in front of the mirror. She had the strangest feeling her reflection was fading in front of her.

'It's probably nothing to worry about.' Gert was trying to sound cheerful. 'Most likely your father just wants to know how you are, that's all. So please, mistress, try not to anger him. He does get so ...'

Jade stood up. She kept her back straight and her hands clasped in front of her, walking like a girl condemned as they made their way along the passage and through the door to a gallery. The wooden walkway ran along all four sides of the room to the sweep of the stairs at the far end. Jade felt a wave of dizziness as she looked down into the well of the room. She steadied herself, leaning slightly on the rail of the banister. The room was laid out below, her father's high-backed chair facing the fireplace. To one side, stood her portrait, painted by Rembrandt van Rijn: the portrait her father had commissioned for their trip to England and which had first caught the rich English goldsmith's eye. It was to be a wedding present and she hated it – loathing what it represented – even now covered by a velvet cloth.

She could hear voices as Gert led her along the gallery and down the stairs. The door that connected the back of her father's accounting chamber to the grand room below was open. She caught a glimpse of him sitting at his desk with his back to her. He didn't look up from his papers as she was ushered in.

'That will be all, Gert!' Her father dismissed the maid without looking up. 'I will send for you when I am ready.'

Gert bobbed and retreated with obvious relief. Jade stood very still. She didn't look at her father. He was signing some papers and Goltz was sanding the ink dry. For a while, the only sound was the scratch of his quill and the rattle of the sand on parchment. When all the papers were done and, with nothing more to occupy his immediate attention, her father was forced to look up.

'I have decided,' he started awkwardly then stopped to begin again. 'Yes, perhaps, Doctor Munck ...' He folded his fingers together then unfolded them. 'A chair, Goltz – find her a chair!'

Goltz produced a chair.

'Not there!' her father snapped. 'Put it further away – back against the wall! There, yes *there*.'

Goltz moved the chair back under the great map of

the world that was nailed to the wall. He returned and led Jade by the hand, dusting the seat of the chair before bowing slightly in a sign for her to sit down. This done, Goltz returned to his position at his master's side and for a while another awkward silence engulfed them.

Jade didn't look at her father. He sat drumming his fingers. He stood up, knocking several scrolls on to the floor. They rolled about and Goltz went to pick them up, only to be waved aside impatiently.

'Isn't there something you should be getting on with?' her father asked, his irritation growing.

Goltz nodded and mumbled something about the ledgers.

'Well, go on, then!'

Goltz retreated through the door leading into the panelled waiting room and the relative safety of his desk facing the door to the Street of Knives.

'I thought you might like ...' her father started. 'Damn it, girl! Why are you looking at me like that?'

Jade lowered her gaze to her hands in her lap.

Her father's knuckles whitened, his fist punched into the top of his thigh as if he hadn't meant to speak so sharply to her. 'You're no fool, Jade, so I won't insult you by pretending this is my idea. It's just that the doctor, well, I mean – it's not good for you to stay up in that room all day and all night. So I thought you might ... Well, I'm not sure what I thought ...'

His explanation trailed away. Jade stared at her hands.

He looked at her critically. 'You look awful, girl. So thin and so very pale. Are you taking the tonic the doctor has prescribed? He is costing me a fortune, you know – a gold piece a day for his potions alone.'

'I'm sorry.' She spoke for the first time since she had entered the room.

'You're *sorry*?' He let his exasperation show. 'I'd pay double if it would make you well.' He cast around for someone to blame. 'It's that maid's fault.' He stood and went to the door. 'Gert!' he roared. 'Gert! Why is the girl never around when I want her?'

Gert came running with her skirts and apron hitched up. She arrived, breathless and flustered at the door, only to be accused of not doing her job properly.

'Bring my daughter her tonic!' Hugo van Helsen said. 'And be quick about it!'

The girl bobbed and hurried off. This done he had nothing else to do but return to his desk. He sat down and the gulf between them was filled by a silence that seemed to scream. He tried to ignore it by busying himself with some small matters among the papers in front of him, but found he couldn't concentrate. Gert wasn't the only one who was flustered and it made him more irritable than ever.

'Where is it? Where is that list? It was here – just *here*,' he muttered searching furiously among the papers on his desk. 'Goltz! *Goltz!*'

Jade stood up and went to pick up a scroll of parchment that had rolled further than the others and had been left lying forgotten on the floor. She held it out to him without a word. He glanced at it briefly then snatched it away with a curt nod. Goltz hurried in.

'Damn it, Goltz!' her father took it out on his servant. 'Why can I never find anything around here?'

'But you sent me to do the ledgers, sir.'

'I don't care about the ledgers! How can I do

anything without a proper system for filing these papers?'

'I have been saying for some time that I need an assistant to help with such matters –'

'An *assistant*?' Her father hammered on the table. 'You mean more expense for me and less work for you!'

They were interrupted by a knock at the door. Gert appeared with a small earthenware bowl on a tray. The banker rounded on her furiously and demanded to know why they had been interrupted.

'You sent me to fetch the mistress's tonic, sir!' Gert explained in a trembling voice.

He remembered. 'Oh, very well. Hurry up, girl!'

Gert delivered the tonic into Jade's hand and stood back with the tray, waiting for her to finish. Jade sipped at the heavily spiced liquid. It tasted of nutmeg. Her father watched her, grunted and returned to his papers, only to sigh and look up again.

'This isn't working, Goltz,' he said, lowering his voice but not enough. 'I can't concentrate with Jade in the room.'

Goltz leaned forward and spoke quietly in his ear. 'Then may I suggest you find her something to do?'

Her father seemed surprised. 'This is a place of business. She is a girl – what could she do?'

Goltz considered it briefly before coming up with an answer. 'We do need a clerk, sir –'

'A clerk? My *daughter*? Don't be ridiculous.'

Goltz bowed and said it had only been a suggestion. 'Now if you'll excuse me – I have the ledgers to attend to.'

Hugo van Helsen glanced uncomfortably at his daughter and stopped him. 'On second thoughts, the doctor did suggest ...' Another pause brought him to a decision. He cleared his throat and addressed Jade soberly. 'I have decided that you should begin to earn your keep around here. If nothing else it will keep your mind occupied. So I require you to help Goltz in certain matters of my business ...'

Jade glanced up in surprise.

'What is it, girl? Is there something wrong?' he asked. 'Suddenly there is a slight colour in your cheeks.' He looked to the maid for an explanation. 'What was in that tonic you gave her?'

'Vervain and betony, spiced with nutmeg – just like the doctor said,' Gert assured him.

Hugo van Helsen sat back in his chair. 'I'd never have believed it, Goltz – but I think the good doctor's tonic actually *works*.'

17. Van Helsen's Land

Jade awoke with a shiver. The heat had gone out of the fire and the night's chill had crept into her bedroom. She lay in the darkness and was overwhelmed by a sense of the inevitability of her destiny.

A week had passed since she had been called to her father's accounting chamber. Was it only seven days since her life had changed? she wondered. Gert no longer needed to force her to eat and, even though she was still thin, her strength was returning little by little. Each day was better than the one before.

The work wasn't difficult – if anything, creating a system for filing her father's papers was routine and repetitive – but for the first time in her life she felt as if she had been allowed into a place she had only ever seen in glimpses before. This was her father's secret domain, a place into which he retreated on a daily basis, and at last she had found a way in.

At first, he had been afflicted by the same tongue-tied awkwardness he had shown before in her presence. As the days went by, however, and her work on the files progressed, he had begun to appreciate the

238

methodical way in which she went about storing the scrolls, wax seals and ribbons facing out so they were easy to match and find. Her attention to detail was equal to his own. Soon, without realising it, he began calling on her rather than Goltz to fetch the papers he required. And her confidence grew with even the smallest indication of his appreciation.

The daily work of a banking house continued around her. She would listen as the deals were struck. The thrill of it surprised her and she found herself calculating the profit her father made, listening for as long as she was allowed. Every so often she would look up from her work and see him watching her. He would see she had noticed and look away immediately, without giving any indication of what he was thinking. But once, caught off guard by an idle thought perhaps, he had spoken:

'You learn about business quickly for a ...' He stopped. There had been real regret in his eyes then – as if somehow no matter what she did, no matter how hard she tried, she would always be a disappointment to him.

But Jade was not the sort to give up easily. She persevered, making herself as useful to him as possible until the evening she came across the map.

It was getting late. The September nights were drawing in and the shadows were returning earlier and earlier to haunt the house on the Street of Knives.

'The lists, Goltz!' Her father snapped his fingers impatiently. 'Where are the lists of Atlas van der Stolk's business interests?'

'I'll just go and look, sir,' Goltz said.

'No! You'll take too long. My dinner is on the table – ask Jade!'

239

Jade didn't wait to be asked. She took up the candle and shielded the flame with her hand as she moved along the shelves, searching among the boxes and papers that were now all placed in alphabetical order. She found the relevant box and put down the candle so she could lift the casket. A square of parchment slipped off the top and fell to the floor.

Jade thought little of it – other than it was an oversight of filing that jarred at her new sense of order – and picked it up. She unfolded the parchment. It was bigger than it looked folded and she spread it wide, moving closer to the candle to see where it belonged. The candlelight washed over an expanse of ocean where strange sea creatures crowded around the ragged outline of an island. In the feeble yellow light she picked out a compass star and the faces of the four winds with bulging cheeks as they blew curls of breath across the page. The title and all the details were written in old-style Spanish script and, not for the first time in her life, Jade wished she'd been born a boy so she might have been better educated and understood what it said.

'Where's that list?' her father called.

She was about to fold the map away when her eye was caught by a name. It jumped out at her from among the other words because the ink was darker and she realised it had been added to the map recently. She recognised her father's hand in the spidery scrawl, but she had to read it twice to be sure she had not made a mistake. For there, marked clearly on the map, was the name 'Van Helsen's Land'.

'What's keeping you, girl?' Her father's voice was suddenly closer.

She glanced up to see him coming and hurriedly tried to fold the map.

'What have you got there?' he asked, making her show him. With that everything changed. His expression fell to a scowl and he snatched the map away, clutching it to him protectively. 'You've no right to look at this – no right, do you hear? This is my business – *mine*.'

'It was on top of the box ... It fell –' Jade wasn't given a chance to explain.

'I'll have no more of your spying! Get out of my chamber.' He turned on his heel and stormed to the door. 'Gert! Geeeeeeeert!' The maid came running. Jade was ordered to her room. 'And see she doesn't come out until I say!' Her father's shouts had set echoes warring in the hollow heart of the house.

That night it was as if the darkness had returned to Jade's soul.

Doctor Munck looked up. 'Hmm,' he said, reaching for his pipe. 'Something has changed,' he said. 'Changed for the worse too.' He glanced at Gert. 'Have you been administering the tonic as I asked?'

Gert nodded and bobbed into a curtsy. Hugo van Helsen stood sullenly looking down into the Street of Knives. He had his back to the scene behind him. Jade was lying in bed, propped up on pillows. The doctor stood over her, with Gert in attendance near the door.

'I could try bleeding her again, sir,' the doctor said, sounding dubious about the difference it would make. 'I don't understand it. The patient was making such good progress ...'

Doctor Munck reached for the knife and the bowl.

'Wait!' Hugo van Helsen turned to face the room. 'How much do I owe you, doctor?'

The doctor responded in the way of someone who didn't want to lose a wealthy client too quickly. 'The treatment is only half completed, sir. There are other medicines to try. Secret potions only I know –'

'No more potions. You may as well drink them yourself for all the good they'll do my daughter.'

The doctor was shocked. 'But you said yourself they were working so well.'

'Here is a purse of monies,' the banker cut him short, pulling a leather pouch from his belt. He held it out. 'More than enough to pay your extortionate bill. Take it and your vervain and betony, your nutmeg and your bleeding bowl and leave at once! I think I now know best what ails my own daughter.'

'But you could jeopardise her treatment.'

'Leave us!'

The doctor reluctantly moved away from the bed. He had to take several steps to reach the money, plucking it away with practised fingers. 'I cannot be responsible for any relapse.'

'Would you bleed me dry too, doctor?' Hugo van Helsen said. 'No, I see now that your expensive potions and tonics will make no difference. In this way, at least, you have helped me. So I am paying you off in full.' That said the banker headed for the door. He paused briefly to look at Jade before moving on to speak to Gert.

'See that your mistress is given something to eat and drink. I will expect her back in my accounting chamber first thing in the morning. First thing, mind.

242

She must not be late.'

Gert bobbed and he was gone.

So it was that Jade was allowed to return to her work. But it wasn't the same as before. That soon became clear in the crystal silences that once again began to separate them. Her father tried surprisingly hard to make her feel welcome, but Jade no longer felt any of it had the same meaning. If nothing else the incident over the map had proved it. She had been deluding herself. She hadn't really broken through to her father. He had let her into his life only as far as was necessary to make her well again. No matter how he tried to hide it, she knew his intolerance of her remained.

To make matters worse, her work on the files was soon completed and where before she might have undertaken other tasks willingly, now she took to sitting for long periods on the chair by the wall until some small job was found to occupy her time. All the while she was filled with a growing sense of her own powerlessness. One thought became her obsession. It gnawed constantly at her like a voracious worm: the thought that no matter what she did, no matter how hard she tried, she would never be good enough for her father.

So this strange half-life went on. Days became a week and nothing changed, until one cold mid-morning an unexpected knock came at the door of the Street of Knives.

'All right, all right, I'm coming,' Goltz said as the knocking became persistent.

Jade was sitting alone in the accounting chamber. Her father had woken with a head cold and, some time before, had taken himself off in a clouded mood to warm himself by the fire in the galleried room next door.

Jade heard Goltz muttering under his breath as he opened the small trap in the door and looked through the grill to see who was outside. His reaction surprised her.

'It's you, sir!' Goltz's voice rose to a higher pitch. He snapped the small trap closed and there was genuine urgency about the way he drew back the bolt, fumbled with the key and finally opened the door. 'Come in, sir! Come in out of the cold! We were not expecting you back so soon. You must have had fair winds indeed to make such good time.'

No answer. By the crunch and scuff of the footsteps, Jade judged more than one person had entered. This was followed by a general rustling as Goltz fussed around with gloves, hats and cloaks, before ushering them to the door.

'This way, gentlemen.' He almost fell over himself such was his hurry. 'Of course, my master will want to hear the news of your discoveries at once.'

A tall square-shouldered man wearing a dark coat and breeches entered first. He had a pointed beard, a long straight nose and his eyes were the colour of hazelnuts. He made a striking figure with his mane of brown hair swept back from a high square forehead.

Behind him came a shorter, younger, olive-skinned man. He was of a wiry build and dressed in a buff-coloured coat over a waistcoat, white shirt with baggy cuffs that protruded from his coat sleeves and he wore maroon pantaloons. His eyes were quick and very dark; his face was round and clean-shaven, surrounded by a mop of jet curls.

Neither of them noticed Jade sitting quietly to one side, her chair pushed back against the wall. Goltz was so perplexed to find her father wasn't at his desk that he forgot all about her. He spluttered through an apology, assuring them that his master wouldn't be far away as he pulled up two chairs. The taller of the two sat down and leaned back. The other remained standing by the door.

'Yes, well, if you are more comfortable there, Mr …?' It was clear Goltz hadn't met this man before.

'This is Captain Valerius,' the taller of the two said, introducing him as a business associate.

'Valerius,' Goltz repeated. 'I think I've heard the name before –'

'Impossible,' the one called Valerius dismissed the idea. He spoke Dutch with a slight lisp and a guttural accent that might have been southern Mediterranean. 'I've never been to Amsterdam before.'

'But I'm sure –'

'Are you going to stand there and keep us waiting all day?' the other interrupted.

'No, of course! I'm sorry. I shall fetch my master at once.' Goltz ducked into a bow, assured them he would be back shortly and slipped out of the accounting chamber into the galleried room behind.

'I don't trust anyone with a head for names,' Valerius said into the pause that followed. 'Questions now would mean trouble.' Only then did he notice Jade sitting to one side. 'You there! What are you doing hiding in the shadows? Speak up! Are you simple in the head, girl, or did they cut out your tongue?'

'One moment, Valerius,' the other said, raising a

hand of caution. 'The moneylender has a daughter.'

Something in the way he said it made it sound more like a warning than a statement of fact.

'A daughter?' Valerius backed off a little. He looked her up and down and licked his full red lips. 'What's your name, green eyes?'

Jade returned his gaze steadily.

'You will have to forgive my associate,' the other spoke from his chair. 'We have been at sea for many months on a voyage of exploration. And you, well, you are a little thin and pale, but you are still charming enough to the sailor's eye –'

'Atlas!' her father interrupted. He burst into the room and spread his hands wide, half-turning to chide Goltz over his shoulder. 'Why didn't you tell me sooner that Mr van der Stolk was here!'

Goltz's attempts to assure his master that he had wasted no time went ignored.

'I see you've met my daughter, Jade,' he said, shaking the taller man warmly by the hand. 'I hope she has been entertaining you in my absence.'

'Jade,' Valerius repeated her name without taking his eyes off her face. 'A strong name.'

Jade's chin came up. He recognised her defiance and smiled.

'You must be the brave Captain Valerius,' Hugo van Helsen said. 'Atlas has told me much about your voyages of exploration.' The banker sneezed loudly into his handkerchief and blew his nose. 'This weather will be the death of me.'

'Oh no, Hugo,' Atlas van der Stolk laughed, settling back into his chair. 'It won't be the ague that carries *you* off to a better world.'

Jade sensed more truth than humour in what he said, but her father seemed oblivious of the rising tension in the room. Far more surprising to Jade, however, was the way they acted like old friends. Atlas van der Stolk constantly called her father by his first name. She had only ever heard others call him Mr van Helsen or van Helsen or sir before. This show of friendship was new and she felt there was something forced about it, even if her father didn't appear to notice.

'What am I thinking? Where are my manners?' Her father made a show of it. 'You must be in need of some refreshment. Goltz! Quickly some wine!'

'Brandy,' Valerius stopped him.

Her father hesitated, forced to change his mind. 'Yes, bring the best Cognac!'

Goltz soon returned with a bottle. He poured the amber spirit and the men took up their glasses.

'We've had our differences in the past, Atlas,' Jade's father said by way of a toast, 'but our disagreements are behind us now.'

'To the future, Hugo,' van der Stolk nodded, raising his glass. 'I have a feeling I am going to enjoy doing business with you again.'

'To cold hard beauty,' Valerius said, raising his glass to Jade.

If her father heard, he pretended not to. He blew his nose loudly. The glasses were drained and put down on the table.

'Enough of this,' her father said. 'We have much to discuss. I cannot tell you how I have dreamed of your return.' He spoke breathlessly, like a child expecting some longed-for toy. He flapped his handkerchief at the large map on the wall. 'The American Islands –

drawn up by a mapmaker who owed me some money. As you see, Atlas, it is not yet complete.' He picked up a quill and dipped it in ink before holding it out to the man sitting opposite him. 'You are the kingmaker, Atlas. You do the honours – and mark the place.'

Atlas van der Stolk leaned forward and took the quill. 'It's true, Hugo, we have a good tale to tell you, but perhaps a little more privately?' He indicated towards Jade with a slight inclination of his head.

Her father followed the direction of his nod. 'Leave us!'

The men watched Jade as she moved across the room, her skirts whispering softly. She was aware of Valerius smiling, one side of his upper lip curled. She didn't look directly at any of them as she made a half-hearted curtsy. But her father was already calling van der Stolk to the map on the wall. Goltz opened the door into the galleried room and she passed through to be greeted by her maid. The door closed. Before it shut, Jade heard her father laugh.

'I was not blessed with a son, gentlemen,' he said. 'That's why I have to live my adventures through brave men like *you*.'

'I'm sorry, mistress,' Gert said, 'but your father says he will be busy all day. He says he does not require your presence in his accounting chamber today.'

The news came as no surprise to Jade. Three days had passed since Atlas van der Stolk and Captain Valerius had arrived at the house on the Street of Knives. Three days she had been told to stay in her room.

Jade crossed to the window and looked down into the Street of Knives. It wasn't long before she saw the carriage pull up outside. Two grey horses stood quietly in the traces, their breath misting on the cool air. The coachman jumped down from his place at the back and put a small wooden stool on the ground. The curtain door was pulled aside and Atlas van der Stolk appeared. Jade eased back out of sight when Valerius followed him out of the carriage and, as if some animal cunning enabled him to sense her watching, glanced up at her window. By the time she looked down again, the two men had been ushered inside.

The strength of her feelings surprised Jade. The mix of emotions was enough to set her blood racing, hot in her veins. What had started as resentment, had soon become jealousy and finally, in the sleepless hours of night, pure hatred.

What, she wondered bitterly, was the secret discovery these men had made that had so transformed her father from cold-hearted banker into a dreamer? *Why* was it that when Atlas van der Stolk spoke he commanded her father's complete attention in a way Jade had only ever dreamed was possible?

During the longest stretches of the smallest hours, Jade had stared into the darkness, creating scenes in her head that would tear this new friendship apart. Briefly she revelled in its destruction, only for her false sense of achievement to turn sour once more. It was all the more bitter because she became convinced they could not be trusted. But the hardest part of all was the feeling that since Atlas van der Stolk had arrived she had finally been completely rejected.

In the end, it wasn't her anger and resentment that drove Jade to take matters into her own hands and act. It was something far more surprising to her – it was the desire to *protect* her father.

'Mistress? Mistress – wait! Where are you going?' Gert was caught completely off guard.

Before she could be stopped, Jade had crossed the room and was out through the door. She banged it shut and twisted the key that Gert had carelessly left in the lock on the outside. The maid's muffled shouts followed her down the passage, but Jade's determination drove her on. She turned right through the door leading to the gallery, made her way swiftly along two sides of the wooden walkway and almost flew down the sweep of the stairs into the room below. The door to the back of her father's accounting chamber was closed, but she could hear a hubbub of voices coming from the other side. She didn't hesitate, she didn't even knock, she just burst in, much to the surprise of all present. She found the men gathered in front of the map.

'What is the meaning of this?' Her father was the first to react. 'I thought I told Gert –'

'You have to listen to me, Father,' Jade said. She felt breathless and light-headed and, now she was facing them, uncertain where to begin.

'What are you talking about?' He looked around. 'Is the house burning down?'

'No – at least not yet.' She looked at the two men and her chin came up. 'I don't know what business you have with them, but I don't trust them – and neither should you.'

'You don't … *what*?' He was incredulous.

Jade stood her ground. 'There's something going on – I just know there is.'

Valerius's reaction seemed to confirm it. He moved

one hand to the hilt of a knife hidden under his coat. Van der Stolk moved too, but only to arrest the younger man's hand.

'Why can't you see it?' Jade went on. 'What have they told you to make you so blind?'

'How dare you!' her father said, recovering now from his initial surprise.

'I'm your *daughter* – why won't you listen to me?'

'And because you're my daughter you think that gives you the right to barge right in here, throwing accusations about?'

'I know I'm right about them, Father. I can feel it – right *here*.' She jabbed a thumb at her heart.

Her father turned to the men and apologised. 'Do not pay the slightest attention to her. She is just a silly girl with an overactive imagination.'

'Don't worry, Hugo,' van der Stolk was irritatingly reassuring, 'I have a daughter of my own and I know them to be emotional creatures – especially at this age.'

Valerius grinned.

Jade hated them then. She threw in everything. 'They say they've been on a long voyage, but I don't believe it. I've been to the waterfront. I've seen ships returning with their crews half dead from scurvy. Not so long ago a captain told me what a voyage was like. But look at them, Father! They're healthy and well fed.'

'Are you calling these gentlemen liars?' her father stormed, striding across the room to take her firmly by the arm. 'How dare you insult my guests in this way? What could you possibly know of business? What could you know of the character of these men?'

'That's just it, Father – I don't know. But there's something wrong, I can feel it in my bones.'

'I've heard enough. Leave us at once!' Her father pulled her towards the door. 'You're just a stupid little girl who thinks of no one but herself. God help the poor goldsmith who has to tame you! Well, you've caused me enough trouble and I'll be glad to be rid of you.' He pushed her away. 'All I ever wanted was a son to follow me into the business. Was that so much to ask? And what do I get – a daughter like *you*.'

And there it was, said. At last, it was out. Her father had finally opened up to her and all she had found was festering resentment at the accident of birth that had blighted her entire life. He knew he had said too much. It was clear by the expression on his face. And yet even as he tried to make amends he was still blaming her.

'Why do you do it?' he breathed his fury. 'Why do you make me say these things?'

Jade backed away from him to the door. She felt as if she had been stabbed through the heart. The invisible knife had gone in and the pain was like nothing she had ever felt before. It brought tears welling up to scald her eyes, but she would not let them see her cry. Her head was spinning as she staggered back into the galleried room and fled up the stairs.

18. The Gauntlet

'He's never wanted me,' Jade murmured. The truth left her numb.

Across the room, her mirrored-self turned as she looked up. Darkness surrounded the candle, its flame guttering slightly in the draughts. Behind her the door was closed and locked, with Gert sleeping in the passage outside.

'He wants a son, not a daughter like you,' her reflection sneered.

The blade drew her gaze back. Jade stared at it in her hand. The yellow light caught on metal and ran smoothly along the razor edge, flicking off the point in deadly glints. And suddenly all the years of pain and hurt she felt seemed to burst within her.

'So he wants a boy, does he?' she hissed. She took a handful of her hair and attacked it with the knife, hacking it away to let it fall. There was a pause. She sat staring at the locks lying on the table in front of her. Then her fury came upon her again. A raging, boiling, desperate fury that set her slashing and cutting, pulling great handfuls of her hair away. She hurled the locks aside and grabbed more. Again and again the knife flashed, until her long dark tresses lay about her. When it was done, she dropped the knife and hugged her stomach where the hurt was deepest, slipping off her chair on to the floor, curling into herself as she gulped at the air in great jarring sobs.

When Jade opened her eyes again, the candle had burned out and her room was filled with moonlight. The heat had gone out of her fury, leaving her feeling cold. She lay there, with her cheek pressed to the floor-boards, staring at the locks of her hair. It took all her strength just to lift one hand to feel her head. Her fingers probed and found her hair was slashed back to the scalp in places. She forced herself to sit up then came wearily to her feet to face herself in the mirror.

She hardly recognised the person staring back at her now. As she looked at herself, something Bartholomew de Leiden had said came back to her. The memory of his words forced her lips into a twisted grimace.

'Maybe my father'll *respect* me now,' she spoke bitterly.

And in that darkest of moments, Jade found herself wishing she had never been born. She was certain it would have been better than knowing the sorrows of her father's house. She felt the weight of the darkness press down on her; it was as if she were sinking into the shadows, and like a drowning sailor, the images of her life raced through her head until her thoughts blunted against the image of Adam Windjammer.

She found herself wondering if he would ever come back, then her thoughts fled from him to the Bourse and Quadrant and the troubles that awaited him there.

She decided then that none of it mattered any more. It was over.

'You're just the moneylender's daughter,' she spoke to her mirrored-self. 'And that's all you'll ever be – until you become the goldsmith's wife.'

Jade's image faded as she turned away from the world beyond the glass. Tiredness came upon her then. It drove her to her bed and she buried her face in the bolster, resigning herself to the trouble the morning would bring. But her mind was drawn back to the Bourse again. She tried to force the confusing strands of her thoughts away into nothingness, but they dragged her back until finally she gave in to them. She rolled over on to her back and lay staring into the darkness, wearily running through the events once more. She found nothing new in Cornelius Yort, Ahmed the Turk and the rest. Nothing, that is, until she remembered Valentino and the others.

What was it he had boasted? Jade struggled to remember Valentino's exact words. In the end she had to settle for the gist of it:

'*If there's something to know,*' her lips moved through the words, '*ask us ... We know more about what's going on around here than most of these fine merchants ...*'

Jade sat up. A wild thought had set her heart racing. She swung her legs off the bed and sat very still. Surely, she reasoned with herself, her father would have to believe her about Atlas van der Stolk if there was proof. No, she decided. What was the point? She eased back then sat up again as the full realisation of what it might mean struck her. For in that moment, Jade realised this was her chance – her chance to prove herself. In this at least, she could prove a daughter could be just as worthwhile as a son.

She made up her mind as she usually did, quickly, giving herself no chance to change it. Dressing in a black woollen dress and boots, she chose a simple cloak from the wardrobe and went to the mirror. Her image seemed to pulse in the moonlight. She slipped the cloak around her shoulders and tied it at the neck, pulling up the hood to cover her hair and looked at herself critically. It would have to do.

She spent some time gathering up her severed locks and then hid them behind the panel in the wall. The blood was pumping hot in her veins again as she slipped quietly to the door and pressed her ear to the wood. She could just make out the sound of Gert's breathing. The maid was asleep in the chair in the passage outside.

Jade knelt to look through the keyhole and was relieved to see her maid had been careless again. She returned to the desk, picked up the knife and spent some time hunting for a suitable square of parchment among the writing materials on her table. She returned to the door and spread the parchment out flat on the floorboards, sliding it smoothly under the door. She positioned it below the keyhole as best she could then probed the lock with the blade of the knife. The key on the other side resisted. She pushed harder and it gave way suddenly, dropping on to the parchment below with a sharp knocking sound that was picked up by the hollows, echoing alarmingly. Jade froze, listening. In the passage outside, Gert stirred and settled again.

Jade breathed her relief and pressed her cheek to the floor, squinting through the gap under the door. She could just make out the shape of the key lying on the corner of the parchment. Carefully – very carefully – she drew the parchment back under the door, bringing the key with it. It came smoothly until the key snagged on the bottom of the door and dropped off.

The parchment rasped as she withdrew it. She took up the knife and hooked at the key with the blade. It took several attempts, but finally she managed to flick it under the door. A moment later it was in the lock and the door came open with the faintest of clicks.

Jade was careful to hide the knife and the parchment before she slipped out into the passage and closed the door behind her. She locked it and was about to leave the key in the lock when she changed her mind and took it with her.

She paused, looking down at Gert. 'I'm sorry,' she mouthed the words, knowing that everything depended on her maid not finding out she'd gone too soon.

The maid slept on peacefully enough in her chair, unaware of the trouble to come as Jade stole away into the night.

Dawn broke in an array of pinkish light. Jade watched the sunrise as she sat huddled by a tree close to the Rokin, the water of the canal reflecting the new day. The city began to stir around her and there was the smell of peat smoke. She was cold and hungry, but still just as determined. She stood up and eased at the stiffness in her back and legs. She knew it wouldn't be long now before she was missed at the house on the Street of Knives and she had already planned her move to a safer place. A few early risers were about as she made her way to an alleyway with a good view of the arch of the bridge and the gates of the Bourse beyond.

The next few hours were the longest. The morning wore away on itself and her nerves. She sat in the doorway and kept watch on the Bourse across the canal. She was frightened to take her eyes off the cobbled square in front of the great wooden gates even for a moment in case she missed them. In the streets around, the shops and stalls opened for business and soon people were coming and going and, only very occasionally, turning to hurry down the alleyway where she was sitting. When this happened, she drew back into the corners of the doorway and kept her hood up and went unnoticed. When it was safe, she returned to her vigil, watching and waiting once more.

The clock tower struck the hours away mournfully until, shortly before the noon bell, the crowds started to gather for the opening of the Bourse. Soon the Calvinist was standing on his box, preaching to a small following just as she had seen before. Others came, rich merchants and burghers of the city and many more too. More people than she remembered and she was concerned that the crowd would grow too big and make it impossible to watch everywhere. The gates were thrown open right on time and the people flooded in. She longed to cross the bridge and mingle with them, but she knew it would be a mistake. So she forced herself to sit and watch until at last – not long before the Bourse closed after two hours of hectic trading – she heard a commotion.

With a hubbub of noisy calls and whistles they announced their departure from the Bourse. Valentino led the way, with Tobias, Aert, Raphael and Luckless Rony crowding in close around. They seemed to be celebrating a win and roundly cheered the Calvinist minister for making a valiant attempt to save their souls.

Jade came to her feet and moved quickly along to the end of the alleyway, watching as they came up over the curve of the bridge then turned along the canal side. She followed, ducking into a shop so she could watch them from behind a barricade of enormous cheeses.

'Can I help you, miss?' the cheese seller asked, peering around her hood for a glimpse of her face. Her lack of interest in his Goudas and Edams was obvious and he grew suspicious.

Jade slipped quickly along to the next shop, paused among the bric-a-brac, then moved on to the next, immediately feigning an interest in the latest in blue and white tiles from Delft. She watched Valentino and the others out of the corner of her eye. They pushed and shoved each other playfully as they walked, until finally they passed under the painted sign of a tavern called The Gauntlet and disappeared, one after the other, through a dark wooden door.

The Gauntlet was a traditional tavern: one large room with low wooden beams and long tables and a warren of smaller rooms leading through to a door, which in turn lead to a canal at the back. Ale was flowing into pewter tankards and there was movement and noise everywhere. Few noticed the girl with her hood up as she pushed her way in through the heavy door and stood with her eyes smarting from the belch of a hundred tobacco pipes.

Jade looked around. Gradually faces appeared between the skeins of smoke. Men and women were sitting on benches and around tables, lunching on smoked and salted meats carved from the haunches hanging from the beams above the landlord's table.

The door opened behind her and Jade's heart quickened as a group of men stepped in. She stood back as they greeted the landlord; it was hard to know whom to fear. She feared almost everyone – even children. With some difficulty she forced herself to remain calm and tried to act normally as she moved through the tables, searching the faces about her.

She ignored the enquiring looks that now searched for a glimpse of her face under her hood, until one man reached out and stopped her.

'Are you looking for me, darling?' he asked, laughing. He wouldn't let her go. 'Don't hide that pretty face.'

'Then perhaps you like my hair?' she said when she found she couldn't shake him off. She pulled back her hood and smiled sweetly at him. 'Pretty, isn't it, sir? The very latest style.'

The leer faded from the man's lips and he turned back to his beer pot quickly. She pulled up her hood and stepped into the passages beyond, peering into the warren of smaller rooms and drinking snugs that opened on either side. In each she was greeted by turned heads and the same blank looks. A dark stairway climbed to the floors above and she hesitated at the foot of it. There was a door at the back of the tavern and she was just beginning to think Valentino and the others might have left by the back way when she heard a voice she recognised.

'… So I said to him,' Valentino was saying, '"Call yourself a baker? You can't even make decent dough."'

And he said, "Do you want to make a meal of it with me, then?" And I said, "All right – as long as it's *wholemeal*."'

Jade was drawn along the passage by the sound of their laughter. She found them in the third room on the left and paused outside to gather her thoughts. All morning she had been rehearsing in her head what she would say, but now the moment had come she hesitated, suddenly self-conscious about the way she would look to them. She made sure her hood was in place and was just smoothing her skirts when the door at the end of the passage opened. The light from outside was dazzlingly bright and she shielded her eyes. She could see the water of the canal that ran behind the tavern shimmering in the sunlight, and then a woman and a small child stepped in.

Jade, alert to danger, ducked into the room to her left. She peered around the doorframe, watching with growing horror as she recognised Mother Race. The seer arranged her sack-coloured skirts, took her stick in one hand and laid the other on the boy's shoulder. Jade turned, looking for a way out, but found Valentino, Tobias, Aert, Raphael and Luckless Rony sitting around a table covered in half-empty beer pots, watching her. Before they could say anything she silenced them with a finger to her lips.

'I need help,' she whispered.

If this surprised any of them, it didn't show. It was almost as if mysterious girls were always bursting in on them in taverns and asking for help.

'You had better sit down,' Valentino said, offering her his stool.

'I need somewhere to hide – *quickly*.'

'And no one would ever think of looking on that stool,' Tobias said sarcastically.

'Well, can anyone else think of a better place?' Valentino asked.

The others glanced about. Apart from the table and the stools, the small room was totally bare. Jade realised she had no choice and sat down. Valentino squeezed in beside her and made Tobias and Aert pull their stools around so they all had their backs to the door.

'Have you heard the one about the rich burgher of Haarlem?' Valentino started loudly, acting as if nothing had happened.

Jade pulled her head down into her shoulders and tried to make herself as inconspicuous as possible. She could hear footsteps; the scuff of a heel, the drawn-out pull of clogs on floorboards. The sounds came closer, then closer still. She cowered away, hardly daring to breathe as the footsteps stopped in the doorway.

'Can I help you, Madam?' Valentino asked politely.

He was answered only by a strange sniffing sound. Then the boy led the woman in. Jade screwed her eyes tight shut and cringed away. Mother Race reached out and the boy guided her hand to Jade's hood.

'Now see here, you can't just –' Mother Race's stick slammed down on Tobias's shoulder, silencing him.

Bone-hard fingers probed into the muscles of Jade's neck and ran up over the fine wool of her hood. Jade ducked her head forward and screwed up her eyes, unable to escape the hand. Valentino and the others were objecting. Then her hood was pulled back with a jerk and everyone went quiet as Mother Race clamped her hand on Jade's head. The woman felt quickly, only to withdraw just as suddenly with a furious hiss.

'The girl has *long* hair, you fool!' Mother Race cursed the boy at her side. She shook him viciously by the neck, before pushing him towards the door. Jade just sat there, her head down close to the table, her eyes still tight shut. She listened in disbelief as the sound of Mother Race's clogs scuffed away. When she finally dared to open her eyes she found Valentino and the others gawking at her. She fumbled as she pulled up her hood.

'Let me guess,' Tobias broke the silence that followed. 'You've had an argument with your hairdresser – am I right?'

'*That*, if I'm not very much mistaken,' Valentino said, 'was old Mother Race.'

'Mother Race? But she's a *seer*,' Tobias said.

'Yes, but she's no teller of fortunes,' Valentino said grimly. 'She's as blind as a pillar of salt without the orphans she takes in, but she'll find anyone if the price is right – spies, runaways, witches.'

'Are you a witch, then?' Luckless Rony asked Jade with genuine interest.

'Of course she isn't!' Aert hissed.

Luckless Rony shrugged. 'I just thought – maybe that's why they cut off her hair?'

Valentino ignored them. 'So we meet again,' he said. 'I think it's time you told us what's going on – and you can start with your name.'

Suddenly all eyes were back on Jade as she sat huddled on a stool trying to keep as far away from the door as possible. She glanced towards Tobias who was supposed to be keeping watch on the passage outside, then looked from face to face around the table.

'My name,' she said at last, 'is Jade van Helsen.'

'Van Helsen?' Valentino repeated it thoughtfully. 'There's a moneylender on the Street of Knives called van Helsen.'

Jade nodded. 'He's my father.'

'Your *father*?' Tobias sounded surprised. 'No wonder you ran away.'

'Keep your voice down!' Valentino hissed. He drew nearer to Jade. 'So you're the moneylender's daughter, are you?'

'Did your father cut your hair off to stop you running away?' Tobias asked. 'I heard he's a hard man.'

She pulled the hood down over her forehead a little further. 'I did this to myself,' she admitted.

Luckless Rony looked around the table in amazement. 'Why would she do a thing like that if she wasn't a witch? Unless she's just plain crazy, that is.' He regarded her thoughtfully through slitted eyes. 'Mind you, her old man must want her back or he wouldn't have set the seer on to her. Hey, maybe there's a reward –'

'Shut up, Luckless,' Tobias growled, 'or the only reward you'll get is a slap in the face!'

Luckless Rony hunched his shoulders. 'I just thought maybe … her father being a moneylender and all.'

Aert shoved him off his stool. Luckless Rony came up, protesting. Valentino seemed quite used to it.

'It's no accident that you're here, is it, Miss van Helsen?' he said.

Jade dragged her gaze off Luckless Rony with some difficulty. She didn't like the way he was looking at her.

'Don't mind Luckless,' Valentino said, noticing. 'He's harmless enough – unlike that blind seer out there.'

'I came,' Jade said at last, 'because ... well, I needed to talk to you.'

'How did you know where to find us?'

'I knew you'd be at the Bourse. You make a lot of noise.' She shrugged. 'It wasn't difficult to follow you here.'

Valentino folded his arms. 'I thought you said you didn't want to know us.'

'I'm sorry.'

'So what changed your mind?' Valentino asked. 'Why would a rich moneylender's daughter come looking for the likes of us?'

Jade hesitated. She knew she was treading a fine line. Despite everything that had happened, she wouldn't betray her father again. It wasn't just because she risked another beating. It was much more than that. She was no runaway now – she was a van Helsen and determined to prove it.

'Answer me this first,' she said. 'Is it true that you know more about what's going on at the Bourse than most of the merchants?'

Aert guffawed loudly. '*Whoever* gave you that idea?'

Valentino kicked him hard in the shins under the table. Luckless Rony sniggered. It was Aert's turn to grumble.

'For the love of life – let the girl speak!' Valentino silenced them.

But Jade was on her guard now. 'So it isn't true.' She looked directly at Valentino. 'You lied to me?'

He shrugged and seemed slightly uncomfortable. 'Perhaps I exaggerated a bit,' he admitted. 'But that doesn't mean I don't hear stuff – especially if it's worth my while.' He leaned back in an Is-it-going-to-be-worth-my-while? sort of way.

Jade gave him a searching look and came to the conclusion she had been a fool. She stood up without another word and started for the door.

'Where are you going now?' Tobias barred her way.

'Back to the Street of Knives,' she murmured. She felt as if she was playing a part in a play – a tragedy of errors. 'They will have missed me by now.'

'*Back?*' Aert said. 'You can't do that!'

Luckless Rony hunched his shoulders. 'Told you she was crazy.'

Jade turned slowly and surveyed their faces. 'I'm sorry I wasted your time. I thought you could help me, but you can't even help yourselves. I should never have come here.'

'Not so fast!' Valentino reached out and pulled her down on to the stool with a bump. 'That's *Mother Race* out there. Sooner or later she's going to work out she's made a mistake and come looking for us. We're all involved now whether we like it or not. So the least you can do is tell us what this is all about – you owe us that much.'

'I owe you nothing,' Jade said flatly.

'That's not good enough,' Valentino insisted. 'Besides, how do you know we can't help? You haven't even asked us the question yet.'

Jade looked around the table. Her confidence in them had evaporated into the smoky air. But she had no other plan and little choice. She sighed and leaned forward. Like conspirators in a plot, they drew in around her to listen.

'A man came to my father's house,' she started uncertainly. 'His name is Atlas van der Stolk.'

'Atlas van der Stolk!' they repeated and nodded almost as one.

Jade was encouraged. 'You've heard of him?'

'Of course,' Valentino said. 'Everyone's heard of Atlas van der Stolk at the Bourse. There's no finer merchant.'

'No *finer* merchant?' she repeated as if the words tasted of dust.

'Bit of a hero, is your Mr van der Stolk,' Valentino said. 'Before he became a merchant he earned a reputation for fighting Barbary pirates in the North Sea.'

'They say he led the attack on a slave galley and captured the pirate captain,' Tobias said.

'Killed ten men to reach him,' Aert agreed.

'There was blood and guts everywhere,' Luckless Rony laughed.

Jade's head had begun to buzz. The revelations about Atlas van der Stolk's fine character left her feeling sick deep in the pit of her stomach.

'What about Captain Valerius?' she asked. 'He has dark curly hair and wears a tan-coloured coat ...'

'Valerius.' Valentino repeated the name. His glance around the table was met by shrugs. 'Never heard of him.'

A pause. Jade came to a heavy conclusion: 'Then I was wrong.'

Valentino frowned. 'Wrong about what?'

'It was the way they acted,' she said, speaking more to herself than them now. 'I just couldn't believe they had been away on a long voyage.'

'This is getting confusing,' Tobias said. 'What voyage?'

'A voyage of discovery,' Jade said. 'A voyage to the

267

American Islands.'

'Don't tell me,' Valentino laughed. 'They've made a great discovery and called it Van Helsen's Land!'

The others laughed. Jade just stared at him.

'Why did you say it like that?' she hissed.

The smile faded from Valentino's lips. 'You mean they *did*?'

'Tell me!'

He shrugged. 'It's just that it's happened before, that's all. It's a big world out there. It's hard to know what's real and what isn't. There's a lot of money to be made by buying land for plantations. Tobacco, sugar, spices – everyone wants them these days.'

'Especially sugar,' Luckless Rony said, licking his rotten teeth.

'What do you mean – "what's real and what isn't"?' Jade pounced on his words.

Valentino was forced to explain. 'Captains come back with stories to tell. They talk of the rich islands they've discovered. They have maps and pictures drawn up. If they're lucky they find someone with money to back a venture, promising returns of one thousand times or more on the initial investment. Greed does the rest.' He paused. 'Listen, why would a fine upstanding gentleman like Atlas van der Stolk be involved in something like that?'

'I don't know that he is yet,' Jade said. 'Just tell me the rest.'

'I'm not saying it always happens,' Valentino was careful. 'It's only sometimes that things aren't quite as good as they seem. By the time the rich investors find out they've invested a fortune in a piece of barren rock in the middle of nowhere, the captain and his associates have long gone, taking the money with them.' He forced a laugh. 'But it's ridiculous – there's no way a hard-nose moneylender like your father would get sucked into something like that.'

'Unless they knew he had a weakness,' Tobias said.

'A weakness?' Jade turned to him.

Aert nodded. 'They say everyone has their price.'

And Jade, above all people, knew that was true.

'Does he?' Valentino enquired cautiously. 'I mean – does your father have a weakness?'

'I'm beginning to think so,' Jade answered him under her breath. She looked up sharply. 'I have to find out more about this Captain Valerius. Will you help me?'

Valentino inspected the tips of his fingers casually. 'That depends –'

'It'll be worth your while.'

'How much?'

'A thousand guilders. My father will pay.'

Valentino whistled. 'That's a lot of money.'

He stood up and called the others together in a huddle by the door. They talked quickly and quietly, often glancing towards Jade, until at last they came to a conclusion.

'It'll take time,' Valentino said. 'A day, maybe two. Even then we can't guarantee we'll find out anything.'

'That's too long – the seer will find me.'

'Then we'll just have to find you a safe place to stay,' Valentino said. 'With a thousand big ones at stake, I don't want Mother Race spoiling things.'

'But where'll we take her?' Tobias asked.

Valentino smiled. 'I know just the place – Inga will help, she always does.'

* * *

269

Some time later a group of youths was seen crossing Dam Square. No one paid much attention to them as they made their way through the crowds, seemingly unconcerned with the daily hustle of the merchants and traders and hawkers. They crossed the bridge and headed for the university, working their way into the streets of the old part of the city, until a series of narrow alleyways led them to a small cobbled square where a washhouse stood. They approached one of the houses and knocked at the door. When it was opened they talked briefly to the woman there, before one among them was ushered in: a hooded figure that glanced back just before the door closed.

The others broke up. A sudden gust of wind blowing up a flurry of dead leaves and sending them hurrying their separate ways.

19. The Return of the *Draco*

Adam Windjammer felt the wind change as he stood at the ship's rail. It veered suddenly into the north-east and caused the first mate to order the helmsman to steer two points to starboard.

It was Thursday, 30th September 1637, eight long weeks and five full days since they had sailed from New Amsterdam. The North Atlantic currents had brought them home. But Adam knew he was returning to an uncertain future.

The news of Bartholomew de Leiden's death had been waiting for them on arrival at New Amsterdam. If Adam had been in any doubt what the loss of such a prominent backer meant to the Quadrant Shipping and Trading Company, Hendrik Honthorst had soon spelled it out.

'We've already delayed too long,' he had told them. 'And now it may be too late. Quadrant may already have slipped out of our control.'

They had veiled the news in secrecy and no time had been wasted in unloading the paying passengers. Only Madam de Witte and her maid had remained aboard until her cargo was safely unloaded. They had replaced it with wood and furs from her company's trading post on the Hudson River, and had taken on supplies of food and water for the long journey home.

When the moment had come for them to say their goodbyes, the widow had been forthright in her opinion. 'You are stubborn, headstrong and too wilful for your own good, Adam Windjammer,' she had said. 'And I don't know yet if you'll make the businessman they are training you to be, but while I am out here seeing to my late husband's affairs ...' she had glanced around at the rudimentary colony of rough timber houses perched on the tip of the island they called Manhattan, '... I can think of no one I could trust more than a Windjammer to keep his word and make sure I am supplied.'

'Does that mean we have your business, Madam?' Hendrik Honthorst had asked, barely able to conceal his excitement.

The widow had simply nodded and handed over the papers. 'But don't thank me,' she had said, pausing just before she had gone ashore for the last time, 'thank Clara. For some reason she likes you, Master Windjammer – and in my experience she is very rarely wrong about people.'

The memory of Clara's smile remained with Adam even now as he returned home to Amsterdam, sailing in across the Zuider Zee just as his father had done and his grandfather before him. He was older – he had turned sixteen on the 12th of September, the day they sighted the French coast – and perhaps a little wiser. And for the first time since his father had died he felt at peace with himself.

His hand went to the ring on the chain around his neck. In recent weeks he had felt the weight of it lift. The burden of the House of Windjammer, the burden he had carried for almost a year, seemed somehow easier to bear now he had found the *Sirius* and brought back Hobe.

'Hobe?' He remembered the boy and looked around. 'Where are you? You have to see this!'

Hobe hop-crutch-hopped to stand at the ship's rail and peered with some difficulty over the side.

'It's no good,' Adam sighed in frustration. 'We can't see clearly from here.' He glanced up into the rigging of the main mast. High above he could see Govert on lookout in the crow's nest. The captain wasn't on deck. Mr Glass was busy elsewhere. 'Come on,' he said. 'We're going aloft.'

'Aloft, Master Adam?' Hobe glanced down at the flap of his trouser leg. The stump was healing well, but it was still too tender to take a wooden peg. He depended on the crutch now. 'But I can't,' he said.

'We'll see about that.' Adam kicked off his boots and took off his coat, pulling himself up on to the bulwark at the main chain plates. He reached down to Hobe. 'You're not going to let a little thing like a missing leg stop you seeing the finest sight in all the world, are you? Come on! I'll help you.'

Hobe refused again, but Adam insisted. The boy left his crutch against the bulwark and hopped on the spot. Adam caught hold of his hand and pulled him up.

'See – it's easy,' he said.

Hobe put one arm over Adam's shoulders and together they started up into the ratlines that ran up from the bulwark like huge rope ladders, narrowing at the top. They climbed slowly, unsteadily in a three-legged way, until they got the hang of it. The main rigging soon narrowed and Adam was forced to let go of Hobe briefly, pulling himself up on to the lookout's platform that marked the halfway point of the main mast. He reached down and helped Hobe up and they rested side by side, three legs dangling over the edge.

Adam looked down, down past the bulging sheet of the main sail, down to the deck below. Already the length of the *Draco*'s deck seemed terrifyingly small.

'Are you all right, Master Windjammer?' Hobe asked anxiously.

'I've never liked heights much,' Adam admitted. 'But we've come too far to stop now.'

He took several deep breaths and helped Hobe up. The next set of the ship's rigging ran up the top mast to the crow's-nest where Govert was standing under the Dutch flag flying from the masthead. Hand over hand, they went, with the ratlines rough on the soles of their feet. The rigging was narrower now, less stable and, more than once, they were forced to stop, swinging dangerously about as the ship pitched and rolled.

'You'd best go on alone, Master Windjammer,' Hobe panted.

'Not far now,' Adam said, trying to sound more assured than he felt. The topsails billowed and flapped around them, making a sound like thunder, and he tried to steady the violent swaying of the rigging and mast by sheer willpower.

'Young master?' Govert looked down as they reached the top. '*Hobe?* Is that you? But he can't come up here, not with only one leg!'

'Tell Hobe that,' Adam said drily. 'Now give me a

hand and help him up!'

Between them they managed to pull Hobe into the crow's-nest. Adam followed, dragging himself on to the wooden platform.

'Mr Glass'll have me slopping out bilges for this,' Govert groaned.

Adam wasn't listening now. The view had stolen what little breath he had left. Ahead of them the great city was spread out, the sunlight catching on the slopes of the roofs and shattering into a million glints on a thousand windows.

The sight of it set Adam's spirit soaring. He became a creature of wind and air and when at last he regained control of his thoughts and remembered Hobe, he saw there were tears streaming down the boy's face.

'We're home, Hobe,' Adam said. '*Home* at last.'

The sounds of the waterfront hit them. It washed over the ship's rail, surging around them as the galleon was drawn finally to rest by the tightening rope hawsers at her bow and stern. High in the masts above men were hanging in the rigging, cheering and waving. Others were tying the sheets of the *Draco*'s sails to the yards. Everywhere Adam looked there was movement and noise. The bell was ringing on the Schreierstoren tower that dominated and protected the waterfront – announcing their arrival to the city. The sound of it brought people running to see the great ship that had returned to port safely. The crowd gathered at the quayside to witness the event, the people milling about with dogs and children chasing around their legs in all the excitement.

Adam had felt that excitement before. As a small boy

he had often watched the returning ships and felt the rush of the waterfront, but it had never been like this – so full of utter joy. Only in his dreams had if been this way.

The *Draco* wore the scars of the voyage on the outside. In many places her timbers were split and splintered by shot; her sails were patched and worn. Weed grew thick on her hull among the barnacles, but her cargo was safe. Whatever was to come from the death of Bartholomew de Leiden, the Quadrant Shipping and Trading Company had delivered on time.

The gangplank was sent sliding across by eager hands and the men poured off. Allart, Govert, Manfred and the others went striding down to be greeted by their families. Some fell to their knees to kiss the ground; others turned their faces towards heaven, thankful for their safe deliverance. Children were hoisted high on to shoulders. Dogs barked furiously. It was a sight Adam would never forget.

'Adam!' He heard his name being called and looked to see his mother waving as she hurried along the waterfront. His sisters were close behind and he ran to greet them at the head of the gangplank as they came aboard. He fell into his mother's arms and breathed in her scent as she wept tears of pure happiness at having him safely back.

'You look thin,' she said. She noticed the flash of silver in his hair. She touched it then hugged him to her breast until it became embarrassing. He managed to break free and immediately felt a tugging at his sleeve and found his sisters looking up at him.

Adam bent down to gather one in each arm. When he let go, he reached deep into the pockets of his coat and pulled out two spiny murex shells. Their eyes sparkled as he held them up to their ears so they could listen to the sea.

'Is that where they are now?' Rose asked.

'Uncle Lucien and the others, she means,' Viola explained.

Adam thought for a moment then nodded. And that, it seemed, was enough for them.

Shortly afterwards, Captain Lucas stood on the quarterdeck and called for quiet. The crowd listened in silence as he read out a short statement from a roll of parchment, detailing their search for the *Sirius* and the other lost ships of the Windjammer fleet. The news had been long expected. '... God rest their souls,' the captain finished.

He looked around and beckoned to Hobe. The boy hopped forward to the ship's rail and leaned on his crutch.

'Is there anyone here to claim this boy?' the captain asked. 'He goes by the name of Hobe.'

The people stirred and looked around. No one spoke up. Hobe stood leaning on his crutch. He seemed so small, so alone.

'Then does anyone know where we might find his father – the shipwright?' the captain tried again.

'Aye, sir!' a voice spoke up. 'He lives down on Marsh Lane in the Jordaan.'

The captain thanked him.

Hendrik Honthorst's smile remained fixed. 'Now it only remains for us to attend to the matter of our shareholders, Master Windjammer,' he said. 'I suggest we go straight to West India House and find Cornelius Yort.'

Adam glanced at Hobe. The boy was still standing, looking out forlornly over the ship's rail.

'There's something I have to do first, Mr Honthorst,' Adam said.

The streets near the shipyards on the western edge of the Jordaan were always crowded. Behind the warehouses, between the taverns, the houses squeezed streets into alleyways. The dwellings in the stews and slums that had grown around the marshy edges of the great city sagged under the weight of their poverty. The thoroughfares were ankle deep in mud and rutted by cartwheels – so unlike the scrubbed cobbles in the centre of the city – and the air hung with the smoke of cooking fires and the belch of the forges and pewter factories. The industry of people turned Marsh Lane into one of the busiest parts of the Jordaan.

Through this maze of sounds and smells and houses and alleys, Adam helped Hobe, searching out a house the boy barely remembered. Finally they reached the corner and were confronted by its low door and windows. Hobe stood, leaning awkwardly on his crutch, hanging back as if afraid.

'What if he doesn't want me back, Master Windjammer?' he asked. 'What use am I to my father now with only one leg?'

Adam had often wondered on the long journey home what would happen to the boy. He glanced around. Life didn't come much harder than down there on Marsh Lane.

'I'll find you a place at Quadrant,' Adam said. 'There'll be work – I promise.'

Hobe just looked away as if he suspected it would be

a promise Adam wouldn't keep.

The house was dark and empty. Adam rubbed at the grimy panes of glass with his sleeve and looked in. The one room inside was deserted.

'You'll not find the shipwright here at this time of day,' a neighbour said when they enquired. 'He'll be at work at the docks.'

So they went to the shipyards, dragging with them the burden of the boy's fears. Adam helped him to climb down one of the wooden ladders from the parapet to the mud on the riverbank below. There the shells of unfinished ships lay in line on ramps. The *Draco* had been born out of the mud and sweat of that place. Adam remembered how he had stood and watched the dragon figurehead being raised into position on the prow.

Now other ships towered there, half built. Skilled men laboured at the skeletons that stood on the slope of wooden ramps. They were supported on stocks cut from trunks of hundreds of trees. High above men worked on platforms: cutting, shaping and pinning the timbers into place – made insignificant by the sheer size of the ships they were building – and there was a rich smell of sawdust and tar.

A labourer pointed out a lone figure to them. Hobe's father was a giant of a man with a badly scarred face and an eye turned milky-blind. He was shaping timber with an adze, wheeling the flat-bladed tool with easy precision, chipping away at a piece of oak with a swinging motion of his arms. He didn't notice them as he worked.

'Father?'

The big man stopped. He stood very still, just staring

at the piece of timber at his feet. Then very slowly, he looked up. His blind eye was unevenly matched with the bright one to its side: a singular gaze that travelled from the boy's face down to his one foot then back up again.

'You've come to the right man for a new leg, boy,' the big man spoke at last.

And for a moment that seemed to be it from this man of few words. He just stood there for what seemed an eternity before he let the adze fall into the mud and broke into a lumbering run that ended with him sweeping the boy into his arms. 'My boy,' was all he could manage. '*My boy.*'

And then it was over. Adam's work was done. What had begun with a shipwreck ended here in the mud of the shipyards. So he left them with a promise to come back when he could. He paused as he reached the foot of the ladder. Father and son were sitting side by side on an unfinished timber, as if deciding how to carve it out together. Strangely, he envied that boy now. He would have given more than a leg to have his own father back.

He started up the ladder, unaware of the price he would pay for this small victory of life over death. For even as he made his way back to the waterfront the wheel of Adam Windjammer's fortune had turned once more.

20. The Bitter Taste of Coffee

Adam first heard the rumours as he arrived in the fine courtyard of West India House. He had come straight from the shipyards and was looking for Hendrik Honthorst among the merchants gathered under the lines of square windows. He soon heard the news about Cornelius Yort.

'It's a sad business,' one of the company clerks told him from behind a mahogany desk. 'First it was Mr de Leiden, now this. They say he's ruined – lost everything.'

'*Everything?*' Adam repeated. 'But he's a rich man – he even owns ...' The danger to Quadrant dawned then. 'Who did this to him?'

The clerk shrugged. 'They don't tell people like me things like that.' He glanced both ways and leaned forward. 'But just between you and me, I heard he lost half his fortune on tulips and the rest to some moneylender on the Street of Knives.'

Adam burst out into the courtyard and hit the cobbles running. He barely heard the complaints of the merchants, the shouts that followed him out on to the

281

waterfront. He ran along the line of great ships, his feet thumping into the quayside, tearing breaths from the air. He avoided the goods being hoisted in and out of the holds, jinking between nets of barrels and the slow swing of the wooden cranes, running even though he knew it was already too late.

He blunted into the shoulder of someone coming the other way. A dishevelled figure with wild hair and even wilder eyes stared down at him. It was a shock when he realised he was looking at Cornelius Yort himself.

'It's over, boy,' the merchant hissed through his beard. 'There's nothing any of us can do to stop him now.'

'What's over?' Adam gasped. 'What's going on ...'

'Go see for yourself, boy!' the merchant raised a trembling hand to point at the *Draco*. 'You'll find out soon enough. Then he'll do to you what he's done to me. You mark my words. Yes, you'll see!'

And with that Cornelius Yort shuffled on, looking for all the world like a ragged prophet determined to return to some distant wilderness. Adam went after him a little way, but soon gave up – drawn back to the *Draco*.

By the time he reached the quayside everything had changed. The waterfront had become alien and unfriendly, filled with rats and the stink of the water slopping about the hulls of the ships tied up in line. As he raced to the *Draco* he saw a notice nailed to the newel post at the bottom of the gangplank; one corner had come away and curled up. Adam smoothed it back and saw it was official: signed and sealed. The *Draco*, it said, had a new owner – Hugo van Helsen.

'No!' He tore it down and scrumpled it into his fist.

He started up the gangplank to be met by strangers. They were hard-faced, brutal men who went about their unspecified business as if the ship were theirs. One saw Adam and stopped him.

'Who are you?' the man asked. 'Who gave you permission to come aboard?'

'Since when ... do I need permission ...' Adam was gasping for breath, '... to come aboard my own ship?'

'You'd have to ask Captain Hoorengarde about that.'

'Captain Lucas is master of the *Draco*,' Adam insisted. 'I'll speak to him.'

The man shook his head. 'Not any longer, he isn't. So you'll just have to go ashore.'

Adam was forced to retreat to the gangplank. He argued every backward step of the way until the man lost patience and threatened to throw him off. And things would have turned rough had Merrik the mapmaker not appeared at that moment.

'Adam, thank goodness!' the mapmaker called, hurrying across the main deck.

'What's going on, Mr Merrik? Who are these men? What are they doing here?'

'You saw the notice, Adam. They arrived soon after you left with the boy. Captain Lucas was sent ashore along with all our men. Hendrik Honthorst went to the Bourse, I believe, to try and sort out the mess. Your poor mother! She left – taking your sisters home in case you went there first.'

'But you're still aboard, Mr Merrik!'

'They want my charts and maps, Adam. I refused to leave them, of course, so they had to let me stay ...'

Just then a man appeared carrying some plants in

pots. He took them to the ship's side and started throwing them overboard.

'Those are botanical specimens, you fool!' the map-maker gasped. He just managed to save some of them, cramming them into his arms. One pot fell with a crash. 'Philistine! Ignoramus!' he seethed and turned. 'They must be stopped, Adam ... Adam? Where are you going?'

The Street of Knives cut into the heart of the city: a twisting line of cobbles that turned between the shops and houses, leading through to a string of market squares.

Blind fury took Adam there now. He moved through the streets, the houses passing in a blur of windows and doors. He crossed Bread Street and cut along the Street of Cheeses. At times on the voyage he had been almost overwhelmed by longing for food like this. Now his stomach cramped at the thought of it.

Across the narrow thoroughfare and some way along, the Street of Knives opened to him. The butchers were hard at work in their shops on either side, their knives flashing in metallic glints. There was a clammy, damp feel to the place, a smell of blood and sawdust that carried on the breeze, funnelling its chill between the buildings.

The house on the Street of Knives was just as he remembered. A dark-timbered building with narrow leaded windows, it stood on the corner, squat and brooding behind the iron-studded door. A sign swing-ing gently in the breeze marked it out as a house of lending – five golden florins painted on a black board.

If the house had not changed, Adam had. It was a

very different Windjammer who presented himself at Hugo van Helsen's door that day. He was older, stronger, taller and fitter too, and – so it turned out – totally unprepared for what would happen next.

He glanced up at the windows. The glass reflected the sky and the clouds. He had once seen Jade at one of those windows and he wondered if she was there now, watching him as he slammed his fist against the door until at last a voice called, 'All right, all right, I'm coming.' A small trap opened among the iron studs and someone looked out through a grille.

'Open this door!' Adam snarled. 'I've come to see Hugo van Helsen.'

The trap snapped shut. Adam thumped furiously on the door again. A bolt was drawn, a key turned and the heavy iron latch snapped up. Adam pushed in without waiting to be asked.

'My name is Adam Windjammer,' he announced, 'and I demand to see your master at once.'

'I know who you are, Master Windjammer,' Goltz said with a slight inclination of his head. He closed and locked the door behind him. 'If you would follow me, please. Mr van Helsen has been expecting you.'

'What is the meaning of this?' Adam hurled the crumpled notice he had torn from the *Draco*'s gangplank down on to the table in front of the banker.

Hugo van Helsen was sitting at his chequer – a table covered with a black and white chequered cloth – counting coins into piles of ten, stacking them up neatly on the squares: silver on the white squares, gold on the black. He had been weighing the coins in the brass dishes of some scales, testing the gold pieces with an assortment of tiny lead weights. He didn't look up from the delicate act of balancing he was undertaking as Adam stormed in.

'One can never be too careful,' the banker said, making a small adjustment to the weights. 'Some coins look genuine, they feel genuine, even *smell* genuine but, in fact, when they are weighed in the balance they are found wanting for a grain. It pains me greatly the way unscrupulous people will shave the edges and hoodwink honest men so.'

'You're a van Helsen – you don't know the meaning of the word *honest*,' Adam spat back.

Hugo van Helsen's pale eyes flicked up from his gold; his gaze searched Adam's face. 'I expected more of you, Adam Windjammer, than cheap slanderous jibes.'

'I don't care what you expected. You've no right to take the *Draco* – no right!'

The banker sat back and interlocked his fingers under his chin in a thoughtful sort of way. His smile was thin and slightly stretched. 'Does an owner not have a right to his property?'

'What are you talking about? You don't own the *Draco*. I want my ship back'

'*Your* ship? But surely the *Draco* belongs to Quadrant.'

'My father built the *Draco* and Bartholomew de Leiden bought her when he set up Quadrant,' Adam said. 'We have delivered on time. We have new contracts. We don't need you or your money. So you can order your men ashore.'

'Surely you've heard the unfortunate news about Cornelius Yort by now?' the banker said casually. 'He has lost his fortune.' He paused before adding, 'You can imagine my surprise when I found out I now own a sizeable share of the Quadrant Shipping and Trading Company.'

'You don't fool me. Besides, there are other shareholders. Hendrik Honthorst told me so.'

Hugo van Helsen nodded. 'It is true. Bartholomew de Leiden divided the company up well between his friends to protect your family. From what I hear you will benefit personally from his will. It seems his final wish was to leave his share of the Quadrant Shipping and Trading Company to you and your mother.' Another pause, and his expression took on a look of regret. 'Of course, I do not yet have *all* Quadrant, just enough to take control'

'Never! I'll stop you if it's the last thing I do.'

Van Helsen disagreed. 'You made one big mistake, Adam Windjammer. You put the dead before the living and went in search of the *Sirius*. As soon as I heard the news I knew I had my chance.'

'As soon as you heard the news ...?' Adam picked up on it at once.

'A letter. From your last port of call. You see, I have been keeping a careful eye on you, Adam Windjammer.'

'You've been *spying* on me?'

'Oh, don't look so shocked. In business it pays to be one step ahead of the rest.'

'Who is your spy?' Adam's mind raced through the possibilities before settling on one. 'It's Allart, isn't it? I never trusted him.'

'This is of no importance,' the banker said. 'The fact is – you must deal with me now.'

'I'll go to the Council of Merchants,' Adam said. 'I'll stop you – no matter what it takes.'

'Too late,' Hugo van Helsen said. 'I already have Cornelius Yort's share of Quadrant.'

'And I've seen what you did to him to get it!'

'He destroyed *himself*. Debt enslaves the strong and weak alike.' The banker's pale eyes searched Adam's face. 'Of course, thanks to my daughter's misguided actions, I was denied an outright takeover of the company.'

'Jade?' Adam glanced about as if he expected to see her. 'What's Jade got to do with any of this?'

'It's a long story,' the banker said. He sighed deeply. 'God forbid you ever have a daughter. They bloom like roses but are covered in thorns.'

Adam reeled back, struggling to understand what he was being told. His rage was rapidly turning into panic. Everything seemed to be slipping away from him as if he had scooped up a handful of dry sand.

'It is true,' Hugo van Helsen went on thoughtfully, 'gaining control has taken all my considerable skills.'

Adam frowned. 'But –'

The banker stopped him by raising a hand. 'Have you ever tasted the juice of the cocoa bean? They call it coffee. It is quite bitter to the taste, but I have a fancy it has a future.'

'I don't care about coffee,' Adam snarled.

'Oh, I think you will, Adam Windjammer. You see, there's someone you must meet.'

Dam Square beat like a heart in the centre of the city. A cobbled and flagstoned plaza built on the great barrier that had been constructed across the River

Amstel. By an astonishing feat of medieval engineering, huge wooden piles had been driven by hand through the ooze and the clay to the bedrock, the natural course of the river dammed and diverted, its waters channelled into a system of the canals that fanned out through the city on either side. Here stood the New Church, the thirteenth century town hall and the weighing house known as the Waag.

A vast assortment of goods was arriving all the time, brought up on smaller boats from the ships at the waterfront. In Dam Square these goods were weighed for tax at the Waag before being loaded into the river boats and barges to be transported to the towns inland. Masts lined two sides of the square, up river and down, poking up over the stone parapet of the dam. Beyond, winding away into the distance, the river's widening course reflected the sunlight like a shining highway.

The carriage rattled to a stop. Hugo van Helsen pulled back the curtain door and stepped out. He settled his cape and adjusted his gloves before pointing with his silver-tipped walking cane.

'This way,' he said as Adam climbed down from the carriage. 'It is not far.'

Adam reluctantly fell into step beside him. They descended some stone steps and made their way along the Rokin for some distance. Narrower streets opened to their right. Here were the print shops and paper makers, the writers, thinkers and artists that were making Amsterdam a beacon of free-thinking and a leading light in the publishing world. And there, next to the striped pole of a barber-apothecary's cabinet, stood Ahmed the Turk's new coffee house.

'Mr van Helsen! This is indeed an honour!' Ahmed

the Turk greeted them with a reverential bow as they arrived. 'I was not expecting you, but you are most welcome.' He clapped his hands and several servants appeared to sand the flagstones around a suitable table in the open front of the shop.

At first Adam refused to sit down. 'Are you going to tell me what this is all about?' he said.

The banker nodded. 'All in good time. First I wish to partake of Ahmed's finest beans.'

'Of course, Mr van Helsen,' Ahmed said. He turned away and clapped his hands. Servants came running.

It wasn't long before the coffee was served. It came in several earthenware pots and was poured steaming out of spouts into thick glass goblets. One pot was served flavoured with powdered cinnamon, one infused with cloves and another with ginger. It was brewed bitter and strong, and sweetened with sugar or wild honey.

'The taste takes some getting used to,' Hugo van Helsen admitted, 'but I think you might be on to something here, Ahmed.'

'I wish the good people of Amsterdam would agree,' Ahmed said, bewailing the fact that his coffee shop was almost empty.

The banker sympathised. 'You are ahead of your time, Ahmed.'

Ahmed beamed. 'Thanks to you, Mr van Helsen.' He withdrew with a deep bow.

Adam had heard and seen enough. 'Why did you bring me here?'

Still the banker didn't answer directly. He waved his stick about. 'Ahmed has grand plans and big ideas. I have been forced to invest a lot of money. Goltz calls coffee "the Turk's folly".'

'Then *you* own this coffee shop? I hope it sinks!'

Hugo van Helsen smiled. 'You have not changed that much, have you, Adam Windjammer? You are still the headstrong boy that left Amsterdam in the spring. But it is time you started using your head. Sooner or later you will see that it is easier to work with me than against me.'

Adam stood up. 'I've told you before – I'll never do that.'

'*Never* – such a difficult word to define, don't you think?'

'Never means *never*. Now if that's all?' Adam heeled around and started to walk away.

'There are more ways than one to cook a fish, Adam Windjammer,' the banker called after him.

Adam stopped and stood very still before turning back to face him. 'What's that supposed to mean?'

'It means that in return for my investment, Ahmed here has signed certain papers.' He raised his voice. 'Isn't that right, Ahmed?'

Ahmed the Turk smiled, nodded and bowed.

'He has given me certain ... guarantees,' Hugo van Helsen went on. He feigned surprise. 'It turns out that our Turkish friend here knew that old fool de Leiden quite well.'

Adam felt his heart race.

'It seems about a year ago, Ahmed had some money and he was persuaded to buy a sizeable holding in the Quadrant Shipping and Trading Company. Thanks to you it has been a good investment for him and I was only too happy when he offered his share as a guarantee for the money he has borrowed from me.'

Only then did Adam realise what Hugo van Helsen was telling him. The banker smiled; it was the smile of someone who knew he had won.

'*Why?*' Adam gasped. 'Why are you doing this to us? Why can't you just leave us alone?'

The banker finished his coffee and stood up without paying. He thanked Ahmed with a nod of his head and stepped forward to pat Adam on the shoulder.

'I find myself in need of a ship,' was all he said before walking away.

'Mr van Helsen!' Goltz seemed very relieved to see him as he opened the door.

The banker stepped in from the Street of Knives, handed his servant his cane and began peeling off his gloves.

'Someone's come, sir,' Goltz said. 'He arrived not half an hourglass ago. He would not give a name, but it is about Miss van Helsen. He insists on seeing you in person.'

'Where is he now?'

'In the kitchen, sir. I had cook prepare him something to eat.'

'Very well.' Hugo van Helsen nodded. 'Take me to him.'

Goltz bowed and led the way through the house. He reached a flagstoned corridor leading to the kitchens and hurried ahead of his master to open the door. The youth was sitting at the table under the watchful eye of the cook. He was hunched over a bowl of stew, chewing at the meat noisily, the juice dribbling down his chin.

'Have you eaten your fill yet?' Goltz asked.

The youth shrugged. 'I likes pancakes, me. Pancakes with sugar.'

Hugo van Helsen stepped into the room. 'Where's my daughter?'

The youth glanced up. 'So you're the moneylender everyone's talking about, hey?' he said, looking unimpressed. 'I'm not saying nothing before I get my money.'

'You'll be paid well enough.'

The youth stretched out a hand, palm open. Goltz glanced at his master. The banker nodded and Goltz reached for the purse on his belt. He slapped it into the outstretched hand. The youth checked the contents carefully before making the leather pouch vanish under his coat.

'You'll find Jade at the washerwoman's house. It's in the old part of town,' he said. 'I'll show you the way if you like.'

Hugo van Helsen gave him a curt nod. 'What's your name?'

The youth wiped his mouth on the back of his hand. 'They call me Luckless Rony,' he said.

'Well, *Mr* Rony,' the banker said. 'If you are telling the truth, I have a feeling your luck is just about to change.' He called the cook out of the shadows. 'See the boy has some pancakes – with plenty of sugar for his trouble. Come, Goltz, we have work to do.'

21. Out of the Shadows

Inga was a small woman with a very big heart; a washerwoman by trade and a landlady to some of the poorest in the city. She was well known for taking in more than just the linen that came by the cart load from the fine houses across the Rokin.

Her house was a warren of small rooms on three narrow floors – one door at the front, one door at the back – it was built of brick with small shuttered windows. A large room on the ground floor served as the kitchen and sitting room. Here, a rectangular table dominated with benches on either side, the wood scrubbed until most of the colour had been bleached out. Washing hung on rails in front of the open fire where she cooked stews for her paying guests. In reality most of the people who came to Inga's door were so down on their luck that they couldn't pay. But she never turned them away if she had room and a spare bowl.

'We don't ask questions here,' Inga said. 'That's not our way. We take as we find and don't judge.'

Jade sat on the bench and watched her going about

her work. A hard life had made her broad and thick-limbed and her greying hair was pulled back and tied behind her head. Every so often she would return to stir the contents of a large pot hanging over the fire.

'I can't pay you now for your kindness,' Jade said. 'But I will.'

Inga smiled to herself as if that was what they all said. She tasted the stew, seemed satisfied with its progress and placed a lid on the pot to let it simmer. She turned, wiping her hands on her apron.

'If you don't mind me saying, my dear, your hair looks a fright.'

Jade touched it self-consciously and looked away.

Inga came to sit beside her. She took her hand. It seemed so small resting in the washer woman's broad palm.

'In my business you can tell a lot from someone's hands,' Inga said. 'Yours tell of your fortune.'

Jade glanced down at her palm, wondering if her life was somehow mapped out in the lines and contours she saw there. 'Can you read the future?'

Inga laughed, her cheeks balling up. 'I'm no fortune teller,' she ran the bowl of her thumb over Jade's palm, 'but your skin is soft and smooth. Where I grew up we couldn't afford to have hands like that.'

Jade eased her hand free.

'I don't know what trouble you're in and I don't want to know,' Inga said. 'But others will soon enough, if you go out looking like that.'

She reached out and smoothed down the uneven spikes and longer strands of Jade's ruined hair. She stood up and took down a pair of metal clippers and fetched a comb. Jade drew back in alarm.

'Someone has to finish the job,' Inga explained. 'It won't take long.'

Jade saw the sense in this at least and nodded. Inga began to cut. When she had finished she produced a small piece of mirror and Jade stared for a long time at the result.

'Try these on for size,' Inga said. She had dug out some clothes and returned chatting on in a matter-of-fact way. 'They belonged to a young man who stayed here once.'

'A young *man*?' Jade was surprised.

'You're tall – try the coat on for size.' Inga held it up. The coat was dark brown with brass buttons, cut long with vents in the back. With it went an off-white shirt with puffed sleeves and a lace collar, and a pair of fawn-coloured breeches.

'I can't wear these,' Jade said.

'It's your choice, my dear, but dressed this way you'll go less noticed with your hair cropped short.'

Jade looked at the clothes and suddenly saw the irony of it. 'My father always did want a boy,' she said, beginning to undress.

Some time later, with the evening drawing in, Inga's house began to fill up. The men working in the local pewter factory arrived, their faces blackened with soot from the furnaces. Inga made them wash before she allowed them to settle at the table. Others came too. From their talk Jade worked out there was a boatman among them, an unemployed carpenter and several others who seemed to have little else to do but beg. They were all treated with the same bluff kindness. Each was served with hotpot in a wooden bowl, given a hunk of rye bread and a mug of a brew they called small beer.

Jade sat among them, unnoticed after the first few sideways glances. The light from the smoky oil-lamps caught in the wrinkles of their faces. They talked, exchanging the news of the day without seeming to notice the young man wearing an oversized coat who was sitting in their midst.

'Eat now,' Inga said, placing the bowl in front of Jade. She was treated like the others, as if to do anything else would only have drawn unnecessary attention to her.

So Jade ate the stew seasoned with herbs and served with shallots and the leaves of the wild marsh flower. Food had never tasted so good. It warmed her belly and she felt stronger for it. And after they had eaten, the men took out their pipes. Their shadows grew longer against the wall as the darkness settled outside, night drawing over the house like a great thick blanket.

Only then did Valentino return.

'How goes it at the Bourse, Valentino?' one man greeted him.

'Never better,' Valentino replied confidently, but he glanced back out into the dark before closing the door.

'Creditors after you again, hey?' the man laughed.

'It's time you found yourself some honest work,' another said. 'There's work at the factory if you want it.'

Valentino thanked the man and said he'd remember that when he was desperate.

'Hark at him!' the man said. 'Always dreaming of being rich, but never wants to work for it. They'll catch up with you sooner or later, lad. Then it'll be *you* they fish out of the canal, face down.'

Valentino ignored their warnings, glanced around the table and had to look twice when he saw Jade. He forced his way on to the bench, making room beside her, and tore off a hunk of bread, stuffing it in his mouth and chewing hugely.

'You have to keep your eyes open and your ear to the ground in my business,' he spoke to the company with his mouth full. He glanced meaningfully at Jade. 'It's amazing what you learn if you do.'

'Perhaps it'd be better if you kept your nose to the grindstone instead,' Inga said, placing a bowl in front of him. 'You're late,' she scolded, but of them all, she seemed to have a soft spot for Valentino.

Jade was forced to endure the rest of the meal wondering what exactly he had meant. It was only as the others had left the table that Valentino leaned closer and lowered his voice.

'I always knew you were one of us,' he joked, admiring her clothes. 'You'd fit right in at Mr Books's table wearing that lot. Where did Inga get that coat? From some poor unfortunate they pulled out of the canal, I shouldn't wonder.'

Jade shifted uncomfortably. The clothes already felt strange and they clung to her body in places she wasn't used to. The thought that they had belonged to a corpse only made it worse. Valentino seemed amused by her discomfort.

She lost patience. 'This isn't a game to *me*. Tell me what you found out!'

Valentino glanced about to be sure they weren't being overheard. 'Quite a lot, in fact,' he said, inspecting the tips of his fingers in that way of his. 'It seems your father and Atlas van der Stolk have done business before.'

'Is that all! He does business with a lot of people.'

'Ah, but the word is,' Valentino said, 'that they fell out over it. Some time ago, when van der Stolk was just beginning to make his fortune, they got involved in buying land together. The deal went wrong and your father pocketed a considerable sum.'

That came as no surprise to Jade either. Nevertheless, it made her think. 'Now you come to mention it,' she said, 'I remember my father making a toast and saying something about them forgetting the past.'

'That must have been it.' Valentino nodded. 'But the good bit's still to come.'

'The *good* bit?'

Valentino leaned closer. 'Do you remember I told you how Atlas van der Stolk made his name fighting Barbary pirates? He killed ten men and took a slave galley.'

'I remember.'

'Well, it turns out the pirate captain was a Moroccan who went by the name of the Red Hand. His real name – wait for it – was Valerius.'

'*Valerius.*'

'Shhh!'

'But if he's the Red Hand, surely he'd have been hung for a pirate?'

'That's what I thought. But when I started asking around, I found that the story didn't end there. It seems that somehow the Red Hand managed to escape before they could bring him in. They say he bribed one of the crew aboard Atlas van der Stolk's ship to let him go.'

'Do you think it was van der Stolk himself?'

Valentino shrugged. 'Who knows? But the way I see it, if van der Stolk and Valerius are in this together they make strange partners.'

Jade thought it through and came to a conclusion that set her head buzzing. 'Do you think Atlas van der Stolk could be using this Valerius to get back the money he lost?'

'And more, I'll wager. *Much* more.'

'I still need proof.'

'That's the hard bit,' Valentino said. 'But I've always believed there's no smoke without fire. The trouble is, poking about in other people's business can sometimes lead to burnt fingers.'

Jade sat very still. She ran through it again in her head. 'Then I am right! I know I am!' she said, and she felt the sudden burn of excitement in the pit of her stomach.

'Maybe,' Valentino said, then sighed. 'Listen, I don't know what you're trying to achieve here, but has it occurred to you that you're doing this for the one man who seems to want to hurt you the most? If it was me, I'd –'

'Well, I'm *not* you,' Jade stopped him. 'I don't expect you to understand either. But I think this could be the chance I've been waiting for all my life – my chance to prove myself to my father. The old man told me it would be this way.'

'The old man?'

'Bartholomew de Leiden. He said I had to prove myself. He said, "Without respect there could be no ..."' She paused. 'It doesn't matter what he said.'

'Respect?' Valentino repeated. 'The only thing a moneylender respects is money.'

'That's not true!'

Valentino leaned back, startled. He searched her face, looking deep into her eyes, leaving her feeling very unsettled. 'You really believe that, don't you?' he said at last.

'I have to,' she said, looking away.

'If this is the same Valerius, then he's not a nice man. It could be very dangerous.'

Jade nodded.

Valentino sighed again and shook his head. 'I thought that might be your answer. So I sent Tobias and Aert to the waterfront to find out what they could about van der Stolk's businesses. It turns out he has a warehouse on the eastern dock. Tobias said it all looked normal. There was no big ship at the quayside – only a lugger called the *Haarlem Queen*. When Aert asked around, the word was that the lugger had been seen running out towards the marshes more than once. Only there's nothing out there but wild birds.'

Valentino eased back from the table at this point and glanced towards the door as if his next thought had made him feel more than a little uncomfortable.

Jade noticed. 'What is it?'

Valentino hesitated, then shrugged. 'It's just that I sent Raphael and Luckless to see what they could find out about Valerius in the alehouses along Kalverstraat. We arranged to meet back at the Gauntlet two hours ago. Only Raphael showed.'

Jade came to her feet.

'I'm sure it's nothing – Luckless probably got lost or fell in the canal or something.'

'And maybe he decided to trade me in for a reward?'

Jade said. 'I can't risk staying here – not now.'

'But where will you go?' Valentino tried to stop her.

'To the waterfront. I want to see this *Haarlem Queen* for myself.'

'I'll come with you.'

She shook her head.

'You don't trust me?' Valentino said.

She reached out and touched his cheek. 'I trust you, Valentino, but you've done enough. You don't know what my father's like. He has a long memory. If he finds out you've helped me he'll destroy you. But I promise, when this is all over I'll come back and find you – I'll bring the money like we agreed.'

Valentino smiled. It was the smile of someone who had known from the start that she would never be able to pay. 'Like I said – you're one of us now, Jade van Helsen. And we look after our own.'

Inga opened the door and peered into the night. She nodded the all clear only to pause and listen. Then she stepped back suddenly and closed the door.

'Someone's coming.'

Jade went to the window and looked out into the small square. She could just make out the washhouse in the shadows. At first she didn't see anything unusual, then torches appeared and a line of men came striding into the square.

'If I lay my hands on that Luckless ...' Valentino muttered, flexing his fingers.

'There's no time for that,' Inga said. 'You'd best go out the back way.'

'Too late,' Valentino said. 'You have to know the alleys around here – they'll catch you for sure if you get lost.'

'But I can't stay here!' Jade gasped.

'You can and you will,' Valentino said. 'Sit down there. Bury your face in your arms like this.' He showed her. 'Inga can say you're drunk. All you have to do is stay slumped over the table. I'll do the rest.'

'The rest?' Jade protested as he pushed her down on to the bench.

'People see what they want to see,' Valentino said. 'They're looking for a girl remember.' He turned to Inga. 'I'll need her cloak.'

Inga produced it and hid the rest of her clothes among the washing. Valentino tied the cloak around his neck and pulled up the hood just as a tremendous thumping started on the door.

'I'll go out the back way and run them around town,' he told Jade. 'Wait until they follow me, then go out the front. Take a hat. Keep the brim down and act normal. No one will think to stop a boy.'

'Why would you do all this for me?' Jade asked, amazed.

Valentino shrugged and smiled. 'I had nothing else planned.'

His smile faded as the front door juddered under the weight of many shoulders. He pulled the hood of the cloak down over his forehead and darted to the back door, glancing back briefly before vanishing into the night. Inga gave him a head start before going to the front to allow the men in.

Jade buried her face in the crook of her arm and slumped over the table, pretending to be asleep. Her father led the way in with several men following, passing so close to her she could have reached out and touched him.

'Where's my daughter, woman?' he snarled when a search of the house proved fruitless.

'Your daughter, sir?' Inga said. 'Does she have a name?'

'Don't play games with me!'

'Begging your pardon, sir, but plenty of people come through here – I can't be expected to remember them all.'

'She was brought here today, woman!' her father interrupted. 'I have proof.' He glanced over his shoulder. 'Where's Rony? Tell him to get in here now!'

Luckless Rony was pushed in and sent staggering to cower in the middle of the room.

'She's lying, I swear it!' he whimpered when Inga denied Jade had come in earlier. He cast about and spotted Jade without recognising her. 'If you don't believe me – ask *him*!'

'I will.'

Jade had an almost overwhelming urge to run as her father came across and shook her by the shoulder.

'Oh, leave that boy be, sir!' Inga said. 'He's drunk too much wine.'

A shout from outside set her father spinning on his heel. He crossed to the window and looked out. He swore under his breath and turned to the others. 'It's her! Quickly! She's getting away!'

'It seems you've had the wrong house, sir,' Inga said tartly.

Jade heard a furious hiss of breath, then her father rounded on Luckless Rony. 'Get out, you little rat! I'll deal with you later.' He stormed out and sent the men running. 'Thirty silver pieces to the man who brings my daughter in!'

The sound of their footsteps began to fade. Inga shook Jade gently by the shoulder and she jumped, startled by the touch. When finally she came to her feet, she found she was trembling all over.

'If you don't mind me saying, my dear,' Inga said, 'your father needs you more than he knows.'

'Here you, boy! Have you seen a girl come this way?' the man called from the bridge.

Jade hunched her shoulders into the oversized coat and kept her face turned down as she hurried past the bridge end.

'Hey! I'm talking to *you*.'

She realised she couldn't ignore him and stopped in the shadows, only half-turning her face to look. Her heart sank when she saw the man was coming across the bridge. He was holding a torch, the flames guttering in the breeze. She glanced over her shoulder. There were other torches in the streets behind her; their flickering light sent the shadows of the men leaping up into the branches of the trees and smeared burning streaks on the dark stillness of the canal.

'I said – did you see a girl?'

She shook her head and walked on. The Old Church was not far ahead of her now and beyond lay the eastern dock.

'Not so fast!' the man called. 'Where are you going?'

Jade stopped and stood for a moment as she tried to think. She remembered the Windjammers' house was nearby. 'Home,' she lied. 'It's just over there – past the Old Church.' She nodded in the direction of the *hofje* where the Windjammers lived.

The man approached and she did her best to avoid

the light from his torch. He peered under her hat, giving her a long hard look before grunting as if he'd been mistaken about something.

'This girl I was talking about,' he said, 'she's about your height, but wearing a cloak with a hood.'

'I haven't seen anyone,' Jade said. 'I have to go home now.'

'I'll wager she's long gone,' the man nodded. 'You live down here, you say? I'll go with you – I'm heading that way.'

Jade thanked him, but said she would be all right.

'I've got a torch,' the man said. 'Besides, you look too young to be out at this time of night. You meet all sorts down here, you know – and some of 'em aren't as nice as me.'

He gave her no choice but followed beside her, talking constantly as they made their way under the lowering shadow of the church.

'Just between you and me,' he said, 'this girl we're looking for is nothing but trouble. They call her Jade van Helsen and she's run away more than once. This time they say her father's going to have her whipped and I don't blame him. A girl owes her father some respect, don't she? You aren't one for talking much, are you, lad?' He stopped. 'This is it, then?'

She nodded.

'Well, go on!' he said. 'I'll wait here with the torch so you can see your way in.'

So Jade was forced to start towards the door. She walked slowly, hoping he would lose patience and leave.

'And remember, boy,' the man called after her, 'if you see this girl be sure to go to the moneylender's house on the Street of Knives. There's a reward for the one who brings her in.'

Jade didn't look back. She kept walking towards the house as slowly as she could without making him suspicious. The candles were lit inside. She could hear muffled voices through the shutters. All too soon she had reached the door and found the man was still watching. She made a show of searching her pockets for a key, all the while glancing sideways at him, praying he would leave. But he didn't and her fumblings became desperate.

'Locked out are you, lad?'

He started towards her. She began to panic. Then, just when she thought she had no choice but to run, a shout rang out in the street behind. The man turned to look and Jade ducked into the shadows, scuttling away to the nearest corner. She came up flat against a brick wall and stood very still, breathing as quietly as she could. When nothing happened, she risked a look. She could see the man talking to two others. They discussed something urgently before setting off in different directions. The man took several steps towards the door, realised she had gone, muttered and turned back, dragging the tongues of torchlight behind him.

Jade breathed her relief and eased back against the wall. She forced herself to calm down so she could think. It was clear that she wouldn't reach the waterfront without drawing attention to herself. She needed somewhere safe to hide for a while.

Her gaze was drawn to the lights coming from the Windjammers' house. There was smoke rising from the chimney, blotting out the stars. She eased out of her hiding place and crossed the shadows to look through the cracks in the shutters.

'The Windjammers?' she murmured. She forced the thought from her head, began to walk away, only to stop and turn to look at the door once more.

22. The Price of Friendship

Adam Windjammer couldn't remember much about how he had found his way from the Street of Knives to the Herengracht. He must have walked, but he had no memory of it beyond a blur of houses and canals, and the faces; oh yes, he remembered the faces – the faces of strangers looking at him as if somehow they could see he was dragging the whole weight of his failure.

He must have walked over the bridge and turned right along the canal, but he didn't remember doing that either. He remembered only standing in front of the large flat-fronted house on the corner of Deer Street. He remembered the stone steps leading up to the front door. He remembered the watery reflections of the sunlight catching on the windows where someone else now lived. And there he had stood, just staring at the house that had once been his home, the house that had been taken from them and sold, until finally he heard his mother's voice.

'Adam?'

Adam stirred, coming out of his thoughts. Now his

mother was looking at him across the table. Rose and Viola sat beside her.

'You must eat,' his mother said.

The joy that he had felt on his return had gone. It had been replaced by something much heavier, something invisible that seemed to press down on them all, filling their small house in the *hofje* so that it became stifling. Now, sitting at the table in the tiny kitchen, words came only with great difficulty.

'You haven't touched a mouthful of your dinner,' his mother said.

'I'm not hungry.'

The twins watched him with large, fascinated eyes.

'Will we have to leave?' Rose asked simply.

'This house too, she means,' Viola explained.

'Like we did the other one.'

'When Father died.'

'Why can't you shut up?' Adam snarled.

'That's enough!' his mother's voice cracked across the table.

Adam hunched his shoulders.

'Your brother is just tired after his voyage,' their mother explained. 'Everything will be better in the morning.'

'How will it be better, Mother?' Adam hissed.

She nodded at the twins. It was time for their bed. They stood up from the table and kissed her good-night, hesitating, looking uncertainly at Adam as if he were a stranger.

'Thank you,' Rose said at last.

'For the shells, she means.'

'They're only shells,' he said.

They glanced at each other as if this person he had

310

become couldn't possibly understand. Then they were gone.

'Anyone would think I'd brought them back jewels,' Adam forced the words into the silence that followed.

'Those shells are treasures to them,' his mother said. 'It's just a matter of how you look at things.'

Adam sat forward. 'Can we live on shells, Mother? Will *shells* put bread on the table?'

'Calm down, Adam.'

'Calm down? How can I calm down? It's happening again, don't you see? Hugo van Helsen is out to finish what he started. He wants to destroy us, Mother – destroy the Windjammers.'

'Hugo van Helsen is a businessman. He must have a reason for wanting the *Draco*,' his mother said. 'But Bartholomew de Leiden has left us a considerable share of Quadrant in his will. We are not beaten yet.'

'You didn't see Cornelius Yort,' Adam said. 'There was madness in his eyes. He's been ruined and all because that moneylender wants Quadrant.'

'Ahmed the Turk agreed with me not to sell,' his mother pointed out.

'He might as well have done! Do you know what the moneylender said to me? He said, "There are more ways than one to cook a fish." Do you know what that means?' Adam gave her no chance to answer. 'It means he has found a way to control Ahmed. And if he controls the Turk, he can control Quadrant.'

'We will wait and see what Hendrik Honthorst has to say about that.' His mother remained the voice of reason. 'Who knows – maybe we can work something out with Mr van Helsen.'

'How can you say that, Mother, after the way he tore

us apart? How can you think of even talking to him?'

Mary Windjammer leaned forward and fixed her son with a hard look. 'I will do anything it takes to protect those two girls upstairs, do you understand? They have been through enough in their short lives. We *have* to ensure this family stays together – even if it means doing business with a man we dislike.'

'And what about our contracts with Madam de Witte? She is out there in New Amsterdam relying on us to –'

They were interrupted by a sudden knock at the door.

Mary Windjammer looked up. 'I'm not expecting anyone.'

Adam went to the window and peered out through a crack in the shutters. He could just make out a shadowy figure on the doorstep.

'Looks like a messenger,' he said. He picked up a lantern and the cool night air rushed in as he opened the door. 'Yes?'

'It's you!' came a startled reply.

'Who did you expect? I live here.'

'But you're back. I didn't know ...'

'What's it to you?' Adam's frustration overflowed. 'What do you think you're doing knocking on people's ...' His voice trailed away. He raised the lantern higher. 'Take off your hat!'

After a brief hesitation, a hand moved up and drew the hat down in a sliding sort of way. 'It's me, Adam.'

Adam stared at her. '*Jade?*' A long pause. His heart seemed to thunder up into his throat, making it hard to speak. 'But ... What are you doing ...? Your *hair* – I mean, what happened to you?'

She glanced over her shoulder then back to him. 'I need your help, Adam. Can I come in?'

'Let me see if I've got this straight,' Adam said, pushing his chair back from the table and coming to his feet. 'Your father is involved in some shady business and you've run away because you think the men he is dealing with are trying to swindle him out of a fortune?'

Jade nodded.

Adam shook his head in wonder. 'And now you've come here – to our house – because you want us to help you stop what's going on?'

'I know how it sounds –' Jade said.

'How it *sounds*? It sounds like madness.'

'Adam!' his mother cut in.

'Don't you see what she's asking us to do, Mother? She's asking us to help her save the man who is trying to destroy us.' He rounded on Jade again. 'I'd rot in hell before I helped you do that. I hate your father and everything he represents.'

She came to her feet and stood, hugging her elbows. 'I thought …'

'Yes, what *did* you think, Jade?' he snarled. 'Once, some time ago, you had your chance to help us. But you chose to be a van Helsen then. You stole the Black Pearl from me.'

'I gave it back.'

'Yes, but it was too late,' Adam snapped. 'Take a look around you, Jade! Do you think we like living here? No. The fact is, I couldn't sell the Black Pearl after the market in tulips crashed. Your father took everything we had and threw us out. If it hadn't been for Bartholomew de Leiden we'd have been begging on the streets. So if I could, I'd go to this warehouse on the East Dock and find Atlas van der Stolk and his Moroccan friend and I'd shake them both by the hand. In fact, I'd push that boat of theirs out if it helped them. Yes, I'd have the name *Haarlem Queen* carved over our door and sing praises to –'

'That's enough!' his mother stopped him.

But Adam was filled with a strange sort of rage now. Part of him hated her for who she was and what she represented, and yet part of him wanted to reach out to her and pull her close. He wanted to crush her, break her, hold her. The emotions were so intense they hurt, tearing at him inside and forcing ever-crueller words from his lips.

'Look at her, Mother! She's a van Helsen!' He spat the name like an insult. 'We are Windjammers – *Windjammers.*'

'She's also a person, Adam. And she's asked for our help.'

Adam's fury at his mother's apparent betrayal sent him spinning on his heel. He began pacing the room, only stopping when Jade spoke.

'You think you are so hard done by, don't you, Adam,' she said quietly. 'You think my father's to blame for everything that has happened in your life. It's not true. No one forced the Windjammers to borrow from him. My father didn't arrange for your ships to sink. I can't say I'm proud of the way he brought down the House of Windjammer, but it's no secret that he's a hard businessman. So if you are looking for someone to blame – try looking to your father first.'

'You've got no right to speak about my father like

that!' Adam was shouting now. 'He was ten times the man yours will ever be!'

Jade just looked at him and there was sadness in her eyes. 'Bartholomew de Leiden was wrong about you.'

'Bartholomew de Leiden,' Adam hissed, 'is *dead*.'

'Maybe so, but before he died he told me you were someone special. But you're not, are you? You're just like everyone else. You're out to get what you can and you'll do and say anything to save your precious company.' Jade shook her head. 'I was a fool to listen to him. I wish I'd just kept right on running instead of going to the Bourse.'

'The Bourse?' Mary Windjammer intervened.

'Don't listen to her, Mother –'

Jade's chin came up slightly. 'I made the biggest mistake of my life when I tried to help you.'

'*Help* us?' Mary Windjammer frowned. 'What did you do?'

'She'll say anything –'

'Let her speak!' His mother brought the flat of her hand down on the table.

Jade glared at Adam. 'The old man asked me to find Ahmed the Turk. He asked me to warn him not to sell out his share of your precious Quadrant to my father. So that's what I did. I betrayed my own father for *you* – and I'm not proud of it.'

'You're lying,' Adam said.

'No, she's telling the truth,' Mary Windjammer cut him short. 'When Ahmed came to me that day with the news of what had happened, he told me that he had been warned not to sell to Cornelius Yort by a strange girl with green eyes. At the time, I thought he was just being dramatic. I was too concerned with my worries

315

for you and the *Draco* to think much of it …'

'I still don't believe it!' Adam said.

His mother looked at him. 'I love you, Adam. I love you more than my own life, but sometimes you can be so pig-headed and stupid.'

Silence. They noticed the twins standing nervously at the door, brought down from their bed by the row. They ran to their mother.

'I'm sorry we woke you,' Jade said. She picked up her hat and started for the door.

'Stay a while, Jade,' Mary Windjammer stopped her. 'Please. I want to talk to you.'

It was the same dream: Adam running into Dam Square to be met by Hugo van Helsen and his beautiful green-eyed treacherous daughter.

Adam hovered on the edge of waking, clinging to the dream a little longer than usual. 'You'll do and say anything to save your precious company, won't you, Adam Windjammer?' her voice came slowly, distorted to the ear. But it was the look in her eyes that tore into him – the look of someone hurt to the point of hatred.

'Wait!' He tried to stop her, but she just walked away and no matter how hard he tried he couldn't reach her now; he couldn't get her back.

Adam came awake with a gasp, sitting up suddenly. He was sweating, lying fully clothed on his bed. It was just beginning to get light. He blinked at the small attic room with its heavy beams, struggling to remember where he was. It came back to him and the weight descended on him once more.

He dragged himself off the bed, went to open the window and took a deep breath. Outside, the city was

316

stirring as the dawn shot blood-red arrows through the mist and smoke from the chimneys.

The letter he'd been writing was addressed to Jade, but the words were exhausted. On the floor lay a dozen scrumpled attempts. He had hoped it would be easier saying it in a letter. He had hoped by writing it down he would be able to make her understand why he was going to stop her: how this was as much his chance as hers, how it made good business sense to exploit her father's weakness, how his responsibility was to his mother and sisters and Quadrant ... He wondered why it always sounded so hollow when he read it back.

He returned to face the page again. He picked up the quill and sat for a while before his frustration burst out of him and he crushed the paper in his fist, hurling it away.

The narrow wooden stairs creaked as he made his way down. He looked into his mother's room. Rose and Viola were still asleep, curled up in the same bed as their mother. The door to the only other bedroom in the house was closed. He opened it and peeked in to see if Jade was awake.

The covers were drawn up and the early morning light made it hard to see much more than the outline of her form in the bed. Very quietly, he closed the door again, pulled the knife from his belt and slipped it into the latch, jamming it shut. Then he continued downstairs to stir life back into the fire in the kitchen. He sat down at the table and gazed gloomily into the flames. He was still sitting there thinking about what he had done when he heard someone at the door.

'Mr Merrik!' Adam said as he answered to the mapmaker's timid knock.

'Adam, my boy!' the mapmaker said, peering at him through a new pair of lenses. 'My goodness, it is good to see you!' He removed his battered hat. 'I hope you don't mind the earliness of the call, but I just had to come.'

'What's happened, Mr Merrik?'

'I was hoping you could tell me that. They're talking about moving the *Draco* to the East Dock.'

'Moving her?'

'Hendrik Honthorst came to object, but was ordered back ashore. You have no idea what it's like aboard that beastly ship now. The crew are so rough. When will it end, Adam? Do you know?'

Adam glanced past him, then stood back. 'You'd better come in.'

They settled at the table by the fire and for a while the relief of seeing a friendly face overwhelmed all other thoughts. It wasn't long, however, before their talk returned to the *Draco*. Adam explained as briefly as he could what had happened.

'Then this man, van Helsen, has taken the *Draco*, Quadrant – everything?' the mapmaker concluded.

'Not yet, Mr Merrik,' Adam said. He felt sure the mapmaker of all people would understand. 'You see last night, Jade van Helsen – the moneylender's own daughter – came here. She's upstairs right now.'

'*Here?* Now?' The mapmaker lifted his lenses and peered about as if he expected to see her.

'She's asleep.' Adam was suddenly overwhelmed by the urge to lift the burden of guilt. He explained why she had run away and why she had come. Once again it didn't take long for the mapmaker to grasp the situation.

'You've *locked* her in? You're holding her prisoner!'

'I had to do it, don't you see? I have to stop her going to the waterfront today. I can't let her warn her father. It's time Hugo van Helsen learned what it's like to lose a fortune. Then he'll be weak and in no position to take Quadrant from us. This is our chance to beat him once and for all.'

'Why, Adam,' the mapmaker sounded shocked, 'I had no idea that you had such a ruthless streak in you.'

'I'll do anything, Mr Merrik – *anything* to save Quadrant.' He paused. 'But we have to be careful. They mustn't find out where Jade is.'

'I understand. You can rely on my discretion.'

'I know that, Mr Merrik. Sometimes I feel as if you're my only friend in the world. But the money-lender probably has someone watching this house right now.'

'*Watching* us?'

'He's been spying on us all along. He even had a man aboard the *Draco*. Someone's been reporting back to him. He's known our every move from the moment we set sail.'

'A spy in our midst?' The mapmaker refused to believe it. '*No*, Adam, surely not!'

'He told me himself.'

The mapmaker pulled out his handkerchief and mopped his brow. 'And ... did he *name* this spy?'

'No, but I'm sure it's Allart.'

'Allart? Yes, perhaps. But no, it couldn't be – unless ...' The mapmaker stopped, thought briefly and shook his head.

'You suspect someone else, Mr Merrik? Tell me!'

The mapmaker declared he wasn't the sort to speak

319

ill of anyone who wasn't there to defend himself, but Adam pressed him and finally he gave in.

'Well, it's just that I remember something that happened when we went ashore on Hell's Rock. An argument between Allart and Mr Glass. I thought nothing of it at the time, but now perhaps the incident makes sense. If I remember rightly, Allart accused our first mate of watching you.'

Adam remembered now. 'Mr Glass? *Yes.*' Suddenly it made sense to him. 'Still, I can't quite believe it …'

'And nor should you, Adam!' the mapmaker said. 'Just forget I even mentioned it. Mr Glass is a good and honest man – I'm sure of it. How could he be in the pay of Hugo van Helsen?'

But once it had been said, there was nothing either of them could do to unsay it. And the more Adam thought about it, the more it made sense.

'And now,' the mapmaker said, standing up, 'I really must go. I dare not leave my precious maps unattended for much longer. But if you need me – I'll be aboard the *Draco.*'

They stood up and went to the door. The mapmaker lifted his lenses to look up the stairs. He thought for a moment then said, 'Perhaps I should talk to her? Try to explain on your behalf. Tell her that everything will be all right. It may help.'

Adam leapt at the suggestion. 'Would you do that for me, Mr Merrik? It'll be better coming from you.'

'Of course, my boy. I do have a certain way with words.'

So Adam led him up the stairs to the door. His mother appeared from her room, her hair tousled and her face creased with sleep. She was closely followed by

320

Rose and Viola and the twins stood clinging to her nightdress. 'Leave the girl alone – she's tired to the point of exhaustion.'

'Just stay out of this, Mother! I know what I'm doing.'

Adam pulled his knife out of the catch.

'You locked her in?' His mother was horrified.

Adam opened the door and they stepped in, standing by the door, peering into the half-darkness as the mapmaker called softly to Jade.

'Don't be alarmed, Miss van Helsen ...'

Nothing happened. He cleared his throat. Still nothing.

In three steps, Adam was at the bedside. He ripped off the covers to reveal the bolster and a pillow.

Jade had gone.

23. The Red Hand

The dawn broke cold and grey, the pale light crawling out of a thin mist that hung over the waterfront. Jade lifted the collar of her man's coat against the chill and looked around at the warehouses lining the eastern dock. In the dim light they all looked the same, looming out at her, their brick facades studded by lines of wooden doors. Ropes looped from the beams of the hoists that jutted out from the walls above each door like so many empty gallows.

She moved carefully, alert to the sounds around her. Already there was a stirring and movement of people around the docks. She passed an archway at the end of one of the buildings and paused, her attention caught briefly by a group of men standing around, talking about the day's work, stamping their feet against the chill of the morning. She moved on quickly.

It had been her plan to use the Windjammers' house only until the search for her had moved away from the surrounding streets. So she had stayed at Mary Windjammer's request, accepted their food and had even managed to snatch a few short hours' sleep before slipping away unnoticed. Her only regret was lying to Mary Windjammer by promising to stay until morning. She realised Bartholomew de Leiden had been right about Adam's mother. It was Adam who had changed.

Jade still remembered the way her heart had leapt when he had opened the door. It had been such a surprise to find him there. Now she wished she hadn't. He was not the same boy she had kept in her head all those months. In his place stood a bitter youth. But worst of all was the growing sense of the inevitability of it all – of how life was gradually making enemies of them.

Wooden jetties ran off at angles from the quayside disappearing at a distance into the mist. She could see larger ships tied to the piles further out, the galleons and warships, the frigates and merchant carracks; their masts spiking through the white shroud that came rolling in off the wide expanse of the Zuider Zee beyond. To her left, the warehouses were dulled by the whiteness. Each bore the name of a merchant over the door. Among the signs – the offers of spices and sugars, the cloth dealers and grain storage at the best prices – she picked out one name. Atlas van der Stolk.

A man Jade took for a nightwatchman was relieving himself against the wall. He was whistling tunelessly under his breath. A candle still flickered in his lantern as he picked it up and made one last tour of the warehouse before handing over the keys to the men arriving for the day's work. The large doors were thrown open by a burly warehouseman. It seemed it was going to be business as usual on the waterfront that day.

Jade stood back at a safe distance and watched the door. She couldn't see the lugger called the *Haarlem*

Queen anywhere along the quayside and she felt squeezed inside by the thought that it might all have been for nothing. She didn't have to wait long to be proved wrong.

The carriage arrived as the bells on the waterfront were chiming eight. Jade saw the horses first, turning out of the side streets pulling the heavy carriage behind. She stepped back around a corner, catching a glimpse of someone inside through a gap in the curtains. The wheels rattled on the cobbles until finally it stopped in front of the warehouse. The curtain door was thrown back and van der Stolk stepped out. She watched him settle his tall hat. He was dressed for business, wearing a long black coat, and he had a casket under one arm. His breath smoked on the chill air as he took several deep breaths before disappearing through the door at the front.

Jade came out of hiding, pulled down her hat and hunched her shoulders as she walked quickly down the length of the building, slowing considerably as she passed the door. She glanced in and saw the warehouseman sitting at a desk. He noticed her and she was forced to carry on walking. Further along she eased around a buttress wall and wondered what to do next.

The answer came from the sea.

The boat appeared out of the mist. It came gliding in across the water, a man standing in the bow, looking out like Charon, the boatman of the dead. What little breeze there was failed and the lug-sails began flapping limply around the two masts. A dozen men had to take to the oars to bring the lugger in under the quayside. Jade lost sight of the boat briefly then the men came leaping up a ladder and spread out. Jade noticed they were all wearing long coats and she caught glimpses of weapons underneath. Only when the men were in position, did Valerius climb up out of the lugger and step on to the quayside.

Jade watched him stride across the warehouse and in through the door, knowing that this was her chance. The excitement left her feeling slightly breathless. She was scared and excited at the same time, but most of all she was determined.

She forced herself to wait to see what would happen next. The men stood around for a while, before they began loading barrels out of the warehouse, rolling them across the quayside and manhandling them down into the boat. Only when she was sure they were at their busiest, did she ease out of hiding, walk along to the door and slip unnoticed into the warehouse.

The burly warehouseman was at his desk, but he didn't even look up now there was so much activity going on. Jade darted in behind a stack of barrels and let the shadows absorb her. She found herself in the weighing room of the warehouse, the great arm of the scales rising high above her head. Not far away there was a door. It was slightly open and she recognised the voices coming from inside. She crept over to listen, straining to hear what was being said, unaware that she had been spotted.

The first Jade knew of it, was when she was suddenly jerked by the collar and dragged back. Someone slammed her up against one of the wooden posts that supported the beams above, and a face came close.

'What are you doing here?' the warehouseman growled. His breath was rank. He hurled her back against the post again. 'I'll break you in half if you don't answer me, boy!'

The man threw her forward and sent her sprawling. Before she could recover, he had her by the collar again and was dragging her up. She crashed against a stack of barrels, and was left to slide on to the floor. By the time her head cleared and she looked up, others had appeared, attracted by the commotion.

'I found him listening at the door,' the warehouse-man explained, jabbing an accusing thumb at Jade.

The men moved aside to allow Atlas van der Stolk through. He looked down at her and his eyes narrowed slightly.

'Well, well. If it isn't the moneylender's daughter,' he said.

Jade sat on the stool in the middle of the room with her hands tied in front of her. Men stood back all around. She had no hope of escape.

'I'm sorry about your rough treatment,' Atlas van der Stolk said, 'but if you will go around dressed as a boy ...'

Across the room Valerius flashed a grin. 'I could tell she was a wild one from the moment I saw her.'

'You've got no right to hold me here,' Jade said.

'And why exactly *are* you here?' van der Stolk asked.

Jade glared at him, refusing to answer.

'You're a clever girl,' he said. 'Much cleverer than your father gives you credit for, it seems. You've suspected something was going on all along, haven't you? Well, if it makes you feel any better – you're right. There is something going on.'

His look hardened and she saw a slight clenching of his jaw.

'You see, some time ago,' he went on, 'your father almost ruined me in a business deal. He does it to many people, but he made one big mistake – he neglected to finish me off properly. When I made my money back I swore then I would get even. I'm a patient man, you see. It has taken considerable time to come up with a plan. But now my friend Valerius and I are about to teach your father a lesson he will not forget.'

'You'll never get away with it,' Jade hissed. 'No one ever beats my father.'

Van der Stolk smiled and glanced around at the men. 'How touching to see a daughter's loyalty to her father.' The smile faded. 'Shame he doesn't return it to you in kind – from what he says it's clear he thinks so *little* of you.' His words were chosen to wound.

'Oh, he's a clever man, and cautious too,' van der Stolk admitted. 'But they say ambition makes you blind. And your father is ambitious, all right. He longs to be held in the same regard as the fine old families, the merchants and burghers of this city. But they have never accepted him. To them he has always been just an ambitious little moneylender living in an unfashionable part of town.

'So you can imagine how he must have felt when we came along with an offer to advance him beyond his station in life. Imagine how he dreamed when we offered to make him a *king*.'

'Van Helsen's Land,' Jade breathed the name.

'Right again, my dear.' Van der Stolk sounded impressed. 'I am surprised your father has not more regard for you. But then he does *so* want a son, doesn't he?'

Jade's chin came up. She bit her lip until she tasted blood.

327

Atlas van der Stolk smiled and took a scroll from the casket on the table. 'But you're too late. It has already started. I have here an agreement signed and sealed by the Banking House of van Helsen.'

He pulled out a bag of coins and let them spill across the table. One coin edged and rolled. Valerius stepped forward and slapped it down.

'Gold,' van der Stolk said. 'And this is just the beginning. Your father thinks we are equal partners in this venture. I have him so convinced, he has even bought himself a ship and a company called Quadrant. He is making plans to supply his new kingdom across the sea and bring back the wealth of sugar and spices we have promised him.'

'He'll send the *Draco*,' Jade said. 'He'll find out you've been lying.'

'Yes, he'll send his ship,' van der Stolk said. 'But Valerius will be waiting for her. He's quite experienced in such matters. Perhaps you've heard of the Red Hand?'

Valerius flashed another smile. 'The Caribbean can be a very treacherous place.'

Atlas van der Stolk nodded. 'But don't worry, I won't steal everything from him at once. I want to take my time and see how your father squirms. We will bleed him dry. And the beauty of it is, he will never even know that he has been taken for a fool.'

'I'll tell him!' Jade snarled, fighting against the ropes.

A pause. 'Yes, it is true, *you* have now become a problem.' Van der Stolk looked thoughtful. 'What shall we do with her, Valerius?'

Valerius drew a knife from his belt and came around behind her, jerking her head back and laying the steel against her exposed throat.

'Effective,' van der Stolk said, 'but I am no murderer. I prefer a more subtle and yet just as effective way.'

Valerius let her go.

Atlas van der Stolk laid a consoling hand on his shoulder. 'From what I hear this girl is quite a handful. She is always running away.' He smiled. 'What say we help her, Valerius? What say you take her with you and show her the real world?'

Valerius grinned and nodded. 'A girl like that should fetch a good price in the slave markets of Marrakech.' He attempted to look at her teeth, but Jade pulled her head away, her eyes sparking.

'Then again,' he said, 'maybe I'll just keep this one for myself.'

'As you wish,' Atlas van der Stolk said. 'But for now keep her out of sight. Take her to your tower in the marshes, Valerius, and be ready to sail when I tell you.'

Valerius nodded and waved his men forward. 'Take her to the boat – and see she doesn't draw attention to herself.'

Jade was bundled to the door and her hat was pulled hard down on her head. A group of Valerius's men surrounded her and forced her to walk normally out of the front way. As soon as she was outside a knife was pressed into her ribs to keep her quiet. She staggered, half-carried across the quayside, only vaguely aware of the tall man in the battered hat who was pushed so roughly aside. They ignored his protests as he blinked angrily through a pair of lenses. She was forced down a ladder and sent sprawling on to a pile of sacks on the deck of the lugger, and there she lay fighting for breath, trying to force back her tears of pain and rage.

*　　*　　*

There was little to mark the place where the city ended and the countryside began. The houses gradually petered out, thinning into open fields until the eye was drawn away suddenly into the mist and flat expanse of the marshes.

Jade lay on the pile of sacks. The ropes around her wrists were tight and her hands had gone numb with pain. She tried to ignore the growls of the flea-bitten mongrel lying close by. The dog belonged to one of the dozen or so men that sat about the deck of the lugger. She could smell their sweat and sensed the tension among them now she was aboard.

As she looked around she noticed that most – but not all – had the same sun-darkened, Mediterranean appearance as Valerius, and decided they must be his crew. Once they were away from the quayside they had taken off their coats. Some wore leather jerkins, others shirts. They had knives or short swords slung on baldrics and small bags of gunpowder hanging from their broad belts or from loops in their breeches and pantaloons. All went barefoot.

Jade raised her head and looked out over the side. The *Haarlem Queen* sat low in the water, sluggish and heavy under her load of men and supplies. The wind-mills and factories of the eastern side of the city were vanishing behind them. She felt sick and utterly alone. The realisation that no one even knew she had been taken filled her with desperation. She tried gnawing at the ropes around her wrists, but the dog growled and drew unwanted attention from some of the men.

'Here, my beauty,' one said. 'I'll cut your ropes for a kiss.'

Others laughed and looked greedily at her.

'Leave her alone!' Valerius hissed. 'Green eyes is mine now.'

The men scowled and muttered, but they backed off all the same.

Jade soon became conscious of the mill in the distance. The giant cross of its sails marked it out like an X on a map. It stood raised on a dyke close to a point of land and seemed to slide off the horizon towards her. There was something brooding and dangerous about that crumbling tower, its ragged outline silhouetted against the sky.

Soon the helmsman steered the lugger out of the open water and into the mouth of a narrow creek. They slipped in by a schooner lying at anchor, sails furled along its yards, partly hidden beyond the point, and ran the lugger up to a wooden jetty. The dog leapt ashore, barking at the men as they tied up.

Valerius dug at her with his boot. 'We're home, green eyes.' He looked up at the mill. 'It's not much, I admit, but it serves our purposes. You see, it's not wise for men like us to stay around town.'

The mill on the Westerdijk had been abandoned long ago. The pale grey stone was crumbling. From its wide base, it tapered into a tower that was encircled by a wooden walkway about a third of the way up. From this rotting gallery, a cantilevered system of steering beams lifted the eye to the roof where storks had been building their nests for generations. The sails stood frozen, giving it a cold, lifeless feel.

Jade slipped in the mud as she jumped down on to the bank. She lost a boot and the mud squelched between her toes. The men laughed at her as she tried without success to retrieve the boot with numb fingers. She took another step and would have fallen again had one of the men not dragged her up.

'Leave me alone!' she snapped, shaking him off furiously. They continued to laugh at her as she fought her way out of the mud and up the grassy bank.

She paused for breath and glanced at the tower. Thick laurel bushes had grown up to cover the mound on which the windmill stood, crowding in around a square door. Some of the undergrowth had been cleared and she judged from the barrels, wooden chests and smouldering remains of a large fire that Valerius's men had been using the mill for some time.

The men pushed her on. The door in the base of the tower seemed to gape as if the building itself would swallow her up. She recoiled from it, realising she had more chance outside than in.

Jade broke away suddenly, dodging to her left and taking the man behind her completely by surprise. In three bounding steps she was plunging into the bushes.

'Stop her, you fools!' Valerius's furious shout followed her.

A roar went up from the men behind. She fought her way through the bushes with tied hands, until she crested the dyke and went slithering down the steep slope on the other side. She came to her feet, stumbling into marshy ground.

'Help me ... someone ... please!' she gasped hopelessly.

The mill rose behind like a giant stump. She lurched on into the great, flat, misty openness. No matter how hard she tried to get away from it, the windmill still seemed to loom large over her. And all the while she could hear the dog barking and the shrieking calls of the men as they whooped their delight like wild things revelling in the unexpectedness of the hunt.

'No please – *please*,' she begged, her breath coming in gasps. She lost her other boot in the mud and staggered on, the weight of her waterlogged clothes dragging her down until at last she tripped over a dead tree and fell. She tried to crawl away and hide, but the marsh just seemed to suck her in and hold her.

At first she could hear only the thundering of her own heart, then they appeared out of the mist. The sound of their laughter filled her with terror and loathing. They pulled her to her feet and dragged her back to where Valerius was waiting.

'Like I said – you've got spirit, green eyes.' He grinned. 'And I like that.'

24. The Hol Lands

'I have never known such rudeness,' Merrik was complaining when he met up with Adam again.

Adam ignored him. 'I know this is it, Mr Merrik,' he said. 'I'm sure this is the warehouse Jade was talking about.'

The mapmaker raised his lenses and peered at the name over the door. 'Atlas van der Stolk? That's the name of one of the finest, most upstanding gentlemen in Amsterdam. You would have thought he would employ people who are a little less brutal.'

Adam glanced about. Men were loading and unloading, hoisting and lowering goods, stacking and unstacking barrels. Everything seemed normal: just another ordinary business day at the warehouses on the eastern dock.

'She must be hiding around here somewhere,' he decided.

The mapmaker had insisted on coming with him to the waterfront. 'You'll need help if you are going to find her, dear boy,' he had said as they had hurried down to the eastern docks. Luckily Jade had told

Adam enough for him to know where she was going and he was too consumed by his determination to stop her to listen to the mapmaker. They had split up, searched and now were left wondering what to do next. And all the while Adam couldn't shake the feeling that there was something in all of this that he had missed.

'A boat,' Adam said. 'Jade said something about there being a small boat ...'

'A boat?' the mapmaker repeated. 'That reminds me, I was going to tell you –'

'It must be around here somewhere,' Adam said, ignoring him. He went to the quayside and looked along the line of boats. 'What was it called?' he asked himself without being able to remember. 'The *something Queen*, I think.'

'I was walking along minding my own business,' the mapmaker was saying. 'Anyone would tell you.' He lifted his lenses to peer around and spotted a group of youths who were talking to one of the boatmen. 'They must have seen what happened. That fair-haired one was right there,' he pointed. 'I saw him. Those ruffians almost knocked him into the water. I didn't like the look of any of them. They were hard men.'

'*Men?* What men?' Adam frowned.

'The ones who came out of the warehouse,' the mapmaker said with a hint of exasperation. He pointed to the ladder. 'Yes, I am sure the boat was down there – that's where they took the young man. If you ask me, he didn't look as if he wanted to go with them and I can't blame him!'

'What's this got to do with finding Jade?' Adam asked. 'They were probably just loading ...' He paused.

'A young man, did you say? What did he look like?'

The mapmaker shrugged. 'Hard to tell. His hat was pulled well down. But I would say he was a little shorter than you – not much older.'

'Jade!'

The mapmaker's eyebrows shot up. 'No, Adam, I assure you it was a young man I saw.'

'Wearing a brown coat that was too big?'

The mapmaker seemed surprised. 'Yes, did you see him too?'

Adam didn't answer. He looked towards the group of youths. 'You say they saw what happened?'

The mapmaker nodded. 'Now, Adam, we don't want any trouble …'

But Adam wasn't listening again. He moved quickly along the quayside to the place where the youths were standing. They were wearing an assortment of coats and breeches, all of which had seen better days. It soon became clear that an argument was going on.

'… but someone's *got* to take us!' a fair-haired youth was shouting now.

The boatman folded his arms, giving a fair indication of how he felt about that.

'It's a matter of life and death.'

The boatman glanced from face to face. 'Do I look stupid to you? Do I look like the sort of man who takes four moneyless youths out for a boat ride? If you want to go in my boat you have to pay my rate.'

'But we haven't got that much.' The fair-haired youth caught the boatman by the collar of his shirt.

Suddenly there was a knife in the boatman's hand. 'Back off – *all* of you!'

'I'm sorry, I didn't mean it. It's just they've taken a

friend of ours – a girl ...' the fair-haired youth pleaded with him.

'A girl?' The sound of Adam's voice made them look around.

The mapmaker dragged at Adam's arm. 'I really don't think this is wise ...'

Adam stood his ground. 'You said a *girl*.'

The youths forgot the boatman and formed a line to confront him. 'What's it to you?' one of them asked.

'Did she go in a boat? The *something Queen*?' Adam asked.

The fair-haired youth's eyes narrowed suspiciously. 'And who's asking?'

'This is Adam Windjammer of the Quadrant Shipping and Trading company,' the mapmaker intervened importantly. 'He's young but very well regarded – so there had better be no trouble!'

'*Quadrant?*' the fair-haired youth repeated the name. 'Do you hear that, my friends? *This* is Adam Windjammer.'

They exchanged glances.

'You know me?'

'Oh yes, we know all about the Windjammers,' one of the others spoke up.

'And how your father lost a fortune,' another added.

'We just don't know *why* you're here now,' the fair-haired youth finished.

'For the same reason as you, I'd say,' Adam came to the conclusion. 'Looking for Jade van Helsen.'

'Then you're too late.'

'They took her?'

The fair-haired youth was cautious. It was the others

who gave it away by glancing out at the harbour without thinking.

The boatman confirmed it. He burst through their ranks. 'I'll tell you what I've told them,' he said to Adam. 'I'm not taking my boat out to the marshes unless I get paid. And even then I don't like it.' He glanced about as if he suspected they might want to murder him and steal his boat. 'In fact I want double rate. No less than a guilder – *two* if you want me to bring you back.'

'That's robbery!' the fair-haired youth exclaimed.

'Someone should complain about you,' another agreed.

'Done!' Adam interrupted, causing a stir.

The boatman showed his delight. 'Now that's more like it!' He held out his hand. 'I'll see the money first.'

'Half to take me, half when you've brought me back,' Adam said. 'Mr Merrik here will pay.'

'Adam,' the mapmaker said, reluctantly handing over the money, 'I strongly advise against this course of action.'

'I have to go, Mr Merrik,' Adam lowered his voice. 'I have to find Jade first. If I don't I could lose Quadrant.'

'Is it worth risking your life? I saw those men.'

'I can look after myself.'

'At least let me come with you.'

'No. Go back to my house and tell my mother to expect us. When I find Jade I'll take her there or she'll go straight to warn her father.'

'You would kidnap her again! I thought she was once your friend.'

'She's a van Helsen, Mr Merrik. She can never be anything but that banker's daughter to me,' Adam lied. 'Just meet me here. But remember, he has spies everywhere – so don't tell *anyone*. Will you do that for me?'

The mapmaker sighed. 'Well, of course, you know I would, but –'

'It's agreed, then.'

The mapmaker nodded. As Adam turned away, however, he reached out and stopped him. 'We all do things in life we regret, Adam – you know that, don't you?'

'This is right for me, for my family – for Quadrant, Mr Merrik,' Adam said. 'People are relying on me. Hobe, Hendrik Honthorst, Madam de Witte – we have contracts …'

The mapmaker drew his hand away. There was a strange sad look in his eye. 'Money changes everything – even *you*. I can see that now. It's a blessing and a curse. Sometimes it's even used as a weapon. Will you remember that, Adam, when next we meet? Promise me – *please*, so we can discuss it.'

'We'll have all the time for talk later. I have to go.'

Adam slipped past him and went to the ladder. He was surprised to see the fair-haired youth and his friends already sitting in the boat.

'What are they doing in there?' Adam asked the boatman.

'We're coming with you,' the fair-haired youth answered for him.

'No, you're not.'

'Then you'll have to drag us out, Windjammer.'

Adam glared at him.

The fair-haired youth smiled. 'You might as well get to know us. My name's Valentino. This is Tobias, Aert and Raphael. They don't look much, but they're useful in a fight. And there's going to be a fight, Windjammer, you mark my words.'

'Why are you doing this? What's Jade to you anyway?' Adam asked. He was surprised by the twinge of jealousy he felt.

'It's a long story,' Valentino said. 'Maybe I'll get Raphael to write it down for you. But all you need to know for now is – she's a friend.'

'One of us,' Tobias agreed.

'And we look after our own,' Aert added.

Raphael just nodded.

After a brief pause, Adam gave in to the inevitable. 'All right, you can come along,' he said. 'But you do what *I* say, right?'

'*Right*,' Valentino said and grinned as he watched Adam climb down.

Adam sat in the bow, apart from the rest, looking up at the tall ships as the boatman worked his small boat out of the harbour. The wind was light and the small sail struggled to catch the breeze. He looked back at the waterfront, watching the mapmaker until he was out of sight. He sensed more had been meant than said, but he had other things on his mind now.

The eastern marshes stretched away in front of them. It was a lonely place, vast and open, the wetlands steaming a gentle mist. Great flocks of waterfowl turned on the wing: oyster-catchers and lapwings flicked to and fro. Bird calls as sharp as pins pricked the air. The ghostly song of the curlews – their shrieks like the voices of lost spirits calling – increased the sense of loneliness; as formations of ducks and geese fired across the sky like arrows falling somewhere out of sight.

340

Then the mill came sliding across the horizon. Blunting up against the sky, it's brooding shape dominated everything. They were still some way off when Tobias noticed the smoke of the fire drifting up out of the mist to smudge the lowering clouds.

The boatman stood at the tiller, frowning. 'The old mill on the Westerdijk's been empty for years – as long as I can remember.'

'Looks like someone's at home now,' Valentino said.

Adam searched the widening expanse of water to their left for any sign of a sail. The Zuider Zee spread away into the fog, empty as far as they could see. He turned his attention back to the mill and the jutting point of land beyond.

'Why don't we sail in and take a closer look?' Tobias suggested.

'And why not bang a drum instead?' Aert said. 'That way we'll be sure to let them know we're coming.'

'I say we go ashore,' Valentino said. 'They won't be expecting anyone to come from the marshes. But then you're in charge, Master Windjammer.'

Adam detected a hint of sarcasm in his tone. 'Listen to me – all of you,' he said. 'I didn't ask you to come along, but you're here now so if we're going to find Jade and bring her back then we're going to have to work together.'

Valentino nodded. 'He's got a point there.' He paused and gave Adam a long hard look. 'Just one question. Why do *you* want Jade back so badly? She's the daughter of that moneylender – how can she be a friend of yours?'

A pause, then Adam answered him, 'This is business – just business.'

'Somehow,' Valentino hunched his shoulders, 'I doubt that.'

They told the boatman to steer in towards the shore and he did so reluctantly.

'Them there's the hol lands,' he warned. 'There are bogs out there so deep they'll swallow a man and leave only his hat floating on top for others to find.'

'His hat?' Tobias tugged at his pot-shaped Tudor cap and eyed the marshes nervously.

'Then there's the marsh witches,' the boatman went on, clearly a superstitious type. 'And fairy folk – the goblins, imps and gnome people – not to mention the *kabolas*.'

'What are kabolas?' Aert asked as if he didn't really want to know.

'Only madmen can see them – but the kabolas bring bad luck wherever they go. They'll steal your children and bring the plague and they can make people vanish into the air, just like that.' He clicked his fingers.

'Here, Raph!' Aert said. 'You want to put all that into one of your stories.'

'Will you keep your voices down?' Adam hissed.

'You heard him,' Valentino said.

The boatman steered in under the dead branches of an ancient elm. They jumped ashore.

'I want my return fare now,' the boatman said. 'You'll not be coming back – not from there. If you ask me you all belong in the madhouse.'

Valentino tied the boat firmly to a branch.

'You'll get your money when we come back,' he said. 'And just in case those kabolas of yours come along and make you forget all about us,' he added drily, 'we'll leave Raphael here to keep watch. He doesn't say much, but he likes stories – don't you, Raph?' He settled his hat. 'And I have a feeling this is going to be a good one.'

25. The Old Mill on the Westerdijk

Distance plays tricks on the eyes in a flat place. In the marshes each tussock of reed grass seems the same as the next and the mist thickens the waterlogged ground to swallow the unwary as the open flats stretch on and on.

Only the mill stood out, one constant in a place that seemed to shift around them endlessly in swirling eddies. Adam, Valentino, Tobias and Aert walked in single file and for a while managed to keep a straight line towards it. Gradually, however, the land settled into long stretches of peat bog and it soon sucked them in. Walking became harder, their stops for rest more frequent. Eventually the ground became so water-logged they thought they had stumbled upon a river only to find the water formed small lakes. They were forced to go around and it wasn't until some time later that, muddied and bedraggled, they approached the windmill along a winding stream.

'We'll go up and take a look,' Adam whispered to Valentino as they crouched among the bushes on the slope of the dyke. 'You two stay here and keep quiet!'

They crawled closer, worming into the thicker bushes, making their way towards the base of the tower. They paused and studied the wooden walkway that ran around the outside of the mill. A man with a musket was standing sentry on the gallery. He walked slowly to and fro, keeping watch. But he appeared to expect trouble to come from the sea and was paying scant attention to the marshes behind where the mist turned everything vague.

The smoke they had seen from a distance was rising from a fire that had been lit close to the base of the tower to one side of the door. There, another of Valerius's men was sitting on his heels, feeding pieces of wood into the flames. Every now and again he would turn the spits over the fire as he cooked an assortment of waterfowl. The fire hissed and crackled as the fat dripped and the rich smell of roasting duck carried on the air. The only other sounds came from the sucking wetness of the bogs.

'I count only two,' Valentino whispered.

'Three,' Adam said. 'I saw one inside.'

'There were more of them at the quayside than just three,' Valentino assured him.

Together they made their way further up on to the dyke to get a better view. As they reached the top, the marshes on the other side were revealed to them, stretching away to the point of land that jutted into the wide expanse of the Zuider Zee. And there they saw the schooner.

A bluish haze hung over the water and made it seem as if the whole scene was glazed into a piece of Delftware. The ship lay at anchor, the sails furled fore and aft on her two masts. There were no flags flying from the mastheads to distinguish her.

Valentino nudged Adam and pointed towards the water's edge. Below the dyke, some way off, half a dozen men or more were unloading supplies from a lugger.

'Can you see Jade?' Adam asked.

Valentino shook his head.

'Then she's either aboard the schooner or there.' Adam glanced up at the mill.

'It looks like they're eating and sleeping here,' Valentino said, 'so my money's on the mill.'

'Let's hope you're right,' Adam said, easing back.

'Where are you going?'

'To take a look inside.'

'You'll never get past the guards.'

Adam glanced up. To his left, he could see some steps leading to the walkway on the outside of the windmill. From there one of the mill's sails rose to meet the three others forming an X at the hub. The canvas on the sails had rotted away, leaving the cross-pieces of wood exposed. It reminded him of a giant ladder leading up to a small door at the top.

'That door must've been used by the mill keeper to reach the sails.' Adam pointed it out. 'If I can climb up there, I should be able to get in.'

'Aren't you forgetting someone?' Valentino nodded at the sentry patrolling the walkway underneath.

'That's where you come in,' Adam said. 'You have to think of a way to draw them all around to the front just long enough for me to get inside.'

'Have you lost your wits?' Valentino hissed. 'They'll kill me on sight. I'm beginning to think that boatman was right. We must be crazy coming here.' A pause. He thought about what he had just said and dismissed it.

'What is it?' Adam gave him a hard look.

'Just something the boatman said – something about the kabolas.'

'*Kabolas?* What have they got to do with it?'

'Just that they bring bad luck and misfortune,' Valentino said. He looked thoughtful. 'Only a madman can see them, that's what the boatman said – and I'm mad enough to be here ...'

'I still don't know what you're talking about.'

'Well, maybe I've just thought of a way to get you into that mill,' Valentino said, beginning to look pleased with himself. 'But I'll need Tobias and Aert's help.'

'You'd better make it fast. The rest of them won't be unloading that lugger for much longer.'

'You let me worry about that. Just be ready to make that climb. I'll see that the guards don't bother you. Whatever happens, whatever you hear, just get in and find Jade if she's there. We'll meet back down there in the stream beyond the bushes.' He looked Adam in the eye. 'Don't let us down, Windjammer.'

And with that he was gone.

Adam crouched in the bushes and looked at the steps leading up to the walkway. They were weathered to a gnarled grey and rotten in places. He wondered now if they would take his weight. His legs felt unwieldy and heavy as if his insides had been sucked down into them, leaving the rest of him empty. He wiped at his mouth with the back of his hand. A quick glance down towards the jetty told him the men had almost finished unloading the lugger.

'Where are you, Valentino?' he murmured.

It started with a high-pitched, giggling kind of laugh; crackling on the quiet it brought everyone to a sudden alert. Through the bushes, Adam could just see Valentino sitting cross-legged on the grass. He was now wearing Aert's hat and to the men at the mill it must have seemed he had appeared from nowhere. The sentry was so startled he fumbled and almost dropped his musket. He strode along the walkway to the front and looked down.

'I've told you before, haven't I?' Valentino's voice rose, a slight sing-song quality in the pitch. 'I've said a dozen times you're not to come here bothering these good people.' He leaned forward and shook a finger at the space in front of him. 'Now, there's nothing to go smiling about. I don't want any trouble.'

The cook appeared around the corner. He had a club in his hand. Another – the third man Adam had seen – appeared at his shoulder and they exchanged looks of complete amazement with the sentry on the walkway.

'What's that you say?' Valentino spoke loudly, looking down at thin air. 'No, no, no – you can't do that.'

The sentry recovered from the surprise first. 'Who are you? Where did you come from?'

Valentino glanced up. 'I live here,' he replied happily. 'And so do they.'

'No one lives in the marshes.' The sentry raised his musket threateningly. 'What are you talking about? Who else is there?'

'Only them.' Valentino pointed to the ground at his feet. 'Handsome, aren't they, but very nosy. I've told them before not to come bothering others. In my experience people just don't understand them.'

The men exchanged more glances. 'I can't see no one,' the sentry said. The others glanced about. Neither could they.

'I've told you before,' Valentino said, speaking to the ground again. 'You have to wait to be invited to dinner. And don't you make that face at me!' He glanced up with an exaggerated sigh. 'They can be so rude sometimes.'

'You're a madman,' the sentry concluded suddenly.

The others seemed relieved and agreed. And – as is often the way with people who don't fully understand something – they began to laugh.

Adam took his chance. He slipped out of the bushes and over to the steps. Climbing quickly, he did his best to avoid the rotten treads and came up at the level of the walkway. Around the curving wall, he could just see the sentry's shoulder. The sail of the windmill laddered up, but he needed to stand on the walkway's wooden rail to reach it. He eased up, teetering on the edge before he made the jump on to the sail. The wood creaked alarmingly as he kicked his legs and swung himself up.

'What was that?' the sentry said, looking around.

Adam froze, pressed flat against the sail. The curve of the wall meant he was just out of sight as long as the sentry didn't move.

'Oh, don't you worry, sir,' Valentino came to his feet. He did a little jig on the spot, drawing the sentry's attention down once more. 'It's only them playing games.'

'Them? *Who* are you talking about?' The sentry was growing agitated. He levelled his musket and pointed down into the bushes.

Valentino showed no hint of concern. 'Now look what's happened!' he said. 'You put that back!' He shook his head, tut-tutting. 'I can only say I'm very, very sorry for what they've done.'

'Done?' the sentry rounded on him. 'Stop your raving! What are you talking about?'

'About your dinner, sir.' Valentino pointed towards the fire. 'They've gone and helped themselves – without even asking.'

All turned towards the fire now. Adam began to climb.

Hand over hand, he went. Testing each strut quickly before trusting it with his weight. The sail creaked and he thought it might tear away from the hub, sending him plunging to the ground. But there was no going back now. He heaved himself up with his breath coming in short pulls and had almost reached the top when one of the struts gave way under his foot. He went down with gut-wrenching suddenness only to come to a jarring stop as the strut below held. For a moment he was thrown wildly off balance, swinging giddily over the drop until he managed to drag himself back against the sail, clinging on, hardly daring to look down. When he did, however, he was relieved to see the men below were all looking at the fire.

'I tell you there were two of them.' The cook's words carried up to him. 'The finest ducks – *gone*.'

'Yes.' Valentino nodded sadly. 'They do like a good duck.'

'How did you do that?' the sentry called down.

'Don't look at me, sir,' Valentino said. 'It was *them*.'

Adam pulled himself up on to the hub of the sails and found he could easily reach the small door. It wouldn't budge. He tried again, prizing his fingers into the gap around the edge. It gave suddenly. The drop dizzied away beneath him. In a surreal moment he hung there, with Valentino jigging and dancing far below, shouting, 'You put them back!' Then he recovered his senses and eased back the door. No one saw him as he crawled inside.

The smell hit him at once, the ammonia from the guano excreted by generations of storks caught in the back of his throat. Adam slithered in their droppings, crawling in under the nests, squeezing between fallen roof supports and a complex interconnection of broken wooden cogs to reach a trapdoor in the floor.

The trap was open and he found himself looking down into the main body of the tower. A wooden shaft had once connected the sails to the pumping mechanism at the base of the mill. They drew his eye down through the floor into a great volume of darkness crisscrossed by thin grey lines of daylight coming through slitted windows, catching on the motes of dust suspended in the air.

There were no steps down from the trapdoor, so he eased his legs over the edge and slipped through to hang by his fingers, hoping the rotten floor would hold his weight when he dropped. He rolled to break his fall and came up into a crouch. The thump set dull echoes running around the walls and disturbed a pigeon. The bird flapped up with a sharp snapping of its wings, startling him. It settled again and fixed him with one bright eye.

Adam listened. He could still hear Valentino talking and laughing, but there was a slightly strained tone to his voice now. It seemed the men were beginning to grow weary of the show. Adam glanced up at the trap above him. It was too high to reach. There would be no return that way.

Steps led down to the floor below and he ducked to take a quick look under the beams. As his eyes adjusted to the dimness he picked out objects lying around: a table, a sea chest, a lantern among other things. He counted at least twenty straw mattresses. A door led on to the walkway outside. It was open and he could see the sentry standing with his back to him.

'What have you done with the captain's ducks?' The cook's voice rose to a bellow.

'I think you'll find them over there in the bushes,' Valentino replied.

There was a pause while the third man went to see. 'He's right!' he called back. 'They're here – half eaten.'

'Well, don't say I didn't warn you,' Valentino said.

The cook was furious. 'Can you see anyone?' he called up to the sentry.

Adam had to dodge behind the open door, pressing his back into the wall as the sentry made a complete circuit of the tower, scanning the bushes below with his musket ready, before returning to the place where he had started.

'No – no one,' he announced.

An uneasy silence descended on them.

Adam went down on to his hands and knees and looked through the gaps in the floor. Light was coming through the open door in the base of the tower. He picked out the huge cogs and wheels of the windmill's machinery. He could smell the ancient horse fat that had once been used to grease the wheels. There was a table and several stools and … He moved holes several times until he could see clearly.

Jade was lying on a pile of sacks, tethered by the neck to an iron ring in the wall. He could see her wrists and ankles were tied.

'Psst!' he hissed. 'Jade. It's me – Adam.'

He called several times before she stirred and looked around.

'Adam?' she murmured.

'Up here!' he whispered.

She looked up and saw him through the hole in the floor.

'What ... are you doing? How did you find me?'

'Shh!' He made a cautious descent of the steps, passing the open door with great care. Valentino was still doing his very best to confuse the men by having a furious argument with himself over who was to blame for stealing the ducks.

'I heard someone talking,' she said. 'Laughing.'

'That's Valentino.'

'*Valentino?*'

'No time to explain,' he whispered. 'Right now we have to get you out of here – *fast.*'

Adam pulled at the knots with his teeth. She winced as the blood flowed back into her hands and feet.

'Can you walk?' he asked.

She nodded, but she found it hard to stand up at first. Adam helped her over to the steps and they were about to start up when events outside took a turn for the worse.

'I've had enough of this,' Adam heard the cook say. He saw what happened next through the open door. The cook pushed Valentino aside and started jumping up and down and clubbing the ground. 'There – *that*'s what I think of your invisible friends!'

A stunned silence followed. Valentino just stared at the ground. Then he sank to his knees. 'You've killed him!' he wailed. He buried his face in his hands, blubbering. But all the while he was looking through his fingers.

Adam left Jade and went to the door. He gave Valentino a signal, a sign that it was time to go, then fled with Jade up the steps. Behind them, a change came over Valentino as he rose from his knees and turned to the men, his face set, his expression grim. The sentry saw danger in it and called out, 'Stay where you are – or I'll blow your head off!'

'You killed him!' Valentino snarled. 'And now there's nothing I can do. They'll take a life for a life, that's what they'll do. They'll make someone vanish into the air, you mark my words!'

Adam helped Jade in behind the open door leading to the walkway and together they waited to see what would happen next. There was a long pause, then the cook started laughing, setting off the others until the tower echoed with their grunts.

'And which one of us will they take?' the cook finally huffed. 'Come on – tell us! We're all waiting.'

Valentino's reply cut the laughter dead. 'It's not *you* they want. It's *her* – the one you've got inside.'

Silence.

'Wait for it,' Adam breathed.

Then everything happened at once. The sentry spun on his heel and burst through the door into the storeroom. He thundered on past and took the steps down at the run to meet the other two as they fought their way in through the door below.

'No – it can't be!' the sentry snarled.

'She's gone!' the cook gasped.

'Vanished into thin air!' the third man said.

Adam and Jade wasted no time slipping out from behind the door and on to the walkway. As quickly and as quietly as they could, they made their way around the curve of the tower and down the steps. They dodged under the overhanging walkway and flattened themselves against the wall just as shouts exploded inside the windmill.

The men inside had remembered Valentino and wanted blood now. The sentry thundered back up on to the walkway and made a complete circuit without seeing Jade and Adam right under his feet. By now the cook and the third man had armed themselves and rushed out in front of the mill, bellowing.

'He's gone! Vanished just like the girl!' the cook said when their search for Valentino produced no result.

'What kind of witchcraft is this?' the sentry asked nervously.

Suddenly all three were seized by superstitious dread and began discharging their muskets, firing wildly into the bushes. The noise reverberated through the tower, scaring an assortment of birds from their nests in the roof.

'I think it's time we were somewhere else,' Adam whispered.

26. Something Lost, Nothing Gained

'Jade!' Valentino caught her as she came sliding down the dyke and dropped into the cut of the stream.

'Valentino!' she said and hugged him in relief.

Adam slid down and glared at them, that same jealousy burning his insides. '*I'm* the one who got you out, remember!'

'You couldn't have done it without me,' Valentino said. '*And* you took your time in there.'

'It's not that easy climbing up and down windmills, you know –'

They were interrupted by an urgent whisper from the bushes above.

'Any chance of a bit of help here?' Aert hissed through gritted teeth. He was helping Tobias along, his arm tucked under one shoulder. 'He's been hit.'

'I'm all right,' Tobias said. But there was a red stain growing fast between his fingers as he gripped his side. 'They got in a lucky shot when they started blasting, that's all.'

'I warned you not to go back for that duck,' Aert said.

'Well, I was hungry.'

There was a lot of blood and Valentino took a quick look. 'The ball's passed clean through,' he said. 'It's deep, but you'll live ...' He heard shouts from the mill and added, '... for now at least.'

They could see the men from the lugger swarming over the dyke, their shapes dark against the sky as they closed in around the mill. A dog was barking furiously.

'Time to go, I think,' Valentino said, slipping his shoulder under Tobias's other arm.

They set off along the cut of the stream, vanishing into the mist. Behind them, Valerius pushed through his men and aimed a kick at the dog.

'What happened?' he asked in a dangerous voice.

'It was witchcraft – pure sorcery,' the cook assured them all dramatically. 'The marsh spirits came and took her away. There were hundreds of them. They were horrible to look at –'

A hand lashed out and smacked him hard across the face. The cook clutched at his cheek and cowered back as Valerius strode away around the tower. He stopped when he reached the bushes where the carcasses of the two half-eaten ducks lay. He spotted something among the twigs and reached out, catching its wetness on the tips of his fingers.

'Marsh spirits, you say? Then these spirits *bleed*!' he snarled into a turn. 'Get the weapons! Spread out! I want green eyes back and whoever's with her *dead*.'

The pursuit began with a series of terrifying howls and shrieks. Adam had just helped Jade up the slippery bank and was waiting to lend the others a hand with

Tobias when he heard the blood-lust noise rising above them.

'They're on to us, then,' Valentino said.

Adam glanced about. Ahead of them, the marshy flats stretched away into the mist. There was nowhere to hide and, without a fixed point like the mill to guide them, he knew it was going to be very hard to find the boat quickly enough to escape. He drew an imaginary line from the mill back to the dead elm. It was a guess, little more. He knew their only real hope lay in cutting up to the edge of the marsh and following the shoreline until they came across the boat.

'We'll never make it,' Aert said, when Adam explained what they had to do.

'Would you rather end up going around in circles until they find us?' Adam asked.

Valentino thought and saw the sense in his plan. 'Windjammer's right – we could be lost out here in the fog for ever.'

So they made up their minds and stumbled on, dragging an increasingly listless Tobias with them. But no matter how hard they tried to go around it, the marsh just seemed to suck them in. As before, they kept finding their way blocked by stretches of peat bog and tracts of open water. More than once they had to go back or around. To make matters worse, the mist seemed full of half-imagined shadows. Each eye-tricking swirl struck terror into them. They were driven on, their feet sinking into the ooze at every step. And all the while they could hear the sounds of the pursuit behind them, drawing closer and closer as they were remorselessly hunted down.

'I can't go on.' It was Tobias who brought their run

to an end. He was weak from the loss of blood. 'You'll have to leave me.'

'We're in this together,' Valentino said.

'But I'm only slowing you down,' Tobias insisted.

It was true and they all knew it. But they would not leave him out there to die and struggled on.

Adam stumbled into it first. He had slithered down a jutting peat bank and taken two steps when he felt himself sinking. He went down with surprising speed and was up to his knees before he realised he had stumbled into a quagmire. He shouted a warning over his shoulder and threw himself backwards, landing flat.

'I'm sinking!' he called, fighting a rising panic as he tried to backstroke through the ooze. 'Quick – pull me out!'

Valentino and Aert left Tobias propped up against the peat bank and dragged at Adam. It took Jade's help to free him and they all collapsed against the bank, panting for breath.

'We'll have to go around,' Valentino said.

'We'll never make it,' Aert gasped. 'Anyway, Tobias has had it.'

Tobias's face was very pale. He sat propped up against the bank with his eyes closed. He was shivering and mumbling. Valentino took off his coat and spread it over him.

So it was there, at that line of peat, trapped against the sucking ooze of a deadly quagmire, that they finally decided to make their stand. A quick check for weapons produced only Adam's knife.

Aert forced a laugh. 'Maybe we can scare them away by making faces.'

'Don't worry,' Valentino said, giving Aert back his

hat. 'I've ten stuviers that says they won't find us in the mist.'

For once, no one took the bet.

After that, all they could do was wait. They pressed their backs into the sodden earth, with the rich dead smell of the ancient peat filling their nostrils, listening to the sounds of the approaching hunt. It soon became clear that Valerius's men were strung out in a line and coming straight for them.

'I'm sorry I got you into this,' Jade whispered when it was clear they wouldn't escape.

Valentino smiled. 'Like I said before, you're one of us now.'

'And we look after our own, don't we, Tobias?' Aert added.

Tobias managed a smile and a nod.

Jade looked away. Adam sat staring at the quagmire in front of them. If there were words for him she couldn't find them. Instead she stood up.

'It's me they want,' she said. 'Maybe if I go to them I can make them believe you're lost in the bogs or something ...'

'No!' Valentino and Aert said together.

'Don't let her do it,' Tobias gasped.

'It's the only way,' Jade insisted. 'If I don't they'll kill you all.'

'Well, let's not shout too loudly about it,' Valentino said. 'We don't want to make it easy for them ...'

It was as Valentino spoke that Adam's ideas suddenly came together. Strangely, it was something Jacques Talon had said that brought the strands of a plan together. 'If you can fool your enemy,' he murmured, 'you can outmanoeuvre him ...'

'What did he say?' Aert asked.

It came to Adam then so rapidly he wondered why he hadn't thought of it before. He looked up sharply. 'You're right, Aert – we will have to scare them off. Only we won't be making faces. We'll be making noise – *lots* of noise.'

'How did you ever get mixed up with him?' Valentino asked Jade with a roll of his eyes.

Adam ignored them and pulled off his coat. He scrumpled it up into a ball and hurled it as far as he could into the quagmire in front of them.

'Give me your hat!' Adam said to Aert. Before Aert could stop him, he had snatched it off his head and sent it spinning after the coat. 'Now start shouting, all of you! Scream, yell – do anything you can to draw their attention.'

'Has the marsh sucked out your senses?' Valentino hissed. 'You'll bring them right to us.'

'And when they get here, all they'll see is clothes and a hat on the marsh. They'll think we've been sucked down. They'll think we're dead.'

'And just *where* are we going to hide?' Valentino asked.

'Right under their noses.' Adam pointed out the way the peat bank rose and curled over slightly at the top. 'They won't be able to see us unless they come right to the edge.'

'It'll never work,' Aert said.

'Have you got a better idea?' Adam asked.

Aert hadn't. Valentino thought about it and decided he hadn't either.

'Maybe there's more to you than I thought, Windjammer,' he said.

They started uncertainly, but soon got into it, trying to outdo each other, shouting, screaming, bellowing and calling for help: 'I'm sinking!' 'We're drowning!' 'The mud, the mud!' Their calls became increasingly desperate until, on Adam's signal, they stopped one by one and lunged against the bank.

Adam was the last one standing. He shrieked one final gurgling wail just as he saw shadows appearing out of the mist. He threw himself into the side of the bank and scrambled up beside Jade who had a view over the top between the tufts of marsh grass. Everywhere they looked now they could see wraith-like shapes advancing out of the whiteness. The shapes formed themselves into men and they came on cautiously, stopping a little way from the top of the bank. One pointed at something floating on the marsh ahead of them.

The men spoke in low voices and a mixture of languages, only some of it was in Dutch. But there was no mistaking the fear. Superstition and dread had gripped them, brought on by the mist and the terror of the marsh.

'I know the hol lands,' a Dutch voice spoke up. 'Only a fool would go into a hole like that. The mud sucks you down – we all heard the way they screamed.'

Then one among them pushed his way through and stepped forward.

'Valerius,' Jade breathed.

Their captain had the dog on a rope. It was pulling hard, straining to be free. He began shoving his men forward, but they refused to go any further.

'You'll do as I say or I'll set the dog on you!' Valerius snarled. But no matter how he lashed out, no matter what threats he used, the men still hung back.

Fear gripped them. The line wavered as one by one they stepped back. Valerius released the dog, but to his surprise it didn't go leaping forward. It must have sensed the danger too, because it turned with a yelp and ran.

'I told you!' one man spoke up – it was the sentry from the mill. 'Even the dog can sense it! There's witchcraft here.'

'And death too,' another agreed.

They glanced at each other, standing in line for a short time longer before one among them turned. The rest broke suddenly and fled back through the mist towards the windmill.

'Stand, damn you! *Stand!*' Valerius drew his blade and slashed at the air. But nothing could stop them now. He gave up on them and turned.

Jade ducked down the bank. Adam followed her and they curled themselves under the overhang. They soon heard the sound of Valerius's breathing. It was short and ragged, drawn sharply in over clenched teeth. None dared look up as he came to stand at the top of the bank.

'You're here – I know you are!' he called out, so terrifyingly close.

He scanned the mist around him, his head turning slowly on his neck, this way and that as if it was detached from the body below. The line of the peat bank caught his eye and he followed it back until inevitably his gaze was drawn right down to his feet.

'So you've been playing games, have you?' he said when he saw them.

Valerius launched himself off the top of the bank

with a snarl. It was a huge leap designed to stop them escaping. He landed with a shout, his boots plugging deep into the sucking ooze. But he was lithe and fit and full of fury. He came around with a sharp twist to face them.

'Come back, you cowards!' he called to his men. 'I have them – like crows in a trap.'

His lips pulled back, baring his teeth like an animal as he cut at the mist with his blade. They shrank away from him. He tried to take a step towards them. Only then did he realise the fatal mistake he had made.

Valerius grunted and looked down at his feet. He tried to lift one leg, but only succeeded in forcing the other in further. Before he knew it, he was up to his thighs and struggling hard.

'Arrrgh!' he snarled and slashed wildly about with his blade. He was drawn in over his waist and, with surprising speed, up to his chest. His eyes grew wider and he stabbed furiously at the marsh as if it was something he could kill.

'Darius! Gregor! Salim! Help me!' he called for his men. 'I'm sinking, damn you! Going down.'

It all happened so fast. Adam and the others hardly had time to move. They looked on, half-fearing Valerius's shouts would bring his men back, half-mesmerised by the terrible sight in front of them. It was Jade who took a step forward. She tried to reach Valerius, only to be pulled into the mud herself. Adam and Valentino hauled her out by the arms. By the time she was safe again, Valerius was pleading with them for help.

'I'll let you go!' he shouted. 'I give my word on it. I'll give you anything. Money, money, you *must* want money! Everyone wants to be rich – *rich*. Just get me out of here.'

But there was nothing they could do. Valerius saw the hopelessness of it and began to panic. His struggles only made it worse. He sank up to his neck. His screams became more and more desperate, but with a remorseless suck the quagmire drew him down as if the Devil himself had reached up and caught him by the ankle.

'Damn you – damn you all!' he snarled at the last. His eyes grew wide and staring, his lips twisted. 'Help meeeeeeeeeeeeeeee …'

Jade turned away as the mud ran into his mouth and choked off his shout. The mire closed over his face, the slime churning thickly as he struggled to the last, one hand sticking up, the fingers hooking at the sky until it was drawn under.

And after the noise, a terrible silence descended upon them – filled only with the endless suck and ooze of the marsh.

The boatman eased his boat along the quayside. He turned to look at the muddied and bedraggled group in front of him.

'I don't know what happened out there,' he said, eyeing Tobias's wound, 'and I don't want to know. But maybe you'll listen to me next time – them marshes aren't the place to go.'

It was beginning to get dark and it had been some time since they had struggled out of the mist and into the boat. Tobias had lost a lot of blood, but once he was able to stop moving the flow had stemmed.

The boatman shook his head. 'I'll have my money

now,' he said. 'And a stuvier or two more if you want me to forget I ever saw you.'

'It's all right, boatman,' a voice called from above. 'I'm here to pay for them.'

Adam looked up and was relieved to see the map-maker on the quayside, peering down through his lenses. 'Are you all right, my boy? You look terrible.'

'We need a doctor, Mr Merrik,' Adam said.

'A doctor!'

Aert and Raphael helped Tobias out of the boat and together they manhandled him up the ladder.

Adam reached out to Jade. 'You're coming with me.'

She pulled her arm away and stood up, rocking the boat.

'Not if she doesn't want to,' Valentino said.

'You stay out of this,' Adam hissed at him.

'You'll have to make me, Windjammer.'

'I can look after myself,' Jade spoke up.

'I know that,' said Valentino, 'but I just want to be sure you're safely on your way.'

'See to Tobias first,' she insisted. 'He needs you more.'

Valentino reluctantly made his way up the ladder.

Adam leaned forward. 'There's no use running,' he warned Jade. 'Mr Merrik's up there. I sent him for help.'

Jade held his gaze, chin up. 'You're just like all the rest,' she said, a slight curl to her lip. 'I suppose you think it's just business, don't you? But it isn't, because it never is. It's about people's lives and dreams. You of all people should understand that.'

She jumped across the gap between the boat and the ladder and climbed quickly to the top. Adam wasted no time in following her up. As he came level with the quayside a scene unfolded before him. Everyone was standing very still: Jade with her back to him, Valentino to one side, Aert and Raphael kneeling beside Tobias, and the mapmaker facing them all. There was great sadness in his eyes.

Adam pulled himself up and came wearily to his feet. 'What is it, Mr Merrik? What's wrong?'

'I'm sorry, Adam,' the mapmaker said. 'I had no choice.'

With that he stood aside and Hugo van Helsen stepped forward. Adam just stared. The banker's gaze ran over them all before settling on Jade. He beckoned her forward and, after an uncertain pause, she obeyed. She walked, straight-backed, to stand in front of him. His pale eyes narrowed as he looked at her hair and clothes.

'Is this some pathetic attempt to be the son I always wanted?' her father asked quietly.

Jade looked stunned.

'I asked you a question,' he said, raising his voice.

'I only wanted to help you –' she started.

His fury came upon him suddenly and he slapped her hard across the face, sending her stumbling back.

Adam took a step forward.

'Stay out of this, Windjammer!' Hugo van Helsen rounded on him. 'This is between me and my daughter!'

Jade's chin came up slightly and for a moment she stood defiantly before him. Then the girl who had always been so full of spirit, so determined and strong, lowered her gaze and stared at her feet.

'That's better,' her father said. 'As for you, Adam

Windjammer, be thankful that I am glad you have brought my daughter back safely. From what Mr Merrik here tells me, she has been more than fortunate.'

Adam saw the truth of it then. He looked at the mapmaker. 'It was you all the time, wasn't it? *You* were the spy ...'

'Adam, please –'

'You pretended to be my friend,' Adam hissed. 'You *lied* to me – you even blamed Mr Glass.'

'Mr Glass was keeping an eye on you too.' The mapmaker clutched at the truth. 'Only he was in Bartholomew de Leiden's pay.' He stood wringing his hands. 'I never wanted to do it. I had no choice – I owed Mr van Helsen money.'

'Oh, come now, Mr Merrik. You are being too modest.' Hugo van Helsen took pleasure in exposing the lie. 'Why don't you tell him about the new appointment you have been hankering after – the one I have secured for you as official mapmaker to the East India Company?'

'I tried to tell you, Adam,' the mapmaker said weakly. 'Really I did. But everything got out of hand –'

'I don't want to hear it,' Adam interrupted. You lied – you sold me out.'

A thin smile pulled at the corner of the banker's lips. 'You see, Adam Windjammer? Everyone has their price. But then you know that. From what Mr Merrik tells me, you have a ruthless streak I wasn't aware of. I'll have to watch that in future. But for now I suggest you go home.' He snapped his fingers and Goltz stepped forward. 'Bring Jade!'

Valentino rose to her defence. 'She only wanted to

help you!' he faced up to the banker. 'She only wanted to stop you making a fool of yourself with Atlas van der Stolk.'

'I will deal with van der Stolk in my own way,' Hugo van Helsen said.

'*Now* – yes,' Valentino stood firm. 'But you'd never have known anything was wrong if it wasn't for Jade.'

Hugo van Helsen's lips drew into a tight line. 'Give this ... *person* ... a purse of monies, Goltz. Tell him to take it, and his friends, and leave Amsterdam.'

'You can't make us,' Valentino said.

'Oh, I can,' the banker said, 'and I will. And I'm warning you, if I hear one word of this business at the Bourse I will have you hunted down and dragged to the House of Correction. Believe me – I'll see you rot there for ever!'

Hugo van Helsen took Jade by the arm and led her away. As she passed, Adam saw the look in her eyes: they were cold green now, as if some spark – some essence of her life – had been snuffed out.

27. Dam Square, 13th October 1637

The morning: a vigorous breeze was blowing off the
North Sea. It brought bursts of rain to dampen the
streets of Amsterdam. In the New Church on the edge
of Dam Square the guests huddled against the cold. A
small crowd of the interested uninvited had gathered
on the cobbles outside to watch. Soldiers of the Civil
Guard, wearing helmets and breastplates and carrying
halberds were lined up to keep them at a distance.

The Englishman, Henry the goldsmith, stood under
the great arched door with the weight of the church on
his right side. He was finely dressed in red velvet and
brocade; a tall hat covered his greying hair, pressing
out his ears into a vaguely farcical look. Perhaps he
had been handsome once. Now, at fifty-five years old,
he was just wealthy. To Jade he was an old, old man.

The carriage rattled across the cobbles. She felt each
jarring rut and guttered drain. Her father sat on the
bench opposite and hooked back the curtain with one
finger, looking out at the assembled crowd. He had
never known success so huge and so complete. Jade
watched him passively, submissively; the golden dress

she wore was drawn so tight at her ribs it felt suffocating. The coach rattled to a stop and the curtain door was thrown back. Faces looked in, people were smiling at her pain. The voices sounded like sea birds crying on the wind and all the while the church bell struck at the air, tolling now for her.

Adam Windjammer pushed his way through to the front of the crowd and stopped under the orderly stare of one of the soldiers standing with his halberd sloped. Adam didn't know yet how he would do it, only that he had to talk to Jade; he had to try and explain. On the way there, his head had been filled with wild visions of riding across the square on a white horse. He imagined himself galloping up and sweeping her off her feet, riding away into the sunset. But it was a sunless morning and he had no horse. He didn't even have a plan, just a vague determination to somehow make things right.

Polite applause rippled through the crowd as the carriage pulled up. The horses stood blowing through their noses, shifting in their traces, stamping at the cobbles. Hugo van Helsen stepped out on to a red carpet and greeted the crowd with a wave, then turned back and held out a hand to help his daughter down.

Jade emerged, pale, into the chill. Her cropped hair was now disguised, wreathed in golden leaves and looped with silk to match her dress and slippers. She appeared to have been gilded and she shimmered as she moved – as if, like King Midas, her father had turned her to gold with his touch. Just the sight of her left Adam feeling breathless. He had never seen her look so beautiful, or so tragic.

'Jade!' he called out, one more voice in the crowd. He attempted to get around the guard as the people moved forward for a better look. They were met by the flat shaft of the soldiers' halberds and pushed back.

Adam worked his way along, weaving through the people, losing sight of Jade briefly behind the carriage and horses before he drew near the rising stone arch of the church door. There he found Valentino. Despite the obvious danger, he had been drawn to watch.

'I didn't mean to,' Adam tried to explain. It sounded so weak. 'I never meant any of this to happen.'

'Tell *her* that,' Valentino said, without looking at him.

Adam pushed his way through to the front again and came up alongside Hugo van Helsen as he led Jade along the carpet to the church door.

'Jade!'

He saw her stiffen slightly. She turned with a look that was empty and cold – as if somehow she was not really there. Her father's hand clamped hers firmly into the crook of his left arm.

Jade looked away without a word, staring straight ahead. In that instant Adam knew it was too late. He felt it like a wound somewhere deep inside. He could only stand and watch now as Hugo van Helsen led his daughter towards the gaping maw of those church doors. To Adam they were the gates of hell – only the hell he feared was on the *outside* with him.

This was it: Hugo van Helsen's crowning moment, the moment of his ultimate victory. The self-made man, the man who had started with nothing and had worked his way up by ruthless determination could hold his head high as the great and the good of Amsterdam looked on. They had come knowing this alliance would make the House of van Helsen one of the most powerful banks in Europe. They had come to witness his accomplishment, knowing that this could affect them all. He raised his hand in triumph and waved to the crowd without noticing the dishevelled figure of the merchant standing close to the church door.

Cornelius Yort came out of the crowd suddenly. He was hunched over, carrying something close to his chest hidden under his coat. He reached the step in front of them before the guards even noticed him. And his eyes were filled with the madness of revenge.

Hugo van Helsen stopped. For what seemed an age, the two men just stood looking at each other. Hugo van Helsen showed no fear. He faced the merchant down. It was the courage of a man who believed himself completely in the right.

Cornelius Yort's shoulders slumped. His chin descended on to his chest as if in that final moment his courage had failed him. The guards stepped forward, but the banker waved them aside.

'That will not be necessary,' Hugo van Helsen said. 'This merchant was just leaving.'

And something in his tone, some element of contempt or thinness in the banker's smile was enough to ignite the spark of fury and hatred in the merchant's eyes once more.

'You've taken everything from me, van Helsen,' he said. 'Now I'll take everything from *you*.'

There was a gasp, a scream from someone in the crowd as he drew the knife out from under his coat.

The blade flashed up and an animal snarl twisted the merchant's lips. Hugo van Helsen saw the knife just a little too late. He had no time for thought. He moved instinctively, stepping forward to shield Jade from the blow that was aimed at her heart. And in that unconscious action he proved there was more to him than just money.

The knife plunged in. The merchant's arm drew back and struck again. The fatal blow dealt, he pulled away, staring as if in horrified disbelief at what he had done. He let the blade fall. The guards were on him even before it hit the ground. He made no attempt to resist as they wrestled him down and pinned him to the cold stone.

'Father!' Adam heard Jade's cry.

The banker staggered back. He turned, stumbling, lifting his hands to stare at the blood with genuine surprise – as if for the first time in his life something had happened that he had not expected. He stood for a moment before the horrified crowd, then his knees buckled and he fell into his daughter's arms.

Jade struggled to hold him. Her father's weight was too much for her and he dragged her down on to the step of the church. The crowd surged forward and was pushed back. Adam fought his way through, trying to reach her. As he burst to the front, the sight stopped him dead. A red stain was spreading about the banker. Jade knelt in the blood. It was everywhere, on her hands, on her face, on her dress: crimson obliterated gold.

Goltz broke through the crowd and dropped to his master's side.

Hugo van Helsen dragged at his sleeve. His lips

worked through words. 'Tell her, Goltz,' he wheezed. 'Make her see I only wanted what was right for her. Was that so wrong ...?' A trail of blood broke from the corner of his mouth and ran down his chin. He slumped back into her arms.

Jade just knelt, cradling his head, staring at her father as he died.

A screech broke from Goltz's lips, a thin wail of misery and pain aimed at the leaden sky. Hugo van Helsen's head rolled to one side, his pale eyes staring straight at Adam as if they had searched him out one last time.

28. Business, Just Business

Adam Windjammer came out of the darkness suddenly, arching up on to the points of his elbows. He struggled, still caught in the net of his dreams until the images melted into the low beams above his bed.

He lay back again, dragging for breath, only to sit up almost at once and listen. He could hear the sound of footsteps. Someone was running across the square below. There was a sudden halt and the dull thump of a fist on wood. He slipped out of bed and over to the window. Looking down he saw a messenger dressed in a blue coat standing on the doorstep below.

'State your business!' he called.

'If you're Adam Windjammer,' the messenger called back up to him, 'then you're to go to the moneylender's house on the Street of Knives at once.'

'Jade!' Her name turned to mist on the chill.

'I knew she would come round in the end,' Adam said to his mother as he picked up his hat and headed for the door.

376

'Well, be careful what you say, Adam,' his mother advised. 'She will still be mourning for her father.'

'She's better off without him.'

'Adam!'

'Well, it's true.'

'That's enough,' his mother said. 'It's time to forget the past and move on. We have Madam de Witte's business and we've enough to think about now Bartholomew de Leiden's will has been settled. I want it to be a new start for us all when we move to the house he left us on the Keizersgracht.'

Adam shrugged her off. He was too excited to think of such mundane matters. This was it – the call he had been waiting for – his chance to make everything right. He had dressed quickly: white shirt, black fustian coat and breeches, socks, garters and shoes. He wanted to look the part of the merchant he was fast becoming, even if he didn't feel it yet.

'We saw her,' Rose said.

'Jade, she means,' Viola expanded as usual.

'In Dam Square yesterday.'

'She looked different.'

'Sad,' they chimed together.

Adam was too busy settling his hat over the streak of silver in his hair, too concerned with his look in the mirror by the door, to hear a warning in it.

He left the house and ran through the streets towards the Rokin, moving quickly along the side of the canal in the watery sunlight, darting between lines of lime trees, crossing bridges, running by churches. As Dam Square opened to him, he had a strange feeling he was dreaming again.

But only ghosts waited for him there. Dam Square

came and went and he moved through the streets, the houses passed by in a blur of windows and doors. He crossed Bread Street, cut along the Street of Cheeses and ran to the Street of Knives. The house on the corner hadn't changed. It stood squat and dark-timbered, hunched over its iron-studded door where the sign was still swinging gently in the breeze.

He shook off a growing feeling of dread and knocked. The small trap among the iron studs opened and an eye looked out through the grille.

'I've come to see Jade,' he said. 'I mean, Miss van Helsen.'

The trap snapped shut without a word. There was the sound of a bolt being pulled. A key was turned and the heavy iron latch lifted. The door opened with Goltz standing back to one side. He bowed slightly as Adam stepped in, then took his time bolting the door and turning the key.

'Mistress van Helsen has been expecting you,' he said, leading the way across the room to a door Adam knew only too well.

Jade was sitting in her father's place behind the desk. Ledgers were stacked up on either side of her.

'Jade!' Adam said, snatching his hat from his head. 'It's good to see you ...'

Her eyes flicked up to him. They were the same eyes, beautiful and green, and yet somehow still cold and empty when she looked at him.

'No one came to the funeral,' she said at last. 'Not one person came to show my father respect.'

Adam paused. 'You couldn't expect us to ... Well, I mean, your father didn't exactly go out of his way to make many friends.'

Jade studied his face. Adam felt more than a little uncomfortable.

'He was my father,' she said simply. 'To insult his memory is to insult me.'

'But he didn't care for you,' Adam said. 'He didn't care for anything but money.'

'That's not true! He loved me! I would be dead now with a merchant's knife in my heart if it wasn't for him.'

Adam paused, uncertain what to say. 'Listen, Jade.' He tried to be reasonable. 'You've been through a bad time. I know. I remember what it was like when *my* father died and –'

'And I suppose that makes us even?' she interrupted. 'One father apiece?'

'*No*, I didn't mean that.' But Adam was struggling to say what he did mean. She seemed so hard, so different. He tried again. 'It's just that things will be better now – *easier*. You don't have to marry the English goldsmith. You have more money than you'll ever need and you can do what you want. You can be free at last – *happy*.'

Jade's fist came down, setting the echoes warring in the hollow places.

Adam stood very still. He stared at her for an age before he spoke. 'You've changed,' he said quietly.

'We've all changed,' she said.

'And you called me here just to tell me that?'

Jade turned to Goltz with a nod. Goltz stepped forward and held out a roll of parchment.

'It seems my mistress has inherited half of the Quadrant Shipping and Trading Company, Master Windjammer,' Goltz said in a matter-of-fact sort of way. 'That makes the House of Windjammer and the Banking House of van Helsen partners in business.'

'Never!' Adam snatched the parchment away, unrolled it, saw it was signed and sealed and threw it down on the table in front of him.

'Whether you like it or not, sir,' Goltz went on, 'it must be business as usual between us.'

'You can't be serious,' Adam laughed. 'Nobody's going to do business with a ... Well, you're just a ... just a ...'

'Girl?' Jade found the word for him.

'Yes, if you want to hear it – just a girl.'

'Not just *any* girl, Adam Windjammer,' she said with a slight shake of her head. 'I'm also the moneylender's daughter.'

Adam saw it then – the spark somewhere deep in her eyes. He spun on his heel and started for the door, only to pause and look back. She was still watching him. It was the look of someone who had grown much stronger – the look of a girl who had finally come to believe in herself.

A Brief History of the Windjammers' Times

1300	Amsterdam first chartered as a city. During the Middle Ages the Netherlands did not exist as a nation. It was part of the Holy Roman Empire and ruled from Austria by the Hapsburgs.
1519	The Netherlands come under the control of Charles V, Holy Roman Emperor and King of Spain.
1568–48	The Dutch, under the House of Orange, struggle for independence from Spain.
1579	The Union of Utrecht forms a union of northern states with the most powerful state being Holland.
1588	The Spanish Armada is defeated by the English, ending King Philip II's plans to invade England from the Netherlands.
1602	The Dutch East India Company is formed.
1605	Guy Fawkes returns to London after fighting for the Spanish against the Dutch in Flanders (Belgium). His intention: to blow up James I and the English Houses of Parliament.
1606	Rembrandt born in Leiden (died 1669).
1609	Henry Hudson explores the Hudson River for the Dutch.
1618–48	Thirty Years War. Religious wars rage throughout the European mainland and cause large numbers to emigrate to the Americas.
1621	The Dutch West India Company is formed.
1626	The Dutch buy a small island at the mouth of the Hudson River. It is called Manhattan.
1632	The philosopher Rene Decartes moves to the University of Leiden.
1636	Tulip mania reaches its height in Amsterdam.
1637	The market in tulip dealing is suspended. Prices crash.
1648	Thirty Years War ends. The Treaty of Munster is signed and the Dutch Republic is formally recognised as a country.

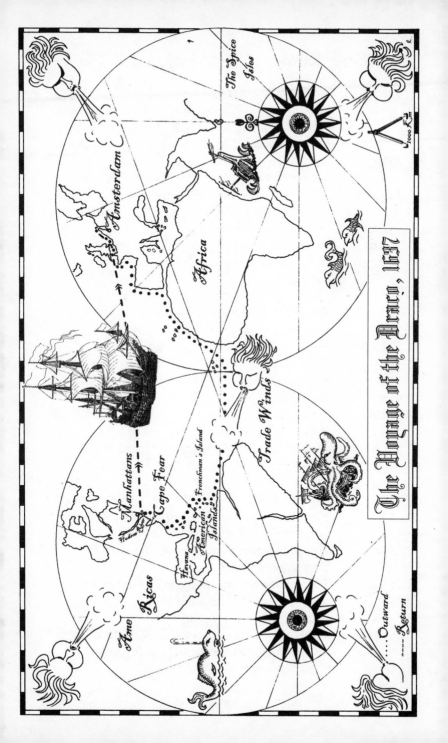

The Voyage of the Araru, 1637